FEAR THE DRAUGR

Book 2 of The Lost Hunt series

Neil Kay

CONTENTS

Title Page
Prologue
Chapter 1 — 1
Chapter 2 — 5
Chapter 3 — 10
Chapter 4 — 15
Chapter 5 — 20
Chapter 6 — 25
Chapter 7 — 30
Chapter 8 — 34
Chapter 9 — 37
Chapter 10 — 41
Chapter 11 — 46
Chapter 12 — 50
Chapter 13 — 55
Chapter 14 — 60
Chapter 15 — 65
Chapter 16 — 69
Chapter 17 — 75
Chapter 18 — 80
Chapter 19 — 83

Chapter 20	87
Chapter 21	93
Chapter 22	99
Chapter 23	104
Chapter 24	111
Chapter 25	116
Chapter 26	121
Chapter 27	125
Chapter 28	130
Chapter 29	136
Chapter 30	140
Chapter 31	145
Chapter 32	150
Chapter 33	155
Chapter 34	160
Chapter 35	166
Chapter 36	174
Chapter 37	181
Chapter 38	187
Chapter 39	194
Chapter 40	199
Chapter 41	206
Chapter 42	213
Chapter 43	218
Chapter 44	223
Chapter 45	227
Chapter 46	232
Chapter 47	238

Chapter 48	245
Chapter 49	250
Chapter 50	257
Chapter 51	261
Chapter 52	265
Chapter 53	272
Chapter 54	278
Chapter 55	286
Chapter 56	292
Chapter 57	298
Chapter 58	302
Chapter 59	307
Chapter 60	315
Epilogue	321
Afterword	325
About The Author	327
Books In This Series	329

PROLOGUE

789 AD. Isle of Portland, Wessex.

"Faster for god's sake!" the reeve screamed as his horse tore along the beach. The ships had been spotted two days ago a mile out from the island of Portland. The messenger who arrived at Sherborne earlier that day had told him, "Too long! The skiffs can't surround something that long and there's three of them!" The reeve had heard rumors of these ships being sighted off the Cent coast before but this was the first time they had decided to turn inwards when the ship suddenly showed signs of movement an hour ago.

Ships did not land on the Wessex coast without being boarded first but the usual fleet of defenders was much reduced in recent times, and as the ships had been satisfied to remain becalmed far from land, the reeve was content with just having a messenger go back and forth with information before the ships made their abrupt turn inland. The reeve had a lot of authority over the coast as King Beorhtric was Offa of Mercia's puppet and what did a Mercian care about the south sea?

The reeve had grown very fat over the years dismissing these annoying little fleets coming out of Dumnonia clad with the odd foul looking flag of a spear going through a snake's eye. "The shores of Wessex have been pirate free for over a century," he'd smugly bellow before turning his gaggle of village thugs onto the skiffs taking "taxes" from the angry Briton sailors. Wessex was one of the strongest kingdoms in the land, he said as he laughed away their claims of offering protection. They'd stopped coming in the end, their pleas to speak to the king rejected. The reeve was the king of the coast and he took a cut of whatever washed up. Including whatever the ships from the east were bringing.

He turned behind him to check that his four bodyguards were alert and armed. They'd made it on time. He had worried that by waiting until the last minute to come ashore, the sailors were hoping to make it to the woods before the reeve would have his due, but he'd cut them off like he always did.

Six men he counted in the first skiff. Hard looking bastards but weak from being out at sea, and not knowing the land well counted as being a man down. Besides who sails across the sea looking for a fight? The reeve had never heard of such a thing.

The first of the men to come ashore turned to face the welcome party. He had a grin like he was privy to all manner of secrets that other men weren't. The reeve knew that blue eyes were usually Saxon and Franks had brown eyes, the Britons were darker still. What land did these men come from to have eyes of yellow that seemed to stare right through you?

The man's grin twisted into a shape that reminded the reeve of a snake twisting through the grass. He bellowed something in a language that sounded like glass scratching glass and charged.

~

The arrows hit with precision. Only the best archers had been chosen. This close to the sea they couldn't allow the arrows to piece any beasts that were in the water. Brennus had been told of what had happened the last time that had happened. Any archer with less than a 100% record had been kept at home.

These arrows carved from yew trees of the forests in Conwy and blessed by priests and monks were the only thing that could mortally wound these creatures.

The arrows were making their mark and ungodly screams were coming from the beach. The archers were unperturbed. Another reason for their selection was that each of them had fired arrows into a creation before. If the sound hadn't driven them mad the first several times, they were deemed reliable.

Brennus stood behind the row of archers. Next to him in mail was a youth with shaggy brown hair and a grin on his face. The grin revealed a prominent canine tooth.

"Everything you expected, young Ecgberht?" asked Brennus.

Ecgberht pointed. "One of them is making a run for the water!"

"No need to mind, as long as he gets struck on land, then the sea will just boil around him. Needn't trouble the fish," replied the disfigured man. A splash and then steam rose from a small patch of sea, the rest of it looked remarkably calm amongst the cries from the shore.

"I think the archers have got all of them," said Ecgberht. He looked up at the flag one of the archers was displaying; a snake's head being pierced by a spear. "I'm going to the beach to take a closer look."

~

The reeve sat on the beach catatonic. The man who had

unsettled him so much with the yellow eyes and disconcerting smile was no longer a man. He or it was the most pitiful and wretched thing he had ever seen in his life. The size of a weasel, completely skinless, vomiting bloody bile and shrieking a sound that made the reeves ears bleed. The same sound was piercing the air coming from other wretched creatures that had come from the ship and it seemed to travel upwards, not outwards. Certainly none of the villagers across the causeway could hear it as no one had appeared from the huts with torches, but the sound was going upwards that was for sure. Every now and then a bird would drop from the sky stone dead from the air where the screams were being emitted to.

"Seagull tastes like leather so it's no great loss that we are forbidden to eat anything killed by the arrows no matter how indirectly," came a voice from over him. The reeve looked up. The young man's grin was disconcerting under the circumstances.

Ecgberht continued pointing his sword at the skinless weasel-like creature now in perpetual agony. It had been a burly six-foot tall man yellow of beard as well as eyes before the archers had had their way. "A small taste of what he's dealt out to others and if what the priests say is true, then this is merely a warm up for what's to come for him once the sun comes up and takes him to his eternal reward."

The reeve was snapped out of his stunned state by the sound of violent gurgled death throes from each of the equally catatonic bodyguards as spear tips shot out of their mouths. Four archers had left their vantage point and were cleaning up the carnage on the beach.

"Oh, I should have mentioned, the old man doesn't want any witnesses to what happened here so you get to find out what's on the other side now," Ecgberht said. "I would have done it after I become king anyway. All of Offa's creatures can expect the sword. I serve Wessex!" The reeve's head bounced onto the sand after Ecgberht made one swing of his long sword.

~

Later at the biggest fishing village hut, Ecgberht pressed a silver penny with Offa's face on it into the palm of the village chief while his wife served salted haddock to them. "Them others eat outside," she insisted, annoyed by the archer's inability or disinterest in addressing her in Saxon. Telling her that without the archers, the invaders would currently be eating her face would be a waste of time, plus maybe she'd gotten a smell of Brennus. He whispered to the chief, "Raiders came, killed the reeve and his crew, took a look around and didn't like what they saw so got back on their ship, okay?"

"Ships gone anyway," the chief said after scraping one of his few good remaining teeth on the coin. The reminder made Ecgberht frown.

After cleaning up the mess on the beach; more or less chasing away the skinless weasel things, now rendered harmless he'd leave the choice to them to continue existing in a state of never-ending torture or to walk into the sun and take their chances with the next world. They had tracked back to the fishing village where they'd arranged for smaller boats to be pushed out immediately ready for them to board. Blessed arrows were strapped to the point of their spears to be more effective in the fierce fighting that was soon to come at close quarters on the ship's deck.

But the instant they were ready to depart from the beach, the three long ships glided off at a speed that shouldn't have been possible even in strong winds with a full crew on the oars. From Ecgberht's view, only about ten oars or so on each side were being used and the breeze was calm. Despite this, the ships sailed to the east at a speed that was beyond chase.

~

Outside, the twelve or so archers and Brennus sat around a fire. They greeted Ecgberht as he brought out the fish and ale. "The Atheling makes a good kitchen wrench!" joked one of the archers, although in Western Brittonic the first syllable of 'Atheling' came out as a wheeze. According to Brennus, what was spoken in Dumnonia and the kingdoms of Cymru used to be the same but the two tribes hadn't been able to understand each other for over a century. "West Saxons carved out too much land and separated them, I told them not to..." Brennus had once said in his cups before changing the subject. Ecgberht had noticed the much older man was prone to saying such strangeness. He was the second oldest man Ecgberht had met after Merlin. How many years had he lived and what had caused the wounds that had rendered his face a twisted collection of cracked and curved folds of skin with just one eye peering out of the folds?

~

Brennus was looking over the Saxon youth carefully, he claimed to be an Atheling that was true but son of a king from a different Saxon kingdom called Cent, his father disposed of after he had displeased King Offa in Mercia. Landless, without an army and fueled by a hatred of Offa and Mercia, he declared Wessex as his new kingdom and his survival was owed to two things. First, Beorhtric and Offa probably not knowing who the hell he was, and when they finally heard of this boy idiot going from village to village trying to raise his own fyrd with coins that he had acquired god knows how, he had already attracted the Hunt's attention. In the middle of the night at the foot of a mountain in the Hunt's current base in Eryri, Brennus and

Merlin awaited the arrival of the bound and gagged youth they had ordered the kidnap of. When he tore off Ecgberht's hood revealing the prominent tooth and shaggy hair, Merlin turned to Brennus. "Do you see now why?" Brennus had nodded.

~

That had been six months ago. He had proven to be a quick learner once he'd learnt the alternative to training to fight for the Hunt was being trussed up and dumped on Offa's doorstep. Merlin's spies had told him that Offa's mint in Lundenwic, newly created in the shadows of the haunted Roman ruins had been ransacked explaining how this Centish, dispossessed Atheling was running around carrying coins with Offa's face on them. "He's not ready but we have enough warriors already! We need friends in Saxon lands like we once had!" Merlin had spat at Brennus.

"We've done well to contain whatever has been thrown at us the past few centuries. Surviving creations, fools mixing in the black arts, Saxon monstrosities, even the beasts that roamed this island long before Spurius but ships are getting bigger and longer again, the number of people is growing. Soon new threats will arise." Merlin was quiet for a long, long time after that. "Spurius wasn't the only one she made," he said finally. "I am in touch with Charlemagne of the Franks, he has broken with Offa and sends news of ships. Ships full of worse things than Romans, Angles and Jutes, worse even than Saxons. You will go to Wessex in secret and deal with one of these errant ships that has turned its nose in a northern direction. Once dealt with, you will send the Atheling across the sea. He will study at Charlemagne's court and we will bring him back at the right time."

CHAPTER 1

793 AD. The Frisian Sea.

Ulf vomited on the deck. He'd be beaten for it but didn't care. There was a long line for the bucket and leaning over the side of the ship would be suicide with the sea this way. He heard something shouted from the skipper but in these rains he could barely see the figure ten meters in front of him and the sound was just a faint bellow. He pulled the oar and hoped the things under the deck were asleep. He'd never seen lightning so clear and vivid in the daytime and couldn't help but wonder if the things were responsible.

~

Thorleif the skipper was ready to vomit himself and not just from the storm, strong as it was, the waves seemed to beat against the ship's hull eerily, as if they were making some sort of rhythm. The drums the shaman of the northern people, The Sami used made a slow, similar sounding thud when their seers were trying to see into the future or contact other realms. He shivered, he was scaring himself needlessly. He had never heard the Sami drums himself. The only reason they came to mind was the blonde stranger claimed to have come from the far north himself. "Empty villages for as far as any man can walk," the stranger had said with a cruel smile before he made his offer to Thorleif. Could it be that the two things under the deck were Sami? Or had been once?

Thorleif was also frightened by the growing realization that he had no idea where they were. The blonde stranger had promised he would find land beyond the sea with his charms and Thorleif had believed him. Among the skippers of the various chieftains fleets, the past five years had come about a frenzy of rumors about this stranger who traveled to and from the market towns along the fjords appearing randomly. He was said to promise the skippers and chieftains with charms that would guarantee passage to the rich western lands. Thorleif had doubted the stranger's existence, especially due to the claims he was as tall as two men and could snap a tree trunk with his bare hands.

When the stranger finally sought him out and they arranged a meeting at his chieftain's mead hall, he found a tall, strong looking man but a man nonetheless, he just wasn't prepared for those amber eyes. Eskil, his chieftain cursed and raised his hands to his wife when she found herself pouring the mead on the floor, captivated by those eyes but halfway through his bellowing he'd caught the eyes himself and had forgotten what had caused his rage.

The stranger explained to Eskil and Thorleif that he had the gods' favor and would perform the rituals that would assure passage to the fertile green lands of legend. "Your ship will be weighted down with gold, silver and slaves on the way home," he'd said with a smile. "There are other fine things in the Saxon kingdoms as well but for now rest assured I'm firm friends with Thor and we will get you there in one piece. I only ask in return that you carry some cargo for me."

Later in the woods the stranger had grinned as the seers slit the oxen's throat and then his smile went right up to the corners of those beautiful eyes when it was time for the slaves to be sacrificed. Each of the crew members offered a trinket which was hung in the branches alongside the entrails of man and beast. Finally the stranger said, "It is done." By now it was dark and then they came. Stumbling through the woods, a naked man and woman. They reeked of rotting meat and their pale white skin was riddled with jet-black lines which marked their bodies from head to toe. They raised their heads and their eyes were wide and bulging like eggs, not a fleck of any other color but white apart from a single black dot in the center of them. Their teeth and gums were black and their cheeks a light blue shade. The black veins were twisted across their foreheads. Long seaweed spilled from their heads instead of hair.

They were by far the most repulsive things Thorleif had seen in his life. He heard behind him muttering and heavy breathing before someone screamed "Draugr!" and in a blur a figure charged forward with an axe. It was over within a second, the female draugr gave a light swat with the back of her hand and the attacker's head flew off.

"Strong eh?" said the stranger with a laugh that sounded almost feminine. "Two of these on your ship, below decks during the day mind and you will hit land to the west, I promise. These two may even be useful once you hit dry land but the important thing is you let them loose in these new lands." He looked at the headless man and said, "I'd burn him if I were you," before disappearing into the woods with the two draugr following him. Thorleif checked the corpse. "It's Kalf," he told the chieftain, it had happened so fast he wasn't sure until he checked the body.

"He died axe in hand, he will go to Valhalla," Eskil said, sounding unsure. Thorleif himself wasn't in a hurry to ask the seers what happened if creatures of Hel were the cause of death. "We burn him here, tell his woman bandits fell on us and he died of his wounds." Eskil decided.

The next morning they boarded the ship. The stranger was there to see them off. "Your guests are under the decks already, I saw to it myself. I have spoken to the gods and you will make good speed lads! Southwest sharp, not straight south, that takes you to a narrow sea, one that divides the Saxons and the Franks, not sending another ship that way, not after last time. Southwest it is for you lot hah!"

~

That had been days ago, they should have found land by now. The stranger lied Thorleif thought, if they had sailed straight south, they would have stayed in range of the coast, past the land of The Danes and the Frisian lands after could be easily raided. But to sail straight into sea, into waters no Norseman knew of was sheer madness. The stranger was Loki sent to deceive, perhaps they were destined to sail for the remainder of days until Ragnarok, the foul draugr keeping them alive, keeping them away from Valhalla. He kept one hand wrapped around his sword in case a wave took him as it took Eskil two days ago.

He decided to inspect the rowing benches, there was slightly more cover down here and he could relieve any oarsmen who were exhausted. They'd lost too many men to the sea. Only thirty of them remained, he couldn't lose anymore. He caught eyes with Ulf, the pointy nosed young lad on his first voyage. Always smirking that one, until he saw the draugr, Thorleif hadn't seen the lad smile once since then. Their eyes locked and Thorleif was about to offer to relieve the lad when they heard "Land!" bellowed from the direction of the ship's prow. While the rest of the crew reacted with cheering, the two men felt a coldness. Sweat went down from Thorleif's widow's peak to his nose. "Something feels off about this land, familiar but off." He was talking to himself but Ulf nodded, Ulf understood every word, yet Ulf felt a warmth which he told himself was his body reacting to the prospect of an open fire once ashore.

CHAPTER 2

Lindisfarena Island, Kingdom of Northumbria,

Brother Aindrea put down his quill, he remembered the novice had brought some food. How long ago he couldn't remember, he had chased the young lad away with a sharp whistle. It had been hours since he'd last eaten. He ripped off a piece of bread and dipped it in the halibut broth. It was stone cold. He stared out of the scriptorium window, the small slit giving a view of the island's southern coast now obscured by the clouds and heavy rain beating against it.

He finished the cold broth and started to resume copying the letter Saint Cuthbert had written giving an account of his interview with the holy abbess Elfleda on Coquet Island. It had been fascinating, at least the first time he'd copied it, six weeks of copying it meant Cuthbert and Elfeda's rather one-way conversation had lost its appeal somewhat.

He decided to give himself a break and walked to the window. Only an hour or two of daylight remained but the storm meant the beach was just a blur. He looked up to the sky. The lightning looked beautiful, he'd never seen it twist across the sky in a horizontal form before. Then just as the sky darkened a little, there was another twist of lightning. His blood ran cold. The lightning had made the shape of a snake and that snake's head turned as if it were looking straight at the priory.

~

Ulf was feeling more and more excited as he marched with the others along the beach. Only not wanting to be mocked by his shipmates had prevented him from kissing the beach once they were on dry land. They were now walking in a group of twenty-eight, two had been left guarding the ship and the things on it. They could barely see a thing and were keeping to the beach to guide their way along the coast. They began a war chant to warm themselves against the rain. *"The land is holy that lies hard by. The gods and elves together; Ånd Thor shall ever in Thruthheim dwell, Till the gods to destruction go."*

~

Thorleif was chanting away but was also thinking hard. He could make out the outline of a few hills on land a bit further away beyond a different stretch of water that told him they were on an island not far from a bigger body of land. The land looked sparse and marching through it during a storm would sap his men's strength. He decided to look for shelter on the island and waiting the storm out before advancing to the mainland. He gave a bellow of triumph when he turned the corner and saw a crudely made harbor, some small boats tied to a long wooden pier and a row of huts at the far end of the beach. A few of the boats were smashed into two or cut adrift due to the storm. The huts had large stones wedged against them in an effort to prevent them being washed away.

Thorleif charged toward the huts waving his sword, screaming, *"Odin owns you all!"* His men repeated the cry. Thorleif noticed halfway through the charge on the beach that on the higher land next to the beach was a building that was made completely of stone in the distance beyond the huts.

~

Brother Aindrea was at Vespers when he heard the noise. He was smiling at brother Heregod the young former novice who had recently taken his vows as he sang, *"Deus, in adiutorium meum intende. Domine, ad adiuvandum me festina."* The young man's voice was as beautiful as his face. Aindrea didn't get to hear it enough with silence being the norm for most of the day. He was in the priory church with the other brothers and the prior, twenty in all. The rain had ceased suddenly and angry shouts came from somewhere. Aindrea who had sharp hearing was the first to say, "That's too many voices to be from the fisherfolk? Can anyone understand what is being said?"

Prior Aldred scowled and hushed him but Heregod spoke too. "No, I hear it too, listen!" Soon all the monks were muttering to each other as the angry voices grew louder and angrier.

The ancient prior started to whine, "Of course it's the fisherfolk, no one else could reach our gates in this weather. Disturbing Vespers! I will have the wretches flogged! What ingratitude! The salvation we provide brings more to this island than mere fish and…"

Heregod stood next to Aindrea making him shiver. He whispered into the older monk's ear, "They're not speaking Northumbrian or Pictish, you have the most tongues of us, brother Aindrea. What do you think?"

Aindrea spoke Goidelic, his language since birth, had learned Mercian during his fighting days and Northumbrian since coming to the priory, he knew enough Pictish to communicate and could read and write Latin which was why he was often assigned to the scriptorium. He listened further. "Not from any of the Saxon kingdoms nor Frankish, at least some of the words would be the same as…" He then remembered the lightning making the snake shape in the sky and his left eye started uncontrollably twitching. The thrill he'd felt when Heregod had stood next to him was now replaced with terror. The twitching had started during a childhood fever which nearly killed him and only came at times of great danger; before a battle, a storm at sea, once when his horse had panicked after a snake bite and dragged him from the ground. It hadn't happened once since arriving at the priory.

Until now.

"I have to go to the dormitory, I'll be back soon. Do not open the doors to them! Even if Prior Aldred tells you to!" Aindrea said backing away unnoticed, the rest of the monks still distracted by the prior's complaints.

~

Ulf stood with his shipmates in front of the impressive stone building. He had to admit the skipper had done a good job navigating the island in the storm and finding just the right number of sacrifices in the fishing huts showed the gods were looking kindly on them. Despite… those things in the ship. The two men in the huts, one young and one old were too shocked to put up much resistance as Thorleif had slit their throats and thrown them face first into the sea as an offering to Thor. The three women had been driven into hysterics at this and one needed her face caved in against one of the rocks used as storm protection. Face down in the sea, they were now gifts for Odin. They found a skinny cat at the back of the shack and had gutted it before throwing it into the sea, a good sign as it is Freyja's favorite animal. Five minutes after the human offerings, huddled in the cramped huts they let out a cheer as the storm ended.

It was when the cat was killed that they heard the howling sobs from under a crumbling wicker basket made of twigs. Ulf had pulled it off the head of the young woman and pinned her down by the neck as he searched for his dagger. Thorleif very sharply told them that the gods were satisfied as the storm had stopped and this one was to be spared. Ulf thought it was unlike the skipper to show mercy but then he caught sight of the woman's face and her rump which stuck out sharply. *Skipper wants a pretty slave when he gets back home,* thought Ulf with a chuckle. They had left the girl trussed up like a swine ready for the spit back in the huts while they marched onwards to the tall stone building. He couldn't understand a word of what she was screaming but was still happy to gag her with strips of her dress, he doubted what she was saying was useful or amusing and therefore of no use to Ulf.

~

The wooden doors were strong looking and they hadn't brought a battering ram due to its weight. Thorleif screamed at the building, "Open your gates and we will take what we find and spare you!" It occurred to him that he had no idea who was behind these doors. The building was unlike anything he'd ever seen in his life. Built with stones that stacked up higher than the wooden huts and halls back home and the building covered more land than two, no three of the chieftain's great hall. Could the island's king live here? Could his warriors be behind that door? *A Norseman fears no man!* he thought and snapped at the two men standing nearest, "Bjorn! Ulf! Find me an oak! We will break down these doors with its trunk!" Then he heard the slightest hiss before screaming as an arrow struck his thigh, he sat on his arse in shock. He gasped as he saw another arrow sticking out of the gut of a wide eyed and shaking Bjorn who crashed to the ground.

CHAPTER 3

Aindrea had to lean half his body out of the bell tower's window to get a shot off at the intruders. Despite the chill sweat spilled across his cheeks, if he fell all was lost. He had seen the axes, shields and swords in fleeting glances from the view that was visible from the tower. These were not pilgrims come to see the holy bones, nor starving men willing to risk damnation to fill their bellies. These were warriors, come to fight, kill and pillage. He heard shouts bellowed in the coarse sounding language from the one with an arrow in his leg and two other raiders attacked the doors with axes. He knew despite what he had told Heregod, the prior would open the doors totally blind to the possibility that they were in danger. The handful of bandits that had turned up in the past were so pitiful, a few heels of bread had sent them running and as for the ones who may be truly desperate, Aindrea had only hinted at his past to the other brothers but it was an unspoken fact that he kept bow, arrows and sword under his bed, thankfully they had remained unused.

Until now.

He fell back into the tower and notched his bow before leaning outside again. His skills hadn't perished. He took one of the raiders smashing the doors with his axe right in the side of the neck, an amazing shot from this angle if he did think so himself.

No matter what their words meant, he could feel the panic along with the rage as they shouted to each other. The one with the leg wound shouted the loudest and they raised their shields and gathered around him. He was leaning on the shoulders of their strongest looking warrior and shouted some more before they began to back away heading in the direction of the harbor. He had done it! They had won!

~

Nelda had finally worked out that if she kept screaming and sobbing, she would suffocate and she couldn't die now! She needed to give her confession to brother Heregod about... about... what she had been doing with brother Heregod. She couldn't give penance to anyone else or her family... then the thought of what the monsters had done to her parents, her two sisters and her brother. Even Inky her cat had been slaughtered by these demons from hell. It was the thought of hell that terrified her when she realized she might die without receiving absolution. Somehow she managed to get her breathing under control. She heard voices, words without meaning but dripping with surprised anger.

The doorway now just splinters hanging off, it had looming figures blocking it. She couldn't be sure as it had gotten too dark outside to see. They made grunting noises and something was dumped on the floor, from the smell and size she knew it was a man, one of the demons.

The demon was panting and in pain. She turned her head and from the outline she could tell it was their leader, the one who killed her family. His wound was deep. *God is great!* she thought.

~

Thorleif panted both with pain and rage. Bjorn; his son-in-law and Mak both dead and himself struck lame. Arrows! He fucking hated arrows! A coward's weapon and somehow they cause the most blood loss. Thorleif had taken knives to the gut during drunken mead hall fights in his youth and had lost half an ear and scarred his cheeks in battle but his skin was tough, a few days later he'd been as good as new, just a little sore. Why did arrows cause so much blood to pour out? It was nothing like being stabbed.

He grunted and called out to the men who were standing over him, "Wrap the wound tight with anything you can find! Don't pull out the shaft yet. Help me back to the ship!"

~

Ulf didn't want to sail again so soon but rather face the storms than an unseen foe lurking in the shadows. "Aye skipper, we've got the one thrall and a good amount of salt fish. That's not bad for such a miserable little island, if we stick to the coast we should find a village to plunder soon. Might be a healer for your…"

He was shocked at the strength of the wounded man who grabbed him by the throat and squeezed as Thorleif gasped, "We take everything in that stone house and we kill everyone inside, we are going back for the draugr!"

~

Prior Aldred pointed a bony finger at the two corpses they had dragged inside and said "Picts!" in a proud voice. "I knew it was Picts!"

"Old goat told us it were fisherfolk, if not for you, those axes would be in our skulls," came a voice from behind Aindrea. He smiled. Brother Godwin's rough southern Saxon dialect was so distinct from the prior's Northumbrian that he knew the prior wouldn't understand a word.

"What was that Godwin?" The prior's bony finger now jabbed at the Wessexman.

"Picts would've come from the north, same direction storm blew in from! Surely they'd have sheltered instead of walking through it," Godwin said in Mercian; a clearer dialect that most Saxons and Angles could understand. "Besides Picts are Christian and I ain't ever seen a Christian wear that." He pointed to the hammer amulet that was tied to string around the dead men's necks.

This made the other monks who were all gathered in the refectory murmur. Usually silent, it felt eerie to hear voices inside the monastery, no matter how hushed. The cold gale rushing through the dimly lit room made the candles flicker. The prior did not like that one bit and snapped, "What do you know of our land, you southern wretch!"

But then Heregod spoke over the prior. Aindrea flinched, the prior was too feeble to administer the punishment beating that he would surely order on Heregod himself, but he may give the task to one of the more physically able monks such as Aindrea.

"Brother Aindrea has been all over the island as well as Hibernia, would he know where these men came from?" Heregod said.

Aindrea cut in to prevent the prior exploding in rage. "I have never seen such amulets, I daresay they are not Picts. The weaving of their garments, the sharpness of their axes, their shields… It's like nothing I've seen from the north, south or west. I think these men came from the sea… or… or the land beyond it. I should go to the scriptorium, perhaps our forefathers had some knowledge, perhaps the Romans…"

"Silence, need I remind you I am the prior!" Aldred's tonsured dome was bright red as he screamed. "I will…" a gust of wind extinguished all the candles at once making everything go pitch black. A chill went throughout the room and Aindrea heard a pitiful whine; the wind had knocked the angry prior over.

"Prior Aldred? Are you hurt?" Aindrea asked with concern.

"My head, I'm bleeding."

Aindrea quickly took control. He ordered the monks to prop the prior up and surround him to make sure he didn't fall again and led the way out of the rectory, clearing any obstacles. The candles in the hallway were out, forcing them to grope blindly as they left the refectory.

Aindrea said, "To the cloisters, the moonlight will allow us to attend to Prior Aldred's wounds." They shuffled slowly, not a candle in the whole monastery appeared to be lit.

Arriving in the open air of the cloisters, the monks organized. They laid Prior Aldred on the grass and Aindrea examined the gash on his head. "It's not so bad, two of you head to the infirmary, one to guide the other. We need water and honey to wash the wound. There should be a tinderbox too so get the candles lit and…" he froze, his jaw hanging and shaking.

"Brother Aindrea, what is wrong?" Aldred said in a faint whisper. "Why have you stopped? What is happening to your eye? It flashes and twitches. I say, it is most off-putting."

Aindrea was staring at the entrance to the cloisters, the main entrance to the whole monastery. The thick oak doors that had frustrated the raiders were missing. An open space with a strong wind rustling through was all that remained.

CHAPTER 4

The other monks slowly began to notice what Aindrea had. "What is happening I can't see!" whined the prior as the monks backed away and began to pray. It was painful to move his neck so the prior looked up at the moon and heard chanting around him, *"Father God in Jesus' name I implore your mercies against evil…"*

Aindrea wasn't praying or helping the prior anymore. He was running. The prior had ordered him to return his bow and arrow to their hiding place under the stones, beneath his bed in the dormitory after the raiders had fled. Aindrea was a soldier before he became a monk and one who was used to disobeying orders. He wanted to wait at least a day to ensure the raiders had left before burying them again. He had hidden the weapons behind one of the cloister's pillars and took off in a diagonal direction to find them.

~

Ulf was one of the first through the open space where the doors once were. He waited until the draugr had walked past him, one of those giant doors held upright in its fist, like it was toasting a drinking horn. The other one, the one that had once been a woman from the sight of the front of her, had snapped her door into two and was carrying a piece under each arm and wandering away from the building aimlessly. Once both were out of sight, he advanced with his companions, each chanting, *"Tyr!"* hoping to win glory for the war god.

He was stalled for a second by how strange the design of the building was. Pillars of stone holding up more stone, and a building on each side of the grass rectangle, but he quickly charged with his axe sending the collection of tall, gaunt men scattering. He whacked his axe across the back of one's head felling him. He turned the man's body over to face him. "Where is the silver? Where is the gold? Where are the women?" he screamed but the man wept and gurgled, mumbling nonsense sounds. Ulf turned to Baggi, who after screaming the same questions at the old man, laid on the ground and was now hacking his dagger into the old man's guts. "Why do they make their hair look so stupid?" Ulf shouted across.

Baggi shouted back, "Maybe it's because…" Ulf would never hear Baggi's theory as an arrow hissed out of nowhere and took him in the eye.

Ulf did as he'd been ordered to by Thorleif before the attack. *If the archer is still active, then take cover!* He rolled behind one of the pillars and watched the raiders who had followed him and Baggi through the empty gates fall back and find hiding spaces of their own. He winced as he heard another hiss and another crewmate Ari had been felled with an arrow in his back. He wondered if the draugrs could row. They had lost too many men in what should have been a simple raid.

He heard shouts from behind the entrance where Thorleif was being carried on a shield, the man had the strength of an ox to still be conscious, Ulf thought. The skipper's blood loss was severe. Then a strange silence broken only by Ari's dying moans and a gurgle, not from the now dead man Ulf had struck but from the elderly one who had taken half a dozen hacks to the gut from Baggi's dagger. Still alive! *Led by tough bastards on both sides,* Ulf thought with admiration. Then Ari's pants and the old man's babbling faded. Ulf checked and breathed a sigh of relief. Ari and Baggi had died axe and dagger in hand and would feast together in Valhalla. Ulf breathed slowly, he knew what the skipper's next move was to be and put his hands over his face as the smell of rotting meat grew.

~

Aindrea notched his bow for the third time. He'd sent two more of the raiders to hell but too late to save Prior Aldred and one of his other brothers who was laid face down, too difficult to identify at this angle and in this light. He felt a flush of shame for the relief he felt when he realized the body was too short to be Brother Heregod.

He knew three or four raiders were in the cloisters with him but none were within sight. The remaining brothers had fled. He prayed they had made it to the church where the doors were thickest and locked by an iron bar as a latch. He only had three arrows left, he had to make them all count. Maybe the raiders would flee if they lost more men. More likely, in the chaos he could get to the dormitory and find the sword buried under the paving beneath his bed. With sword in hand and knowing the layout of the monastery, he could give the brothers time to find an escape, a way out, a chance to call for help. The raiders had not expected a skilled archer, they would be even more surprised to find a warrior among the monks. Soon Aindrea heard footsteps and breathing. The breathing sounded like a growl.

He saw the profile of the two figures that entered the cloisters. The moonlight seemed drawn to them. First Aindrea thought the black lines bulging all over their torsos and legs were some form of odd clothing, rags wrapped tightly for some reason. It was the eyes that told him, the shape of eggs, glowing in the darkness and with blood trickling from the eyelids. He began shaking and gave a plea to god; *"Oh, that you would rend the heavens and come down. That the mountains might quake at your presence..."*

Then he noticed the smell of rot and the growling getting louder, he fired and hit one of the creatures point blank in the chest. It had been walking toward him, the other turned and he then saw both were naked, he had shot the male one which lay sprawled on its back unmoving. The woman creature bared her decayed lips revealing black teeth. He didn't wait to find out if she was smiling or growling. An arrow took her in the forehead.

Only one arrow left! He ran, he hadn't seen anything to suggest the raiders had archers of their own and hoped in the confusion he could outpace any pursuers. He bolted in the direction of the dormitory and his heart clenched tightly in fear as he heard a horribly familiar growling behind him.

He had seen men break in battle many a time. From well-trained warriors to farm boys armed with poles. Nothing prepares you for the first time you come across dangerous men you must kill or be killed by. He never thought it would happen to him. He had too much experience but it happened now. He couldn't move, he felt growling right behind him. The smell of rotten meat was so strong he started retching and a thin stream of vomit ran down his chin to his robes. It was the woman he somehow knew, she seemed more aware of her movements and surroundings than the mindless male monster. She stroked the nape of his neck with her finger and he collapsed sobbing onto the ground. He felt as if he had been hit in the stomach with a hammer and whacked in the back of the neck with the flat of a thick sword. Blood came out with the next stream of vomit.

~

"STOP!" yelled Ulf as he saw the stinking woman was about to take the archer's head off with one flick of her finger as she had done to Kalf. "Leave this one to me, you dead bitch!" She turned and only after staring at him for the longest ten seconds of Ulf's life did she give him that terrible black toothed grin and shuffled away in the direction of the other draugr. They both still had the arrows sticking out of their chests and foreheads.

Ulf raised his axe over the broken man and screamed, "For

Bjorn and Mak and Baggi and Ari!" The broken man's face peered up at him, his eyes flickering and Ulf had the strangest feeling that he knew this man from somewhere. The few moments of confusion saved the broken man's life as Ulf heard shouting and chanting from behind him.

"All men with me now!" Thorleif bellowed from the shield he was being carried on as he entered the building. "We have found where they are hiding; it must be where their gold is!"

Men must have slipped in during the draugr chaos and located where the robed cowards with the odd hair were hiding. Ulf had already forgotten about the broken, blinking archer. A delay of even a minute could lead to missing out on gold and Ulf needed as much of the plunder as he could get. Ever since he saw the extent of Thorleif's wound back at the fishing hut, a plan had started to form in his head.

He ran in the direction of the rotting smell.

CHAPTER 5

Ulf got to another thick door at the back of the large courtyard just in time to see the male draugr turn it to splinters with one kick, his partner pulled the iron bar back, it stretched into a curved shape before dropping to the floor. Ulf was one of the first to charge in.

Axe in one hand, dagger in the other, he howled at the robed men who ran and wept. He got one in the eye with his dagger and realized none were fighting back! They were weeping and screaming and some were shouting in a grunt-like tongue, some had their hands clasped together and were chanting gibberish while looking at the sky, tears rolling down their cheeks. Sure enough, soon he began to smell shit.

His shipmates were charging in, some went straight for the robed men, butchering them as they whimpered but a yelled order came from Thorleif, "Keep some of them alive! They will tell us where the gold is," as he was carried in, the doorway too narrow for the shield, he was propped up on each arm by a crew member. He then winced as Egil and Gunnar; two raiders who had charged in after him began to fight over a silver chalice they had found. The fight ended when Egil stabbed Gunnar in the gut. They really couldn't afford to lose anymore oar hands.

Some organization finally occurred after much bellowing by Thorleif. Ulf could see the amount of effort it was taking for him to get everyone under control. Panting and clearly in great pain, he arranged the surviving robed men to be bound as he interrogated them.

Pointing to a gold ring he carried in his furs and gesturing around the cavernous stone room, Thorleif managed to get the message across of what he wanted, assisted by grabbing a robed man by the neck and smashing his face repeatedly against the stone floor until it was red goo. As he reached up the dying man's robes to remove his cock and balls with his dagger, Ulf saw the bloodstain around the protruding arrow now covered the skipper's entire upper leg. Maybe the wound smelled bad, couldn't tell with the draugrs lurking in the background. *He'll be lucky if he makes it till morning,* Ulf thought.

The next robed man they asked, the youngest, a right pretty boy Ulf reckoned, wondering what he was doing with a bunch of old men with silly hair was much more helpful. He led Ulf to a raised stone platform at the far end of the room where Egil and Gunnar had found the chalice. Two large planks of wood had been nailed to the wall here to make a cross, Ulf shrugged. Below the cross was a raised, three-sided, wooden platform, this one much smaller than the one Ulf and the pretty boy were standing on.

The pretty boy stamped his foot on the floor a few times and said something in his gibberish. Ulf didn't like that so he slapped him across the face. Weeping, his lip bloody, he sank to his knees and jabbed his finger at the stones under the smaller, wooden platform. He then lifted one of the stones out from the floor they were standing on. *That's what he meant,* Ulf thought in amazement. He'd buried plunder in dirt before but under stone! That was a new one.

He screamed at the pretty boy to move all the stones and despite not knowing any Norse, the boy worked it out well enough. The stones were lifted and a large hollow space was underneath. One of the surviving robed men was screaming at the boy in their nonsense tongue but Ulf didn't care about that.

He was struck dumb by the amount of plunder. There was gold, silver, jewels, coins with the faces of so many different men, bits of ancient faded parchment with strange scribbles on them. All nonsense to Ulf but the pictures looked interesting. They needed something to wipe their arses with on the voyage back after all, he stuffed them to one side.

"What is in that?" Ulf demanded the boy tell him pointing to the long rectangle shaped box that was in the stone hole surrounded by the treasure.

The pretty boy shook his head and repeated a word a few times before clasping his hands together and starting the chant-like gibberish he'd heard from the other robed men.

"No?" Ulf said, repeating the boy's word. "What is a 'No'?" When he got no answer, he head-butted the boy so strongly that his nose exploded and then gave him an uppercut punch that sent the boy flying and his teeth clattering on the stone.

"Heregod," moaned one of the surviving robed men. An annoying noise, Ulf thought.

He kicked a few teeth away, said to the groaning boy, "Not pretty anymore, are you?" He then called to one of the others to help him pry open the box.

Once it was open, he gave a bark of laughter at the sight of a yellowing skeleton inside the box. He put his hands into the box to retrieve some coins and a silver cross that had been buried alongside the bones. The skeleton was also clutching a thick rectangle shaped object, Ulf snatched it away and it fell open, it was full of parchment pieces with curly shapes on them, hundreds of them. He threw the object to one side.

Ulf was confused. This man must have been a great enemy to the robed men for them to trap him in a box under stone for all time. It was known that you burn men, the smoke is their souls departing to Odin's great hall. Women and children, you return to the mud in the hope they get reborn as a warrior and can earn their place in Valhalla.

He turned to look at the rest of the building. The men were in good spirits. Once the treasure had been located, Thorleif had ordered more stones removed from the floor and more plunder was found where there were loose stones. Someone must have found the kitchen or had the draugr destroy every door until it was found as barrels of ale were being rolled in.

As for the robed men, most had their throats slashed; a few unfortunate ones were still alive and restrained by his crewmates. He knew once enough ale had flowed, men would start taking bets on which man would live the longest once their heels were pierced and ropes threaded through the wounds to hang the men upside down.

Staring at him was the man who had moaned a word to him after he'd ruined the pretty boy's face. Somehow the runty looking man had escaped the other men's attention. He was looking at Ulf with sheer hatred. Ulf had to laugh.

He picked up the thigh bone of the skeleton and waved it at the man. "How did this man wrong you to earn such a terrible end?" Ulf was then shocked by the man's strength as he made a giant leap and knocked Ulf to the floor. He looked for Njarl the man who had helped him open the box, bastard was probably laughing as the enraged man rained blows onto his face.

Ulf wriggled and had his hand halfway to his boots where another dagger was stashed when his attacker's head exploded. Ulf felt red hot liquid all over his face and blinking hard through a vision of thick redness, he understood his attacker's blood had sprayed over him.

"I had him well enough," he said to the male draugr who had popped the man's head like a berry. Both draugrs appear to be interested in the bones of the long dead man and peered into the box. Ulf shrugged and grabbed a sheet of the ancient paper to wipe his face clean and fish an eyeball out of his hair. He got his vision back just as he saw an arrow take the male draugr in his right hand. The fucking archer must have recovered, Ulf realized. Can't be in great shape, running low on arrows and they don't seem to harm the draugrs, he wearily thought just before the male draugr unleashed a scream that made everyone in the building stop and fall to the ground clutching their ears. It was a scream from the depths of Niflheim and then the draugr burst into flames.

CHAPTER 6

Aindrea coughed up more blood and bile and lay on the cloister grass looking up at the moon and wondered when the light would come and take him. No, there would be no light for him, not after the things he'd done. But not the fire too, he'd done good work since arriving at the monastery. Slumber in the cold until the resurrection on Judgment Day was the best he could hope for. He muttered a prayer for the souls of the two monks who lay on the grass beside him and closed his eyes before he could pray for himself.

~

He dreamt. It was fifteen years ago. His adventuring had brought him a place in one of Offa's fyrds and they were campaigning against the Cymru kingdoms, which one of them, he couldn't tell, by now Mercians were referring to anything west of them as Wealas. After falling back in Mercian land, he'd been assigned the job of looking after the Wealas prisoners at the border as the dyke was being built.

The earthwork was ambitious but working. A trench now separated the two Kingdoms of Mercia and the Wealas kingdom of Powys. The earth removed from the ground piled up on Mercia's side rather than the front, making the edge of Mercia higher and allowing them to look down into the fields and hills Wealas warriors would be advancing from; a massive advantage. Of course Wealas warriors had charged to prevent the barrier being made but Offa seemed to count on that and made bags of coin available to any man who could fight.

That's how he'd found himself in Mercia. He found some of the tasks such as digging traps for the Wealas raiders and building wooden cages to house them in to be a bit strange, but the coins kept coming at a rate he or any soldier on this island was used to. Soon their number grew and whole fyrds were full of non-Mercians.

He was good with tongues and what the Wealas prisoners spoke was not that dissimilar to Goidelic. He quickly worked out they were in fear of what the woman had in store for them. "Offa's whore" was what they called her; although some of the ones who clutched their crucifixes tightly as they huddled in their pens hissed at even mentioning her.

He saw her often moving around the border camp. Clearly a woman from her shape but that was the only clue as to her appearance. A black gown covered her from neck to toe, snakeskin was wrapped around her neck and an eyeless wooden mask covered her face. Snakeskin wrapped tightly around her hands meant the only visible part of her was the flowing black hair that descended from the back of the mask.

He'd once asked his Mercian captain about her, just over some ale, questions like; is the mask because of burns? Is she the king's kin? Why does she come to camp so often? The man, previously friendly toward Aindrea had put a coin into his palm and said, "Never ask again, if you do..." the flat of the knife against Aindrea's cheek spoke the rest of the sentence.

The few times the King had come to camp, she had never left his side. He saw them at a distance once, she appeared to be whispering into the king's ear. He looked euphoric.

Then came the ceremony.

Nothing like it was done in Hibernia, his land of birth and they had some rituals that outsiders found odd, as did the Britons of Dumnonia and the Saxons of Wessex who Aindrea had both soldiered for on his travels. But this, he wasn't sure it was a local custom. Even the Mercian troops had faces that ranged from bemused to aghast.

The Wealas prisoners in the dead of night with their wrists bound behind their back were lined up toward the trench that separated Mercia and their homeland. There atop a stage was the masked woman. The King had decided not to attend.

Each prisoner was brought before her trembling and from the flickering of the torches, Aindrea finally saw her fingers slip out from under the snakeskin coverings. He was a good twenty feet away, one of a parade of soldiers charged with forcing the line of prisoners forward but he could make out long black nails and the light flickering seemed to show discolored fingers. A trick of the light or could sickness be the cause of her coverings?

The screaming started, those nails sliced through the men's skin like a sword through porridge. Hundreds of severed ears filled the dyke and then Aindrea's blood had run cold. He'd suppressed the memory until, right until he saw the raider's monsters fifteen years later, hundreds of miles to the north of Mercia. But he remembered the chant the woman made in some tongue he'd never heard before. A fire started, hundreds of ears were in flames with not a man nor a torch anywhere near them.

~

His memory was foggy the next day about what had happened the night before. The dyke was finished, the prisoners were gone, the woman, the ears... only a charred meaty smell remained. He was told later that day the fyrd was disbanding and he should leave Mercia.

While lining up for his final bag of coin, he'd overheard a conversation between two Mercian archers.

~

"Won't see her for a while, she appears when the King is in great need."

"What happened to the prisoners?"

"Sent back to their shithole without their ears, mind I had to gut one with my blade."

"Why?"

"Little shit tried to grab one of my arrows after we cut their ropes and kicked them over the dyke."

"Gonna invade us with one arrow, was he?"

"Think he might have been a priest, he was yelling in the priest's language not the Wealas one."

"Priest?"

"Yeah, in nommy patri blah blah… that chant they do. But it was like he was chanting at the arrow, until I made his guts fall out."

"Maybe taking the ears means their wits fall out of the holes?"

"Yeah, that makes sense… "

~

A week later and the events of his final days in Mercia were completely gone from his memory.

Until now.

He knew it was futile, he could barely get to his knees, let alone fire an arrow but he had to try. He clutched his one remaining arrow to his chest and began to chant, *"In nomine Patris, et Filii, et Spirtus Sancti…"*

~

Choking, he crawled and followed the foul-sounding hoots and yelling coming from the church. He couldn't even give a full cry of despair when he saw so many bodies of his brothers spread across the church floor as his body was wracked with pain at every movement.

A strange feeling went through his upper body. Something inside of him was making him fight through the pain and get off one shot, it was too late for him but one shot could save a life, could save many if he could destroy the monsters.

When he saw the young raider raise Saint Cuthbert's thigh bone in a mocking gesture, the mixture of adrenaline and rage somehow got him to his feet. He couldn't save the brother who tackled the raider but got his breath back to aim and fire at the female monster who was pawing her way through Saint Cuthbert's coffin. The male's hand blocked the shot and took the arrow instead.

Aindrea could feel the heat on his face from his position in the doorway.

CHAPTER 7

Ulf's life was saved by Njarl's curiosity about the window at the back of the building, behind the large cross. Unlike the others that were uncovered or obscured with animal hides, this one was glass! Colored glass! If Ulf hadn't been so distracted by the skeleton and the robed man's outlandish reaction to it, he would have joined Njarl in dismantling the glass and breaking it into pieces.

When the draugr turned into a fireball, he ran to the window and leapt out. The window was a little high up so he leaped onto Njarl's head to escape. Njarl was holding a jagged piece of the glass and the first human scream Ulf heard was Njarl's as his head was forced down and the glass pierced his lower jaw.

Lying face down on the grass outside, he heard more human screams soon enough.

~

Aindrea charged toward the fire. He was unnoticed as the raiders were running past him trying to escape. He had to save any of his brothers that he could. He saw one man in a robe, Godwin. He thought to reach the door only to take an axe in the back of the head from a fleeing raider. He couldn't see Heregod, could he have survived?

He stopped when he felt someone clutching his ankle. Before he could look down, he looked at the horror ahead of him.

Men were ablaze and screaming. The monster was still engulfed and trying to put out the fire by rolling on the ground.

The flames weren't receding one bit and anything or anyone the beast touched ignited from head to toe instantly. The flames seemed to be never-ending.

He then looked down at the man clutching his ankle. It was the raider he had shot in the thigh while in the tower. His wound had gone bad; most of the lower half of his body was caked in blood. It was a surprise that he was still conscious. He surely couldn't walk and whoever had helped him into this room was either on fire or fled.

The man's eyes, once so fierce were quivering with terror. The heat got closer and smoke filled the air. "You are scared of fire?" Aindrea asked. "You cannot move?" The man didn't hear and wouldn't have been able to understand, instead he began to whimper and weep in his own tongue.

Aindrea found further adrenaline from the fire and the man's terror. Somehow that strange feeling in his arms and chest returned. He lifted the heavy man, slung him over his shoulder and made for the doorway. He turned back to make a silent prayer for his brothers and even the raiders now cursed to hell. The aflame monster's inhuman shriek continued and Aindrea heard a low groan, like a beast in great pain, a bear caught in a trap. But this was mixed with human-like weeping. He guessed it was coming from the monster's mate. He closed his eyes and tried to run.

~

Ulf smelt her first, then he heard her. The draugr was coming. Howling like the cold winds of Niflheim. He saw one pale white leg, riddled with protruding black veins stretch out of the open window. She had something under her arm.

He got up and ran, grunting with pain, he couldn't go far, he realized screwing his face up. Some pieces of the glass were in his leg. He managed to stagger to a bush and crawled under. About to pass out from the blood loss, he kept his eyes open long enough to see the draugr lay what she carried on the floor. It was the formerly pretty robed man he had beaten bloody.

She bent over his twitching and groaning body. He was still alive, if only just and put her face against his. Ulf gagged from just the thought of how bad the smell must be and cringed in disgust as the draugr stroked her black teeth against the man's cheek. He clenched his eyes shut as he saw the draugr's tongue lick the man's face and then slide into the man's now gummy and toothless mouth.

He made sure to clutch his dagger in his fist as he drifted away. *Valhalla awaits.* He would remember later, much later his final sight of that terrible night being the robed man's face blinking as he sat up. It was pale white and a large black vein began to stick out of his cheek.

Ulf passed out and didn't awake until the explosion.

~

Thorleif pounded on the man's back. He was shocked and ashamed by his reaction to the fire. The man propping him up had screamed and cursed at him to move. To shift his body along, to crawl, "You're too heavy to carry, skipper!" Thorleif couldn't move. The man ran for the door. The fire had rendered his whole body useless. It wasn't just the leg. He saw the men, robed men and his shipmates alike in flames from head to toe after coming into contact with the beast and somehow he knew what they were feeling.

The robed man who grunted at him and then picked him up must be insanely strong, he thought but he could not allow the survivors from the ship to see him be carried like a child. He intended to survive this journey and with Eskil lost to the sea become the new chieftain. He needed the men's respect.

~

Aindrea finally lost the power to carry the man and dropped

him on the grass a minute or two after they had passed the entrance where the oak doors had been. The man groaned but managed to sit upright, his paralysis seemingly cured now they were away from the fire. Still unable to walk and on the verge of unconsciousness, the man screamed words into the fading darkness. Two men stepped out of the shadows. Aindrea gave a look back to the monastery. The shriek of the beast was still piercing the air but it hadn't found its way out of the church. Some human screams and howls were still audible. "We need to go back and see if we can save…" one of the men punched him in the gut and then he felt his nose crush as another fist smashed into it, after the pain he tried to breathe but couldn't and then darkness hit him before he could panic.

CHAPTER 8

Nelda was woken by the sound of boots stamping on the wooden deck she lay face down on trussed up and gagged. She groaned with despair as the horror of last night overcame her and then another memory, one which chilled her to the bone. The last thing she remembered before passing out. The monsters prizing open some planks of the deck, near where she'd been thrown, to reveal a space underneath and then the real monsters had appeared. Two of them, naked as the day, they came into the world, white skin, black smiles and a stench of death. That was the last thing she remembered.

They weren't here now, she couldn't smell them and the men getting on the boat were talking to each other excitedly. They had been struck silent as the demons rose from the bottom of the boat last night.

Dawn was just starting and she felt a thud and struggled to turn her head to see what had been dumped next to her. It was the unconscious body of Brother Aindrea from the priory. Her frantic muffling through the gag was cut off by her being hoisted upright and her restraints cut and her gag removed.

She immediately yelled at the unconscious monk, "What happened? Who are these men? They killed…" Her rambled shouting was cut off by one of the men turning her around and clutching her throat. Certain she was to be killed or raped, she tried to wriggle and kick her way free while screaming only to feel a massive pain in her arse when she was dumped onto one of the benches, an oar was put in her hand and a word shouted at her, "Roa!" She guessed it meant 'row' as that was what the other men on the benches were doing. "Roa! Roa! Roa!" screamed a man striding up and down the boat. There were over twenty men at the beach when she was seized. Now only half that number were on the boat.

It took a couple of slaps to the face but soon she was rowing and the boat was pushing out toward sea. Tears streamed down her face. Where was she going? What was going to happen to her? The boat turned north. She saw at the head of the boat, sitting down, unconscious or dead, the foul man with the arrow sticking out of his thigh. She saw now about half a mile away, the huts on the beach she had grown up in and rising above them, a field's length inland the monastery towering over the land. Smoke was pouring from one of the buildings and she saw flickers of orange flame. The sun slowly rose, lighting up the whole island.

The sun's rays shone into the monastery and as they hit the church, the whole building exploded with a crashing rumble and a giant orange ball of fire engulfed the whole structure. Everyone stopped rowing to watch. They could hear the splashes as bits of stone hit the sea.

~

The rumble woke Ulf up and half a brick to the forehead put him to sleep again. It was an hour later before he limped his way to the beach looking for his shipmates and sank to his knees in horror as he saw the boat as a speck out in the distance. He put his head in his hands and screamed as if the boat could hear him.

Panic overtook him as he realized they thought him one of the dead in the fire and wouldn't return. He was trapped on this awful rock, unable to speak the language or know his way around. He also feared the glass had made him lame. He would be killed or enslaved as soon as he met his first armed man.

It was hours later that he had the idea to return to the scene of the fire. All seemed quiet now but his hands were shaking as he walked past the two charred skeletons in the grassy bit outside the large room where he'd last seen the burning Dragur and peered inside.

CHAPTER 9

796 AD, Aachen, Austrasia,

Ecgberht reminded himself to buy some of those odd tasting seeds on the way home as he took massive gulps of wine. He needed to conceal the smell. Nabila said getting drunk from grapes or dates was bad for some reason, her god was against it and so she only drank mead. Her distaste for wine made as much sense as her claims that their gods were the same. "Why do you hate the nuns if it's the same god?" These discussions never ended well, he had long come to accept they were very different people and he did his wine drinking without her. He wasn't going to drink fucking mead while living in the Frankish kingdom but he knew better than to provoke Nabila into throwing her chamber pot at his head.

Nabila or not, he was getting wrecked today. The news had arrived from across the sea that day. Offa was dead!

Ecgberht had been sent to Aachen to assist with the new palace Charlemagne had ordered constructed. While Saxons were found to be lacking with architecture expertise, they knew from their lands that a palace needed a town to thrive. Eudes the hairy old architect had been happy to assign the increasing number of Saxon exiles with building the wooden shacks and huts they insisted were needed for trade.

Eudes would never admit it but it had been a wise idea to let a small market town grow around the uncompleted palace. More and more coin was being generated and more and more men with building skills that were far beyond any Saxon that Ecgberht had met were arriving with the promise that wine, ale and women were to be found in Aachen. Although with the construction being ahead of schedule, there was talk that the zealously pious king of the Franks may be moving in early and that could cause trouble for Ecgberht's excessive lifestyle.

But the news of Offa, which had been twice confirmed now, meant they would all be sailing back home soon. So that's why the group of Saxon exiles were now waist-deep in the thermal baths of the palace, swigging from amphoras like there was no tomorrow.

"When will the big man give his orders?" Odberht asked, referring to Charlemagne. Odberht, who was posing as a priest, was really called Eadberht, another king in exile. He claimed the kingdom of Cent.

Ecgberht took another gulp and said, "I think that's largely up to me."

"What do you mean?" Odberht said.

"The big man is bogged down, our king doesn't half like a war or six going on at the same time. He's finally pinned down these Avars who live god knows where, no sooner than do the pagan Germans next door here rebel. Anyway he wants to use armies from the Spanish marshes to throw Offa's puppets out of our lands and for that I need to make Nabila my queen."

"The Moor!"

"She prefers the term Saracen, I don't know the difference either."

"She's fair looking apart from the…"

"It's not that, it's that she still refuses to convert and the big man will not tolerate a non-Christian queen."

"But I thought you promised the big man that you could convince her..."

"Yeah, it's been tougher than I expected."

~

With a hangover and his mouth reeking of the bitter tasting seeds, he trudged off to the nunnery the next morning to try and convince the Saracen noblewoman once more.

~

"What do you mean she's gone?" Ecgberht had never gotten comfortable with this particular dialect of Frankish. Even the Saxon words they slipped in didn't help, the Saxon spoken around here was very different from what his ancestors had spoken when they got on their boat and sailed north all those centuries ago.

What was really making it tough though was the elderly nun had no teeth. Hardly unusual but he could tell she had recently lost her remaining teeth by how her jaw was still flapping, spraying spittle everywhere, plus she was embarrassed as her hand was shielding her mouth. The toothless usually talk from the back of their throat and try not to move their lips.

Eventually a younger nun took the hissing old one away and told Ecgberht that a man bearing the King's golden seal had arrived that morning with instructions to take Nabila with him.

"A guard?" Ecgberht asked.

"We're all for the fire if our lord has guards that age!" the young nun said. "I reckon he was older than Sister Dadin and Sister Doda put together!"

"What did he look like?"

At the description, Ecgberht turned and started to run in the direction of the royal palace.

CHAPTER 10

Nabila had risen early to pray before the nuns were awake and was playing her lute while waiting for one of the sisters to bring her morning porridge. Praying was the only thing that kept her sane while being held prisoner in this dump and it had the added advantage of soothing the tyrannical and humorless nuns. She even had seen one of the younger ones tap her feet to the tune. The *maqam* pitch of both the melody of the Oud lute and the notes of her voice as she chanted the poems was obviously unlike anything they had ever heard.

The door opened with no knock and Sister Doda wordlessly put the wooden bowl on the stone floor. The ancient sister was at least rightfully wary of her leaving immediately. Nabila wondered if she was to be in trouble for knocking Sister Dadin's fourteen remaining teeth out when the old hag had gleefully announced she'd mixed pork fat into the porridge after Nabila had finished it last week.

How they could punish her, she was unsure. If they wanted to kill her, they would have done it by now.

She was still astonished at how her life had changed in just a matter of weeks all those years ago. Life as a merchant's daughter in the beautiful plains and valleys of Ribagorza shielded under the giant mountains had been luxurious and peaceful but it had made her restless. She found herself distracted from her lessons and spending hours staring at those mountains from her villa's courtyard, wondering what lay beyond. She now wondered if she was being punished for such thoughts.

Over the course of weeks, she noticed more and more groups of men arriving at her house. Her father began holding court with them in meetings behind the latticed windows. Rumors started that the Franks; infidels to their north, had broken through the mountains! Impossible, she thought.

Soon the roads and valleys were full of groups of soldiers marching toward the mountains. Armed with mace, scimitar, javelin and bows, they would make short work of the savage Franks who were said to be so primitive they only knew the sword and spear.

Her first worry was after her father returned from a battle he and other high-ranking merchants had watched from hilltops expecting a pleasant afternoon of viewing the slaughter of infidel barbarians. Shaking as he returned, she caught him muttering, *"Whoever their king is, he is of greater mind for warfare than any savage we know of to date,"* to his companions.

It had been a few days later when she was woken in the middle of the night with the rest of the household as they piled their possessions into large chests and started to ready their horses from the large stables. She was told most of the family and neighbors were going further inland. To the parts of Al-Andalus, the Franks could not reach, to Isbilya or Al-Lixbuna perhaps. She was about to jump in the back of a wagon her sisters had boarded when she felt a whack to the back of her skull, a horrible pain that seemed to spread eerily slowly and then the darkness.

At dawn she came to. She was bound and gagged, blood running down her neck, and slung over the arse of her favorite Andalusian horse Moonlight.

Her father riding the horse gave the explanation. "We've ceded this land to the savages, in return they've agreed to allow us to retreat into Al-Andalus. They want a guarantee that we won't return with a larger army to retake our land and send them straight to Jahannam. So they've asked for hostages. The most pure of our blood, our princesses, those descended from the Prophet, Peace be upon him, himself…"

Nabila, who was the third daughter of a salt merchant's second wife, began to wriggle desperately and make muffled screams. She was to be sacrificed!

~

Life in the walled city of Worms was more comfortable than she had feared. She was allowed the freedom of the city as long as she was chaperoned and the city's Jewish quarter allowed her to purchase herbed bread and dried figs which was a respite from the slop that was usually served to her and the others.

One day she returned home and saw the sight she knew would come one day. The heads of her fellow "princesses" Husna, a slave and Zinat, a girl abandoned by her family after her wits had gradually left her were nailed to the floor of the hut they shared. Her people have retaken their land! She was briefly pleased before reality hit and she turned to run. Her chaperon's fist was waiting in the doorway for her.

~

So to the present day, she had been in the Aachen nunnery ever since. Tormented by the sisters who saw her existence as blasphemous, preached at by priests, then threatened and beaten when she scoffed at their sermons. Never knowing when guards would arrive at the nunnery gates to give her the same awful fate Husna and Zinat had suffered.

Recently there had been a new visitor to preach at her. He had a kind face that wasn't terrible to look at even though his hair reminded her of the plumage of the white vultures that flew north from Africa to the mountains every summer. Staring at the face was all she had as he was so dull-witted, despite being in this land longer than her. His Frankish sounded like he was trying to chew stones while speaking. Much like the priests, he was here to convert her but at least the priests could read and knew of Euclid and Aristotle, men she knew were studied by the Christians of the east. But even these priests, the best in the land to be selected by their king, were appallingly ignorant about the works of the rest of the Greeks, the great Christian thinkers of Alexandria and even The Prophet himself. How could she be preached to by men who thought a bookshelf was a library?

The man with the vulture plumage hair claimed to have read a book once but upon questioning, it had been a collection of riddles on parchment he had committed to memory.

"You don't even know the language your holy book is written in?" she had said flabbergasted during one meeting.

"It's why we have priests and monks, I think," he replied.

He was good for two things. His face was pleasurable to gaze at and he brought her mead.

~

Back in the present, she finished her porridge and was about to pick up her lute again when she heard raised voices from outside her room.

They've come for me at last, she thought, the assault of the nun had reminded them of who she was and that converting her was a lost cause. She looked for a weapon. Years of beatings had led to her losing her meekness. As Sister Dadin, a priest who looked up her skirts with his hands and had his balls kicked black and the vulture plumage haired man, Ecgberht, who ended up with her chamber pot contents on his head after blowing his nose on one of her books, had all found out to their cost.

She had one of her lute strings around the neck of the intruder before he knew she was behind him. She noticed as she pulled tighter that for a guard, he was old and unarmed and although she couldn't see it, the front of his face seemed oddly shaped. She let her guard down for just a moment and the man sent her sprawling with a strong elbow to the face.

Her nose was bruised and bloody as she looked up at the bald, ancient looking man with severe burns and blue dots tattooed on his face. *"As-salamu alaykum,"* he said and then in the same language, "I'm Brennus, we have been looking for you for a long time."

CHAPTER 11

Ecgberht was known to the guards at the entrance and strolled past them into the huge, uncompleted brick hall. At fifty meters long and twenty meters high, it was the biggest building for miles. On each end of the hall, a large dome shape had been constructed, called aspes, the one to the south was already filled with treasures plundered from every part of the Carolingian dynasties conquests. Golden and silver crosses, chalices, statues, jewel encrusted crucifixes and more. This was the part of the hall that had three guards armed with spear, shield and sword patrol at all times. At least thirty guards would be on the perimeter of this section of the building.

Not enough, thought Ecgberht, sooner or later one of the men hammering the curved wooden roof into shape will talk in his cups and an army of bandits will organize. If he knew the big man as well as he thought, perhaps he was gathering so much plunder in one place as a challenge for them to meet his own army.

To the north was another aspe, this was from where Ecgberht had entered and the market town was growing. To his left were two rows of arched-shaped windows which shone light onto the western side of the hall. These windows shone onto the gallery of paintings on the wall to his right. He remembered his first tour of this building being told who these men were. There was the big man's father Pepin, Constantine the first Roman emperor to be Christian and Clovis the first king to unite the Frankish tribes.

"Boy! Get in here right now! We've been waiting for too long. I'm a busy man!" boomed the loud, jolly voice of the king of the Franks from the largest and final aspe on the western side of the hall. This aspe was concealed from the rest of the building by linen wall hangings and had two guards at the entrance.

Despite knowing the guards by sight, he was still roughly patted down and his dagger taken before he was allowed to enter King Charlemagne's private suite for the first time since arriving in Francia seven years ago.

~

On a stone podium, six stairs up, the King towered over him while sitting on a marble throne. A sturdy, broad-shouldered man, over six-foot tall, white hair and gray-bearded, he seemed almost celestial from such a height. A blue silk tunic was over his linen breeches and shirt topped off by a blue cape and a sword with jewels covering the hilt by his side.

At the foot of the podium was a trestle table covered with food. At one end on a stool sat Nabila, swigging mead from a jug and gnawing on a chicken leg. At the other stood Brennus, nibbling at some grapes.

"A Briton, a Saxon and a Moor walk into a King's suite..." boomed the voice from above them, it stopped before "...never mind I'll think of the rest of the joke later! Glad you could join us, boy-king, how many Saxon kings in exile am I sheltering and feeding now? Feel free to take a look around the suite, friends, not many people get to see the paintings I keep here."

Ecgberht noticed the portraits behind the King's throne. These had been painted onto wood rather than papyrus and looked different to the paintings outside the suite. He guessed the artist was a Saxon as the lack of colors and oversized heads reminded him of wall paintings from his childhood. The artist was not without talent. They had managed to capture a lot of detail in a portrait of an unremarkable-looking woman he couldn't help but see flashes of beauty in her messy hair and jagged smile. She was wearing a tatty, brown gown; the same type village women wear today and was clutching a long dagger.

The painting next to her showed a handsome if gaunt-looking man. The artist had captured a sense of worry and sadness in his eyes. Stretching over his left eye like a web was some sort of marking. He was missing his right arm and a great longsword was in his left hand.

"The heroes of Londinium!" Charlemagne shouted, "Brennus, bring me that wheel of cheese!" As he sank his teeth into it, he started speaking at a furious pace, "So the heroes have returned, you think, Brennus!"

Brennus shuffled uncomfortably. "We believe so, Lord King." He then turned to Nabila and spoke to her in a language he had never heard, it sounded like he was coughing. She replied in the same tongue making far more curt and coherent sounds albeit ones still meaningless to Ecgberht.

After a few more of these exchanges, Brennus switched to Frankish and said, "Fine, finish that chicken off and I'll escort you back to the nunnery where you can spend the rest of your life, that is unless King Charlemagne knows of an Avar Khagan who it might be advantageous to offer a concubine to." The big man's eyebrows rose at this and Ecgberht could see him beginning to think before Nabila spoke in Frankish.

"Your face looks like a donkey's arse and smells worse," she said before pulling down the veil that covered her lower face to take another swig of mead. Instead of pulling it straight off, she began to tug at the hooded veil that covered her hair and the sides of her face. When it fell off, her long, black, curled hair fell to her elbows and then, it must have been something Brennus had asked her in her language, she pulled the hair over the left side of her face back to reveal her cheek and temple.

Her marks were black and his were purple but the pattern they made on her face were identical to the man in the painting.

"Rebirth, it is true!" The King gasped.

"For some eternal rewards must wait while there is unfinished business on this plane," Brennus said. "I know of this only too well, my Lord King," he gave the big man a strange look as he said this.

The King ignored him. "But this time they have come back as… is that possible?"

"It appears so," Brennus said.

"And the others from the tales Merlin told me. The slave girl who brought Londinium to its knees, the sister that rid the world of the Nix creature, the brother that could burn stone, the brave child that made the strigoi choke on her own flesh, the Saxon couple that found Avalon, have they returned too?"

"We believe so, Lord King, it's just they have proved more elusive than these two," Brennus finished.

"Do you have any idea what they are talking about?" Ecgberht asked Nabila.

She shrugged as she put her head veil back on. "Thought donkey arse was here to kill me, turned out I got to eat something other than porridge for the first time in three years so I've been working on that." She took another swig of mead and burped before telling him, "You stink of wine and cardamom, it's a disgusting combination."

The King's booming voice interrupted them. "Now let us talk of Northumbria!"

CHAPTER 12

"Northumbria is a land I have taken a great degree of interest in, a most holy place and one in which the church owns a lot of land. His holiness is new to the papacy and has many enemies, it is important to my plans for Leo to remain as the Bishop of Rome for a long time, thus Northumbria must remain Christian!" the King proclaimed.

~

Nabila had never heard of Northumbria before, still if it was having second thoughts about having nuns in it, she figured it can't be that bad. She was examining the suite herself now. The embroidery of the wall hangings hardly seemed kingly, she knew of baker's wives who had better quality stitching done in their bedrooms back in Al-Andalus. Gorging on too much food had made her tired. She tried to concentrate on the King's speech and was helped by mention of a murder. Things like that are always interesting.

~

"The problem with Northumbria is it is full of treacherous, perverse people who have not read Adomnán of Iona's accounts of the divine punishment that befalls those who refuse their kings because they are refusing god himself!" The King's face was turning the same color as the wine in his cups as he continued. "Aethelred has been murdered! The third king of theirs slain since I've taken this throne. I've forgotten how many others have been deposed and sent into exile. You boy, some of your drinking companions might be among them."

~

Ecgberht knew he wasn't the only king in exile living in the palace. Young men from all over the Carolingian sphere of influence who were said to be powerful in their homelands lived here. There was himself, Odberht, Nabila was said to be a great princess whose father commanded large armies in the godless lands to the south. But he couldn't think of a Northumbrian he'd drunk with. A dreary place that served as a barrier between civilization and Pictland was his only impression of it.

Apart from his teacher, when he'd first arrived in Francia, he was unable to speak the Frankish language so was sent to a Northumbrian who was close to the big man called Alcuin for instruction. Alcuin was a softly spoken man, insanely intelligent and unable to keep his eyes off Ecgberht's arse but his lasting memory of the man was a few years ago when he informed the court of pirates or someone sacking some shitty little island in his homeland.

"St Cuthbert's bones, splattered with the blood of God's priests, the holy isle stalked by the devil himself, the smell of dung fouling the air as dead things came from the water!" The poor man had howled at the court with tears streaming down his face. Everything was gone. Not a single survivor, even the residents of the fishing village that kept the monks fed were found feeding fish instead of monks. The priory, one of the great buildings of the north now just charred rubble. Only one fleeing, wounded monk who had died hours after being found gave his account to the shepherds that found him. By the time word reached Alcuin, the information would have been repeated many times over and the pirate's foul deeds surely embellished. Now Brennus had arrived in Francia and the big man was getting interested in Northumbria straight after. Ecgberht started thinking hard.

~

The King continued, "This new king, this Eardwulf is an imposter! Everyone in Northumbria knows Aethelred killed Eardwulf six years ago but amongst the chaos he claims to have returned. Alcuin had influence among the conspirators and put his friend on the throne but the friend turned out to be a fool and lasted only twenty-seven days. Then Eardwulf, now richer than anyone in the kingdom, returns from the grave! It appears these two..." he gestured at Nabila and Ecgberht "...aren't the only ones to rise from the dead, although it's trickery rather than rebirth from Eardwulf."

Shaking by now, he said, "The new Eardwulf has lost half a head of height, his hair has changed color and he speaks Northumbrian so poorly that your Frankish seems competent in comparison..." Ecgberht blinked at this directed toward him "...worst of all, my spies confirm he is a pagan! He worships the same gods that the pagan Saxons to my east do, the same your ancestors did!" This again directed toward Ecgberht.

~

Brennus decided it was time for the King to get to the point. "Lord King, this is distressing news but you command large armies in almost every Christian land and however much gold this Eardwulf has, surely you can provide more to maneuver the situation to both your and Pope Leo's advantage. Why, may I ask you, do you wish the Hunt to be involved, you understand that our forces are only to be used for darker things than the squabbles of men? I am a Briton, Lord King, we are well aware that Saxons rebel and fight among themselves just as pigs roll in shit, it is merely their nature."

~

Ecgberht was beginning to take these barbs a little personally but it was toward him that the King waved a piece of parchment he'd taken out of the folds in his tunic.

"From Alcuin," the King said with great effort. The speech had taken its toll.

Ecgberht stammered at the curved letters on the parchment. He *could* read, it was just he didn't do it very often and it was a perishable skill. Before he could make a stuttering start, Nabila walked next to him and snatched the parchment away.

~

Nabila saw Ecgberht was uncomfortable at being expected to read Alcuin's message and she did for some reason feel pleased at helping him but the main reason she took the message was to practice her own reading skills. She had been taught her letters at a young age as was normal, no husband would want a dull-witted or incompetent wife, she'd been told and upon her arrival in Francia, she found she had a new set of letters to learn and set about it.

Only finding things to read, literate people to teach her or even a fucking sign or two appeared to be beyond the Franks. Not lacking for time, she had found the names of food items written down at the market and committed them to memory. Once her guards mistakenly left a list of names with her and the two other "princesses", she'd memorized what she guessed to be the shift schedule of the guards, some were just marked with a single character but every little bit helped.

By the time she was confined to the nunnery, other than a few scraps of papyrus with prayers written in her native tongue that she'd been allowed to keep, the only thing to read was the nuns' shopping list. Most of the nuns had about twenty words they could read and write with symbols being used for any items they couldn't. Still she poured over the lists and Ecgberht brought her anything with writing he came across in his routine, some of the more learned priests that could read would give her flashing glimpses of religious texts they allowed her to look at but not touch.

And now she had a letter to read. Just as years of porridge had made the King's greasy offerings seem like a lavish banquet, years of smatterings of text made a single letter seem like the famed House of Wisdom in Baghdad.

She began to read.

CHAPTER 13

"Eardwulf is not the man I knew, I have already told of the changes to his person and speech. He is a pagan, he refuses to take Thor's hammer from his neck and refuses all services and consul from the church. He has retreated to the Roman wall where he has rebuilt the fort of Segedunum..." this was where Nabila reading Alcuin's words had her tongue betray her as she gave up after her fourth attempt at pronouncing the Roman word. Charlemagne corrected her and urged her to continue.

"... Eardwulf's gold has built him a great army of both Northumbrian and Pict. There is talk of others coming from the sea to the east but this is not confirmed. Deserters from Eardwulf's army talk of darkness in the depths of Segedunum. A masked woman who has the pretender in thrall, swaying hooded guards that smell of the grave and are capable of great feats of strength. Already the Northumbrian dux are bemoaning their hasty deposing of Aethelred. Osbald claimed the throne and rode for Segedunum demanding Eardwulf lay down his arms. Osbald returned without his army and fled to Lindisfarena. We fear Eardwulf will march on Bamburgh, the dux and bishops have fled to Eoforwic..."

Nabila stopped and silence filled the suite. She was trying to translate it in her head. Had she got the part about smelling of the grave correct? An odd way of describing something. Ecgberht and Brennus looked thoughtful, there was something they hadn't told her. The King looked as if he had aged ten years. He waved at her to continue. There was a small part left.

"...Osbald has been tortured mad, I fear. He mutters nonsense such as 'white of skin, black of heart, black of blood and even black of tooth!' and when I asked about his army's whereabouts, he burst into laughter screaming, 'They don't breathe no more but they walk, they run, they even swim!'

~

"Alcuin and Osbald await on Lindisfarena for help. I do not intend to send ordinary soldiers into what could be the devil's own mouth," Charlemagne said. "Brennus, I want the Lost Hunt to travel to Northumbria and rid the land of it!" He glared at Ecgberht and Nabila and said, "I assume there is a divine reason for having ended up feeding and housing the survivors of Londinium and it's time for repayment."

~

Nabila's confusion at everything since Brennus entered her bedchamber finally boiled over. "Why am I here? What is the Lost Hunt? Where or what is Londinium?"

"It's a bunch of Britons who run around in the mountains of Wealas looking for monsters to kill with magic arrows," Ecgberht explained.

Nabila didn't say anything to that. Instead she turned to Brennus and asked the same questions.

"The island Ecgberht and myself are from has a reputation for demons and darkness so an organization was formed to..." Brennus began.

She cut him off, "The things Alcuin was talking about, could they be ghuls?"

He looked troubled. "What is a ghul?"

"Flesh-eating, deformed and insane demons barred from the heavens." She answered slowly as if a child had asked her something foolish.

"Yes, that could be what we are dealing with here." Brennus looked thoughtful. "Have you ever notched a bow before?"

"Of course," she replied. "It is a Sunnah."

~

Two weeks later in a thriving town called Dorestad, Nabila found herself with less of the privacy than she had in the nunnery. She was sharing a hut with Brennus and Ecgberht, at least she had a tent set up behind the hut to retire to when she needed to. But she didn't miss the nunnery at all and this town was a lot more interesting than Aachen. It was a thin, tall town, a three kilometer strip that rested on the banks of the widest river she had seen. From the town extending out into the river were hundreds of jetties, with storehouses being built alongside the jetties; it was as if the town was being extended into the river.

Brennus, who spent most of the day in the hut talking to Ecgberht, had told her it was safe to walk around.

"Not usually but this city is too important to the King's finances and raiders from the north are getting bolder. The city watch will be large and all will have been instructed that the veiled Moor woman is not to be touched if the soldiers want to keep body parts that they are likely to miss. Take this dagger just in case."

She hadn't needed the dagger. On her first solo walk outside of the hut, she was attacked. She was still fumbling for it when she felt her shoulder grabbed and yanked into a gap between two huts. By the time she had grasped the hilt, the air smelled of shit as her attacker fell backwards clutching his entrails as they oozed out of his belly. The guard who had been discretely stalking her from the other side of the huts had been well positioned to run his lance through the narrow gap.

Since then she had enjoyed the freedom of the town, going up and down each jetty, communicating as best she could verbally and with gestures. She discovered this giant river started many miles to the south among a great group of mountains. Not the ones she had grown up under, these were covered with snow. The smaller river went north to a sea, the one the large men in furs with hammers around their necks would sail in from.

Other ships from the north brought men wearing the same garb as Ecgberht was fond of, longer tunics and cloaks than the Franks indicating a colder climate. From the south ships with black-haired men wearing tights with puffy sleeved tunics and men in colorful robes with brown skin much darker than her own would arrive regularly. The market was loud, full of voices in scores of different tongues.

Silk, amber, fur, glass, swords, pelt, dyes, salt, spices, honey, hunting dogs and slaves all came off the boats. The townspeople had their own coins to trade and sold wool and linen, iron tools and bone combs to both sailors and the merchants who had come to trade.

Nabila was enjoying talking to people from all over the world, seeing what they wore, how they spoke, what they sold. She was interested to see Christians, Jews and Pagans mix freely and she wondered if any of her own people were this far north. She had to return to their hut soon. Brennus used the evenings to observe her archery and horseback skills in the fields behind the village.

Then she came across the slave pen.

~

Ecgberht took another swig of wine and burped. "So did you ever find out what a Sunnah is?"

"No," Brennus was inspecting a Frankish small sword called a seax, "but we have nothing to fear about her skill with the bow nor her horsemanship. In fact it's better than most Briton or Saxon men of good training I know of. I'd worry about yourself, we can't afford a longsword so this seax will have to be sufficient for you."

"It'll do, pugio would be better for fighting at close quarters, the seax is a bit more fiddly when you're going for the throat to stop them from squealing and telling their mates where you are," Ecgberht said.

"Well, stay away from brothels, alehouses and anywhere you might find yourself in such a situation," Brennus advised.

"Shouldn't be a problem on Lindisfarena." Ecgberht sighed. "You say the arrows are coming by sea but why so long? And why not bring the pugio and longsword that are on display in the great hall? You and Merlin always said I'd need that if things went…"

"They have not left that hall for over two hundred and fifty years. The decision to move them is not to be taken lightly," Brennus snapped, beginning to get annoyed at being stuck inside with Ecgberht for most of the day. He didn't really have the face for large towns. He was also frustrated at the delay of the arrow shipment and explained why.

"They are being taken around the coast of Dumnonia. We cannot move overland, since that fucking dyke got built anytime one of the Hunt's men crosses into Mercia, they get ambushed. Some foul magic was done to ensure the Mercians know we are coming, no kingdom has spies that good." Brennus closed his eyes. "Perhaps better relations with Mercia now that Offa is…"

He was cut off by a shout from Ecgberht. Something had crashed through the deer's hide used for a door. It was Nabila, she crashed to her knees and looked up to them wide eyed, sobbing and panting. Her hands were red with blood.

CHAPTER 14

Nabila had had slaves at her family's villa in Ribagorza, they had seemed content, they weren't overworked in her opinion. She came from a big family with a large appetite and those pigeons weren't going to stuff themselves, nor were the stables where Moonlight and his friends lived going to clean themselves. It was only a few young girls, some from the old country across the narrow southern sea, others more fair-haired, from the people who had been in her lands before the Umayyad conquest that had created Al-Andalus.

She'd been forbidden from talking to the male slaves who guarded the walls of the villa and were forced into the militias that patrolled the land, but the women seemed to be in good condition, no doubt helped by the bulging storehouses that ensured no one went hungry. If one was unwilling to work or spoke back to her, a light if firm slap across the face reminded them of what was expected of them. Once every few years, her father would give one of the aging guards if pious enough his freedom. The new freedman would be allowed to select one of the slave women to wed and a small piece of land was given to the couple.

Her father would, in the weeks that followed, take a caravan to the coastal city of Barcelona to load his carts with salt and he would return with replacement slaves who were quickly put to work. Nabila never thought much about where they came from.

~

Now she was face to face with the horrors of a slave pen. She had walked past the part of the market where they were paraded on a stage and they had sold quickly. All young and healthy to survive the journey. Men and women, Christian and Pagan, Frank and foreign, they found themselves in strong demand. There were only a handful that had remained unsold and marched back to the pen she now found herself at.

It was a crudely built wooden cage positioned on the very banks of the river. Too low to stand in, sitting down in it brought the water up to the occupant's chest. The three living occupants were shivering and sick.

She had been drawn to the wretched sight by the sound of her own language being chanted in such a pitiful way it made her skin curl up. *"You are our Protector, so forgive us and have mercy upon us; and You are the best of forgivers."* Even in rags, she knew the man for a Saracen.

"What happened? How did you come to be in such a place?" Nabila whispered, wading into the river. The man turned his head in shock at being addressed and his eyes peered over her head and then looked from side to side. His eyes were cloudy. "Can you see?" Nabila asked.

As his head swung around looking for the source of the voice, she saw a wound in the back of his head, a gaping, deep looking gash that was oozing blood. This man had only hours to live which would be spent in great pain. Panting came from the other side of the pen, the only other two occupants; a young woman and her young child were shivering so hard, it sounded pained. The woman said something to Nabila who shook her head, she couldn't understand but knew the woman was pleading for help.

"Interested in buying the dregs, Moor?" Nabila shot upright at the voice behind her. She turned around and saw the slave trader. She recognized him from the market. A plump belly showed that business was good. He jumped from the top of the bank down to the edge where she was standing.

"Let me show you a trick!" He kicked one of the wooden bars and it came loose. "The others are buried three feet deep but this one barely goes into the ground. Saves on gates and locks, only ones who come back from the market are the runts, even knowing the special place won't help them escape. Look at your mate!"

The Saracen was back to praying. "What happened to him? He's blind and dying!" Nabila said, upset.

"Shipwreck survivor, was found in Benevento at the bottom end of the big boot. Came with the upriver ships. To hear the lads speak of it, the dozy fool was praying for the whole journey. Well, on the auction stand it was beginning to put some of the customers off, very emotional you see and obviously not Christian, people aren't going to like that in their houses! To get him to stop I gave him a few taps with my club, forgot that it had a few nails sticking out of it. Now as for the woman, her child is putting customers off but if you aren't interested, I know a priest who likes them that..."

The man's piggy eyes bulged with shock and then fear as he gave a wheeze and tears rolled from his eyes and drool and blood from his mouth. His face went pale as his knees began to buckle.

Nabila was still clutching the dagger, her mouth opened and shut in shock. She had felt a surge of anger more furious than anything she had ever felt and her body had shook with rage. Seconds later she was stood holding a bloody dagger with the slaver's guts spilling out of his body.

"No, sorry... I..." she cried as she made to push back the red, slimy things coming out of the large wound she'd made when she leaned forward screaming at him. She screamed with disgust at their touch and turned and fled.

~

Now back at the hut, calming her was difficult as she refused wine but Brennus reached into one of the many pouches he carried and mixed some dried herbs into a cup of beer and tipped it down her throat, this eased her breathing and once she was sat comfortably, he asked her in halting Arabic what had happened.

When Brennus had translated her story for Ecgberht, the younger man sighed and said, "We are fucked."

"For once you speak with knowledge and are correct," Brennus said.

"You mean you don't have any plan or magic to get us out of here?" Ecgberht actually sounded concerned now.

"The slaver is or was one of the most important people in town. Even the King's protection won't save us from his friends and family. We should leave town now." He began marching around the hut putting items in the sacks and chests they had brought with them. "It's getting dark, but if we can find somewhere to hide at night and get past the swamps during the day, we will come to a settlement called Antwerpen, we can tell them we are under Charlemagne's protection and they may even remember The Hunt, Antwerpen looked to us when they had a giant problem during Roman times." Brennus huffed out words while packing.

"How big was this problem? It must have been immense if they're going to remember it centuries later," Ecgberht said.

"Not a giant problem, fool! A Giant problem. Beast by the name of Antigoon he was and…"

Brennus was cut off by the second sudden intrusion through the hide door. A filthy young woman covered as much in blood as in mud and dirty water. Behind her was an equally filthy young child who was so frail, it was shocking the child was breathing, let alone standing.

The woman sank to her knees just as Nabila had but the expression on her face was one of pure joy. "God is great!" She screamed. "He has made the heavens flood." Both men looked at each other, heavy rain was thudding on the straw roof and thunder soon followed.

The woman continued, "The demon sent by Satan is slain and the Lord washes away his blood, just as I, his servant, filled his cursed-to-hell corpse with stones and sank him at the bottom of the river!"

The two men looked at each other again. "Did you hear what I just heard?" Ecgberht asked.

"Yes," Brennus replied, "but what form of Saxon is she speaking? It's very distinct from Mercian, I struggle at times with it."

Ecgberht smiled. "It's a bastard to get used to but she might have given us a chance. She's speaking Northumbrian."

CHAPTER 15

The packing continued, Brennus explained, "If she speaks true, then we may have a few hours, the night if we are very fortunate. At the best, tomorrow morning his wife will notice he didn't come back from the brothel or ale house and form a search party. At the worst, Nabila was witnessed and the city watch are on their way!"

Ecgberht looked outside and said, "I think we have the night, there's nothing amiss, fewer people out because of the rain but no one appears to be paying this hut any mind."

Brennus looked at the child with disquiet, he clearly didn't enjoy the company of such an age. Nabila had found something to distract her from the trauma as she made a fire and searched for scraps of furs and hides to warm the child and his mother who announced, "His name is Heregod, after his father," to no interest from the room whatsoever.

~

Nelda smiled as she whispered grateful prayers to herself, she could see her son's skin get less pale as he sat by the fire. Soon a cup of beer was placed in her hands and a bowl of porridge given to both her and the child. She looked at her saviors, a deformed old man, a drunk and a Moor. *He truly works in mysterious ways*, she thought.

After the horrors of that terrible last night on Lindisfarena, her next memory was being shaken awake each time she fell asleep on the boat and collapsing on a stone beach as soon as she was hoisted out of the boat. The last thing she felt were ropes being roughly tied around her wrists.

She had woken in a large wooden building with straw on the floor. Her hands still bound and surrounded with a dozen other wretched men and women in a similar state. Twice a day a pail of grains would be thrown into the room and those that could get to the food in time would fight, kicking and biting each other for the scraps. Nelda lacked the strength to do even that.

Fearing that both her and her unborn child were doomed to starve, her only respite was not being one of the group of slaves that were shepherded out of the hut each morning only to return in the thick of darkness too tired to speak. During the day she was left with one girl with cloudy eyes who stared at the wall and a man with a club foot.

For a week she thought she'd lived on just a few crumbs of grain a day, how she'd survived she didn't know, her memories of this time blurred but she remembered the day when the blue-skinned man entered the hut.

He grunted orders to the blind girl and lame man and then turned to her and said in words she could understand, "So, you're with child, that means you're to be Droplaug's maid."

It took her a while to work out that the blue skin was dye, blue scales and wave like designs had been so overdone that few pink fleshy parts of the arms remained. She knew who used dye from a wild flower to look like that. "You are a Pict?" she asked.

"Aye, name's Bili," said the Pict, "was a fisherman over on our side of the sea till a storm took me too far out one night. Been head slave for ten years now. These folk are Norsemen. They are, they are… different to us."

"But if you are from Pictland…" She pointed to the hammer around his neck.

"Trust me, lass, life is a lot easier around here if you pick the one-eyed god rather than the one who got nailed to a stick." He sighed. "Thorleif, the new chieftain wanted you as his humping girl, he likes them with a bit of stoutness on the arse and thighs but his wife brought the Volva, that's their medicine woman, to check you over first while you were out cold and she said…" He pointed to her belly.

He continued, "Anyway, Thorleif wanted to sell you if he couldn't hump you, they think it's bad luck, you see, but his daughter is in the same way so needs her rest…"

~

Now years later, warming herself by the fire and bringing her son closer to her, Nelda felt vindicated. She had lost the wooden crucifix she wore around her neck years ago, but she had never stopped believing in the words of the lord Brother Heregod had preached at her. The private sermons when he came to collect the priory's fish deliveries that soon turned into something else. She had never taken to tales of multiple gods, all seemingly without love, each controlling part of the heavens. Now safe and warm, she was being rewarded for her faith.

~

"Did the slaver have a boat?" Ecgberht asked the newcomer, jolting her to attention. They had been speaking Frankish for Nabila's benefit while discussing what to do and the woman had been content not to be part of the discussion, smiling with a look of relief on her face. Now it was time to get her involved.

"Yes, the Norsemen brought down two boatloads of slaves. Neither were allowed to dock in the town so he had to make several journeys in his own boat," she said.

"That means a small boat," said Brennus. "And we must wait here for the blessed arrows. We cannot depart without them, not if Eardwulf has a ghul army. It would be suicide!"

"What's a ghul?" the woman said.

Nabila got the gist of the question and answered by rolling her eyes back into her head and making a mock snarl. She briefly had the effect of making her pretty face look hideously terrifying.

"Draugr," the woman whispered. All traces of relief gone from her face.

CHAPTER 16

King Eardwulf as he was always trying to think of himself decided to return from the wooden ramparts and into the fort. At nighttime he knew they would be stalking the hills and plains around the wall. People stayed away from the area around the wall. North and south of the wall, there wasn't a village for miles. It was like people knew to stay away.

The woods north of the wall were full of deer which made the lack of villages even more puzzling, not that Eardwulf was complaining. They were also known to enjoy the woods at night and of late, the howling of the wolves had ceased. As long as he couldn't see them when he was trying to rest at night, as long as he couldn't smell them.

He stayed away from the newly built barracks, guardhouse and headquarters inside the fort during the daytime unless it was essential. The things were lurking there, unable to face the sunlight. Most of the men did the same, preferring guard watch or patrol to coming across one of the things.

The witch could face the sunlight. She was the only one of them who could, she sometimes even removed her wooden mask when she walked with him smiling at his discomfort.

He remembered the first time he met the witch.

~

Ulf, as he still called himself back then, sheltered shivering in the ruins of the monastery. Exhausted, he had slept for most of the day and it was pissing down. He was clutching as much of the gold as he could carry from the box with the bones in. It didn't warm him.

It was then he heard the voices; a man and a woman.

"We've been walking for a week now, for this? A wreck of a building on the edge of the world?" the male voice said.

"I told you. I dreamed it. A wonder, a way of boosting our numbers!" the woman's voice hissed back.

A torch was lit and the man's face became illuminated. Long, straight, brown hair curved down each side of his face and his eyes were the most fierce shade of yellow. He gave the torch to the woman and that's when Ulf, who hadn't understood a word of their discussion, whimpered and gave away his location. The woman would have been beautiful if not for the green scale-like skin and complete absence of eyes.

Soon Ulf was staring blankly into that face as she asked him questions. She took a pouch from her belt and from it dabbed some powder onto her tongue. She then asked him in Norse, "Where are the draugr?"

~

Now back in Segedunum years later, Ulf... no King Eardwulf told himself he did what he had to stay alive. The deal he'd made with Alecto; the eyeless witch, to use the monastery gold to build the fort and use bandits for hire to increase his fortune.

Alecto told him that once there was a race of demons that controlled this whole land which was an island hundreds of miles long. There was one demon that could turn mortal beings into all manner of creatures or 'creations' as they called themselves. But a terrible event brought about the head demon's fall and the event which Alecto called "the great cataclysm" had wiped out many of their number.

"You will control the north and once our numbers have grown

here, we will cross into Cymru, where certain items exist that can return us to our former glory." Alecto had promised. "We will take all the southern lands and will be no threat to you as you have the power of the sun." That was true with the exception of Alecto who had the annoying habit of popping up and surprising him during the day none of the others were ever seen outside, always lurking inside.

He entered the headquarters, a long log cabin and warmed himself by the fire in the middle of the room. He was alone thankfully. He shouted for beer and deer meat and was something close to content when the smell drifted in. His mouth filled with bile and he spat the chunk of meat he was chewing out.

"Pretty boy," he grunted in Norse, and then in Saxon, "come in, Heregod, I can tell you're out there."

Draugr and man stared at each other from across the table. How Heregod could still speak to any extent was unknown, after hearing the story of the night of the raid enough times, Alecto concluded that Heregod had still been alive when he received the woman draugr's kiss. There were about twenty of them now. Heregod their leader but he was still in thrall to the draugr that had created him.

Heregod picked up the chunk of meat on the rushes and sniffed it before tucking it into the inside folds of his robe. He would eat it in a day or two when it smelt right for him. They had started to bury the draugrs food to avoid the men getting sick and the game fleeing. Punishment for minor insubordination was to be the poor soul who dug up their food. Major insubordination punishment and the reason for most troops being too terrified to desert was being given to the She-Draugr. Sometimes she brought them back with blackened veins but none like Heregod.

Finally Heregod spoke. His voice sounded like a wounded animal's cry, it was disconcerting to hear human words from it. He said, "Osbald."

Ulf looked up. "He's stuck on that island now, his army is dead or… like you. We pay him a visit when we take Bamburgh, if he hasn't fled to Pictland by then." He smelled his beer, somehow the draugrs' presence had soiled it. It smelled like ditch water. "Once my Norsemen come up the Tyne, we march."

That was the plan. Once Bamburgh was taken, the priests and bishops in Eoforwic would flee into Mercia if they knew what was good for them. Mercia was in chaos due to Offa's son Ecgfrith succumbing to poison after just a few months on the throne. Alecto had creatures in Mercia too, Ulf suspected. She still needed more numbers for her army, the She-Draugr was the only one who could seem to create new draugrs and even to Alecto, it wasn't an exact science as how to persuade Keres as Alecto had taken to naming the She-Draugr to bring her victims back to life after breaking their bodies. Keres did it when she felt like it. Once the draugrs were enough in number, Alecto would take them south and leave Ulf or rather King Eardwulf secure in his kingdom.

"Osbald," the former monk repeated.

"As I said, he's stuck on…" Ulf began.

"Alcuin… writes… Alcuin… kill… dead… return…"

Ulf put his hands on his face. Alecto once told him that the draugrs dream better than men. Images of their past, images of their homelands; how their world was continuing without them, images of the future yet to come and the future they would have had. None of them could ever articulate these dreams into human speech, apart from Heregod.

"Let's take you to her, see if she can turn this gibberish into words."

~

She was in her tent that was set up in the woods about a mile from the fort. He was glad to get Heregod away from the fort. He insisted they stayed a good distance from where the men slept. Once one had wandered into the barracks and one man had choked on his own vomit while sleeping. Could be too much ale but Ulf doubted it.

They entered the tent. Alecto was reclining on deerskin. Outside there was an empty spit over an extinguished fire. Ulf's hopes that it had been a pig were dashed by the body parts in a basket, charred arms, hands and bits of legs. Alecto's mouth was bloody. "Bandit," was her simple explanation. The tall, yellow-eyed one in the corner of the tent, Ordo, the same man who was with Alecto the night they met, was more talkative. "Shame to burn the outer parts but who knows when one will come…"

"Shut up, Ordo," she said. "You had enough guts to not complain." She felt the two intruders' presence, her fangs had jagged edges which almost glinted when she smiled. "Our soon to be king and his best warrior, what an honor."

Ulf ignored the sarcasm and told her he wanted Heregod's ramblings translated.

"Alcuin… writes… Alcuin… kill… dead… return…"

Alecto gave a wry smile. "I can only tell you what each of these words means to Heregod, Alcuin is a priest, one of the most powerful men in Northumbria. Writes refers to letters he is sending overseas. Kill is what Heregod feels we must do to him. Dead refers to Heregod himself and return also refers to him and someone else."

"Who?"

She shrugged. "This is no language problem a spell can fix. When Heregod received his second life, he was left with only the words he has, I just try to read his veins when he speaks them for images of what he means." She looked thoughtful. "He wants to kill Alcuin, Alcuin is on the island with Osbald.

The island is where he became who he is, maybe someone he knows is still there. We aren't going to stop him from going to the island if he wants to leave before the Norsemen come Alcuin and Osbald have to die eventually. Let him go. Send men to keep an eye on him, even a draugr if you can spare one. But not Keres, she stays near me at all times."

CHAPTER 17

Nabila sat at the bottom of the boat, making sure her bow and quiver were close to her chest and shivered. It was decided she should stay hidden until they reached the open sea. Her clothing and appearance marked her as someone from a distant land and should something happen to Ecgberht, she could become a target and end up in a different slaver's boat under much more dire circumstances.

Her linen tunic and pants dyed in a variety of bright colors were replaced by one of Brennus' coarse hemp robes and her equally colorful veils and headscarves now were the woolen rags that Brennus used to disguise his face when he was outside. The clothes were still damp, they had to leave in haste but Nabila insisted on drenching all of Brennus' clothes she was to inherit in the river before putting them on. She sneezed and reasoned it's better than being a prisoner at the nunnery awaiting beheading, perhaps.

Ecgberht steered the boat along the coast. It was just the two of them. Brennus and the woman who they learned was called Nelda were staying in Dorestad. Nabila had to leave immediately in case witnesses had seen her talking to the slaver before his death or returning to the hut bloody after. Brennus had to stay to await delivery of his arrows, so it was the exiled king and the Saracen supposed princess sailing the northern Frankish coast to find the Briton city of Saint-Malo.

Brennus had explained, "The larger ship that the Hunt is sending with the arrows is to take us up the coast all the way to Northumbria but you can't wait for it and neither will the slaver's shit tip get you across the sea. There are ports nearer to our island but I don't trust them nor the Wessex or Sussex ports. We've already talked about how vulnerable Nabila is at sea, there are also powerful people in the Saxon lands who are aware of your claims of kingship."

During the day they looked for inlets and coves far from the fishing villages and rested there. Taking shifts watching the other sleep, Nabila with bow notched from a hidden vantage point and Ecgberht standing with his sword arm ready in front of the beached boat, she was resting in. Night-time, they rowed.

The occasional fishing boat late at night ignored them as long as they kept their distance. Perhaps they were mistaken for smugglers. They never saw any smugglers themselves but Ecgberht reasoned that not being seen or heard was the point of being a smuggler.

Once in the early morning they reached an inlet and just after they turned inwards, they saw in the distance two longboats glide through the morning mist. They were too far away to be seen and such ships would hardly take the time to divert from course for such a small boat but they wordlessly made shallow breaths until the ships were out of sight. The carved head on the prow of the ship reminded Ecgberht of both the creature on the flag of Wessex and the snake's head on the flags of the Hunt.

~

"Who is Brennus? What is the Lost Hunt? Why am I needed for it?" Nabila asked these questions frequently, unsatisfied with Ecgberht's answers which were too vague. Ecgberht wasn't trying to keep secrets from her, he was simply awful with words in all languages. However when they turned out of a bay and the walls of Saint-Malo became visible, the town clinging to a rocky outcrop, something clicked in his brain. By the time they could see flags fluttering; each representing factions of Britons, Gauls and Franks who coexisted in the city and the flag with the snake being speared in the head among them, Ecgberht had become very talkative.

"Right, so the Romans controlled the island and lived with the Britons but something bad happened. One of the Romans became corrupted and somehow could do otherworldly things, he made more like him and they terrorized the island. The Lost Hunt was formed by the remaining Britons, it was like a fyrd but one with a degree of magic. Saxons from the east arrived and the Hunt retreated west. After about one hundred years Spurius, the Roman demon got cocky, he decided to provoke the Saxons and if the legends are true, Saxon and Briton united to assault the abandoned Roman city of Londinium and the beast was defeated."

"So, the Saxons and Britons work together now."

"Not really, well some of us do like me but the Hunt is mainly Briton still."

"I see, and what are they going to do for us in this town?"

"Hopefully get us safe and discrete passage over the sea to Dumnonia for now."

"Why do I have to come?"

"Brennus said it was important. He was very interested in your archery skills. This looks like a great port. Look at the walls and harbor, it can fit far larger ships than anywhere else we've been. I will ensure that after we return from our trip, I'll get whoever runs things in this town to ensure you safe passage on a boat back to your people."

That made Nabila ask, "Was this city built by my people?"

"No, Romans. Why?"

"The buildings, they are well built. Decent stonework and the masonry done by a builder who has learned his numbers, not wood nailed on top of more wood at disjointed angles like in the other Christian cities I've seen."

~

Their boat sailed under one of the larger piers and they tied it to a post before hoisting themselves onto the pier itself. "The Hunt will have a building and a representative in this town Brennus told me," Ecgberht explained. Knowing it was unlikely they would ever see the slaver's boat again, Ecgberht had a box with their possessions tucked under his arm while Nabila kept her bow and quiver strapped to her back.

Before they could set foot on dry land, two men squared up to them on the pier. "No armed strangers in the town," said the larger of the two, an obese man with orange pigtails. His companion, a shorter blond man with a bushy mustache, was more affable.

"Got any coin in that chest? If so, I'll be sure to guide you around the city, we can spend it together. I know this old man, his ale shack has some concoctions that will blow your mind."

"Leave you passed out in the gutter while we take your coin and see what price we get for the Moor girl at the brothel," the fat man said in Brittonic. They had taken the pair for outsiders at first sight and conducted the conversation in Frankish.

So, the fat man was surprised to have Ecgberhts' sword at his throat. Ecgberht said in Brittonic, "The Bretons still wish to have a representative on the Hunt's table, I assume? Because I can't imagine that Wessex's representative and his companion being threatened at the docks would please Merlin."

"No harm done!" the other man said nervously. "We don't want to upset the warlocks, do we, Karreg?"

"No, we don't," his friend replied. "We were just testing you. We took you for a good Brit at first sight but can't be too careful."

"I'm a Saxon," Ecgberht said.

"A Saxon?" Karreg was confused. "Most of this town was driven from their homelands by you bastards. My great, great, great, great grandmother was from Hwicce until the Mercian bastards sent her family fleeing."

"So what?" said Ecgberht. "I'm not even from Mercia, trust me, I've got more than enough reason to hate them myself."

Karreg raised his hands and Ecgberht lowered his sword. Karreg tapped the side of his head and said, "These Saxons are crazy."

The smaller man said, "I am Stered and this is Karreg, to make up for this misunderstanding, let us guide you to the monastery."

CHAPTER 18

Alcuin paced around the rebuilt monastery. He was now in his sixties and doubted he would ever see it again. He was due to depart to Francia as soon as his passage arrived. King Charlemagne assured him that people more capable were on their way to deal with the threat of Eardwulf. It was just so unfair he would never again see the beautiful stone arches, the tall bell towers or even the cloister lawn. It would take decades to rebuild it as it was, raising the coin, hiring good stone workers; Hibernians or Franks if possible, no Saxon was up to the job, and return the priory to its former glory.

Currently three years after the disaster, the buildings were still made of timber nailed together and piled up against surviving charred, stone columns that made up the skeleton of the one great building. Timer boards made up the floor and the roof was half completed. The brothers slept in tents. Two hastily built log huts with thatched roofs stood on what had been the cloisters and they housed Alcuin and the mad, drunk Osbald.

At least Saint Cuthbert's resting place was secure. Should raiders come from across the sea again, or should Eardwulf's men or something other than men march north, beneath the stones they would find a skeleton of a shepherd's wife who had died of a fever last spring. The raiders could defile her skeleton to their hearts' content, she would be rewarded in heaven for her sacrifice, he told himself. The bones of Saint Cuthbert and the Lindisfarena gospels which had miraculously survived the explosion were safe in a secret location.

He was advising the brothers who he had set to the task of fixing the numerous mistakes the first set of hasty builders Aethelred had sent after news of the attack had shocked the whole kingdom. The whole island was appalled, even Offa in Mercia had sent parchment containing his outrage, although none of his coin for rebuilding.

"Take out that plank, we can use it for the nave benches and it allows a bit of light if..."

"Alcuin, my friend! Come drink with me!" Osbald staggered into the church building.

Alcuin groaned, his friend had always found it difficult to live a good Christian life, he wore his hair in rope-like braids in the pagan fashion, he refused to marry, instead buying women with goods and coin he and his clan had plundered on raids into Mercia and Pictland. But he was a brave man, he was a god fearing man. He was a man who would fight for his god. *Was.*

Bored of the weak beer the brothers drank, and having long since depleted their meager wine stocks, Osbald had formed a friendship with some of the island's shepherds who managed to ferment their sheep's milk and distill it over a peat fire to create something that was going to kill Osbald soon, judging from the vomit and bloodstains on his tunic.

"Dear Osbald, you appear to have forgotten your trousers," Alcuin said.

The barrel-chested man looked down at his hairy legs and cock flopping out from between them and belched a giant laugh. "Hah! Walked all the way across the cloisters like this! None of these monks said a word. Maybe they've forgotten what one looks like! Hah! They all get the gelder's knife when they take their vows, aren't I right, my friend!" the half-naked man put his arm around the shoulders of a passing young monk who looked like he was about to burst into tears.

"It is good to see you in better spirits, my friend," Alcuin walked over to the bigger man, distracting him enough for the tearful monk to escape. "Will you not accompany me to Francia? Their king is a generous man, prove yourself on a campaign, he will knight you, that gives you lands and…"

"Thank you, my friend but I'm no horse lover like those Frankish weaklings. I fight face to face and I must stay. My men and I await their return." By men, he meant fifteen warriors who had returned with him from his ill-fated campaign to Segedunum, he had departed from Bamburgh with sixty.

Alcuin frowned, his friend's jovial nature turned dark so quickly and when it did, the short-term insanity took his wits.

"They will come back, you know? Who will protect the relics and the holy bones then? Yes, you've instructed the monks to be trained with sword and axe but these are hell's creatures. Black of blood, black of tooth, the dead walk!" He was now screaming.

"My dear friend." Alcuin was an emotional man and Osbald's madness pained him. Close to tears, he said, "Just wait, providence is coming, King Charlemagne has told me that he sends help. The Britons to the west he says have knowledge of Eardwulf's tactics and tricks and he is sending experienced men and weapons that can destroy Eardwulf. I know it sounds fanciful but I trust this king, he is perhaps the best hope for Christians everywhere."

Osbald had resumed breathing normally but he was swigging from a wineskin he had tied to his belt. The noxious smell betrayed that it wasn't wine inside. "They had better be fearsome and they had better be here soon. The dead are coming." He broke down and started to weep. "The dead will be here soon, I smell them in my dreams. Please Alcuin, you must leave this island as soon as you can."

"Pray for our deliverance to arrive soon," the older man said, staring in the direction of the sea.

CHAPTER 19

"Why are you here?" said the abbot, this abbot was different to most others Ecgberht had met. He wore the same woolen robes most of them did and he had the plumpness of a man who ate well and seldom toiled, again a common feature of abbots. But most abbots didn't have the speared snake symbol etched on the back of their robes, nor around their necks alongside their wooden crucifix pendants that displayed images of the moon, of tree, of mountains and runes Ecgberht couldn't read. His face was marked with blue tattooed lines and red angry scars. His eyes were alert and wary, like they were used to seeing gruesome things.

The monastery too was unusual. It was a tall church and a small garden right in the center of the city. Ecgberht couldn't see any infirmary, cloister, library or dormitory. He couldn't see any monks either. The church had one wooden statue of Jesus at the altar but the nave was decorated with deer hides that blocked the windows, on parchment more runes declaring god knows what hung from the walls. Dominating the nave on either side were copies of the two paintings he had last seen in Charlemagne's suite, the plain but beautiful woman and the one armed, marked man.

"You are supposed to be halfway up the Frisian Sea by now!" admonished the abbot. "The ship carrying Brennus' arrows should have arrived days ago and his archer and swordsman have been sailing in the wrong direction!"

"We had a bit of a problem in Dorestad. A human problem, a

dead human problem, it was decided that we should split up." Ecgberht recounted Brennus' advice about avoiding Frankish ports.

~

Nabila examined the garden after being shooed out of the church by the stupid looking bald man who tapped his foot on the floor like a child, his bald dome flushing red when she tried to reenter. She was unsure if it was her sex or her religion that made her unwelcome but could do little about it. Stered and Karreg had possession of her bow, abashed, they had allowed her and Ecgberht to keep their weapons but the abbot had refused weapons inside the church grounds.

One half of the garden was devoted to leeks, she wondered if the monks ate anything else. The other flower beds however were an array of colors. She recognized nightshade which was used to heal toothache and sore bones, the purple foxglove which could drive devils out of a man when he started shaking and convulsing for no reason. There were bearberries that she knew were good for fevers.

She turned to the girl tending to the plants and asked, "Are all of these healing plants?" The girl said something in Brittonic and pointed to herself and said, "Ninog." Nabila took that to be her name and assumed she was simple, or unable to speak anything other than Brittonic which she took as more or less the same thing. Ninog certainly had beauty if not brains, her blonde hair complimenting the dimples on her cheeks. Nabila decided to take it slower and identify the Briton names for the plants she knew, Ninog was happy to oblige and made no objection when Nabila started to pluck some of these plants for herself.

She was confused by Ninog's insistence at pushing a certain plant into her hands. It was unlike any flower Nabila had ever seen. The stem, the petals, the leaves, the stigma were all bright green. "What is it?" asked Nabila.

Ninog understood the question. "Chloris," she said.

They were interrupted by Ecgberht leaving the church with another chest under his arm and calling back to the inside. "Thank you for your help, Abbot Donnan." And then muttering, "Miserable bald bastard," under his breath.

The sight of Ninog hit him like a hammer to the face. "Do I know you?" he stammered and then from Nabila's point of view, the two spoke in that sing-song language that was spoken alongside Frankish in this town for what seemed like ages.

~

Stered and Karreg, somehow feeling responsible for the stranger's poor first impression of Saint Malo, and still in hope of foreign coin that would go further than anything made in the town mint, carried the pair's goods ahead of them as they discussed their visit to the monastery.

"Why did you act so surprised to see that plant girl?" Nabila asked.

"It was nothing, I just thought she was someone I used to know. She's no one, just the bastard daughter of the abbot, he has her take care of the garden to keep an eye on her. She knows her plants though and told me you do too. That green flower she called 'Chloris', she said it was special. Most of the Breton Hunt warriors spread themselves far from the city, Brittany is a big place, although it might get smaller if the big man has his way, anyway, this plant apparently repels creations and other such foul things. Only it struggles to thrive and after the arrows, it's the main reason Breton Hunt warriors come to the monastery. She must have liked you to give you so much."

"What did the abbot tell you?"

"Nothing useful about whatever Eardwulf is up to, they mainly have siren and goblin problems here, neither of which sound like Eardwulf's ghuls. But I got a set of arrows blessed by the abbot himself and passage to Dumnonia. As Offa's dyke is cursed, the Cymru lot are going to cross the Celtic sea and meet us there and then we march north overland."

"I have no idea what you're talking about!"

"I'll draw you a map when we are on the boat, it'll pass the time."

~

The ship was not unlike the longboats that they had spied on their journey. It had no beast on the prow and its hull was wider and deeper for the cargo; as well as Nabila and Ecgberht's possessions, it was carrying plenty of onions and wine, Offa may be dead but the coins he minted were prized across the island and beyond. There was a ringed Celtic cross on the ship's flag as well as a smaller speared snake flag flapping underneath it.

That flag was the reason Ecgberht headed to it and passed a bag of coin from the abbot into the palm of the captain who spent so much of his day under the sun, his face was bright pink. *Like the color of a pig's arse,* Nabila thought, she felt ambivalently seconds later with both gratitude and regret about her earlier unkind thoughts toward the captain as he whipped the hand of an oar slave whose hand had crept up her robe, along with a degree of pity for the slave.

They waved goodbye to Stered and Karreg who were waiting on the pier for a foreigner with no connections in town that they could relieve of their coin to appear. They sat in the middle of the hull among onion sacks to avoid heavy waves and Ecgberht began to sketch a map on the hull floor.

CHAPTER 20

The Norse longboat erupted in cheers as the large river mouth became visible and land grew closer. Behind them delayed by a few seconds came the cheers of the other boat. The fort was said to be just around the next river bend.

No one was more relieved to see land than the skipper; a black-bearded, hard-faced man with a patch over his left eye. He held the hammer necklace to his lips and kissed it. "There it is, men, the Tyne!" he shouted to more cheers. Aindrea had been away for three years but it felt like thirty.

~

He had been thrown face first onto the stone beach all those years ago as the raider's boat docked in their home port. A faint memory of seeing Nelda, the girl from the fishing village being dragged away, then darkness.

He woke to dirty water being thrown over his face and being dragged out of a hut which was more of a stinking hole in the ground. Light engulfed his face and his ears exploded with the jeers of what appeared to be a whole village of people. He was pushed and kicked forward to a clearing, his bounds were roughly cut loose and a wooden stick shoved into his hands. He looked around, he saw a crowd of men and women were screaming at him around the clearing in words he couldn't understand. The ground was slippery mud, the clearing was in front of a large hut made of huge logs.

Into the clearing strode a large man, this man had not been

on the boat. His face was lined with wrinkles and his beard flecked with gray. A man deemed too old for the voyage and eager for a taste of glory and blood. He raised his axe and screamed at the top of his voice, *"Holmganga!"*

Aindrea smiled despite himself. Village warriors, fearsome in a gang but worthless in a one-on-one fight. This was going to be fun. He even allowed the man to preen and show off to the crowd. He got down on one knee in mock fear, pleading for mercy and the crowd roared. The old man raised his arms in order to soak up another cheer and then Aindrea rammed the wooden stick into the man's guts.

Once the man was on the floor, he knew the knees were both one of the weakest and most important parts of the body. He smashed the stick down on the prone older man's left knee, destroying it in seconds. Now his opponent would need a stick of his own, permanently.

He felt spit rain down on him from the now angry crowd. He felt someone slap him on the back. He ignored both, he was enjoying this. Another slap on the back, he ignored it and made for his opponent's right knee. A third slap on the back, he turned around and screamed, "What?" It was the leader from the boat. He had been unconscious for most of the journey back. He had dragged his useless leg after him into the center of the clearing and gave Aindrea the most ferocious smack on the side of his head that made his ears ring and sent him to his knees.

The ringing was still going on as Thorleif shouted his instructions to the crowd. Although Aindrea couldn't hear them nor would he have been able to understand them, it was clear from the body language that Thorleif was impressed by his fighting skill and was arguing for his life.

Thorleif then said something else that later once he'd learnt Norse, Aindrea found out was along the lines of, "He can live among us as a thrall, he may have some value for us but I do not like how his eye blinks so fast, it offends the gods, gorge out his left eye."

~

He had spent the next several months with the other blind slaves. Blind men were considered to be good weavers so Aindrea worked, ate and slept in a large hut stitching together linen, animal hides and furs to make clothes and sails. He still had half his sight and used this to help the others. The quicker they completed their tasks, the more ale their guards got, as a result the guards saw to it that the slaves sometimes got vegetables with their gruel and extra firewood for the hut. It wasn't much but it was preferable to field labor.

Aindrea expected to remain as a weaving slave for the rest of his life. He prayed each night, for the souls of the brothers killed, for Heregod, for Nelda, for himself to be forgiven for the grave sins he had committed while soldiering. He received no answer. The guard's stories of Asgard, the home of the gods and Valhalla, the next life for warriors, began to warm his thoughts more. He wondered if these gods could be divine when the priests selected the Pict Bili for sacrifice.

~

That night the village was feasting and tales of the gods rang everywhere. Even the weaving slaves got some gristle mixed into their gruel and half a cup of ale. Under a full moon as the boisterous chants and songs from the great hall were fading, Aindrea found himself being shook awake.

He froze, it was the chieftain, Thorleif One-Leg himself. The chieftain put his mouth next to Aindrea's ear and spoke in a hushed tone, "Bili was picked as it's his lands we sail to next. Would have liked to have him along as he knows the land but the priests know the gods want otherwise." He breathed heavily, the sour smell of mead made Aindrea's eyes water. "You are to come along with us. You must know the coastline and the language better than any of us. Fight well and earn your freedom, try to flee and earn yourself a blood eagle."

The next morning he walked through the woods behind the great hall until he found Bili's entrails hanging from a branch. He made the sign of the cross for the last time that morning.

~

He proved his worth in Pictland again and again. He had spent hours in the monastery scriptorium copying maps of the island and had the river mouths, coves and bays of the eastern coast of Pictland committed to memory. His navigation skills meant they were plundering Pict villages and settlements before the Picts even knew they were there.

Aindrea's violence surprised many of the survivors of the Lindisfarena raid who saw the robed men they now knew were called monks as timid.

Their voyages to Pictland were lucrative. To win his freedom, he had to do one thing.

~

It was a stormy night, Aindrea and two seers, a female Volva and male Seiomenn made their way deep into the forest. An ox and a lame slave with a club foot followed. Aindrea was made to wear the wooden cross he had around his neck the day he came to the Norsemen's land as he disappeared into the sea of pine and birch with his companions.

He never told anyone what happened during the three days and nights he spent in the forest. He emerged one morning, naked, his arms caked with dry blood and instead of his wooden cross, the hammer of Thor was around his neck.

~

At his first feast as a Norseman Thorleif One-Leg took him to one side and told him, "My daughter Droplaug lost her man on the raid where we met you." Aindrea remained still but alert, if somehow Thorleif or anyone in the village knew he was the archer who ensured so many of their husbands, brothers, sons, fathers had not returned from Lindisfarena, he would be given a blood eagle; the most feared fate for a Norseman. The ribs severed from the spine and the lungs pulled out to create a grotesque pair of wings, all done while the victim was still alive.

How had they discovered his secret? In Pictland he feigned ignorance at using a bow and attacked with axe and shield.

Thorleif continued, "Her child is growing up wild without a father, as one of our best raiders, you can provide for her very well. I wish you both to wed."

~

Droplaug was a short, round woman with a flat nose, red curly hair and kind eyes. She made it clear that she was happy with the arrangement. She smiled as their hands were bound together by cloth and they raced each other back to the great hall for an enormous feast.

Aindrea thought that perhaps he had finally found peace. Until he entered his new home for the first time and came face to face with the house slave.

It was Nelda. She stared at the necklace of Mjolnir around his neck with sheer loathing.

~

He shook thoughts of Nelda and her fate out of his mind. He was back, skipper of his own longboat with his own men. They had been hired by this King Eardwulf to help him take this kingdom and take home with them anything they liked.

He saw the fort, they had done a decent job. It rested on the northern riverbank which provided good defense from southern attackers as long as they controlled the river. To the north they had found quarries nearby and rebuilt parts of the wall that had crumbled, giving them a defensive advantage. Any northern attackers would find their advance fatally slowed.

He got off the boat and saw from the fort's entrance a procession of warriors was coming to meet him. His smile faded when he recognized the woman at the head of the procession and the familiar-looking mask she wore.

CHAPTER 21

Brennus watched Nelda pray as the waves washed over the boat drenching the pair of them. Nelda was unmoved on her knees as she clasped her hands together and raised her voice so her prayer could be heard. "Lord, ruler over waves and sea, keep your blessed hand over all seafarers. Give us the strength to survive the hardships of your glorious heavens and…"

The ship's skipper and the men he had with him all approved of the girl's piety. They believed it worked and the girl doing it meant they didn't have to pray themselves. The Hunt's men were all good Christians these days. When Ecgberht had joined them, he expressed surprise at the Briton's holy nature, Brennus had chided him, "We were Christian back when you Saxons were savages praying to the trees, why I remember…" He had stopped himself. It had been nearly two hundred years since the first Saxon king was baptized.

Brennus himself had no need of gods. When he was thirsty, he thanked the river he found, when he was hungry, he thanked the tree which gave him nuts and berries. It seemed more natural than thanking someone you couldn't see, be they named The Almighty or Odin. He did have the luxury of Merlin's gift that meant he didn't have to worry about what comes after this life.

He had been thinking about it more and more. Merlin and other representatives of the Hunt had hinted it was time for him to pass on his gift. Seeing Ecgberht and Nabila together made him realize that Aebbe and Milian had indeed returned. He wondered where the other heroes of Chichester and Londinium were. Nelda reminded him of someone now he thought about it, a grin spread across his ancient and mangled lips.

He had made the right decision to pass on the gift in Aachen now that he knew he'd be back someday.

But for now Hunt business. Something not of the living was afoot in Northumbria and it was their job to destroy it. They had just passed the mouth of the Tyne, their destination was close.

Nelda once calmed down after hitting highs of elation at her and her son's freedom and lows of fear at an uncertain future had told him her story while they were in Dorestad awaiting the ship. He was fascinated with stories of lands to the east. Merlin had once mentioned that lands further east had their own unimaginably outlandish beings. "Look at Wessex's flag, someone from our side has been in touch but even my arts cannot find the answer," the wizard had cryptically complained more than once.

The easterners that Nelda had lived among reminded him of how the Saxons had been all those years ago, even the names of the gods were similar. It was her shaking voice telling him about the legendary undead beast called the Draugr that she was sure she saw the night she was taken that had him jotting runes on pieces of bark he kept for writing.

~

As Northumbria neared, he spoke with the leader of the squad of men the Hunt had sent to Dorestad, Derel was a lean, tall, cold middle-aged man who couldn't help but make a sneering expression when speaking. Derel was never going to be the kind of man one could share a cup of ale with but he kept his men in order and despised all of the creatures the Hunt was made to fight.

"We haven't fought anything like these draugrs before, these tales of unworldly strength trouble me," Brennus as usual urged caution.

"I don't hear much to fear," Derel said. "Walking corpses? The archers will see them coming a mile off." But then he frowned. "People were resurrected through miracles in the Bible, or so the priests say, if someone is using the lord's power for evil ends, it can only be Satan himself. After we kill the Draugr, we must send Eardwulf and whoever has him in thrall to hell."

Brennus wasn't in the mood for a theological discussion but agreed it would be unwise to let Eardwulf live. "When his army is destroyed, the Northumbrians will not keep him alive and he will have nowhere to flee." Another wave drenched the crew. Nelda clutched her child closer to her and began to scream her prayer. "Perhaps we should drop her and the child off in Bamburgh before continuing on to the Holy Isle. Bamburgh is one of the largest forts in the north, surely she can find a servant's job that will provide for her and the boy there."

"They don't use slaves up here?"

"They don't live long enough, the climate you see…" A wave twice the size of any of the others engulfed the boat and they were all thrown to one side. Brennus was blinded and swore loudly as his arm was trapped under something heavy and the pain was overpowering. He heard the crack of wood and panicked shouts from the men. High-pitched screaming from Nelda and then the boat filled with water again. He went cold, this was all his fault. He should have waited until this mission was completed to pass on the gift. Now he had removed Merlin's protection, God or the Gods were hungry for his soul after it had eluded them for so long, now he had killed them all. "Save the arrows! Any of you who live through this will need…" A wave even bigger than the mountain that had doomed them crashed into them, Brennus heard a cry of fear grow distant as whoever had emitted it was lost to the sea and then the part of the boat he was clinging to collapsed and all went black…

~

Nelda sank further and further into the cold, her child slid out of her arms and was lost to her. She sank at a rapid speed. She remembered falling before, off a cliff and agony in her legs but this memory was of something that had never happened to her. This confusion was broken by her legs hitting the seabed and in panic at the memory of the pain of broken legs, she pushed herself up and in a blur found her head crash above the water and she took deep breaths as she tried to calm herself and look around for her son.

"HEREGOD!!!" she screamed, frantically looking around. The sun was beginning to rise and it revealed just ten feet away her son lying unconscious, face down in the water. She swam toward him and pushed his body up, trying to hoist him into the air to get air into his lungs. She needed to get to the beach, they weren't far out, they had stayed close enough to the coast to keep it visible but far enough away to avoid the armed men on board being spotted. Nelda was a strong swimmer, all raised on Lindisfarena were but the shock, the cold and the tiredness was proving too much for her.

Her heart leapt when she saw a piece of driftwood from the ruined boat pass her. It was just big enough for little Heregod to lie on and if she was careful, she could cling on and god willing they would reach the coast. She saw a figure approach through the water in the morning mist. "Help me!" she called out. It was as if the figure was sneering at her, she tried to look closer but then her cheeks shook and she felt pain. A punch struck her, not the strongest one but one that stung nonetheless.

~

Derel had seen the drifting plank in the distance and had swum hard to reach it. He'd lost his helmet but couldn't get his mail shirt off and it was slowing and tiring him. He'd finally kicked off his boots and was making progress when she popped out of nowhere and grabbed the wood for herself and the boy.

"Saxon bitch!" he gasped, not caring if she understood or not. He was weak but he had rocked her with the first punch and the second should be enough to sink her, he could then flip the driftwood over and send the boy to the bottom and have it for himself.

She was crying and screaming at him in the Saxon grunting language, he didn't like hearing that at the best of times so raised his fist to silence her for good.

Then the smell, was it rotten eggs or fish? He twisted his face and retched. "Did you shit yourself?" he asked the woman whose open mouth drooling with bile showed she was smelling it too.

The sun illuminated more of the sea's surface. He had never seen water so black before.

Then he felt it. His foot was caught in something. "I'm stuck! Help me!" he shouted, in mid-shout his blood ran cold. The rock or whatever moved. It had his foot more firmly secured. *Siren!* was his first fear but they usually made sailors pass out before they pulled them under. He tried to wrench himself free but it was like being trapped under rock, fingers of rock. His sneer turned into a trembling grimace and his eyes bulged with terror as he was dragged under the surface.

~

Brennus coughed and sputtered as the sun made him wake up and seawater and vomit spilled out of his mouth. He was lying on a deserted beach alone, there was no sign of the others or the boat. The sea had a few specks in the distance but none looked damaged, fishing boats that must have left after the storm had stopped. The sea looked so calm, it was hard to believe the nightmarish conditions Brennus had been in were only hours ago. He figured it was midday from the sun's position.

The gods have one more task before they take me, he thought as he started to walk north. It would take a few days to reach Lindisfarena, he estimated and as much as he would have liked to go inland and stick to the woods, he decided to trek along the beaches in case any of the arrows had been washed up.

It was an hour's hike and just one arrow found later that he made a more gruesome discovery.

Derel's corpse lay on the beach staring eyeless at the sun. His tongue, nose and stomach were also missing, one leg looked to have been chewed off at the knee.

Brennus was aware that the beasts of the sea were a mystery to even the most learned men such as Merlin and something that devoured with such speed and accuracy could certainly exist but then he remembered something from Osbald's rantings that Alcuin reported, *"they even swim."* He said to no one in particular, "The next time this man is born, make it far, far away from this island," and continued to walk north.

CHAPTER 22

Nabila strained to listen to the fierce argument that she had started. After arriving in the place called Dumnonia, they had no sooner unloaded the onions and replaced them on the boat with bags of tin ingots than a parade of warriors emerged from the woods to the trading post Ecgberht called Escanceaster.

~

The flag of Wessex, a golden-winged snake with legs which reminded Nabila of stories of the famed giant crocodile beasts from the old country flew from the main timber building and storehouse but it was clear most of the people here were Britons, they dressed and spoke the same way as they had in Saint Malo with hemp rather than linen tunics and dresses, the same sort of circled crosses around their neck, braided hair, blue tattoos and the light sounding language of the Bretons. The smaller speared snake flag was also displayed from smaller thatched huts.

Ecgberht went with his bag of Frankish coin into the timber building to make sure the Saxon in charge, "Beorhtric's puppet," he had said, allowed them freedom of the town. Then they sat in the ale hut and waited for the warriors to meet them.

Ten or so men with two women among them arrived, larger shields than the Franks used, she noticed and shield preferred over sword. Their armor was leather jerkins with some having a bronze plate on their chest. They all had the wild hair and bushy beards for the men that were becoming synonymous with Britons for her. Each of them had the speared snake etched on a shield or jerkin somewhere.

They had laughed, even the women when Ecgberht told them this short foreign girl was their archer and it had taken the hike through the forest and meeting up with the men from Cymru or Wealas; Ecgberht used the terms interchangeably, until she had open fields and the chance to show them what she could do on horseback. Her chief bully had been Tegen; one of the Dumnonian women who had taken pleasure in assigning Nabila the task of digging pits for the storage of the night soil the group made on their journey. Putting an arrow through Tegen's ale skin as she drank from half a field away won her nods of respect from the others and a new task for a seething Tegen.

The Wealas warriors were a bit broader than the Dumnonian ones and a few favored the Frankish style seax swords but otherwise not too dissimilar. Their leader Hopcyn was a short man who had a large bushy orange beard and red braided hair that went down to his waist. Most importantly they had bought horses with them. Her brown mare had a yellowish mane so she decided to call her Ninog.

~

The argument they were having right now was due to Nabila wanting to practice her Brittonic. With it being spoken, shouted and chanted every step along the way, along with frequent arguments between the Wealas and Dumnonian warriors over which type to use, she had picked up a lot. Her ear for languages was good. But she needed to use it more to get used to speaking it.

Which is why she had asked, "Who built this?" at the place they were resting at in northern Wessex near the Mercia border.

It was the most amazing thing she had ever seen. In Al-Andalas there were tales of the mighty pyramids across the sea and her father even introduced the family to traders who claimed to have seen them with their own eyes.

This here, she wasn't just hearing about, she was actually seeing it! A ring of standing stones all propped up vertically and inside a ring of smaller stones and further inside this ring were structures where one vertical stone was balanced high in the air; the height of two tall men at least, by two vertical stones. All these stones had been arranged by hand with a great eye for detail. She was desperate to find out the secrets here. Maybe the Britons or Saxons, whoever had built this weren't as backward as she had assumed.

She hadn't expected to cause such fierce debate.

Both Briton tribes agreed the stones came from a place called Hibernia but they differed on who was responsible.

"The devil brought them from over the sea. He threw one at a friar when the friar said he'd reveal the devil's secret that's why the heel stone over there blots out the sun in the morning for a bit, it hit the friar's heel!" Tegen said.

"You stupid dung haired witch! Everyone knows Merlin knew these were healing stones found far to the south where the priests say Eden was. Merlin sent Arthur's own sire to Hibernia to arrange safe passage over the sea!" Hopcyn said, rubbing his temples with frustration.

Ecgberht claimed, "King Hengist built this in tribute to his Briton foes in remorse at having slain so many." He managed to unite Tegen and Hopcyn in outrage at this claim, whoever King Hengist was the Britons didn't seem to like him very much. They pelted Ecgberht with stones at the mention of his name.

~

"Do we have enough men?" Nabila asked later as they hiked north, sticking to the dense woodland to avoid being mistaken for a foreign fyrd or large group of bandits. In total they numbered around twenty.

"With us and the men sailing north with Brennus and anyone we pick up along the way, it isn't a bad number given the short notice Brennus had to arrange messengers and pigeons after we decided to split up but no, it really isn't enough. Best hope is to cause chaos once Eardwulf's ghuls are lit up by the arrows and leave it in the hands of The Almighty."

"Praise be to Allah."

"Of course, we should expect heavy losses though." Ecgberht then looked around and said, "I think we've crossed into Mercia now."

~

"We heard Offa's lad didn't last too long?" Hopcyn asked as they tried to get the horses through some dense forest.

"That's what I heard. Offa spent his last few years arranging for most rivals to the throne to have hunting accidents. Christ, for a while standing in a shield wall was safer than being one of Offa's relatives and going hunting," Ecgberht said with laughter.

Tegen said, "Poison is what is said among the villages in Dumnonia."

Argumentative as ever, Hopcyn said, "Wrong as usual, woman. Offa earned himself a curse for the deal he made with the devil. When he cursed the land between Mercia and Cymru, somehow dark forces knew when our men crossed and the curse rebounded to his firstborn, no sooner was Offa returned to the ground than his son's guts started to turn black and rot."

~

They continued to hike north, they avoided contact with the Mercians partly due to the Briton's skill at living off the land and an almost innate ability to avoid being sighted by Saxons but also the land was sparsely populated. "The new king will almost certainly have uprisings in Cent and East Anglia, probably raised as many fyrds as he could and headed east," Ecgberht said confidently.

He was surprised and quite a bit embarrassed as they were halfway through crossing a shallow part of the river Trent when shouts came from both sides of the river and horsemen charged both riverbanks stranding them in the middle. On each side of them, the horseman at the head of his column flew a flag with a golden cross running from corner to corner on a blue background.

"Shit!" said Ecgberht, "These are…" he tried to think of who these men belonged to, of course the King of Mercia but Ecgberht hadn't learned the new King's name. He had been so certain that Ecgfrith; Offa's son, would be king for a long time he hadn't bothered. He had a feeling that he would be learning it very soon, that's as long as one of the others didn't do anything stupid. He looked nervously at the Saracen woman hundreds of miles from home, the Welshman almost as fond of fighting as he was of his own voice, the Dumnonii woman who washed her hair with mud for some reason and the rest of his companions and prayed they wouldn't say or do anything that would earn them all a spear to the belly.

CHAPTER 23

Alecto and Ordo sat across from Ulf and Aindrea. Ordo was very disconcerted from being so close to two pieces of food in their prime and being unable to do a thing about it. He started to remember the events all those years ago in Londinium that had led to their fall.

He had fled Londinium at the start of the shaking and witnessed the destruction of the city from a wooded area just beyond the northern section of the wall. The bastard Hunt had sent men into the city in the weeks that had followed, throwing their poxy arrows into anything that stirred from the ruins. They had also spread word to Saxon villages to the south and Angle villages to the north that any man with yellow eyes seen at night was to be beaten, clubbed and stabbed and the body chained to a cross to face the sunrise.

Injured and weakened from wounds incurred when dodging a collapsing city, he retreated far from any contact with humans. Too weak to chase down deer or best a boar in a fight, he was reduced to surviving on vermin and insects making his recovery excruciatingly slow. Finally he made it to the northern tip of Pictland where the Hunt wouldn't look to find him and where a supply of cave dwelling hermits had also retreated to. Their blood was thin and weak but it was better than a mole or rat.

It had taken him years to get that far and it would take longer to recover his strength and make his way back south. He hoped the area was so remote that other fleeing creations would find their way there. But nothing, he hadn't even learned of the fate of the others until he'd sought out the woods' witch of Mercia, the one who wore a crudely made mask at all times. The stories about an out-of-season harvest crop failing, snow storms ravaging villages in summer, weevils the size of rats, or slugs that could move as fast as cats. If the witch cursed your village, you dumped every bit of coin and steel that you could at her door. If there were none, then whichever villagers were left standing after going crazed with hunger and killing and eating the others got a visit from the witch with her jagged fangs.

~

"When they eat each other so quickly, the survivors have this fatty liver and the blood is a lot richer. Besides there's something about the taste of the brain when it's a normal man who has just committed murder often of those close to him. Tastes like beef with the sweetness of a ripe fruit mixed in." A haggard Ordo was sitting in the cave of the only other known survivor of Londinium who was telling him how she lived these days.

"Of course the clever ones, the ones with some foresight pay for the famine to leave and as a result I've got quite the war chest, even some silver as…"

"You can walk in the sun!" Ordo interrupted Alecto, he couldn't believe it and when he had spied on her from the hollow of a tree, he assumed he had been mistaken and this was some human who knew some dark tricks.

"At the very end, after the earthquake began…" she began slowly, "the Crux gemmata showed me how. I need it to do it again and those bastards have it locked up with the sword that ended our sire in their mountain surrounded by rotting bastards armed with those arrows." The part of her face where her eyes should be moved, by shock or frustration Ordo couldn't tell.

"The arrows Ordo," she continued, "one came close to getting me, I felt it, it's a fate that cannot be endured by anyone. Not even me."

"What happened... to the others?" Ordo asked with hesitation.

"Dead, gone to the sun or buried under that cursed to Hades city!" she cried. "Some may have walked into the sea to find new lands, I lost any sense of their presence. Morchan and Heslop live but are truly lost beyond my reach and our sire is turned to stone, we have no way of boosting our numbers."

"And Psyche?" he asked.

After a long time she answered, "She lives, not happily and she does not seek company but she lives. I feel her."

~

Alecto spent the years and decades building her wealth and reputation and trying to hunt down every last piece of information to hone her already sharp skills in the dark arts. Ordo was useful for securing unwilling labor and bodies for Alecto with his mark; the scratch or bite that turned humans into his thrall. They didn't eat as well as before nor enjoy the luxuries of Londinium but they lived. Alecto "died" every few decades before reappearing in a different part of the island to throw the Hunt off her scent.

One day a large host of men was seen on the edges of the woods where they were living. Too many to fight and although from the treetops at night Ordo couldn't spot the speared snake flag, he was concerned by the presence of a large number of priests. They patrolled the camping army at night, chanting while incense burned in metal containers they were holding over hoards of praying soldiers.

"We need to run now!" he had hissed. "They aren't Britons but they've worked out how to curse their weapons."

"I fear, Ordo, this is it, this is the end. We are to join the others."

They agreed that Ordo would behead Alecto before walking into the sun praying that it would rise before the army could penetrate the forest. This would send them both to Hades, but the arrows if the Saxons had them...

Alecto had a large axe rested against her neck. Ordo was going to time the blow with daybreak so he would burn up straight after. Alecto was fearful, she had once been told by Spurius that beheading ended a creation but that was before the cross had given her the ability to walk in the sun.

Seconds before the end, a booming voice rang out from the entrance of their cave. It spoke with confidence and force. It spoke in Latin; the language of Londinium. "I am Offa, newly anointed King of these lands. I have been chosen by the great almighty himself to create the greatest kingdom this island has ever seen or ever will see. I have slain my enemies and drenched the fields of Mercia red. It is I who will send Satan's beasts to eternal damnation..." he stopped and resumed in a softer tone, "I still have foes to slay, Hwicce, The East Saxons, Cent, I need strength," then even softer, "greater strength than the priests can give me. Do you hear me, witch? I wish to sit and break bread with you."

~

Their time in the wilderness had ended. Alecto had a new fearsome-looking wooden mask coated with some mixture of dyes to give it a permanently shining effect, made so she could walk among humans without revealing her true self. They remained in the woods to Ordo's dismay. The offer of a thatched hut on the grounds of Offa's palace in the fortified, timber fenced burgh of Tamworth was refused by Alecto who feared spies from the Hunt were active in the town a short distance from the Wealas border.

They were rewarded in other ways. Alecto's counsel and

methods pleased the King. The Hwiccan kings fell to maladies one after the other and their successors were advised to become sub kings loyal to Offa. A famine that only affected Essex soon made the East Saxons subservient and dependent on Mercia.

What Alecto asked for in return for her services was captives. These unfortunate men and women, prisoners of war, those who had displeased Offa, criminals, cripples, hermits, shipwrecked Picts, wandering bandits from Wessex or Wealas; anyone who would not be missed, were given to Alecto. When she departed from the Tamworth palace after long nights conferring and counseling the King, following her was a cart with the top tightly sealed with a deer hide to conceal its drugged and unconscious contents.

Again to Ordo's exasperated whines and complaints, these deliveries were not to be used for food… at least not yet. "We are Offa's servants until we can launch an assault on the Hunt's base and regain the Crux gemmata, that along with the sword and dagger the vermin used on our sire could restore our strength, even surpass it!" Then she explained her next step, "To do this we will need an army, and not a human one, we need more creations…"

"But the boss was the only one who could turn the rotting things into high forms like he did to us."

"Well, he isn't here anymore so I'm going to have to learn. Strigoi appear to be the simplest ones to make, plus I have strigoi blood in abundance."

"Where? Oh."

The following weeks and months frustrated Alecto like no others. She chanted every resurrection spell she knew in dozens of dead languages. She had her captives drained of their blood and poured Ordo's blood down their mouths. She had them bathe in Ordo's blood and even had them eat his flesh.

"It's only a finger! Besides, it'll grow back within the hour." But the closest she got was a runaway slave whose brown eyes faded to black and there were flickers of yellow beginning to appear in the darkness of her eyes before she gasped and died of shock.

Alecto would continue the experiments for all the years she did Offa's bidding. Building an army became her obsession. She needed more knowledge but anything of use on the island was either buried in the ruins of Londinium or secured in The Hunt's fortress in Eryri.

Then she had dreamed of longboats and walking corpses. Black of vein with superhuman strength, she dreamed of one giving a kiss with her decayed mouth to a monk and that monk's veins went as black as ink.

~

Now the Londinium survivors were sitting across from their human comrades. The smirking, fair-haired would-be king and the one-eyed, black-bearded man who led the Norsemen. She could tell they despised each other as much as they despised her. Such hate charging through the room made her smile. She said, "Let us dispense with formalities," and removed her mask.

Ulf or King Eardwulf had seen her face many times before, he was used to it but she remembered how he'd pissed himself and started weeping for his gods the first time she'd shown herself to him, she smiled hoping for the same reaction from the ship's captain Aindrea.

He shrugged and poured himself some ale.

She hissed in annoyance but now wanting to get the humans out of her sight as soon as possible, began to discuss their strategy.

"He has left for the island, is that so, Ulf?"

"Yes, well I would guess that's where he's headed. I sent some men with him but he walked straight into the sea and disappeared. My men weren't inclined to follow him in."

She laughed. "No, he will not need to come up from there for air."

"Who is she talking about?" Aindrea said.

"One of the draugrs, this one can talk… after a fashion, he's still as brainless as the rest of them, anyway he communicated he wanted to visit the place he was made, seemed no harm in it, we have someone there we need getting rid of and Alecto said she could work it into the battle plan."

Alecto showed off her teeth with her next grin and that got a cringing reaction from the one-eyed man that she wanted, he certainly looked paler. "After disposing of the annoying priests on Lindisfarena, Heregod will return to the sea to weaken any fleet in Bamburgh. When we have the town surrounded with no chance of escape, we will send in waves of men to plunder. After our Saxon, Pict and Norse mercenaries have taken the town, it'll be full of corpses for Keres to bless with her kiss. Then with a bigger army we can think about marching south to Eoforwic."

She had surpassed herself this time, she thought proudly. The previously defiant one-eyed man was shaking and sweating. She gave herself a shrill laugh as he leaned over and vomited all over the floor.

CHAPTER 24

The settlement of Snotengaham originally had few buildings, the Angle tribe that had founded it preferring the vast network of caves that lay underneath what was now a growing town. The caves were responsible for its growth. Offa had made the place Mercia's main prison, its caves keeping prisoners secure and its proximity to the mouth of the river Trent meant ships sailed up the river to buy prisoners from the town's slave market.

With good timing or not depending on one's perspective, the slave market had concluded its weekly business the day before so the caves were empty as their new occupants arrived in Snotengaham.

~

Ecgberht found himself sharing a cave with Hopcyn and a mixture of Wealas and Dumnonian warriors from The Hunt. They had only lost one man during the ambush. One of the Dumnonian warriors was speared through the stomach, selected at random by the Mercians to show that they could and to ensure compliance. That had even silenced Nabila who was screaming furiously at the Mercian who was trying to take her horse away. Nabila's silence and distraction had allowed the Mercian to punch her out cold and that was the last they had seen of her.

"Women will be caged in a different cave," said Hopcyn clutching the bars cemented to the cave's entrance. They would struggle to escape even without the bars, it was a labyrinth of caves with the town above full of guards. "If men and women share a cage, then things happen and the town gets a bad reputation if the slaves it sells get weak from carrying a child and have to be thrown overboard too often," he went on.

~

Nabila had more room with only Tegen and Nessa, a younger Dumnonii woman. She listened to them rant at each other in their language far too fast for her to catch anything. The only other person in the cave with them was the hag.

Despite the hag's pitiful appearance, she made Nabila feel very uneasy, there was something wrong about her, something of the night. She couldn't speak or walk, she must be ancient. Her mouth a ruined mess of twisted and torn flesh that left just a small hole she could only emit a whistle-like sound through. She was surely blind, only one eye was visible from the folds of misshapen flesh, half of a milky yellow puddle with no pupil or iris to be seen. She could not stand, there were shapes under the black robe she wore which may have been legs but they were never used, her hands were two useless lumps; a fire must have fused the fingers together or burnt them away. Completely bald, the only real reason Nabila had to assume the hag was a woman was her presence in their cave.

She tried to feel pity for the hag, she should, the woman must have suffered unbearable torment for her body to be reduced to such a state. She lived in the caves unable to see, walk or speak, living in this world but not a part of it. However when she looked at the hag, fear and hatred shot through every part of her body. She was at a loss to explain it. The hag had a snake as a companion. A small thing that curled around her neck. Nabila had no idea how either the hag or snake survived down here.

It was two days later with Nessa screaming and shaking at the bars of their cave that they heard more than one set of footsteps. They had one guard per day bring them a water bowl and a stale heel of bread, it wasn't much for the three of them; the hag seemingly uninterested in drinking, eating or washing. She wondered how the larger group of men split between two other caves were surviving on such rations. But two... no three sets of footsteps approaching now, were they to be moved? "Shut up!" she shouted at Nessa.

Two mail-shirted Mercian guards stood on the other side of the iron bars. They parted to reveal a young, handsome man with curly ginger hair. He was dressed in a fur cloak and leather jerkin. His breath engulfed the cave. Unlike any of the four occupants plus the two guards, this man ate meat a lot. Nabila reeled from the smell, wondering if the man ate anything else, although she was thankful it seemed to be beef.

"I am Coenwulf," the man said, "King of Mercia. It was your rotten luck that the men of Cent aren't as good fighters as they believe. We crushed their poxy rebellion with ease and were returning to the Snotengaham caves with our captives ahead of schedule. You happened to come across an advance party I'd sent forward." He was speaking in Frankish and addressing Nabila but what she said next mystified her. "It's a surprise to see so many savages together, the witch usually can inform us when a group of them intend to cross the dyke but she is absent these days. Wealas and Dumnonian mixing together and a Saxon and a Moor among their number is very strange. I do not like such strangeness." He then turned to one of the guards, "Leofing, give the witch's friend her feed." The guard pushed a half-full clay bowl of sticky looking red goo through the bars. "It's just chicken blood," the King said before turning his back to them and walking away.

The hag hurried forward and crawled toward the bowl, she used her stumps to shepherd it to the dark depths of the cave where she resided. The other three all cringed as a reedy slurping noise came from there. Noise from outside the cave distracted them.

A procession of prisoners being marched to caves of their own. Soldiers she saw at once stripped of armor and weapons of course but some had threads of mail hanging from their ruined and slashed knee-length coats, these coats were covered in bloodstains and the men's linen tunics were now engulfed in dry blood giving no clue to the original color. Nabila grew concerned at some of the wounds she saw, leaking blood from puncture wounds in the gut and groin, men vomiting and shitting themselves due to either shock or illness, she was sure many of these men would not survive the first night in the caves and dead and rotting bodies in an enclosed space would spread sickness quickly.

It was the sight of the men's bellies that enraged Nessa, launching pebbles through the bars at the procession of prisoners. "Saxon bastards! Greedy fucks getting fat off our lands! You think you're so much better than us! Well now you and I are the same now, this time next week we'll be pulling the same oar with a Frisian whip at our back."

"Nessa, wait!" Nabila heard a noise from a distance. She heard mocking laughter and shouting from the Mercians but it was all in Saxon so she was at a loss to the meaning. Until she saw who was the reason for the merriment.

~

Ecgberht had taken Hopcyn's position of clutching the bars when he heard the laughter and shouting. "Here comes the King of Cent! A cave for the King, he doesn't want to share one with the likes of you! A cave with light from the town, our King doesn't like the dark!" Here the laughter got loud enough to hurt his ears as it echoed around the caves.

Odberht! Ecgberht thought, his old drinking friend; the priest from Aachen. No, his real name was Eadberht and he was the Centish king in exile. Could this be him? If so, he could be in trouble. He had the same interview with Coenwulf that Nabila had. They just assumed he was part of a band of Briton bandits and some random Saxon that had fallen among them. Coenwulf was curious but occupied and that gave Ecgberht some time to think of a reason for his and Nabila's presence among the Britons. If Coenwulf found out he was the rightful King of Wessex, he wouldn't even reach the slave ship, he would be executed slowly. What a King of Mercia would do if he discovered he had a Saracen princess among his prisoners he didn't know but assumed it would be grave for Nabila.

If Odberht gave him away. He should retreat into the shadows of his cave but couldn't tear his eyes away from the shuffling, sorry-looking figure separated from the procession of Centish prisoners, walking behind them in shackles.

He recognized his friend's bony frame and bowl-like brown hair and he froze as the prisoner stopped outside his cell. It was as if Odberht could sense him. Odberht turned his face toward Ecgberht and saw nothing.

He had no eyes. Two shallow pockets of bleeding red flesh were where his eyes should be. "Come on, your grace, no stopping," his Mercian guard said mockingly, kicking the King of Cent up the arse and sending him to his knees.

CHAPTER 25

Osbald marched his remaining men up and down the beach where it would arrive as they began what they knew would be the last night of their lives. He looked back at the monastery where the evacuation was underway. He had faith that Alcuin was doing all he could but the beast could appear at any moment.

It was just after midday when they had noticed the black puddle in the middle of the clear blue water. Alcuin had tried to calm him at first. "It is merely a seal, my dear friend, what you saw at Segedunum stays there. Eardwulf will go south and attack Eoforwic in an effort to get the bishops and dux to anoint him." An hour later they began to notice the floating dead fish that rose to the surface wherever the puddle moved to. Osbald and Alcuin went to the beach, the charred remains of a few old fishing huts still lay empty and ruined, new fisherfolk preferring to fish further up the coast deeming the site of the slaughter all those years ago bad luck to fish from. It was an ominous wind that blew in and the smell that came from the water was terrifyingly familiar to Osbald.

"Perhaps a whale has passed onto…" Alcuin tried to remember what he had learnt about the immortal souls of beasts and made a mental note to check his books when he returned to Francia. Dead lobsters and crabs soon washed up and halfway up the beach, they found a headless seal.

"Get everyone you can to Bamburgh!" Osbald roared.

"But that would take all night and some of the brothers are…"

Alcuin fell to the ground as a ferocious slap hit him in the side of the face. He looked up at Osbald, his eyes brimming with tears and saw to his surprise Osbald was weeping hysterically.

"I can slow the evil but not defeat it. Get behind Bamburgh's doors so others may live."

~

Now they waited. He had tracked one of the things before and was the only one of the party to live to tell the tale. No weapon they had could stop it. Clubs, axes and especially fire could slow it and give Alcuin, the brothers and the villagers on the other side of the island a fighting chance to get behind the walled fortress of Bamburgh. He had asked Alcuin himself to perform a rite of absolution in front of the men. "He's the most holy man in Northumbria, maybe the world," Osbald had whispered at his men as Alcuin chanted in Latin, dabbing each man's forehead with holy water. His band of men had committed some dark deeds in their time. The threat of hell lingered with every battle, ale house fight and bout of sickness but they would take no fear of it to their clash with the dead.

They marched in a tight unit wanting to attack the monster all together when it left the sea. Osbald wondered many things, he wondered if the creature could sense them, he wondered if it was one of his former comrades there under the water. Most had just been ripped to pieces but he saw at least two, Dunwin and Taber dragged off alive by the woman monster into a cave and they had reappeared when the rotting corpses attacked them while retreating, this time with milk white skin, black veins and strength, such strength.

His candle clock indicated it had been a couple of hours since sundown. All the more time for Alcuin but he didn't like waiting, what was the creature thinking while submerged? Could the creature think? A loud crashing noise started coming from the sea and then a rumbling sensation started beneath their feet. Osbald landed on his arse as the beach began to sway.

Then the impossible happened. The sea moved. It rose as high as two men about a mile from shore and rushed toward the beach at high speed. Osbald and his men stood rooted in shock for a few seconds before coming to their senses and starting to run from the beach. *I'm sorry, my friend, may god forgive me,* was Osbald's last thought before the wave crashed on him with the violence of a thousand blows and his brains were dashed out on the rocks.

~

Alcuin watched in horror as the speed of the wave rushed toward the monastery. He and a party of ten brothers and a family from the new fishing settlement up the coast had left the monastery just an hour before but with the aged, the lame and children among their number, progress had been slow and they were just a mile north of the monastery about to turn left to take the causeway to the mainland. He sent the two youngest and strongest monks to take the dirt road to the right to warn and evacuate a gaggle of farmers and shepherds. *To warn them from what?* Alcuin thought with frustration when he saw the sea swallow the beach and crash into the partially rebuilt monastery sending timer and logs flying.

"Run!" he screamed and immediately grabbed the hands of two of the children in their group and ran as fast as his sixty-six years would allow him.

Maybe the extra twenty or thirty yards gave them a fighting chance, the wave crashed onto his back sending him and the children sprawling face first into salt water that now engulfed the field they had been hiking through. Several of the group that had been left behind had vanished. A log from the monastery passed them. Alcuin used all of his strength to stop it. The water wasn't so deep now, the wave had lost some momentum and the water stood at his waist when he got upright. He propped the girl child on the log and after some frenzied panicking, he found the boy child face down a minute later and got him on the log just in time. He gave thanks to the lord when the boy coughed up salt water and a bit of vomit and began breathing again.

~

Heregod walked through the flooded monastery which was once more just jagged bits of stone sticking up from the ground like the grasping fingers of the men he pulled down to the depths before opening their belly. He touched one of the stones and tried to remember. There had been warmth here once he could feel. He had the base urge to do something, was it to stay here and remember? No, he felt a feeling at the back of his throat. It was like it was burning, he felt unbearably hot despite the sea water. He remembered how to get rid of the burning pain. He had to eat. That was why he had spent the last few days pounding the seabed with his fists, to make the waters rise and have the bodies ready. He submerged himself in the shallow water and began to swim in hunt of the bodies.

~

Alcuin pushed the log and gave thanks that the water was getting more shallow, just half of the next field and they should be able to walk, he guessed from how far they were getting. It was pitch-black but he had known this island since he was a boy and had walked on every inch of it. Raised land was just ahead he was sure, and if he and the children could make one last sprint, they would be on the dirt road that led to the causeway.

The children were understandably screaming for their family that had been left behind and water was crashing around them. Alcuin couldn't hear himself think but was suddenly alerted to panting shouts from behind him, "Alcuin, help! I can't walk any further."

He looked and saw brother Osric panting. The heavy set monk

was on his knees with water reaching up to his neck. He looked desperate but Alcuin didn't know what to do. He was an old man and couldn't carry the younger, heavier man and there wasn't enough room on the log. The children must come first! No matter how much he told himself to leave the struggling man, his conscience screamed at him to find a way. "Osric, my brother, take my hand." He would drag the fat man all the way to Bamburgh if it broke every bone in his body.

He clutched the man's clammy hands while propping up the log with all his strength. He pulled and pulled and the man's feet began to rise. "Try to move forward now, brother…" Water sprayed in his face and Alcuin himself fell backwards in shock at losing grip so easily. He had dropped the log and the terrified children were back in the water. He quickly recovered and got them back on but was troubled by how silent the night had become. All he could hear was muffled noises from under the water. Air bubbles escaped from a spot twenty feet or so from where Osric had disappeared. "Osric!" Alcuin cried. The water felt warmer.

Moonlight shone over them and Alcuin saw a trail of red in the water. More air bubbles and a pool of red appeared. "Close your eyes, children!" Alcuin shouted and prayed they would before Osric's torso torn into two parts emerged from the depths.

CHAPTER 26

Nelda and six other women gathered around the drawbridge which gave access over the two foot man-made ditch that surrounded the wooden fort. As usual the bridge was slowly lowered to reveal a guarded entrance and the starving women got a brief glimpse of the fort town of Bamburgh. It was enough to make their eyes water and their stomachs growl. They saw well-fed guards, merchants and priests and even the smell of cooked meat drifted out. A young priest stepped out of the gate and said, "Alms for the poor, may the lord bless you." The gate slammed shut while Nelda was giving her thanks and she had to quickly rummage with the other six to get as much of the discarded oats and blackened turnips the priest had thrown out into her arms as possible.

Nelda had been inside the high tree trunk walls several times as a child. When a catch exceeded what was needed for the monastery's supplies, the monks had taken the remainder to sell at Bamburgh's market. Her father and brother usually accompanied the monks but on rare occasions she and her sisters were invited. It was the first time she had ever been off the island and it was like a fantastic other world. The bustle of hundreds of people living together in such a small fort. Tents and crudely built huts extended all the way down to the beach on market and feast days. The smell of roasted pork, priests chanting sermons, on the edges of the rocky outcrop where the fort stood, archery, wrestling and hammer throwing games were all going on and the ale was flowing and coin and punches were exchanged between the winners and losers of the bets. It was as if all of Northumbria was there.

It was also on one of these trips where Nelda, no longer a girl, had fallen in love with one of the novices and she found her feelings reciprocated once her father was passed out from cheap ale and she found novice Heregod walking alone on the beach.

That was a lifetime ago, now she had to ensure not a single oat was lost as she made her way back to the settlement. It was a very primitive village about half a mile from the town. With the land too hard to grow very much and the sea fished by boats from the town, there was little but bark, berries and alms for the group to eat. Nelda and her son had fallen in with the group after she barely made it to the shore and walked north. At first they had no interest in two extra mouths to feed and sent them running, throwing rocks at them. Later Nelda approached the huge man who appeared to be head of the village when she saw him alone on the beach. She revealed to him she had skill at making and repairing nets. He had brought her and her son back to the village where she'd demonstrated her skills and she was allowed to stay as her nets yielded a crab or two for the pot.

Waiting for her was Grimwold, the head villager and her man, kind of. Grimwold offered her protection and a covered dirt patch outside of his hut for both her and her son. His wife didn't mind, she needed someone to distract her huge husband. After their eighth child, she had deemed herself both uninterested and incapable of providing Grimwold with his wants so was happy to have Nelda help out around the house and even took care of little Heregod when Nelda was working, as long as Nelda and Grimwold did their humping far from the village.

"Beautiful morning and some good alms I see in your hands," Grimwold said as Nelda put her oats and turnips in front of the communal cooking fire. Nelda always found herself smiling at his voice, it was so light and elegant sounding from a rough, bear-like man. "Elda is taking care of the small ones and the other girls can take care of the pot, the lads are finished with their morning foraging, should be a good lunch, I reckon." He pushed out his huge chest. "How about you and I head into the woods and bless the lord for giving us this fine morning by uniting man and woman as his lord intended when he made Adam and Eve..." He also had a surprising amount of biblical knowledge for a man who claimed to have been born and raised in the shanty town village, Nelda wondered if there was an untold story there but for now she knew the man's appetite was never-ending.

~

An hour later and deeper into the woods than they usually went, Nelda was panting and hoping that the big man had tired quickly. It usually took three or four times before he was worn out but they didn't usually start until after breakfast. He gestured at her to get back on the floor when she moved to put her dress back on. She thought about mentioning breakfast in case that changed his mind when she heard a sound that chilled her to the bone.

"What are you doing, woman? You look like you've seen Abaddon himself! Get your head away from the hole, it'll just be pilgrims from the south on their way to the Holy Isle, Wessex softies or Mercian rats from the way they are talking like their mouth is full of acorns!"

"Shut up!" hissed Nelda. She stuck her head a bit further up the hole that led to the large cavern under a tree trunk that they were lying in. She listened more for confirmation and the all too familiar noises gave it to her. "They're speaking Norse," she said, her voice shaking.

"What's a Norse? Is it something they ride up north in Pictland? Something they eat? Something they hump?"

Ignoring him, Nelda got dressed and pulled herself out of the hole once she was sure the noises were coming from below the embankment the huge oak grew on. They couldn't see her, they were at the bottom of the embankment on the opposite side of the tree. She crept around the trunk to peer down. She saw them, a column of Norsemen in furs armed with round shields and battle axes, iron helmets protecting their dome and covering half their face. These men had come for battle.

Then a sight that deep down she had steeled herself for since she heard Norse from under the tree. The man at the head of the twenty strong column took off his helmet. Hatred surged through every part of her body at the sight of the one-eyed man with that hammer around his neck.

It was him! The betrayer! The traitor to his people, to his god, to her! Judas Iscariot himself! It was the man who had sold her and her child to slavers; Aindrea.

CHAPTER 27

Aindrea had volunteered for the first foray due to his knowledge of the area and fort. He also knew enough to gain entrance. His Norsemen would have to wait, their speech and manners would mark them as foreigners right away. He scanned the coast and fishing ships were scattered across the seafront, deceptively close despite looking like specks. Hardly a terrifying fleet but one that could still ferry refugees to safety or deliver troops and weapons to hinder them during a siege.

No, his Norseman had better be prepared for a while camping in these woods. He would gain entrance as Father Buadach, a priest from Hibernia making pilgrimage to the Holy Isle of Lindisfarne. He took his father's name just in case there was someone inside those walls who remembered the name Aindrea. Once inside, he would disappear just another priest among many. He would find the places that every fort had, ones with a loose post or a drunken guard and he would sneak his Norsemen in. When the sea was clear and he was sure this sea draugr with the name of his old, dear friend had cut Bamburgh off from any hope, he and the Norsemen would set the fort ablaze. The Northumbrians would be trapped between the sea and a forest that by then would be full of Earlwulf's men and behind them, the other draugr, including Keres with her corpse breath and black lips ready to deliver her kiss and bring back whoever she chose.

Had she done it with Heregod? He hoped the witch somehow had come by the name and its relation to him and merely wanted to taunt him but deep down he knew that somehow the man he loved was under the sea in a godless form. That was the other reason for volunteering; Aindrea knew how to kill draugrs. He could still help his friend, he could send him to heaven.

He decided to concentrate on the present. He left his men with instructions to camp and hunt south of here but to spend the day on the fringes of the forest as he would look for them. He then changed into a priest's robes that someone of Earlswulf's thuggish groups of Picts had relieved its owner of, discarded his hammer in favor of a cross and stepped out of the forest walking the mile downhill to the fort town.

~

They were cautious at the gate. He gave up his axe and dagger, although was allowed to retain a smaller knife for cutting food. He showed them his bag of coins with dead Offa's head on them but still asked him to wait until they could find another priest, it only took five minutes before one was found and he tested Aindrea to recite some blessings in Latin.

"Yeah the hibby knows his stuff," said the gray-haired, muscular priest. "Right this way, Father Buadach, we are in need of all the prayers we can get while you're here. You do know we are at war, mate? Old Eardwulf back from the dead, all the great and good have fled south to Eoforwic, just priests, soldiers and those with nowhere to go left. Most seem confident that Eardwulf has forgotten about us but I know the history of this land. Bamburgh is the capital of the first Angles in the north; our forefathers who chased the Picts and Britons from this land so we could have it. Eardwulf will want Bamburgh if he's a true northman. Get ready for a siege, my friend! Good job we have the sea to live off!"

Ulf wants you but not for the reason you think, Aindrea thought with a grimace. He entered Bamburgh with the strangest feeling he was being watched.

~

"You have to listen to me! You've let in a dangerous man!" Nelda had made it to the Bamburgh gates thirty minutes after Aindrea had entered the town.

"Piss off and get your fat arse back to your shit tip and away from decent people, you turnip breathed wench," the guard who answered her furious knocking replied.

"Oi! Manners, Litwin!"

"She one of yours, Grimwold?" he noticed the expression Grimwold gave when he looked back at her. "Oh, like that is it, thought she looked your type, look I don't want no trouble, you're barred from inside after what happened last time so I can't help you even if she were making sense."

"She claims that the man who came out of the woods before us is part of a pagan tribe called the Norse who are full of raiders and killers, the same that did for Lindisfarena years ago…"

"Let me stop you right there, Grimwold. I've heard of these Norse, some of the Pict refugees who come down after a poor harvest moan about them, let the savages kill each other if you ask me. Anyway you've got the wrong fellow here, he's a hibby priest, was able to talk in gargles like the priests do, wouldn't surprise me if the bastard could even read, had the sly look of a reader."

"No!" Nelda squealed, "It's Brother Aindrea from the Lindisfarena priory, we were both taken as slaves by the Norsemen and he turned his cloak and abandoned our lord and…"

"Well that proves it weren't him. This bloke's name is Buadach!"

The gate slammed in their face.

~

Aindrea found it easy to get along with the other priests. As much as he had enjoyed the company of his companions at the monastery, even Prior Aldred, they were not a learned collection of men, accustomed to the meager comforts of monastery life, their minds had grown relaxed and complacent. Aindrea sometimes found himself frustrated when conversations ended with muttering and silences rather than debates or questions when a topic presented new challenges.

These priests were different. They had traveled all over the island and to Francia and Hibernia, some even claimed to have seen Rome themselves. *I bet none have been as far north as me*, he thought. Their conversation therefore was varied and rich. Aindrea was delighted. Even brawny Father Dreamwulf had been quite the sailor in his youth as an East Anglian smuggler before he found the lord and used his boating skills to navigate the marshes of his homeland and bring word of god to the last pagan holdouts, isolated from the rest of the world by the bog lands. "Born half-fish me!" he said, repeating himself more and more as the ale flowed.

They were inside the main hall. The priests were pretty indistinguishable from the warriors with only men skilled with arms welcomed with a siege expected, priest or warrior alike had sword and axe at their side, mail-coats worn by both and the walls of the hall lined with shields and helmets at easy reach. Children and the elderly were absent, with the exception of old Anlaf; Bamburgh's ancient castellan, a handful of servants were the only women that remained and these women had been press-ganged as working as bed warmers for priests and soldiers alike. "It's a cruel thing," Dreamwulf said, "but not as cruel as what will happen to them if Eardwulf breaches these walls."

You don't know the half of it, mate! Aindrea thought to that.

"We can only pray that King Osbald and his men have not

been idle on Lindisfarena," Dreamwulf continued, "he has a fearsome clan, ties with both Picts and Mercians, our salvation will come from there!" He gestured toward the sea, they had made their way from the main hall to the ramparts to share a skin of ale while viewing the sea in the dusk. "Fewer ships than usual, not liking that, going to need to be well stocked in salt fish soon." Dreamwulf shouted to the nearest guard, "Oi! You know why the fishing fleet is low?"

"High waves," replied the guard. "Every morning we have a gaggle of survivors at the gate asking for refuge, have to move them on of course, they claim their boats get pulled down like the wave was coming from below." He snorted. "It's been calm out there for a week now but still they sink." He shrugged. "Whale, bad boatmanship or freak waves, who knows? Timing is shit I know that's for sure."

Aindrea looked across the sea, was his old friend under the waves? He waited until Dreamwulf was out of earshot and muttered to himself for the first time in years, *"In nomine Patris, et Filii, et Spirtus Sancti..."* He needed to get hold of a bow and a quiver of arrows quickly.

CHAPTER 28

Snotengaham didn't have a slave pen, there was no need of one due to the cave cells being right under the city. Instead they were paraded one by one to the end of a small, wooden pier where men in boats shouted at guards on the pier, translations of these shouts would go down the line of guards and captives on the pier all the way back to the head slaver sitting on a wicker chair; a jowly man whose leather vest over his linen tunic displayed his wealth.

Then he would give an open palmed gesture to the men at the head of the pier. Words would be shouted to those on the boat and a bag of coins was thrown onto the shore. The captive standing at the head of the pier would receive a hefty shove into the river, swimming was impossible with their legs still bound so the men and women in the water would have to grab one of the oars offered to stop themselves from drowning and then they were hoisted aboard to their new lives.

Nabila did wonder what happened if the jowly man and whoever the men on the skiffs were should fail to come to an agreement over money. So far all the bartering had resulted in coins being exchanged for a shove into the river. None of the captives were lame or elderly, rather a mixture of her companions and a handful of Centish soldiers. Most of the soldiers had been met at the slave market by wives or siblings who handed over coin and weapons as ransom for their loved ones. As the day went on, the remaining Centmen scanned the southern horizon for their kin, their eyes a disconcerting mixture of hope and despair as it dawned on them there was no one coming.

Nabila was fourth from the front with the latest splash. Nessa was at the front, she could recognize the frizzy hair even though they were all wearing itchy, coarse wool, smock dresses which made it difficult to tell everyone apart in the line. Behind Nessa was what she assumed to be one of the forgotten Centish soldiers due to his short hair and behind him was one of the Wealas or Dumnonian warriors, they all looked the same to her with bright colored beards and braids.

She felt water hit her face for the first time as Nessa was pushed into the Trent. She looked around to make sure Nessa was attached to the oar and had learnt enough of the Brittonic curse words to understand that Nessa was aboard and would be getting knocked out by an oar to the face soon.

Nabila had to think fast but she was bound, unarmed and surrounded by guards, the skiffs were ferrying the captives to larger boats up river. Once on one of those, escape would surely be impossible. She looked around, she needed Ninog, the arrows that Ecgberht had brought over from St Malo had been attached to her saddle. She knew Ninog was somewhere in the town, she had a strange ability to know where the horses she rode were after she had bonded with them. Another splash of water struck her in the face, the Centish man had been snapped up quickly.

~

Ecgberht was at the back of the line of captives. He turned his head to see sat above the slaver's chair a wooden bench which had been carried out of a wagon for King Coenwulf who sat eating fruits and cheese watching the morning's work. Sat on the ground at the King's feet was Odberht, linen was wrapped around his eyeless holes and the stumps of his amputated hands. They had done that to his hands the first night he was in the caves. The screaming and smell of burnt flesh as the wounds were cauterized was still fresh in his mind. It looked as if King Coenwulf was going to keep the rightful king of Cent as a pet. Coenwulf caught Ecgberht's eye. Ecgberht's story of him being a merchant from Wessex and Nabila his wife who had fallen in with the Britons had failed to convince him to let them go.

He heard another splash and from the language the drowning captive was panicking in, he knew Nabila had been sold, he hoped they ended up on the same ship. This journey couldn't end here, could it?

~

Nabila felt the oar smack her in the side of the head, her ears rang. She felt woozy and terrified that she would pass out and sink to the bottom of the river. She clutched tightly onto the oar as it pulled her closer to the skiff. When she came to, the skiff was sailing away and the line of men and women on the pier was getting smaller. Sat next to her was Hopcyn. "I was just behind you, they dragged me on when you were coldcock from the oar." He leaned next to her. "Three large ships upriver, once the crew is split up, there's little hope, we are going to need to go overboard now."

"How? We would just sink to the bottom without being able to swim."

"Well, the idea I had was..." Hopcyn stopped mid-sentence and swung the oar he was rowing with into the face of one of the two slavers, he was strong enough to send the man overboard but his hands were weak from being bound until he was pushed from the pier to grab the oar. The oar slipped from his hands and the other slaver ran forward screaming axe in hand. The axe would have been buried in Hopcyn's forehead if the slaver's feet hadn't been kicked out from under him by the quick thinking Centish man at the front of the skiff. The axe went into Hopcyn's shoulder and the remaining slaver fell face first onto the floor of the skiff, he turned only to see Nessa's face growl at him and a hideous scream rang through the air as Nessa's teeth tore into his face. As Nabila saw half a nose being spat overboard, the last remaining occupant of the boat rose. Oisan the Dumnonian warrior who had been in front of her in the line on the pier stood up and wrenched the axe out of Hopcyn's shoulder and screamed a war chant before an arrow from the shore plunged into his guts.

Nabila sprung into action grabbing the axe and propping up Oisan and the now unconscious and mutilated slavers' bodies in the direction the arrows were coming from in the hope they would act as shields. She hacked through the rope restraints wrapped around their legs and wrists, she rapidly freed Hopcyn, Nessa and the Centish soldier before herself.

Before she could ask Hopcyn if he actually had a plan, they heard two thuds as arrows struck their human shields. All four flipped the boat onto its side and disappeared into the river.

~

Ecgberht couldn't quite see what had happened at first but he saw the boat turn on its side and then a large splashing sound before it flipped back into its original position now seemingly empty. Coenwulf was on his feet shouting orders at groups of guards who were now lining up on the shore notching their bows. Coenwulf had to sit down quickly, he always appeared to be in pain when he stood.

Soon a group of guards came and lifted Coenwulf's bench with him on it. The flustered head slaver followed. At the foot of the riverbank, he climbed onto a horse and rode in the direction of the larger ships. Then they waited, Ecgberht scanned the southern bank of the river hoping to see Nabila and the others resurface but nothing. A guard returned hours later with news. "Sale's been put off until tomorrow, back to the caves with you, we'll get you on those boats even if we have to truss you up and carry you onboard like swine on their way to the market. Now get going!" Ecgberht noticed his old friend Odberht at the back of the line of captives shuffling their way back into the caves led by a rope around his neck. He gave one final desperate look at the southern shore on the far side of the river to see if they had made it across but saw nothing.

~

On the northern side of the river a few miles upstream, Nabila and Cathwulf the tall, handsome Centish man with a blond bowl shaped haircut were making a fire while keeping guard for any of Coenwulf's men who might fall upon them. "Don't talk much, do you?" Nabila chided the soldier, although as communication was done in Brittonic with Nabila making elaborate gesticulations for most of the conversation to make up for her infancy in the language, he may well have thought himself well out of it, she reasoned.

Nabila had been out cold for a long time after washing up on the riverbank and they feared her drowned. She had felt things while she was unconscious that made her think she had drowned.

Nessa was on her knees spitting into the axe wound on Hopcyn's shoulder, he was burning up, his face redder than before and pus was draining from the wound, Allah only knows what the slaver had coated his axehead with but it certainly wasn't anything good.

"Spit's not going to work, to heal a wound gone bad, we need turmeric," Nabila said.

"What is that?" Nessa said.

"A plant that needs warmth and rain to grow so it's not from around here. You grind it into powder and mix it into his water, it makes the blood stronger. We can patch him up with tree bark once he's strong and move him."

"Where is this plant? What good is it if it doesn't grow here?"

"Grows far from here, further than where any Briton has ever been but someone brought it here, maybe the Romans, maybe my people, but I found it in St Malo. It was in Ninog's saddle when we were taken. Stay with him, I'm going to get it back." She shouted to Cathwulf, "Oi! I'm going to get my horse back, coming?"

CHAPTER 29

Brennus sat with his back to the cave wall and listened to the waves from the sea outside, this would work better if he would chant in rhythm to the waves. He was sweating and shivering at the same time. He had mixed the deadly nightshade, mandrake and henbane he'd foraged into a paste which he'd smeared over his face and body, the remainder of the paste he had broiled into a stew and mixed in the red, white-spotted mushrooms before raising the driftwood he was using as a bowl to his lips and downing the substance in one.

Although none of the three knew it, Brennus had bonded with them during their time together in Dorestad. He did so easily with anyone he spent much time with, the result of being alive so long, he reasoned. In his dreams he could see them, not in detail but he could tell where they were and how they were faring, he saw Nelda lived, a life of hunger and worry but she lived not far from here. Ecgberht and Nabila had fared well to get this far, he'd felt their presence in Brittany, Dumnonia and Wessex but now he felt fear and hopelessness from them in Mercia. He didn't know the details but he knew he had to impart some knowledge to them where they were and that was going to take a lot more than bonding.

His eyes rolled back after downing the stew and he fell onto the rocky ground with foam-like spittle forming around his mouth.

He found Ecgberht first, he couldn't see him but he felt him. He was still conscious and wrought with worry and grief, he could try him later after he was asleep, entering their minds while awake could kill them with the shock, Merlin had warned.

Nabila was sleeping though. He sensed it was a deep sleep, she was also cold. He chanted in one of the ancient Celtic languages that predated even the Britons and he entered.

He felt nothing, he thought nothing, he was nothing, there was no Brennus, no Nabila, no future, no past, just nothing. *I should have asked Merlin what happens when one casts a temporary body swap spell with someone who is seconds from death,* he thought.

Wait! He was thinking there was still life in her. He bolted upright and saw out of two eyes for the first time in hundreds of years, saw from a face that wasn't constantly in pain. He could even smile. He tried and vomited water down a smock that had breasts sticking out from it. That reminded him who he was and why he had to commit his information to the brain he now had quickly.

Confident it was done, he gave one final look around, he saw he was lying on a riverbank, Hopcyn and Nessa who he recognized from their training with the Hunt were there. A blonde man stood over him, looking concerned. Brennus shut his eyes tightly and when he reopened them, there was only one eye to peer out of. He was back in the cave, his face and body returned to what they were. He panted heavily and vomited the mushrooms and stew back out.

~

Alcuin sank to his knees on the beach exhausted, he looked around for the children. He had gotten them over the causeway and onto the mainland, they had waded onto higher ground and when they looked back, most of the isle was underwater. He shielded the children's ears as unnatural screams came from the shallow, marshy bog that had once been an island and blots of red water were illuminated by the moonlight. He didn't know if anyone else from the isle had made it onto the mainland, he had just been focused on using every last bit of energy in getting the children far away from the sunken island and whatever dwelled in the shallow depths.

Now it was too much, he fell backwards on the sand and closed his eyes. When he opened them again, it was morning. He scanned his head around the beach. "Children, where are you?" he shouted with a raspy voice. His body froze with fear when he heard a child's scream from further down the beach.

He ran as far as he could toward the screams and saw the two children run terrified from a small hole in a rocky outcrop cliff that neighbored the beach. "Monsters!" screamed the girl. "Shellycoat!" the boy tearfully yelled.

"Children, children," Alcuin put his arms around the shivering pair, "you mustn't stray too far from me, you know shellycoats aren't real, just things grown-ups say to children to get them to behave themselves and as for monsters…" he cut off, not sure what to say. "The bible mentions a beast called Leviathan that is similar to what we saw last night but surely on land…"

"Shellycoat!" both children screamed in unison. Alcuin snapped his head around and emitted a high-pitched squeal at the shuffling, robed figure with a tortured, demonic looking face emerging from the hole.

~

Later when Brennus had managed to calm the timid trio down and wash his vomit soaked rags in a rock pool, he made a fire at the entrance of the small cave and shared his collection of berries and nuts. The children complained but stopped when Brennus told them, "I wouldn't want to eat anything that's been in the water after seeing what you've seen eh?" He turned to Alcuin, "I know who you are, King Charlemagne sent us to see what plagued these lands and he was most keen to see you back in Francia as soon as possible." He looked around. "I passed by Bamburgh on my way here, I was hoping to meet you at your monastery, you see, anyway they took me for a beggar and sent me on my way with pebbles bouncing off my dome but I could see they are getting ready for a siege. Eardwulf is coming and we've been hearing troubling tales about what's coming with him." He whispered the last part so the children couldn't hear and gave the sea a glance. "Let's cut inland, I know the best paths across where we won't run into slavers, bandits or even worse, Mercians, we can sneak into Wealas and get you safe passage to Francia, you can take the children with you or give them to the Hunt, we'll train them… ah that look, you do know who we are…"

Alcuin knew the stranger was talking sense so he was pained to reply, "But in Bamburgh are the remains of Saint Cuthbert and Eadfrith's gospels…" He explained about how he had swapped the holy bones to a more secure location and after babbling on the verge of tears about the sacredness of the bones and the beauty of the gospel's paintings, "You are a Briton? Then you must see it! The decorations are a mix of Celtic and Saxon styles that makes men of both tribes weep with joy…"

Brennus gave a sigh that told the group they wouldn't be heading inland yet. "Your face and reputation will get us inside with a full belly and some straw to rest on, I suppose, but as soon as your bones and book are bagged, it's to Wealas for us."

CHAPTER 30

Nabila and Cathwulf crept through the woods until they were about one hundred yards from the clearing that revealed the closest cave entrance. Nabila gave the land a careful check, beyond the entrance was a raised hillock on which the town stood. This was bad news if any sound was heard from below, then guards would seal off all routes of escape. The silver lining was she had found the horses they were tied to hastily erected posts by the river bank. The soldiers were passing through the town before heading to wherever the King's palace was or the location of their next battle and didn't want to make the effort to trudge the horses up to the stables in town which would have been a much more daunting prospect.

"I think I died at the bottom of that river," she said, not knowing or caring if Cathwulf understood her. "I think I was in Jahannam, the place you Christians call hell, I think I was in Athara the place of cold and damp, that's all I could feel. My body was bent and broken and when I touched my face, I felt as if I had been turned into a demon."

Cathwulf said nothing.

Nabila went on, "I think I went to Jahannam because of killing that awful man in Dorestad but I know something now that I didn't before, about the plant Ninog gave me, it can help us defeat the ghuls and save my soul from… are you listening to a word I'm saying?"

Cathwulf said nothing, Nabila shook her head and checked that the clearing gave enough cover from prying eyes that might come from the sleeping town above them and gestured for him to follow. "I thought Ninog was your horse?" he finally said.

~

They had scouted the two guards who were taking care of the horses, there were about eight horses for the King and senior soldiers, they probably traveled with a priest who would consider walking beneath his station, Cathwulf more knowledgeable about Saxon army life than Nabila was communicating this to her via gestures and shared jargon. She had half an ear on him but her full attention was on the horses. Ninog was there tied to one of several hastily and sloppily erected posts. The saddle was still on Ninog. The leather bag which Hopcyn had sewn between the seat and skirt of the saddle may not have been discovered.

Cathwulf's plan to distract the guards was predictable but despite her misgivings, she listened. "These two drew the shit stick getting duty tonight, Snotengaham has a reputation for being a rambunctious, sinful town, I've never been, well to the town above at least but it's said there're several women to each man and with the King's coin in their hands they'll be rutting like stoats..." he made a gesture to translate the last part "...good for us for later at the caves but they will send women down for their mates, it's the expected thing to do, way of doing things right?"

Nabila agreed and made a gesture of her own that implied Cathwulf's castration before sending him back into the woods. She was putting a lot of trust in the Centish man she barely knew.

~

"Oi Faran, the lads have done their duty, here she comes!" the sleepy guard with straw-like hair called to his mate who was pissing in the Trent.

Faran returned to his post and squinted. The taller man was finding it more and more difficult to hide from his mates that his eyesight was fading. He thought he saw what he saw but couldn't be sure, not with the beige or brown gowns most of the town's women wore matching the skin color of the woman somehow.

His mate Nyle confirmed for him, "Naked from the waist up, she must have walked all the way from town like that, wants to make a good impression eh?"

"Probably heard about the boar we speared earlier, them up in the town have coin but you can't eat coin, can you?" Faran replied before saying, "She don't look like a Snotengaham girl."

"Nah, she'll be from somewhere foreign like Wessex, but word of King Coenwulf being a worthy successor to Offa is spreading, we can expect a lot of them coming up our way."

"As long as they look like that I'm happy... wait, she's saying something..."

"Don't understand a word of it, sounds sexy though."

~

"You are minutes away from entering the consuming fires of al-Hutama where you will be tormented for all eternity as Allah wills it..." Nabila was stalling for time waiting for Cathwulf to take the men from behind if she had been betrayed and Cathwulf was headed downriver in search of a way back to Cent, then she would kill or maim the men herself, she would keep up the whore pretense until she had the chance to use her teeth on whichever one of the men presented the opportunity first. Lips, fingers, nose or something else entirely, she would take something from the man that would be much missed.

Of course in temper she would be beaten to death, Hopcyn would die of his bad wound, Ecgberht would die an oar slave instead of becoming King of Wishsix or whatever it was called,

Nessa would quickly be caught and enslaved. The ghuls would rule the north and maybe beyond and she would return to that broken tomb of a body in Jahannam, this time forever. All of a sudden a ghazi's death no longer seemed desirable. Where was Cathwulf?

The taller one stepped forward and cupped her arse in one hand and tore away the smock that she had pulled down covering her pelvis, she was now completely naked. She couldn't die now, she was going to have to go through with it. She clenched her jaw with rage at both the traitor Cathwulf and also herself for being such a fool when she noticed the guard as he leered at her privates squinting. Could he have weak eyes? Nabila got a sudden idea.

She grabbed the man's cock and gave it a fierce but not painful twist, designed to annoy or excite the man rather than enrage, she then ran in the direction of the river.

She heard shouts and laughter from the man as she crouched shoulder deep in the water, clutching onto the riverbank, the current was strong tonight due to wind, sure enough she heard a splash, the guard had failed to spot both her and where the bank ended and had crashed face first into the flowing water. She heard panicked screams, the smell of ale on his breath, the strength of the current and his mail shirt led her to believe the fish and eels would have full bellies tonight.

She pulled herself back onto land and walked along the river back to the horses. She had to find her smock and somehow deal with the other guard. She heard a squelching, thudding sound and cries of pain.

By the time she had got back to the horses, the cries had stopped but the squelching continued as Cathwulf was still smashing the jagged piece of rock in his hands into the already caved in skull of the shorter guard. Cathwulf had a deadness to his eyes as he kept on thudding the rock again and again into the dead man's skull. He didn't even notice or care that his hands and smock were bloody. He looked up when he noticed Nabila's approach, saw her nakedness and gave the briefest of surprised blinks before resuming with his thudding.

Nabila searched for her clothing and found it several meters away, when she returned, there was barely anything left of the crown of the man's head and the thudding continued. She had heard some of the guards of her villa speak of this among soldiers, a red mist, they had been particularly prone to it when campaigning against the infidel Franks. Either way she knew words were useless. She pulled Cathwulf off the mushy headed man by the hair and slapped him across the face several times. He finally made eye contact with her, frowned a bit when he saw she was no longer naked but his madness had faded and he sat on the grass, cross-legged and panting.

She left him, she would need him to recover his strength, the assault on the caves was still to come. First she checked the hidden compartment in the saddle and her heart leapt when she felt the shape of the arrows and giving the saddle another tug, she found the tightly bound linen bags with the powders she'd made from the plants, she earmarked the turmeric for Hopcyn's wound but first she now knew what to do with the bright green Chloris flower that hadn't decayed on bit since being plucked in Saint Malo. Somehow she had returned from Jahannam with precise knowledge of what she had.

CHAPTER 31

Things were moving quickly for Aindrea. He could stop the pretense of being a pilgrim on his way to Lindisfarne, no one was heading in that direction after what the refugees had said, it sounded unbelievable, a whole island submerged! But the stories were all the same whether they came from the village on the mainland who were within sight of the isle, the shepherds on the hills above the village who got a sobering view of the isle's fate or even the famed Alcuin of Eoforwic who claimed to have been on the island when the waves crashed over it. There were sobering tales from some refugees from the coastal village that the waters had begun to recede after a day or two and some menfolk had waded across the causeway to look for survivors, none had returned. One woman had wailed as she claimed a foot that had washed onto the beach was her son's, the scarring on the sole from him drunkenly stepping on a simmering beach fire at night.

The refugee camp stretched from Bamburgh's walls right down the rock hills to the beach, it resembled the feast days and open markets of old until you got close. There were no suckling piglets on spits in these tents, no impromptu churches in shacks and under trees of priests with dubious credentials collecting alms and giving blessings, no young men wrestling while heated and violent wagers were laid on the outcome.

No, now the camp was full of fear and broken hearts. Mostly women and children, a few lame and old men, a handful of young men who hadn't been out at sea or on the isle were given clubs and patrolled the beach, there was no room inside the fort town. Aindrea or Buadach as he was known inside the walls still found himself welcome. He had demonstrated his skills with bow and arrow to gain himself possession of the precious arrows he had later blessed in secret. Old Anlaf once he'd heard of Father Buadach's rare talent with the bow had instructed the priest was to be kept inside with bales of straw to rest his head on and a bowl of pottage and a flagon of ale a day. At a time when space inside the walls was only allotted to those with the most value and even monks and priests who were handy with their fists or a dagger were being booted out to share the scraps in the refugee camps, this was a blessing indeed.

Aindrea however was plotting betrayal for both sides that had placed trust in him. His Norsemen were out of the forest and camping on the edge of the refugee camp. They had whined and screamed curses to the gods as he had ordered them to hack their hair off and exchange their hammers for wooden crosses but Aindrea wasn't going to pass up the opportunity to have the Norsemen just minutes away from him when they were needed. "Just keep to yourself and don't kill or fight any of the refugees, in fact it's probably best if none of you spoke at all," he had warned them, they would be needed in days, hours even rather than weeks. Aindrea had found a rusty gate in the cliff wall that revealed a tunnel chiseled by Briton smugglers or Roman sailors however many centuries ago that led to a hole in a well-hidden part of inside the fort walls. The Norsemen would be hacking the soldiers and warrior priests to pieces in their beds if, no when, Aindrea gave them the word.

The other betrayal was the one he planned with the arrows. Heregod would not leave this fort alive, he would not be part of the undead army that would march south slaughtering anyone who came in their way until Northumbria was theirs. He hoped the blessed arrows would free Heregod's soul from the grotesque prison it was now in, so on the Last Judgement it could be judged for Heregod's actions as a man.

~

Ivan and Assur, two of the Norsemen camping with the refugees, were training. They were running from the deer and seal hides propped up in a remote corner of the beach that was their cover from the elements to the gate they were to meet Aindrea at when he sent the signal. Their mates back on the beach would time them by making a notch in the sand every time they counted to five. They were hoping to break their record of six lots of ten notches this time. When the time came, getting to the gate a few notches early could give them a huge advantage. They had just returned back to the camp. "Sibbi, how many notches this time? I think I'm getting used to the thick sand on..." Ivan stopped and threw his hand back to prevent Assur from moving any further. Assur went cold, Ivan's rages were known to be terrible things at the best of times, how would he react as he followed the bloodstains on the sand to the slain bodies of his Norse brothers?

~

Nelda and Grimwold were a good half mile away from the beach when they heard the bone chilling screams from where they had been. Grimwold's dagger was still dripping blood. "We didn't get all of them," he told her.

"Three is good enough, three who are burning in the lake of fire now, three who will never steal from Christian families, orphan Christian children, defile Christian womenfolk ever again," spat Nelda. "As I told you, the only good Norseman is a dead Norseman," the screams were coming from multiple people now.

"As you said, Nelda love, I just don't think the surviving pagans are taking the news too well. Let's walk at a brisker pace."

~

"What on earth is the commotion?" Alcuin asked as they were dining in Bamburgh's main hall. The bones and books and anything else that were precious to the learned man had been collected from their hidey holes and Brennus was keen to hit the woodland and head west until he could hear nothing but Brittonic being spoken but the old man in charge of the town had insisted hosting them for one last dinner before giving them an escort from Bamburgh. Seated near the head of the table where Anlaf was hanging off the holy man's every word, Brennus certainly wasn't complaining about a rare chance to eat meat and was grateful that Alcuin spoke of him as "Brother Brennus". The presence of a Briton in the fort, especially one of his appearance, had a few of the superstitious soldiers and warrior priests, which was pretty much all of them, muttering things like, "cursed creature," and, "warlocks should be burned," whenever he crossed their path. If not for Alcuin's benevolence and the awed respect everyone in the fort town held for the holy man, he was sure a knife would find its way into his belly before long.

Alcuin was asking about the sudden movement of soldiers and the bellowed instructions to open the gates. "Are we being attacked?" he asked nervously, he had the nameless children, neither of whom spoke much close to him.

Anlaf answered and Brennus strained to listen, as well as the whine-like Saxon dialect of Northumbria, the old man was toothless and was a chore to understand.

"Trouble on the beach, some savages are attacking the refugees, foreigners from the sound of it. Bastard Pict bandits must have found out about the savage waves taking out the isle and all our boats. No matter, the men will make short work of them…" He looked at a pale but hard looking man with a rag tied around his head covering one eye. "Father Buadach, we could do with your arrows on the beach in case it's one of Eardwulf's tricks and a bigger gang of Picts are on their way."

The dour, pale, one-eyed man wordlessly left the table.

~

Fuck, fuck, fuck… was the mantra that went on in Aindrea's head as he hurried down the stairs to the square, he watched the last set of men head through the front gates but he knew a quicker and most secret way. He found the trap door in a forgotten basement. Damn it! It was to be this evening that he would light the beacon at the right time to signal to the Norsemen to meet him at the tunnel gate. He was sure the timing was right, since the refugees began to arrive and the sea had cleared of boats, the waves had stopped. He knew now that Bamburgh was trapped between the shipless sea and what lay under it and Eardwulf's approaching army. If only the fucking Norsemen could have gone a few more hours without going on a murdering spree.

~

Aindrea disappeared into the darkness of the tunnel so was deep underground, inside of the cliff unable to hear a thing when the screaming from inside Bamburgh started.

CHAPTER 32

The last set of men to go through the gates Aindrea had witnessed before he dropped into the basement were four lads who had grown up together in the town of Berewic. Berewic had a large fyrd drawn from men from miles around due to its fertile fields being full of both barley and cattle which attracted Pict raiders. When Osbald's broken, tiny army returned from their disaster at Segedunum, it was mainly the men of Berewic who had answered Bamburgh's call for help. Now the Pict bastards had broken through the forces they had left at home, so they thought. Sick with worry of their families back home, their minds were focused on getting down the cliff as fast as possible. They didn't notice the clammy white arm reaching out of a small subterrane hollow on the cliff's surface. It wasn't until they were on the beach that they noticed only three of them remained.

~

Heregod had been waiting under the water. He was hungry and sick of fish, there hadn't been any of the things, the things like the old him in the water for days. He wanted some! He wanted some now! Vibrations on the beach, something was happening, he could smell the thing's blood. Some of it was in the water now.

He rose above the water and roared. There was fighting on the beach, a man was screaming curses and swinging an axe, terrified people around him. Heregod was only fifty yards out. He then howled in pain as the sun crept out from behind a cloud and burnt a hole through his pale cheek and set the seaweed-like substance mixed with his hair on fire.

He whimpered at the bottom of the ocean, he forgot the sun was angry with him and burned him so. He forgot that he could only walk the land at night, he forgot so many things lately. He worried if he was losing Keres' gift and becoming like the others. He started clawing at the sand on the seafloor and began to burrow.

He had burrowed his way as far as he could under the seabed and beach when he hit rock, he frantically searched for a way through the rock and found he could slide into the little cracks and crevices if he cracked and ground up his bones enough to fit, if he mushed his guts and organs into liquid and his bones into powder, he could still slither through the spaces in the cliff's interior. Eventually he found a space big enough to regenerate his body in, agony that it was. He needed food and he needed it now, he couldn't wait for the sun to go down whenever that was.

He was lucky he felt the things stomping on his space and yanked one down. It was dead straight away, he was too strong, he tore too much flesh and too much blood poured out at once, he couldn't knock them out while keeping them alive with a deft, light slap like Keres had learned to do, at least not on land. He had had more luck keeping the ones he dragged down from the sea alive to see him. He preferred the sea, he understood now it just didn't have enough of the things he liked to eat. Ones like the broken thing he'd just yanked down. Whale tasted a little similar now that he thought about it, he pushed his thumb down on the top of the thing's skull and the thumb went straight through. He scooped out a bit of the fatty blobby stuff under and skull and sucked the creamy, bitter tasting blob off his thumb and swallowed it in one. It was then that the thunder began to crash. Heregod cringed at first, he didn't know what it was, but then amongst his whimpering something came to him, one of the memories of before. Thunder meant rain, rain meant clouds and clouds meant no sun. He gingerly reached his arm further and further out of the hole, he felt itching but it was bearable.

~

"Death," said Brennus. The instant the word left his mouth, all the candles in the main hall extinguished. He had no idea what made him say it but the looks he got told him the inhabitants of the fort were aware of the meaning of the Brittonic word.

"Brennus, what do you mean?" a nervous Alcuin asked him, looking around at the angry glares. The foreign warlock had spoken a foul word in his foreign tongue and the sky had darkened and they all suddenly felt very cold. "Children, stay close to me." His effete, quivering voice having taken on some uncharacteristic steel.

They all stood upon hearing a giant sounding thud and then a long creeping sound followed by a massive crash and soon the sound of screaming men. Anlaf staggered to the window hole covered by some of his men. "We're under attack! The front gate and gatehouse are down. Men to arms! Men to arms!"

Chaos erupted and Brennus found himself knocked over. Alcuin gathered up the bag of bones and the holy book and backed away to a corner of the room with the crying children under the folds of his cloak. Brennus crawled to the window space, he thought he had misunderstood Anlaf but he meant down literally. The giant logs that made up the gate and gate house had been snapped like twigs and were sprawled both inside and outside the town. A dying man was moaning, his chest crushed under one giant log.

Soldiers poured out of the main building, having made it down the stairs from the main hall. They stopped not sure what they were looking at or for. There was no enemy.

Then from a large muddy puddle the naked man rose with a

terrible roar. He was the color of mud from head to toe. As he stepped forward, the mud slid off his body to reveal colorless, clammy pale skin and what Brennus had guessed had been bloodstains or wounds turned a black shade by the mud were his veins. The man stood around six foot tall and had damp hair reaching to his shoulders but it wasn't hair at the same time, it looked too perpetually damp. The man gave what may have been a smile, may have been a roar. His mouth was the most disgusting thing Brennus had ever seen, the teeth and gums were a gray-black ruin mushed together. The gums were wriggling and twisting. Brennus couldn't see from this distance but he suspected the mouth was full of worms and other vermin.

The first spear went into the man's stomach and black blood poured out. The creature just yanked the shaft out of the holder's hands. The soldier holding the spear was flung across the courtyard, his head smashing into a stone wall. With one backhanded slap, the thing managed to decapitate the soldier who had been standing behind the spear bearer. A pile of seven or eight soldiers piled onto the man who disappeared under a sea of screaming, rage-filled men hacking and prodding their swords into the thing that lay under them. Brennus saw the men with their backs to him as they leaned over the man and seconds later a red dot appear on the back of the linen shirt one of the hackers was wearing and that red dot expanded in seconds before his torso exploded and guts and entrails were draped around the intruder's fist.

The monster, as it clearly wasn't a man, stood as the soldiers backed away. One fist casually thrown by the creature tore through the mail shirt of a nearby soldier and as the thing withdrew its fist, the soldier's guts and blood poured out of the hole in the man's stomach. One of his companions vomited as the red and purple sludge inside the man slowly oozed out. The rest of the men ran. But there was nowhere to run to.

Several miles away stood Ulf, Alecto, their army and the draugr, grunting and wheezing in covered wagons at the rear of the five-hundred strong army.

"I think it's dark enough to let the draugr walk," Alecto told him.

"Where the fuck is Aindrea's signal?" Ulf said. "Smoke should be visible if Bamburgh is aflame by now!"

"I feel something, something has gone amiss there, not what we planned. Send the men in now, even if we lose a few, Keres can bring them back. No one gets to leave this army." She smiled.

"Why don't we send the draugrs in first? Then we won't lose any men?" Ulf demanded.

"I fear if that happens, then there may not be much left of the men of Bamburgh. We need more draugr if we are to take the north and more. Keres can't bring back someone missing all their limbs and with their body eviscerated," she shrugged and licked her lips, "I mean she could try but I fear it would be fruitless. No, let your men stick them with holes then we bring them back."

CHAPTER 33

Ecgberht had more space in his cave cell. Hopcyn dead or fled, Oisan surely dead, three more of the Centish soldiers had been carried out of the cell after their wounds had blackened, the stench reaching the guards who decided the unmoving, stinking bodies needed to be burnt. One of the Wealas men was sick, writhing in agony at the back of the cave with a strong fever. Ecgberht could do little else but pray, it was god who had made the men sick and it was god who would cure them if it was part of his plan.

He saw the guards had brought rusty and uncomfortable looking metal shackles and had hung them across from the cell, a taunting reminder that there would be no escape tomorrow morning. They would be shackled in their cells and their feet and arms would remain bound until they were far out in the Frisian sea. Ecgberht prayed harder.

He must have fallen asleep but he was woken by a wailing sound that he assumed was the dying Wealas warrior but as his senses returned from the sleep, he became aware the sound was coming from outside the cell, far outside the cell. There was a cave near the entrance the guards used as a drinking room and the wailing appeared to be coming from there. Something was coming which made Ecgberht crawl down to get a better view of the part of the corridor that was illuminated by torchlight. He heard low moans interburst with screams every few seconds and he could sense something getting closer. He searched the ground for a loose rock or stone to use as a weapon but the guards had been meticulous in sweeping the cell and making it clear of any potential escape tools before the prisoners were shoved inside.

A face appeared in the torchlight, he recognized one of the guards but the man was crawling on the floor, convulsing in pain, green bile and unnatural green tears were flowing from his mouth and eyes.

~

"Don't ask me how I know," Nabila had begun just ten minutes before as they sneaked their way to the cave entrance, "but this plant is an unusual substance when mixed with blood or saliva, even to the demons and ghuls, if I can work out the right mixture to smear on the arrows, then we won't even need any fat old abbots or smelly priests to bless them before we kill Iblis' creatures."

Cathwulf said nothing, he had been breathing heavily since killing the guard so she asked him to wait ten feet behind her while she chewed the chloris flowers as carefully as possible. She didn't know what would happen if she swallowed some and didn't want to find out. Her throat instantly went dry and her mouth was full of a gooey salty texture that stung the inside of her mouth. The first few times she gagged, once so loudly she was sure that she'd alerted the guards but finally, unable to breath, she could walk with the disgusting goo in her mouth.

~

Ecgberht tried to beckon the wounded guard toward him. He gasped when he got a look at the man's face. Giant red welts were on his eyelids, forcing them to be half shut. He doubted the man could see much anyway, his green tears were congealing into blobs that covered much of his remaining vision. The man vomited some more bile and then collapsed onto his belly, convulsing in violent shakes. Ecgberht strained his eyes looking for a key and then plunged his hands through the bars and into the darkness to the unlit area the man had collapsed into.

He yelled in pain when he reached out and felt one of the blobs on the man's face. It was like a bee sting. More stings as he groped the man's body and touched parts of his tunic that had bile on it but finally he found a leather pouch which felt like it might have the keys in it.

~

At the other end of the subterranean network of tunnels and caves, Cathwulf was worried. Not about the guards, it had only been a skeleton shift and once Nabila had spat the green mist in their faces, they ran away screaming. The screams had faded quickly which told him they didn't get far. A few other guards had the pleasure of kissing his rock which now was coated with the blood of multiple Mercians. He was definitely going to keep this rock if he lived through this which he was less confident about now that a devil appeared to be loose in Nabila's mind, she was shaking and green foam was coming out of her mouth.

He was torn about what to do, he knew Nabila had come here to free her comrades but he needed to get out of here before reinforcements came. He had hesitated when he entered the guards' drinking room and found three naked whores there. He smashed in the brains of the two guards that were watching them undress but stopped himself from doing the same to the women giving them the chance to run. He cursed himself for his reluctance, they would be running through the streets of Snotengaham raising a hue and cry. They needed to be on horseback before men started pouring down the hillock and cutting off their escape route.

"Nabila! Wake up!" he screamed, slapping her across the face twice. When nothing happened other than blood began to trickle from her temple, he realized he still had the rock in his hand. "Shit!" he spat. "Fucking shit!" he shouted when he heard the boozy yelling of Mercians make their way down the hillock. He dumped Nabila's twitching body in a crevice and stood at the cave's entrance with his rock in hand hoping to take out at least two of the bastards.

He could get two, if he spread his body across the cave, he thought. He had been on the attacking side in the past when drunken soldiers got told in the middle of the night that they were needed. Half asleep and many would have forgotten to bring their full kit. Still the numbers meant he was unlikely to live. *For fuck's sake,* he thought. He'd have to get in the crevice and slit Nabila's throat so the drunken Mercians filled with bloodlust didn't take her alive. He was sure she'd prefer death to that no matter what her god thought.

It was while he was fumbling in the dark searching the tunic of one of the dead guards when he heard the shouting from behind him. Had the blinded guards recovered somehow? Then the nature of the noises told him these were the prisoners. The caged Britons and Centishmen had somehow escaped.

He pulled Nabila into the guard's drinking cave as he watched the hellish spectacle of the two sides crashing into each other in the cave's mouth. Blood flowed as the Mercians who had brought their daggers hacked into the surging prisoners despite being unarmed. The prisoners were furious and sober and used their hands and teeth to attack. Cathwulf gave a shocked whistle as he saw a savage bearded man take out a Mercian's eye with his teeth.

The prisoners were losing, sober or not. When a dagger went into one of them, they went down and stayed there and within five minutes of the fighting, their number had been cut in half. Just as it looked like the Mercians were going to break through and Cathwulf put the small blade he'd found on a guard against Nabila's jugular came the chains flying out of the darkness.

~

Ecgberht and Tegen screaming guttural curses in their respective tongues, charged forward waving the shackles that they were due to wear tomorrow. The surviving prisoners knew what was coming and parted, leaving a space for the rusty chains to swing into the Mercians, smashing teeth and tearing through lips.

Ecgberht threw a pile of chains onto the stone floor, the crashing sound and increased chanting by the prisoners disorientating the Mercians further. Each of the remaining prisoners grabbed a chain and after a few more wild swings and a few more ruined Mercian faces, the Mercians who were still standing now numbered just six, they looked at each other and ran.

Ecgberht gave a shrug at the blonde man who jumped out of nowhere and was using rocks to cave in the face of the stunned and maimed Mercians on the floor and ordered the others to strip their bodies for weapons, coin, leather and anything else of use. He then saw her inside the guard's drinking cave. She looked peaceful but unmoving. "No, please, please," Ecgberht crawled toward her and propped her head up, her eyes rolled open but there was nobody home. He moaned as he laid her on the ground and his heart raced when she started coughing violently and her left foot started to twist. "Help!" he called.

CHAPTER 34

Aindrea stalked the courtyard in the dead of night with his bow notched. Heregod was within the walls but no one knew where. In the chaos after the men who tried to kill the draugr were slaughtered and the rest scattered, they seemed to have lost him. No one was sleeping tonight, unable to go on the offensive, the men were acting as lookouts and bodyguards to the defenseless. Alcuin and his two children had good men surrounding them. Anlaf and the warlock were deemed too old to fight, Anlaf had men loyal to him but he doubted the Briton would last the night before finding a dagger in his belly from a superstitious soldier and…

"I've heard you're a good shot, Father Buadach but those arrows still won't work on it."

He spun around and saw the Briton warlock peering at him with his one eye. His Saxon was very good when he wanted it to be, Aindrea wondered how much of the haggard old man who spoke with gasping, accented breaths was a feint. "I've dealt with these creatures before, these arrows will work," he said.

"Then the arrows you used back then must have been blessed by a most holy man indeed. But those arrows have been blessed by a pagan." Aindrea looked at Brennus with loathing. "I do not mean to disparage your gods, I do not doubt their power and perhaps other rituals performed by your godly men and women across the sea may repeal the ghuls but the blessing must be done by a member of the Christian religious orders, priest, monk, nun, bishop and so on..." Brennus stepped closer to Aindrea, "Alcuin has a memory like no other for holy men of this island. A learned man who has his letters and many tongues and is both a fighter and an archer would surely be known to him, but no, he claims he knows no Father Buadach." Aindrea of course knew Alcuin, he had even had the pleasure of meeting the wise man on his visits to Lindisfarena. He was relieved that age and the lost eye meant Alcuin no longer recognized him. Alcuin was a good man and he didn't want to kill him.

Well, he was right about the Briton getting a dagger in the belly tonight, Aindrea just didn't think he would be the one to do the deed. As he reached for the belt hidden between his robes, the old man surprised him by stepping forward.

With surprising strength and speed, he grabbed Aindrea by the wrist and hissed, "I could tell Alcuin and Anlaf that one of their warrior priests is a pagan probably in the pay of Eardwulf but I know a man who has seen the darkness. You are serious about killing this ghul or draugr or whatever it is so take this!"

Aindrea felt an arrow being pressed into his hand. "Brought them north along with men to fire them, the waves did for both the men and most of the arrows but a couple washed up. These were blessed by a holy man I never met but they come direct from the Hunt's base in Cymru so they will work no matter how wet they get! If you need more, get Dreamwulf or one of the others to bless the contents of your quiver! They still have the power although they might ask why you can't do it yourself."

And with that, the old man slunk into the shadows and footsteps receded before stopping suddenly. Aindrea still felt the man's eyes on him. He put the handful of arrows the man had given him to the front of his quiver and continued to keep watch.

He should tell the man to escape even if his arrows worked

against Heregod, then the others would come. It was supposed to be tonight but with his Norsemen now dead, their throats slit or axes smashed against their foreheads once Bamburgh's guards had put down the melee, he didn't have the men to set the fort alight. Tomorrow morning he would try to get the pair of old men and the children they had picked up along the way to the beach and tell them to head south and never look back.

No refugees left on the beach, those who had survived the melee now camped up hill outside the main gates. Only Ivan, Assur and their mates remained on the beach making the crabs fat.

~

Nelda, Grimwold and several other members of their little tribe had moved through the woods deftly. Grimwold was raised in these woods and knew every twig. Right now in the middle of the night, they tracked the army that was slowly and carefully below them at the foot of the forest's hills and embankments making their way through the woods.

"They want the nobs in Bamburgh to get a nasty surprise when they wake up tomorrow and see them camped outside. Don't seem to have considered that Bamburgh has the sea at its back. Mind, now I think about it, I can't remember the last time I saw a ship on the sea that is a stumper. Anyway, looks as if the nobs are going to have to get used to the taste of haddock," Grimwold said.

"How many have we knocked out so far?" Nelda asked.

"A dozen, all from the rear sections, don't worry about our aim, even in the dark our slings go where we want them to go. Those of us who grow up groveling outside the nobs gates and scavenging on the beach soon learn that seagulls taste so bad that the nobs don't chase us away when we hunt for them like they do when we try to fish too close to the town. Hah! Must be half gull me, the number of them I've had down my gullet!"

"I don't think that's how it works… a dozen that's not enough!"

"Well Nelda, it was you who suggested stalking them although I must confess you've surprised me with how well you know their movements, I know you lived among them but I thought it was as a slave."

"That cursed-to-hell bitch Droplaug spent two summers as a shield-maiden before she started her family. Never used to shut up about how they could do a night's crawl through any type of terrain and surprise the enemy hours ahead of schedule. They fight people called Frisians and Danes who live on flat land and sand and… never mind, can't we boil some water and dump it on them?"

"I think even though these old mates of yours might be deaf from the liberties we've taken, they ain't blind enough to miss fire. No, girl, you've done us proud by letting us know what's about to descend on us. Without you, they'd have torn through our fine home while we were having our morning shite, but it's time to tell the nobs that Eardwulf is marching faster than expected. Space for us and the children is the least they can give in return…"

~

Aindrea and Dreamwulf had taken to patrolling the top of the ramparts. They'd worked out most of the guards since fleeing had taken up residence outside the walls, patrolling among the refugees, doubtless some were at the beach. Pushing the men further out might be for the best, Alcuin thought. They could work on deepening and widening the moat, organize the refugees into foraging groups, use the woods for hunting while they still could, maybe make some fortifications around the edge of the hill. It occurred to him that he was thinking like a Saxon. He knew there would be no time for any of this.

He looked down at the empty courtyard, where Heregod was, he could not say. The rain had been sporadic and the mud was thick. He could be down there buried and resting, perhaps his time in the water had disoriented him. He had heard many tales of the draugr during his time with the Norsemen. Some said they had other skills besides superhuman strength, shape-shifting, fire-breathing and so on. He had seen no evidence of this from the gruesome crew at Segedunum but he'd also heard that sometimes they could see the future events that were yet to happen were as accessible to them as memories were to living men. As the draugrs couldn't communicate, he had no way of knowing if that was true. It unsettled him, Heregod could be waiting for the exact time his targets would be vulnerable.

The rest of the fort-town had retreated behind thick wooden doors, latched with iron bars, as if Heregod couldn't smash them into splinters with just a flick of his wrist. It gave them comfort, he supposed.

Then he heard a noise from the courtyard below them. It grumbled and moaned like a man in great pain but then it rose in pitch to become a horrific, shrill shriek. He strained his eyes, the moonlight wasn't strong but the muddy courtyard was moving, it was as if it was bubbling. Aindrea notched his bow.

He thought about offering Dreamwulf one of the three arrows that Brennus had given him but the bog man from the east was a middling archer at best. He hadn't asked the muscular man to bless the remaining arrows either, Aindrea didn't want the man to ask awkward questions, he also thought it for the best if there wasn't a quiver of destructive draugr killing arrows when Ulf's lot turned up. The draugrs wouldn't attack him as the witch had worked out how to guide them well enough but if they all got lit up by the arrows, Ulf suspected betrayal. Aindrea shuddered at the memory of the blood eagle rituals he'd witnessed and how once he had come very close to that fate…

He turned his attention back to the rumbling courtyard, the

shrill pitch was making sense, whatever was down there was chanting and making sounds, recognizable sounds, he could hear the pained, piercing cry, the first time he'd ever heard a draugr make intelligible sounds. *"Alcuin, Alcuin, Alcuin!"*

A white damp hand shot up from the mud and the earth and Aindrea fired. The huge chunk of earth that flew through the air, striking him on the forehead and rendering him stunned meant he couldn't tell if he'd hit the target.

CHAPTER 35

"Twelve men? How the fuck did we lose twelve men walking through a forest?" Ulf twisted the top of the messenger's tunic tighter and shook at it as he spat his question at the man. The sun was coming up and the draugrs were back under cover in the wagons as the men marched on.

"Deserters?" offered Ordo from under cover in his own wagon.

"These weren't the Saxon or Pict troops, these were the Norsemen, where are they going to desert to? The sea? You idiot!"

Ordo blinked, he was used to humans living in terror of him, not insulting him. This wasn't the first time the fake king had directed his anger toward him. In another time he would have picked him up, smashed his knee through his spine, turned all of the squishy bits inside of him to goo with a few punches and turned him into a giant flagon with the blood flowing from his mouth to Ordo's. Alecto had told him that time would return, that they would once again use the humans as meat and drink but first they needed to work together with them as the kingdoms of the island squabbled among themselves. Once they had their undead army, they could march across Offa's dyke and take the sword, the remaining pugio and the crux gemmata back and rule the island again.

But first they needed an undead army larger than the handful of draugr they currently had so Ulf was to be indulged, too bloody much. Ordo fumed.

Alecto didn't like the sound of unexpected obstacles. They gave her the same knot of dread in her stomach that she had whenever she remembered her final moments in Londinium, talking to Ulf gave her a similar feeling at times now she thought of it. She reasoned it was unnatural for her to be dependent on a human. She didn't show her discomfort, she didn't want a row, not with her first legion so close to being created. She spent a few seconds imagining the look on King Eardwulf's face when she and her new army of monsters returned from Wealas with the jeweled cross, all of them walking in the sunlight. She even thought she might keep him as a pet.

That was for the future, for now she decided she wanted to take the town as quickly as possible to get ahead of any major surprises. She literally had all the time in the world and had been looking forward to a siege. The skin stretched tightly over the rib cage of a human was a sight that delighted her enough for her to overlook the piss poor taste of such a specimen, but not now. They were going straight in. She wanted Keres among the dead recruiting by nightfall.

She looked ahead, her vision was amazing. Now out of the woods she could see for miles and miles. All the way to the gates of Bamburgh. "Their men have moved outside, we've been betrayed!" she screamed as she was thinking of fates for Aindrea that would make her sire proud when she noticed something else. "Wait, they are camping and most of them aren't soldiers, it's like a smaller tent town. I see some villages, shacks mainly, deserted so they know we're coming but the tent town is disorganized as if they just emptied the fort so they don't know how close we are. March!"

~

Nelda and Grimwold had been in heated conversation with a guard at the new shanty village the refugees had constructed, they were shocked and angry to find most of Bamburgh's garrison and the warrior priests now squatting inside the tents instead of bringing everyone inside into the fort. The fort's massive gate had been crushed to splinters and rubble, men were guarding the gaps its destruction had created and some tree trunks and logs had been hastily erected as barriers.

"They're coming! They'll be here in an hour, maybe less! Let us through!" Nelda screamed at an armed priest, her son and all the others from the village behind her. When the priest pushed her arse-first into the mud, Grimwold with an almost casual swing of his elbow sprayed most of the man's teeth across the mud.

"Stop blocking the entrance now!" he bellowed, "Or everyone out here is going to get slaughtered."

"You don't understand," moaned a man in tatty mail, "inside is something from hell, unarmed. It killed three of us without breaking a sweat."

"I'll take on this creature if the rest of you let me and mine inside!" Grimwold said with a growl.

~

Aindrea came to, he hadn't been out for very long. He notched his bow, fuck – the arrows had scattered onto the rampart floor, he had no way of knowing which were the blessed ones Brennus had given him and which ones he had blessed himself, he now considered Brennus correct, as a pagan his blessings were worthless. He peered into the courtyard below being vaguely aware of some sort of commotion outside and gathered the arrows and put them back into the quiver as best he could. No sign of Father Dreamwulf on the ramparts and no sign of his former friend. Sunlight was beginning to illuminate the town. He remembered all those years ago, his final sight of Lindisfarena; the explosion of the perpetually burning draugr when the sun rose, from the Norse longboat he had seen the whole monastery destroyed. Maybe he wouldn't need the arrows! But Heregod had had enough self-preservation to slink into the shadows. Aindrea leapt down to the courtyard and began searching for the beast.

~

"I need to talk," said Ulf, with Ordo and Keres both hiding from the sun, he had a rare chance to talk to her alone.

"Now?" she snapped. The Norseman was becoming more and more irritating as their destiny inched closer.

"The gold and jewels from the island where we met, I need more of your spells to recreate them. My supplies have been waning ever since the building of Segedunum and the excess men we've been recruiting and feeding and not to mention word of the draugrs has spread, travelers to rob and settlements to pillage are low... well in other words, after the fighting I don't have enough to pay the men. I know you've made the treasure last a long time because of your spells so I was wondering..."

"Send any men who are wanting payment to me. I will give them a just reward." The wooden mask hid the gruesome smile she was making.

~

Brennus paced around the hall he shared with five others. Alcuin, the two children, Anlaf and an aging warrior called Norbert. Alcuin had spent most of the night in frenzied prayer while Anlaf and Norbert had barricaded the door with whatever they could find in the room. Pots and pans, a wooden board once used as a bed and logs used for firewood were propped against the door along with the two men leaning back as hard as they could. Brennus' contribution had been to calm the children. They were used to his appearance now, but rubbing some stinging nettle roots onto their gums had ensured they slept well.

Now they heard the shrill cry, *"Alcuin, Alcuin, Alcuin!"* It was getting closer.

Alcuin stopped praying. "I will go to my fate," he said with pure steel in his voice.

They then heard a thud and the shrill cry turned into a grunt of pain and then a howl of rage.

Another voice rang out, "Alcuin? Warlock? Where are you?" It was Aindrea.

~

The courtyard was surrounded by posts, propping up the inner part of the ramparts. Underneath the ramparts, ditches had been dug to create walkways under the ramparts and cramped into the small space remaining boards and crumbling bits of stone had been erected to provide shacks; housing for the servants and storage for tools, food and weapons. It was in one of these darkened walkways that Heregod was stalking, shrilly calling Alcuin's name.

Aindrea shot and the arrow took Heregod straight in the forehead. He knew immediately that this wasn't one of the Briton's arrows. The grunt was of annoyance and not a blood-curdling scream of fear and rage. But Aindrea got lucky, the blow pushed the beast into the courtyard where the sun's rays were enough to make it howl in pain as a sizzling sound and smoke came from its naked body. It dived straight into a muddy puddle, this provided respite from the sun but the puddle had receded enough to make the sizzles start again and a desperate Heregod leapt with all his might to the nearest shade which was the walkway on the opposite side. Aindrea now had some time to find the others, but he was too far away for a kill shot, even if he knew which of the arrows worked.

A terrible scream came from the direction Heregod had escaped to, Aindrea heard a sickening cracking sound and the scream reached a pitch that told him it was too late. He gave a prayer to Odin to make Dreamwulf's death quick. He hoped priests were allowed in Valhalla if they had their weapon in hand as Dreamwulf surely did. He ran to where the screams had come from and found nothing, the thing that had been Heregod had vanished somehow. The puddles in the shaded walkway the beast had retreated to were crimson red. His priority now was to rescue the old man and the children.

~

Grimwold stopped when he heard the inhuman noises from inside. "Still want to go inside?" said one of the guards who had stepped aside. Then in the air came faint chanting noises.

Both the guard and Grimwold gave each other a look of confusion. It was words, sounds that neither of them had heard before. "BlooðfyrirOdin! BlooðfyrirOdin! BlooðfyrirOdin!" It was getting louder and louder.

From behind Grimwold with her son in hand and organizing the others from Grimwold's shack, Nelda said, "It means 'blood for Odin', the Norsemen are here."

"What the fuck is an Odin when it's at home?" the guard asked.

"The devil himself!" yelled Nelda with zeal.

"Got anymore of those weapons in there?" Grimwold asked with urgency.

Then they heard it, the sound of the crunch as the advancing army came through the morning mist and crashed into the mass of refugees and soldiers who were given no time to escape. One deafening crash was the sound of fractured skulls, broken bones and torn flesh. Soon those who weren't instantly killed or maimed in the first contact were screaming and pleading for mercy as the newcomers smashed their axes down upon them.

Nelda pushed the children in front of her and urged the others to run and then they were caught in the crush. Half of the makeshift village were being chopped to pieces by the advancing army and the other half surging to get through the space where Bamburgh's gates had been to avoid becoming part of the other half. This created a mass of bodies while only a bottleneck of people were squeezing through the gap in the walls.

Nelda held up her son for someone to grab and reached down to try to find another of the children to aid. A knee rammed into her back and she fell to her knees, crying in rage and pain as her child slipped from her grasp. She heard familiar voices behind her as the others from Grimwold's village fell deep into the crowd. She heard Grimwold's woman Elda scream in terror as she got pulled down and the sickening bone-crunching sound followed. That sound was punctuating every few seconds, Nelda knew she had to pull herself up. "Heregod!" she bellowed her son's name is desperation, the adrenaline giving her a few precious extra inches of space. Soon she was upright and saw she was close to the entrance.

~

Aindrea found them in the main hall on the raised wooden structure that overlooked the courtyard. They were wise to remain on upper ground, he wasn't sure if the creature could climb ladders, although he feared he would be disappointed when he got his answer. He booted the door and found the old men and children being protected by a toothless, squinting warrior who had seen better days. "I know of a trapdoor, we can get to it and avoid the beast, he got penned into a space, he can't live in the sun, it makes him burn up." He saw the warlock nodding. "But there's lots of shade in this fort, I lost him and one swipe of his arm could completely redraw the map of the place. I say we get the children and their protector to this trapdoor, it's in one of the deeper basement pits and has a tunnel that leads to the beach. I fear Eardwulf is closer than you expect too…"

"Fear or know?" asked Brennus.

Ignoring the question, Aindrea said to him, "Once they are secure I will not rest until the draugr is…"

The sound from outside the gates had been growing and Anlaf in particular charged with Bamburgh's defense was impatiently looking outside the window slit for activity. He finally saw something that forced him to cut Aindrea off. "The gate! I mean what used to be the gate. There's a surge." The others turned their attention to what the old man was looking at.

A swarm of bodies was blocking the gap. The cries and desperate, slow surge of people through the gap told them people were being crushed trying to get through, angrier cries from the back of the surge that was now moving through the gap and into the courtyard showed axe waving hands hacking and a sporadic spear or sword would thrust out of the mass of bodies to repeal and strike back. Soon the courtyard was full of people. They were free of the crush but the bearded axemen continued to inflict terror upon them and the mud and puddles were turning what was for Aindrea and Alcuin a horribly familiar shade of red.

"What the fuck are you waiting for? You one-eyed hibby ox arse for brains!" Anlaf screamed. "You're our best archer, get to the ramparts and send as many of Eardwulf's men to hell as you can!" He turned to the old warrior. "Norbert! Get the holy man, the warlock and the children to the trapdoor, I know which one he's talking about. Follow the ladders as far down as they go!" Aindrea moved to the door. He shot one last look at Brennus whose face betrayed nothing.

CHAPTER 36

Ulf and Alecto were almost the final two to enter Bamburgh. Alecto's hideous grin grew even wider when she sensed how little resistance there was. "Whatever happened here was to our advantage. No defenses and most of their army outside the walls unaware we were right on them. It couldn't have gone better really." A handful of Bamburgh's defenders were left standing, one or two went down fighting; disappearing under a flurry of swinging axes. Others surrendered holding up the crucifixes they wore around their necks. The Saxon and Norse members of Ulf's army began screaming at each other in their separate tongues about what to do with these prisoners. The Norse wanted to remove the body parts of the warrior priests one by one and gamble on which one died last.

"Why are the Saxon mercenaries protesting? It's perfectly fair sport." Ulf was bemused.

"They fear their god will punish them, so are pleading for their holy men to be killed instantly or sold as slaves," replied Alecto. "I would urge a quick death, reports of torture of priests could anger Mercia giving us complications should they move against us before our army is complete, also it would please me if Keres would give her kiss to any of the holy men."

Ulf shouted instructions and the largest of the Norsemen began to hack at the neck of the priest he was holding. The others followed his lead, indifferent to the cries from the unarmed prisoners.

~

One of these prisoners was Nelda, her fear for her missing son submerging her despair at being in Norse captivity again. Everyone was dead. Those from the shanty village who had survived the crush had been hacked down in the courtyard as they stood, even the women and children, none of the crazed soldiers cared, the wretched savages were less than beasts. She didn't believe it at the time but now she could see that some of these were tattooed Picts and others Saxons speaking the same language as her. They had surely damned themselves.

Grimwold looked almost defiant even in death, his blue eyes wide open staring at the corpses of the Norsemen who had attacked him. An axe stuck out of the side of his neck, somebody had struck him from behind as even unarmed, he had snapped the neck of two attackers and crushed the dome of a third. Forcing a surge of men to take down an unarmed man had surely saved lives. Most of those who still lived did so as the attackers had attacked so fiercely that they exhausted themselves quickly and were forced to accept surrender from their defeated foes as they could barely swing an axe anymore. The captives were disarmed, restrained and execution or slavery awaited them.

Nelda owed her life to something more than simple exhaustion. This wasn't the first time she'd experienced the violence and bloodlust of the northern men so instead of screaming and running around like a headless chicken, soon to become a headless human as most of the other women and peasant men had done, she had crept around the fighting to covered spaces where she could ride out the violence until the men had exhausted themselves.

She had one stroke of luck. She had stumbled at a crucial point in her journey and attracted the attention of a Norseman. She was unsure if she was to be killed or raped, or if both in which order as the man had his cock in one hand and an axe in the other. She shouted out loud praise for god when the arrow came from nowhere and ripped the man's throat open.

Now she was near the end of her journey. Returned to Norse enslavement, she knew there was no escape. All that remained was Heregod, her son. She must find him or his body, she had baptized him herself back in the Norse lands but being a layperson and a woman, she wasn't sure if it counted. She needed to give him a burial in consecrated grounds to ensure his soul's place in heaven. And maybe, just maybe the lord had spared him somehow…

~

Ulf was inspecting their losses. "If big Keres wants to bring back any of our dead, she had best avoid those three clapping cod who got whacked by one man, big and ugly as he is. They can stay in Niflheim!" He came to another dead body from their side. "Why has he got his cock out? Wait! That's an arrow that's done for him. I told Aindrea to sabotage any archers they had, knock off the arrow heads, put little cuts in the bow strings, idiot must have missed one. There had better not be a live archer on the loose!"

He turned his head and got another one of many unworldly sights he'd had in his short life so far. Alecto, the demon, the witch, the blood drinker, the immortal sunwalker was on her arse shaking with fear. Vomit and blood were seeping from the bottom of her mask.

After what seemed like an age, she stood up, took off her mask, not caring who saw her outlandish face, both beautiful and hideous shifting from one to the other each time you looked at it. She hurled up a red-green mixture from her mouth and took several deep breaths. Finally, she turned her face to Ulf's. "Bring every arrow you find in Bamburgh to me, make sure to bag and cover them so no part is left exposed. A snake skin bag would be best but leather will do. I need to perform a ritual to burn them."

"What are you talking about? We can reuse these."

"DO AS I SAY! OR I WILL MAKE YOUR INSIDES MELT AND HAVE KERES MAKE YOU MY THRALL FOR THE REST OF TIME!"

Ulf gulped and decided there was somewhere else he wanted to be. He gave the witch a nod. "Do not allow a single one of the dragur to touch a single arrow in this town," she hissed as he turned his back and finished with, "They say the castallen survived, bring him to me. I will find out the identity of the archers of Bamburgh and they will die slowly. My sire taught me a few things about prolonging death."

~

Aindrea darted through the back alleys of the fort-town easily avoiding the new conquerors of Bamburgh. He needed to dump the bow and quiver before he was spotted with it. Archers were seldom popular with invaders who had just charged into a town, having usually suffered casualties from the ramparts, also Aindrea was not known among the Norsemen as an archer. A line of questioning being started that would lead all the way to a blood eagle on the banks of the Tyne before they sailed home was something he wished to avoid.

But before dumping his dangerous load, he had to make one final attempt to save the soul of his old dear friend.

~

Nelda was surprised to find she had the freedom of the fort-town, as did most of the other prisoners. Only the old man who was in charge of the place and a smattering of important looking priests were restrained, she guessed they would be kept alive for information or ransom and would travel with the army to wherever they plan to pillage next. For the rest of them, why waste good rope when they were all unarmed and weak? The only exit point was the space where the gate had been, now guarded by the invaders and logs had already been put to barricade the space. She knew they would be leaving as soon as tomorrow, either the newly enslaved survivors, she counted around twenty, would be placed on a ship for the Norse lands or they would be put to the sword and Bamburgh burnt to ashes. She remembered the clear sea from that morning as the sun rose, she had never seen it so deserted. She used her childhood memories of the alleys and slipped into the darkness. Before death, she had to find her son one way or another.

~

Norbert and Alcuin each had a child on their shoulders as they were descending the seemingly never-ending set of ladders, with so many rungs rotted away and a long plunge into the darkness, it was thought best to carry the younger ones. Brennus made up the trio of old men, following last. Each ladder ended in a cramped cavern basement with a network of small caves and crevices leading out of it, none were big enough for an adult and they had to grope around in the dark to find another ladder that descended further. Brennus proved his worth here, the Briton had an uncanny ability to see in the dark.

"The tribe who built Bamburgh were the Gododin," Brennus explained. "They had a seat on the Hunt before the Angles defeated them. They had worked closely with the Romans and learnt a few secrets. See in the Roman's lands, there're mountains that spit fire and are hollow, they saw that type of rock here and decided to build on it and then start chipping away at the cliff they stood on; found their way through quickly, maybe these rocks used to spit fire. Anyway, good to have hidey holes when Spurius ruled these…"

"What in god's name are you talking about? I've understood none of what you've just said and liked even less!" moaned Norbert.

"I have heard of such mountains, the fire has been less frequent since the Romans accepted Christ I am told, all part of the almighty's plan I'm sure but I don't see how this story explains your good eyesight Brennus, especially with one of your eyes... er... hiding?" Alcuin tried to remember his manners as best he could. Thankfully both children had passed out from exhaustion.

"After the fall of Avalon, Merlin decided to build deep into the depths of The Eryri for our new headquarters, it made the Hunt's operations a lot more secret, even among our own kind. Our king ruled from Gywnedd and soon even Arthur's line forgot about us, buried deep in the mountains. In other words, I've spent decades in the dark." They landed at the foot of another ladder. "Here now," Brennus finished handing the bag containing the bones and book to Alcuin.

This cavern was more spacious than the others and was very, very dimly lit from the tunnel that led to the beach acting as a long window. A rusty metal grate covered the entrance but it was easily knocked off. The children were small and the adults so used to hard living and hunger that getting to the beach should be simple. Alcuin did reflect he was acquainted with a fair few priors and abbots who would struggle to pass through.

As Alcuin moved toward the grate, they heard it, a growl, then a whine. Something was down here with them. A hound couldn't have gotten down the ladders, when they heard it move its body in the darkness, they were praying for the biggest rat they had ever seen. It stank down here, some of the caverns were used as a latrine, Brennus guessed, but once the thing in the corner awoke from its slumber and dusted itself off, then the all too familiar smell of something that was not of this world reached him.

The whine increased in pitch, *"Alcuin! Alcuin!"* The cavern's temperature plunged. It was Norbert who remembered his duty and charged forward toward the now standing outline of a human figure in the darkness. He disappeared into the shadows and seconds later, a thunderous clapping sound came from there. The now awake and petrified children were sent into hysterics by the hot blood that engulfed them. Alcuin dived onto the bag of bones as pints of blood crashed onto his back. Brennus was standing close enough to get most of the entrails and guts, it winded him but protected the other three from the sheer weight of the blow. Brennus was a lot stronger than his frail body indicated, physically he was terribly weak but he knew tricks of the mind to endure and find hidden, temporary strength. He wasn't happy that a stray piece of Norbert's mail shirt took off one of his earlobes. He had lost enough parts of himself already, he could do without losing anything else.

Perhaps, this was time for him to go now, the gift had been passed to the next man to receive it. A man Alcuin would be meeting soon. Brennus wanted to pass on a message but instead shouted to Alcuin, "Get them to the beach now! He can't pursue you in the daylight!" He took a long pace forward, the last of the arrows tucked into a fold of his rags. No bow to fire with. The monster's face became visible. Its mouth a ruin of crushed, black bone of what had once been teeth, a recognizable human face; this had once been a young man. Man or monster, he wasn't sure which of them was more surprised when from the ladder came an infant's voice, "Dada?"

CHAPTER 37

"Dada?" The light from the tunnel had been growing wider. It must be close to noon, it was blocked out now by the three adventurers making their way to the beach. Brennus breathed a sigh of relief when the light from the beach resumed; it meant the others had made it to the beach. It also gave Brennus a bit of space to back into, hopefully out of the thing's reach, and hopefully, weak as the light was, it would be enough to deter the beast. In between them had crawled their unexpected intruder. "Dada?" it piped again. Brennus staggered in surprise, could this be Nelda's son? He guessed they all looked the same at that age, but he had the look and his last sighting of the child hadn't been too far from here. He turned to Brennus and said, "Dada?" and then turned back to the monster and repeated the single-word question.

That removed any question; Nelda's boy had a terribly stunted vocabulary, as did most children raised in slave pens, Brennus reasoned, he had never thought about it much. He addressed Nelda with "muma", he said "bread" when hungry, "jebus" when his mother was frequently praying and "dada" to any male he encountered.

"Boy! Is your mother here? Come to me, boy! Come to the light!" The boy looked into the face of the undead thing and saw something. The sparkling egg-like eyes of the creature were damp wet. Brennus just reckoned they were clammy like the thing's skin. It couldn't be the thing could cry after all, could it? Brennus gave a wordless gasp of horror as the infant started crawling toward the draugr.

The thing scooped the child up in its dank hands and Brennus' world stood still, he couldn't react or distract the beast in anyway; the merest flick of the draugr's fingers and the babe's head would pop like a berry. It was waiting for something, it just held the child in its arms. Then it opened its black, decayed mouth and the whole upper half of its head tipped back in an inhuman splitting display. Nelda's son was raised high in the air and that's when Brennus charged forward, arrow in hand.

The draugr saw him coming, its hands full, it kicked up a cloud of dust. It clearly sensed there was enough danger in what Brennus was holding to avoid making direct contact with him, the force of the dust was enough to blind Brennus sending him sprawling and choking as he crashed into the wall of the cavern. He had dropped the arrow and groped wildly in the dust for it.

He heard a crashing noise from the opposite side of the cavern. His heart raced as he recognized the thumping sounds of notched arrows being released and the thud as they hit their target. Brennus, who unsurprisingly had better hearing than the average man, clenched his toothless jaw in frustration as he recognized the clinking thud of the arrows rattling against the stone walls. Whoever was firing was either the most useless archer he'd ever come across or was blinded by the dust too.

Desperately hoping for the latter, Brennus spread himself on the ground and made wild sweeping gestures on the ground, he supposed he looked comical, like a man swimming on the ground but he had to find the arrow somehow, it was the only thing that stood a chance against the creature. He thought little of a second crashing sound from the foot of the ladder.

The dust was clearing. Screaming told him the child was still alive, the beast must be waiting to dispose of the intruders before eating lest they disturb him. As the dust cleared, two thuds sounded like they hit flesh. He saw Father Buadach standing, arrow notched, the child had been dropped onto the hard floor and was wailing and crying in pain and distress. The monster had arrows sticking out of its waist and knee and it was snarling, spitting jet-black saliva down its chin and neck in rage.

Nothing should have surprised him at this point but as he was propping his body up, the sight of Nelda leaping on Father Buadach's back and trying to rip his ears off with her teeth while screaming, "Judas bastard, turncoat, Norse scum, pagan vermin, you will burn in the fire until the end of time! What have you done with my child you cursed to hell treacherous…" Father Buadach finally dumped her to the ground cursing, and Brennus saw he was not the only one to have lost an earlobe. Nelda scooped her son toward her and was caught in the same transfixed look of shock and horror that Father Buadach was, madly enough the monster had a similar expression, it hadn't been crying before when it saw the face of the boy because now thick inky tears were pouring from its milky eyes.

"Heregod?" whimpered Nelda. That was the name of the child, wasn't it? She had the child in her arms now but they were still too close. The beast could with one flick of his hand turn them all into red paste as they had done to Norbert if its mood changed.

It was now or never, clutching the arrow he had found on the ground tightly, he ran forward and plunged it into the beast's neck.

~

Heregod was distraught at the sight of the two figures in front of him. They had been fighting but were now staring at him like he was an abomination. He had seen that look before and didn't care, he usually took their heads off with a swat of his palm straight after but the two in front of him were different. He knew them, he liked them, he cared about them. Their names he couldn't tell you if he tried, he kind of knew one was a man and the other a woman but which was which and why that mattered escaped him. All he knew was he had the most unbearably yearning to be alongside them, not facing them, to be like them... *again!*

The third figure, the meal, he now knew it was connected to one of the two figures and therefore to him. He was wrong to try to eat it. He would eat the other one he had knocked to the ground and wait for nightfall before hunting again.

Then he felt the prick in his neck, it was irritating like the pricks in his knee and waist. He decided to twist open the skull of the one who had jabbed him, something told him the brain of that one was going to be something special.

Then he heard a crackling sound. He was standing in complete darkness, this was different, he wasn't in the other dark place, the two figures that he loved, their child, the insect that had bit him were all gone. But he wasn't alone.

Standing in front of him was a youth, a mess of reddish hair and a tattered tunic. The youth had no jaw, no eyes, no nose. Heregod knew this youth and he knew who had done this to him. It had been one of those first few confusing nights on Lindisfarena, he and Keres crossed the causeway to find places to hide during the day, a cave, a cavern, even a wooded area, there was nothing on the isle so each morning they had to flee.

They met the youth and his companions just after coming off the causeway. They were camping and just waking up. Bandits, pilgrims, desperate men looking for work, he didn't know or care, those words were already beginning to become meaningless.

While Keres was roaring and swinging the men by their ankles, dashing their brains to pieces on the stone below, it was Heregod who had plucked off the parts of the youth's face that he fancied. He was his first.

His second stood behind the youth; a shepherd with his torn

and ruined cheeks drooping down his neck and a hole in his stomach, the shepherd's tortured family stood behind him, behind them some fishermen, a Pict hermit, a party of nuns and their puny bodyguards; all with butchered bodies. All looking at him, right at the back would be the last one; the man he turned to red paste with one clap. They had come to see him at the end.

He felt it like a punch to the gut, a punch from god himself. Heregod realized he hadn't thought of that word in quite some time. He was feeling everything the youth had felt both inside his mind and out as he died slowly and this was just the beginning. The pain was unbearable. Heregod sank to his knees and howled and wept.

~

Back in the cavern, the three adults looked in horrified awe at what was happening to the monster. "He's crying," said Nelda, the thing's face was covered in the ink-like substance pouring out of his eyes, his ears, his mouth.

Then it happened. The black fluid seemed to sparkle and shine, it slowly turned brownish red and then bright orange in color. The orange substance glowed brightly and then even standing as far as they could from the beast, the others could feel the heat coming from the substance. The creature, now on its knees howled a cry of pain that had the other clutching their ears in agony.

"Quick! To the beach!" Brennus urged. It was useless, the howls were too loud but Nelda saw where he was pointing toward and instinctively ran toward the open grate and dumped her screaming child into the tunnel, following straight after. Brennus went next and only the man he knew as Father Buadach remained.

~

Aindrea took one last look at his old friend. What on earth had the warlock's arrow done? This was different from the draugr back in Lindisfarena that one had just burnt until the sun had risen. What was happening to Heregod was far more gruesome and the sun couldn't reach him down here to release him. The bright globs, some orange some sheer white were clinging, unmoving, to his face which was contorting into unnatural shapes. He saw that the black, damp, seaweed locks that had once been a beautiful tonsure were beginning to glow the same color.

Aindrea wanted to help his friend but couldn't risk Heregod following them down the tunnel, not after what had happened to the first draugr once the sun hit him. He ran to the ladder and slapped it a few times. "Brother Heregod! Brother Heregod! Up, go up the ladder to the sun and heaven awaits my friend!"

Praying to both Christian and Pagan gods that he had been heard, Aindrea squeezed feet first into the tunnel and fastened the grate back in place before pushing his body downwards.

CHAPTER 38

They were now racing along the northern banks of the Trent and their number was reduced to six. Tegen had insisted on accompanying them when she learnt Nessa was with the wounded Hopcyn but Ecgberht could also see she was deathly concerned for Nabila's well-being. It was Tegen who realized Nabila was choking due to her tongue blocking her throat in the caves and started aiming savage kicks at Nabila's shoulder blades. Ecgberht had looked for a chain to knock her out assuming the Dumnonii woman was attacking Nabila, however seconds later he heard panting and retching and Nabila was breathing normally once Tegen had calmed her. She passed out straight after and there was no time to do anything else but escape the chaos of Snotengaham.

The blonde man, Cathwulf, had tried to drag Nabila away and the two ended up in a shouting match with Tegen slapping and punching away at both men. The other prisoners were beginning to fight among themselves, torn between the looting of the Mercian corpses and those who favored escape before Coenwulf sent more men. Cathwulf had thrown Nabila over his shoulder and said one word that convinced the other two to trust and follow him: "Ninog".

They slumped Nabila over the horse's saddle and once the horse was free of its restraints, it took off along the riverbank followed by the three humans. The crazed barking of hounds pouring down the hillock from Snotengaham told them that news of the escape had reached the town. Their main hope was that with so many men fleeing into the woods in different directions; some hoping to find a familiar route back to Wealas, others Dumnonia or Cent that the hounds would get confused. All three groups would need to find a shallow crossing of the Trent to find their way home, putting the hounds off their scent and leaving the group who were heading north even more exposed. They had to make haste and leave Mercia by sunrise.

Ninog proved to be an able and nimble horse even as the terrain grew thicker as they left the town behind. They found Nessa and a feverish Hopcyn in the clearing where Cathwulf had seen them last. After embracing, Nessa told them, "Tur... turnip... wait, I've got it! Turmeric, that's what she said would heal Hopcyn, mix it in his water, make him strong again."

"Which one is turmeric?" Tegen asked, pointing to the variety of plants in the saddle compartments.

"How the hell am I supposed to know that?" Nessa shouted.

So, it was with Hopcyn and Nabila slumped over the back of the horse that they left the riverbank and turned north.

~

Ecgberht gaged the motivations of his four remaining comrades as they headed toward god knows what. Hopcyn and Nabila were in no condition to give their approval to continuing the mission but with Nabila so far from home and Hopcyn senior in Hunt rank, he guessed they would agree to continue north. Wild-eyed Tegen with her black and white hair jolting out in random directions was crazily in love with either Hopcyn or Nabila, maybe both. Nessa was clearly most comfortable in her countrywoman's company. He turned to Cuthwulf with suspicion and said, "Why did you not return to Cent?"

Cuthwulf said nothing for about a mile or two and then said, "Missus and me have been having trouble lately but I never expected her to leave me to a life on the oars."

"Maybe she was delayed on route, maybe Coenwulf's messengers didn't reach her?"

"Right and maybe the coin I put aside to bribe the reeve into getting me out of the fyrd for that mad, blind bastard's drunken fancy ended up in my brother's pocket by mistake. Only thing is I've seen the way my Colley looks at him and her fear when the reeve came around to announce we'd be leaving the next day wasn't for me." He stopped and said, "She always moaned I was too silent, in a world of my own."

Ecgberht didn't know what to say, but asked, "So, Odberht wasn't a good king then?"

Cathwulf snorted. "Wanted to be everyone's friend. Francia had made him, soft half the army were toasting our great king who had liberated us from Mercian yolk with our extra ale rations when Coenwulf's men ambushed us." Another long pause. "It wasn't right what they did to him though. Every Mercian I meet from now on dies slowly." A longer pause. "Where are we going anyway? What's up north?"

"Something worse than Mercians, the only thing that can kill them is the arrows in Ninog's saddle. It would be nice if our archer ever felt like waking up. What on earth did she put in her mouth, it did a number on the guards, not that I'm complaining…"

~

Nabila stood at the top of a mist-covered mountain looking down into a deep valley. Standing next to her was a cloven-legged, short man with the strangest tuft of white hair.

"Long time, no see," said the little man. "Enjoyed your fight in Londinium, few twists and turns and she saved you right at the end. So, the soul getting a new body, didn't know that happened. At least you grew your arm back, grew a couple of other things too!" the man finished with a leer.

Nabila didn't have the slightest idea what the ghastly little man was talking about but she knew his name somehow. "Puck?" she said.

"Fucanglong is down there waiting for your rescue but you ain't here for that, are you? You've come alone and I don't know why."

"I have no idea what you are…"

"Chloris! Chloris! Chloris! I can smell it on your breath, on your skin! You've eaten some of it! That's how you've ended up back in Fae! How on earth are you still alive? You should be waking up in a new skin right about now if that is what your soul is want to do!" He stamped his little legs up and down and asked, "How did you get it?"

"The green flower? It was growing in the garden in Saint-Malo and…"

"So, those druids and warlocks have been looking into what grows here and elsewhere eh? One of these days Queen Mab is going to have to get that Merlin down to Fae for an audience. It's made you dry, too dry. All things in your realm die if they get too dry, weak little things they are. All things remember."

"I don't know what you mean?"

"Time for you to go now, next time bring Digoth, you both have a debt to pay!"

"What? Who is…"

~

Nabila choked and choked, she felt as if she'd swallowed a mountain of dust and sand. She opened her mouth to plead for water but no sound came out. She realized with horror her skin was shedding, first just flakes of the outer skin but then the flakes got chunkier and a pained tight feeling gripped her. She looked at her hands and froze as wrinkles appeared that went deeper and deeper, she felt a cracking sound as the wrinkle turned into a ravine that plunged all the way down to her bone. Her hand was now useless and the rest of her body was going to become the same if she didn't get water soon.

She wriggled and flailed on the saddle violently earning an angry groan from whoever was sharing the saddle with her when one of her flailed kicks hit the side of their face but it got someone's attention.

~

It was Tegen who noticed that Nabila was awake first and took her off the horse. She shooed away Cathwulf and Ecgberht, getting Nessa to snap her teeth at them when they became insistent. "Men healers?" she said as if someone had suggested giving the job to the horse. "Men Saxon healers?" more incredulous this time as if they'd proposed summoning horse healers from the sky.

In a clearing, Nessa's threats and snapping gave them a degree of privacy. Tegen examined Nabila's conscious but wheezing and distressed body.

~

Nabila remembered passing out from the pain but her body was restless, it had slept for too long so her head soon jerked herself awake. She screamed when she realized she couldn't move any of her body from the neck down. "Tessa! Negen! What did you do to me!?" her voice shook loudly, she didn't seem to notice she had regained the power of speech.

Sitting on a log across from her, Cathwulf said, "You are buried up to your neck in mud, well mostly mud, Ninog contributed a bit too, that was Tegen's idea."

"Contributed how?" she then took a smell. "Oh..."

"They said they needed to make you as damp as possible, it was weird like you were turning into a dry riverbed, it seems to have worked." He yawned. "Course it was a bit of guesswork, especially with the two Briton wenches stuffing everything they found in the saddle apart from the green flowers into your mouth, turned out to be the smelly purple flower that healed you, didn't do the Britons much good they've been puking their guts out since touching it. Oh well, never mind. Most of your plants are intact, a bit mixed up together. Nessa and Tegen have gone to get you water hoping the walk will do their stomachs some good. No stream near here, we had to use Ninog to wet your throat."

"What do you mean? How did N…"

"Your Majesty! She's awake!" Cathwulf called and Ecgberht emerged from the trees a few minutes later.

"Don't call me that, I can tell you're taking the piss." Then Ecgberht said to Nabila, "How are you feeling?"

"I feel like someone has buried me in horseshit."

"It's an improvement on how you looked before." He turned to Cathwulf. "Let's dig her out and see if she's ready to travel."

She was but with one terrible consequence of using the Chloris plant when assaulting the cave. "I knew it would wound the guards but I also knew I couldn't swallow it or get any inside my body, some must have got inside by mistake. It's too light to throw and my reach isn't strong enough to punch or slap the guards with it on my hands. I should have chewed it carefully and put it on the head of the arrows but we had to move quickly." Her voice echoed with dullness as she looked at her right hand.

It had withered to half the size of what it had been, the skin was the texture of dirt, it was cold to the touch, a thumb and three fingers were permanently locked into a clawed position, only her little finger could move a fraction and at the cost of great pain to its owner.

Tegen had returned and sprinkled water on it which did

nothing so she pulled Nabila back by the hair and poured the rest down her throat. "Everytime you look at that hand, remember the rest of your body could have gone the same way, you'd have made the hag from the caves look pretty in comparison. Horse muck kept your good looks, my mother always said it was the best ointment for the skin."

Nabila knew she was trying to be kind although the cultural differences were a little too high for her to fully appreciate it. She therefore resisted the notion of burying the Dumnonii woman's face into her beloved horseshit and got to the task of mixing the turmeric into Hopcyn's water to calm his whining and stop him from tearing the terribly itchy bark and moss that was healing his wound right off.

"Just a poxy nursemaid now," she muttered in Andalusi Arabic so no one would hear her feeling sorry for herself. "I'll never shoot an arrow or ride a horse again." She blinked back tears as she mixed the turmeric.

CHAPTER 39

Alcuin watched in disbelief as the warrior priest Father Buadach lay helpless on the ground while the peasant woman kicked him in the ribs, face and finally between the legs. It's true Father Buadach wasn't fighting back but the ragged-looking woman still threw him to the ground with ease. She might have loose skin from hunger but the bones were big, he could tell that. The young boy with her was watching with eyes like the moon.

"The unquenchable fire awaits you, you fucking Judas pagan scum, slaving filth!" Another kick, this one to the side of the head. To use such foul language, to compare a man of faith to the lord's betrayer! Such blasphemy! The poor young woman was damning herself. He did what he could, he sank to the sand on his knees and prayed and wept for both their souls.

Standing behind him, the boy said to his sister, "I want to go home. Is the isle still underwater? Did father swim away in time?"

Ignoring him, the girl shouted encouragement to the woman, "Kick him in the balls again!" Alcuin turned his head back to give the pair a distraught look before resuming his praying and weeping.

Brennus knew he had to get some semblance of order going but his hearing had not yet returned after hearing the monster's howls in the enclosed space in the bowels of Bamburgh. He ran to the sea and submerged his head. It didn't give him back his hearing but it reduced the pain of the bleeding from the ears and allowed him to stagger toward the ferocious Nelda and the prone body of Father Buadach.

"Nelda, please, he's a priest, I thought you were a devout Christian, surely you can see…" A swing of her elbow sent Brennus sprawling.

Nelda cried out, loud enough for everyone on the beach to hear, "He's no priest you blubber-faced sack of bones! He's a pagan, pirate, slaver! He's with them who attacked the town and killed Grimwold and the others! He's a Norseman from across the sea but he wasn't always that way. He was born a Christian man and served as a brother at the priory in Lindisfarena!"

All of a sudden Alcuin was on his feet, he rushed toward who he knew as Father Buadach and pulled him up by his tunic and looked into his eye. "Aindrea!" he gasped and looked as if he was about to pass out. "I should have recognized but the eye and we searched the priory after the pagan attack, there was surely no survivors, you, you, you were the brightest light at the priory. Prior Aldred used to sing your praises in his letters to me…"

"Did he?" Aindrea gave a surprised groan.

"Oh yes! Your skill with languages, the beauty of your writing, the maps you drew, the histories you recorded. We had high hopes you could make Archbishop. Praise the lord you are alive! Praise him!"

Nelda looked at the pair with sheer loathing. Brennus was rummaging through his robes frantically. Alcuin noticed both reactions and said, "The girl is clearly mad, you the shining light of the priory a pagan! What piffle! A pagan monk! Like a seal wearing a hat! Completely inconceivable!"

He then saw Aindrea's mournful eyes full of shame and stared deep into them before sinking back to his knees howling and wailing in sorrow that rivaled the monster in terms of passion and volume.

Brennus searched harder and harder for the powder tucked away in his robes. Alcuin had stopped howling and had joined Nelda in their assault on the fake priest, he wasn't as fearsome or as violent as Nelda who was working on the man's kidneys now with kicks to the stomach but he darted in and out of the melee departing each time with a jabbed kick to a place he knew would hurt.

Brennus found it at last. He took out the small hemp pouch and flung the powdery white contents into the eyes of Alcuin and Nelda. Both Christians turned to face and confront him but crashed to the sand unconscious before they could speak or move further.

"Weever fish, the spines have venom, I crush them into powder," Brennus said as he helped the one-eyed man to his feet. "They'll be out for a few hours and when they wake, they will be too nauseous to beat you. Why didn't you fight back? You could have swatted the pair of them away. By the way the powder also means by the time they wake, they will both need to stop to piss every five minutes for about a day so we need to make haste and get far from Bamburgh. I shudder to think what will happen at night."

"More draugr," the one-eyed man gasped.

"You have a lot of explaining to do, Father... no wait, it's Aindrea, that's what he called you. Yes, a lot of explaining and a lot of questions to answer. In the meantime you take Nelda, her bones need a younger man to carry, speaking of bones, I guess I'm going to have to drag Alcuin's bag along with his body. Oi!" he shouted to the two children. "You two take care of Nelda's lad Heregod." Aindrea's face went white at the boy's name. Brennus continued, "Alcuin was never going to ask so I will, what are your bloody names?"

"Gymi" said the boy.

"Hagona" said the girl.

Brennus assured the pair he would pass their names that he had already forgotten to Alcuin once he awoke and began to drag both man and bagged skeleton down the beach as Aindrea hoisted Nelda onto his shoulders.

~

Ulf had been on this island long enough to hear stories of the Christian hell. He found it funny that the Saxon word was similar to the name of Loki's daughter and the underworld realm she ruled which overlapped Niflheim, the real hell. Niflheim was far more terrifying with its coldness and silence than the screaming and fire of hell that the priests screeched at the dumb Saxon peasants to keep them in line. Or so he had thought…

The courtyard in Bamburgh resembled a scene from the priest's twisted imagination. Dead bodies had been carefully lined up and covered most of the muddy ground. Some of these bodies would walk again this coming night. In the center of the grisly display tied to a post was a man and a woman, each would stay alive to see if Keres would favor them with her kiss while they were still breathing. The fools were praying loudly, they probably believed they were to be burnt. *No such luck, Saxons or Angles or whatever you are! Alecto wants to see if her pet can make another Heregod!*

They were going to need a new one. The hell-like sight of the corpses was complemented by the hell-like screams of Heregod in the depths of the structure. The smell of burning flesh lingered heavy in the air. The Norseman who burned their dead were used to it but his Pict, Angle and Saxon men who were more want to bury their dead were gagging. *Best get used to it, he isn't being put out anytime soon!*

When Alecto had been informed he was wounded, she was horrified to see him halfway up the ladders, an arrow sticking out of his neck and those orange blobs on his face as he shrieked. "Burn the ladders! Throw torches down there to blind and choke him! He is not to come to the surface!"

She told him, "The explosion of the monastery in Lindisfarena happened when the sun hit a draugr! If that happens in here, the whole place will be destroyed! The corpses burnt to a crisp! Our army destroyed! All our efforts wasted, if could even disturb Keres and the others who are resting exposing them to the sun!"

"Why does he want to face the sun? He knows it's fatal to him."

"The arrow in his neck, he is experiencing pain of body and mind that is incomprehensible to mortal men like you."

"What are those orange blobs on his face? I've never seen anything like it before."

"Most of the mountains that can spit fire in the northern lands have been dead for longer than we know. I have seen this before when I was human, a young girl living in a place called Milos. The mountain launched rock turned to fire and to be in its way was a terrible thing. Lava, the Romans called it. That's what's on Heregod's face and it isn't ever coming off. That's why he yearns for the sun."

CHAPTER 40

Archbishop Eanbald paced furiously around the Roman wall of Eoforwic followed by his assistant who had been born Eanbald but thankfully Alcuin came up with the nickname Simeon to avoid confusion, Alcuin who was surely dead. Out of the scores of fishing boats and skiffs that acted as passenger boats between Eoforwica and Bamburgh, a mere four had survived to sail up the river he kept insisting was called The Usa as it was written in his books despite the insistence of the mostly illiterate townsfolk who pronounced it 'Ouse' in their Northumbrian dialect.

He had more important things to worry about than the inability of his simple flock to pronounce the name of the bloody river! Lindisfarena sunk! Bamburgh with no support from the sea and now certain to fall to Eardwulf! And the rumors about what Eardwulf had heard in his ranks.

Simeon looked like a young, short version of Eanbald which frustrated the older, tall, gaunt man who fumed that his chubby, lame assistant had his face as well as his name. It made the townsfolk chuckle to see the humorless archbishop have a comical looking doppelgänger follow him around. He took out his frustrations on poor Simeon.

"Come on! Keep up or I'll wrap your knuckles with the crosier again!" he snarled as he inspected work in the gaps between the walls where towers were being hastily erected. For all his faults, Eanbald was efficient as the most senior churchman and de facto ruler of Northumbria due to the lack of a king.

The land surrounding the city had been stripped of crops and they were well provisioned inside. Eardwulf would have to feed his entire army with whatever the Usa could provide. The nearby village of Loidis had been stripped bare of anything that may be of use and had yielded a surprisingly high amount of iron and stone that was going into building these towers. The residents of the village Loiners, the townsfolk called them, were camped around the giant wooden church that dominated the view inside the city walls from every direction.

So Eanbald had done all he could but one question still tore at him and kept him awake at night. *What had happened at Bamburgh?* It made little sense for Eardwulf to leave his secure home at Segedunum and turn north instead of south. A quick march from Segedunum to Eoforwic and forcing Eanbald to anoint him at sword point was what he expected. Maybe he was recruiting Picts up there? Unlikely, his army was big enough already and the further south you got, the less reliable the already undisciplined Picts got. A symbolic capture perhaps? Bamburgh was the old capital, its roots going back to pre Angle days when the Britons ruled the land. No, he shook his head, the man claiming to be Eardwulf was clearly a foreigner with no...

"Archbishop! Archbishop!" he frowned, it was Baga, one of the Loiner refugees. Grubby peasant hadn't learnt his manners yet.

"You address me as Your Excellency or Your Grace, you Loiner lackwit!"

"Of course, it's just that... it's just that Your Excellency or Grace, it's just that there's strangers at the south gate!"

"Coenwulf has sent emissaries! Even some troops!" It was more than the old man could hope for. Letters had been sent to the Mercian king reminding him of how undefended his northern border was as well as Eardwulf's fierce ambitions and the murky creatures in the shadows whispering in his ears. No response had come. The general reason for the inaction of the usually meddling Mercian kingdom had been Coenwulf had committed to campaigns against Cent and Wealas at the same time, the young fool! Spies also claimed that Alkmund, a former Atheling of Northumbria who Coenwulf was keeping as a puppet to put on their throne had disappeared. Some said into Pictland, others said Francia. Finally was the most chilling rumor; that the witch who had supposedly brought Eardwulf back from the dead was a creature of Mercia.

So, it was with disappointment but not much surprise that the archbishop's shoulders sagged as Baga wiped a slug off his cheek which must have been resting there unnoticed since the Loiner peasant woke up this morning in the dirt and began the most remarkable story.

"No, they are wearing slave smocks, can't understand most of them. An angry, big Wealas dwarf just like in the stories, a big Saxon lad who talks funny, two Dumnonii warrior maidens… well that's not exactly the word I'd use but all the others I've got in my head are impolite and you're like a priest, right? There's a beauty there, skin the color of a tree trunk and one of her hands is like a crab, oh, and they have a horse and some weapons in the saddle and their leader is the king of Wessex."

"Baga, have you been eating foxglove again? You are aware we have ample supplies of turnips, you should be getting one twice a week."

"Lost my turnip playing dice," the peasant sullenly replied, but he was insistent that someone of interest was at the gate and something tugged at Eanbald's curiosity.

~

Nightfall fell on Bamburgh. The two unfortunates tied to the post were sweating and shaking, tears streaming down their face but they weren't making a sound, they couldn't. Red bloody streaks ran down their faces from their temples to the bottom of their cheeks. Ordo turned his back to them and licked blood off his long nails and repeated the instructions, "Complete silence from now on, you are not to distract Keres when she inspects you both!" He walked to the edge of the courtyard, stepping over the bodies. When his face met the waiting Alecto's, she nodded and said, "A small one, a child." Ordo gave a nod of gratitude and fished around the corpses before picking one up and taking it away to feed from it.

The only sound was the rain violently hitting the mud and Heregod's cries from the depths.

Alecto then got to her knees and whispered a prayer in Greek, "To my sire, we will find the sword, we will find the crux gemmata, we shall return to our glory, we shall finish what you started," then she rose and screamed, "Keres!"

Her footsteps on the mud gave a squelch that sounded pained as if she was hurting the mud. The guards turned their backs, the soldiers not on duty inside wanting no part of this. Ulf paid well, very well. The Saxons, Angles, Picts and Norsemen ignored a lot for gold. They told themselves in their cups that the things they glimpsed in the dark were weapons. No different from using hounds to guard a prisoner or a war horse to charge an enemy's host. There had been rumors after the assault on Segedunum that some of Osbald's troops had been added to the draugr ranks, a trick of the light that gave the beasts a familiar face and after enough ale and enough gold even if the rumors were true the bastards deserved it!

It was different now, even if the guards averted their eyes, they would hear and feel it. Other guards outside the gates were restraining the other draugr with torches, once Keres had finished, they would be instructed to let them through the gates. They would see the draugr eat, they would see what it eats.

More deserters means more meat on the road, Alecto thought with a grin. She removed her mask, any man who saw would soon find her face the least of their problems. She had grown tired of their greed, it was easily satisfied with illusion spells, making worthless seeds look and feel like piles of coins or altering the soldiers perceptions when he was handed gold or coin making him believe he was getting double or triple what was being pressed into his palms. The greedy soldiers were prepared to put a lot to the back of their minds now they had purses full of seeds. Doubtless she could make real gold with enough effort and access to ancient scrolls and charms now buried deep under Londinium but for now seeds and dirt were the soldiers reward for betraying their land, betraying their kind. After tonight she wouldn't need them, any rebellion or revolt would be quickly quashed, heads popped by draugr and perhaps Keres giving her kiss to…

She was shook out of her thoughts by that just happening. Keres had been wading among the bodies for a minute, her damp seaweed hair shining under the courtyard torches, the milk-colored skin glistening with both its natural clamminess and the rain bouncing off it. Keres was naked as she had been ever since Alecto had met her. None of the draugrs had need of clothes, the newly turned ones simply wore their final mortal dress until it turned into rags and then dust.

She scooped her four-inch nails on the ground, taking skin off the bone like spreading butter on a blade, disgusting slurping noises came from her direction as she sucked and chewed the strips of skin. Then she gave an excited squeal, it sounded almost girlish. She raised a corpse, it was female. From the bloodstained rags being linen rather than hemp, Alecto figured that this had been a serving girl rather than a camp follower and perhaps a bedwarmer too as one side of her face was whitened, maybe by bloodletting. The other side of her face was a ruin of torn flesh and mangled bones, an axe or the flat of a sword had ripped away the skin on the cheek and lower jaw.

Keres held the corpse aloft in the air and brought it downwards, closer to her lips. The slurping faded, she was enjoying the taste of the woman's face as she nibbled and licked before brushing her lips against what remained of the corpses. Lightning flashed across the skyline and the ruined part of the woman's face began to twitch and bulge. Soon the eye on the good side of her face flashed open, it was milky white and had no pupil or iris; just a tiny black dot like the others, it shined in the darkness. The black veins began to spread across her pale, white cheek. Keres then threw the corpse to the group. It slowly got onto its hands and knees and raised itself upright.

Keres repeated the process again and again, soon half of the courtyard were standing. Looking around disorientated, the low telltale groan of the draugr echoing around Bamburgh. One of them, a peasant Alecto guessed from his worn smock reached down and plucked something off the floor, a piece of meat or something that belonged inside one of those still laying on the floor. The former peasant took a sniff, made a growling sound and then tore into it with his now blackened teeth. Soon all of the draugrs were ripping and growling and slurping into the bodies that had not been chosen. Alecto smiled as she sensed Anlaf, the old castellan stumbling among them, she had taken both his arms while interrogating him about the arrows. A physical description had told her that 'Father Buadach' was the Norseman's leader Aindrea. A man linked to or with knowledge of the Hunt's methods inside these walls! Armed with those infernal arrows! Ulf had been charged with hunting Aindrea down and bringing him to her.

Keres was circling the posts the man and woman were tied to, keeping the other draugr well away. She had decided on the name Orthrus if she chose the man and Phaea if she chose the woman. Both humans were unable to make a sound due to Ordo's mark and he had also forbidden them from passing out. The last thing they were going to see was what happened to the corpses, what was about to happen to them. The last thing they would hear was the grotesque slurping and growling of the feeding draugrs. At least it was drowning out Heregod's screams. Fitting, Alecto thought as Heregod's replacement was about to be chosen.

CHAPTER 41

Eoforwic's slave pen was being used as a pig sty for the extra swine brought in from surrounding villages. As a result the six escapees from Mercia were confined to tents among the Loiner refugees. They had been first shepherded into the vast stone basement underneath the giant wooden church only for the archbishop to charge in after hearing of where they were headed, throwing pails of water at them. "Alcuin's writings are down here!" he had screamed at their escorts, a mixture of mailed guards and peasants. "These people are probably covered head to toe in vermin! They can't be allowed near such precious parchment!" Ecgberht sighed with relief when it became clear that the archbishop didn't speak any type of Brittonic as Nessa's threats of biting his balls off were just noise to him that he waved off. Ecgberht also had an eye for the treasures in the basement as they're ushered out. This was a very wealthy city, not that you'd know it from the state of the townsfolk.

Although technically in captivity as the archbishop, followed by a limping shorter version of him had made mutterings about "Returning the slaves to their Mercian owners as a good neighborly Christian act," no one seemed bothered enough to prevent them walking around the city as they pleased. Chats with the head of the city guard in which both Ecgberht and Cathwulf assured them that they could fight and were aware of the threat from the north, that the Britons could be trusted, well Ecgberht did cross his fingers behind his back when he said the last part, and not only did they have the freedom of the city, they regained access to Ninog stored in the stables and half the arrows and plants in her saddle. They were even promised weapons and armor. "When the time comes," the chief city guard had told them.

Despite learning about the tragedy of Alcuin's death and the knowledge that if Brennus and his team hadn't made it up the Ouse yet, then they probably hadn't survived their journey to collect him. Eoforwic seemed as good a place as any for their last stand. They trained with wooden poles smashing them into straw-stuffed dummies, while none of them, apart from the maimed Nabila, were archers and planned on giving their blessed yew arrows to the bowmen on the wall. Cathwulf suggested binding some to poles or spearheads for the attack. They paid their way in other ways, Nessa could make turnip and grass stew last for a lot longer and actually stay down with some herbs and a special recipe she had. A rapidly recovered Hopcyn left the city walls and returned with a slain boar under his arms, it was the talk of the town as the boar was the same size as the Wealas man and he had left the city unarmed. And as for Tegen, the children of the city were much better behaved and less unruly since their mothers now had the threat of, "I'll send you to live with the Dumnonii witch if you misbehave!" All seemed well considering, apart from Nabila who was in the throes of the darkest mood she could remember.

She was tending to the small garden she had made in a remote space between the far end of two tents for the hundredth time that morning. She had managed to salvage seeds from most of the plants before they had perished and was devoting her time to making a new supply of medicine while the others trained and hunted, things that were now beyond her. Nessa had some talent with the art of herbs and medicine and was mixing the dead crushed plants into various stews, pastes and ointments. Nabila's job was to grow and tend to new plants. *A nursemaid to flowers, some comedown from being an archer and a faris warrior,* she thought to herself, growling so much in her head that she gave herself a headache. The Chloris she hadn't grown anymore of, she didn't want to but she didn't need to either, the bastard plant would not die. It looked as fresh as it did the day a gloved Ninog had plucked it out of the ground in Saint-Malo. For safety she had put the plant into a linen sack and buried it deep in a ditch bordering the Roman wall where no one was accidentally going to come across it.

Now, while the others were fighting and hunting, even Tegen was giving lessons to the women and girls of the city of where to keep a dagger or whittled down sharpened wooden stick if need be hidden and how to use it on both attackers and themselves should Eardwulf prevail and his men make it over the city walls. She was stuck teaching Baga and his family how to keep plants alive, *it's just as important as what the others are doing,* she told herself, *their family is growing, keeping plants of their own could keep them alive if there's a bad harvest or the village chief cheats them once they return to Loidis.*

Baga's wife had no teeth despite being too young to have had them fall out. "She's a chatty type, once she said too much to the wrong person and got the foreman's hoe a few times to the face." It made her speech some rapid spitting noise which only Baga could understand. They had a son, a slow talking lad who appeared to regard Nabila with distrust. Baga's wife unintentionally watered the plantbeds by launching into a long speech. Baga translated by saying, "She wants to know why you just don't pull the bowstring back with your feet now your crab hand can't do it no more?"

"That's the most ridiculous idea I've heard since…" She stopped as Ecgberght's idea of poisoning the river so the advancing army couldn't fish from it had only been made that morning, Saxons seemingly knowing or caring little that once something is poisoned, it stays poisoned. The silence made her stop feeling sorry for herself and consider it for a second. Was it ridiculous?

They had made their way along the beach knee deep in water as soon as Nelda and Alcuin could stand. Brennus snapped at the two to keep in the water. It's likely they were being tracked once the tormented beast with the arrow sticking out of his neck was discovered so were not to leave footprints. Brennus had little Heregod on his shoulders while the stronger Aindrea propped up Gymi and Hagona. The two Christians were both weary from the poison, they were unable to argue or do anything other than try to keep up at the rear. The water had the boon of washing away the piss and vomit they were projecting regularly due to the poison's hangover.

Brennus charging forward wagged his boney finger at a cave at the far end of the beach. The cave was connected to the sea via jagged stones and rock pools with a curved piece of rock acting as a bridge to the cave. "Inside! Inside! We rest there tonight but not for long and do not touch the sand! Leave no trace of you there!"

The cave went deep enough that Brennus forbade a fire lest the smoke choke them or even disturb the rocks. He lit some twigs to dry and calm the shivering and crying children who soon fell into an exhausted sleep. He found another bundle of twigs from the seemingly never-ending folds in his robes and lit them faster than any of the other three had ever seen a man make fire. He used the twigs to illuminate faces of each of them in order; the mother, the holy man, the warrior and turned to the last of them, the one-eyed man with the Hibernian brogue and said, "Speak!"

Aindrea aware that all three sets of eyes on him were hostile and two were murderous briskly began to recount his journey from the moment he decided to head to the priory bell tower to train his bow on the raiders all those years ago to deciding to fire on Norsemen when they followed the crush and rushed through where the gates had been at Bamburgh. "I think I saved you," he said to Nelda who spat on the ground at that, "after the battle was lost, I had to find Heregod, save him somehow." His one eye was wet and brimming with tears.

Alcuin was next to speak, "These three days and nights you spent with their priests in their wilderness, it was a test! A test you failed!"

Aindrea shook his head. "What I saw, I saw. I saw Bifrost reaching down from Asgard to this land; Midgard! I saw its destruction, I saw the fire giants arrive signaling Ragnarok, I heard Heimdallr blowing the Gjallarhorn. It sounded like doom." His voice trailed off, the last four words sounding like a child. Alcuin began to weep.

"Never mind that pagan shit!" Nelda snarled. "You and that flat nosed pagan bitch sold me and my child into slavery."

"I was getting concerned about the tension between us since I came back and started wearing the hammer. Droplaug just told me to beat you harder but I knew that you knew I knew Heregod had told you that I was an archer. If you let that slip and you would have done sooner or later, if they'd connected me with the monk in the bell tower that sent so many of their kin to Valhalla..."

"Hell! Hell! You sent the Norse Pagan scum to hell! Same place you are going and soon if I have anything to do with it!" Nelda's rage made Alcuin weep harder.

"If they found out it was me, Droplaug's husband, her son's father, the chief's son-in-law was among the fallen, I would have been given a blood eagle. I had to get rid of you but I couldn't bring myself to slit your throat as you slept. I found a dock a few villages down, they said they sail down sea to Christian lands, it would be better for you both I told myself. I..."

"You knocked me out and took us both to the docks yourself, I remember!" Nelda was now starting to cry.

With caution, Brennus said, "Let us now discuss the matter of the draugr. Nelda I heard you mention the same word in Dorestad…"

"Pagans who somehow escape hell are doomed to walk as dead men and shades! No heaven for pagan vermin!"

"And Heregod?" Aindrea said ever so quietly. "He was no pagan yet he is dead but he walks."

"Heregod will have met the sun by now. The arrows will give him no choice," Brennus said. "He is at peace I am sure."

~

Ulf had searched every inch of the fort-town, he and his men had unleashed their Elkhounds into the woods at the fort of the hill the fort stood on. The woods had yielded three deserters and a few men who had missed the whole attack, claiming to have been knocked out in the woods. He hanged the latter for cowardice and sent the former back for Alecto to deal with. There was no one accounted for left alive inside Bamburgh's walls. Several corpses, both walking and prone once, had one eye missing, but they had mostly been recently lost in the fighting and the bodies were too old, short, young, tall or female to be the betrayer.

It was the morning after Keres had taken her pick of the former soldiers, priests, servants, peasants and slaves of Bamburgh. The ones she had chosen were all the same rank now, the ones she hadn't chosen too, he reasoned. He was running out of time, they were to leave Bamburgh that night. He was combing the beach for the last time, the hounds hadn't picked up a scent the first time and it was a rocky descent that he didn't think the bowman would have attempted with safer options. The wind was howling and rain drops splattered against his face like pebbles. A storm was coming. He heard it. Heregod's screams.

Scream was the wrong word for it. It didn't sound like any scream he'd ever heard before and he'd heard a lot of screams in his life. They needed a new word for it. It sounded like the death throes of a burning village or a slain army all at once but going on for twenty-four hours a day.

And it was loud down here on the beach. That made Ulf snap his head at the dark cliff face and he walked toward the source of the noise. He would never have seen it if the noise hadn't drawn him to it. A small grate! Leading to where Heregod was trapped in the darkness in his never-ending torment. This must have been how he escaped. Aindrea must have stuck the draugr in the neck with his charmed arrow and made his escape through the tunnel, Heregod either too big or too pained or too stupid or perhaps all of these to follow him.

Ever since he'd learnt of the arrows, a troubling daydream kept tugging at Ulf. In the dream he was holding one of these arrows that made even Alecto shit herself but his hands were tiny. He was somewhere dark and he was scared but he was going to shove that arrow right down that bitch's throat in revenge for... it was at this point he snapped out of it with the faint voice of a girl saying, *you're on the wrong side!* The voice faded away as he blinked back tears.

The rain had ruined any detailed footprints but there were still impressions leading from the grate that told him someone had come out of this hole and headed south and it was more than one person, more than two or three from his best guesses.

He gave one lingering thought to the noises and that creepy young girl's voice in his head gave him a shudder, he decided to loosen the grate and after taking a gulp started to wriggle up the tunnel.

CHAPTER 42

The disunited collection of escapees from Bamburgh headed inland. The dampness of the caves and the harshness of the storms was causing fatigue and coughing fits for all of them with the three children most affected. Around a fire Brennus spooned a stew of berries and nettles into each of the children's mouths with a stick and the three other adults glared at each other. Violent hostility reduced to sullen sulking which Brennus took to be a positive sign.

"Eoforwic is the nearest settlement to here, we can get a skiff down the Ouse to Barton-upon-Humber which will have ships bound for the Frisian sea," Brennus began. "Now we are larger in number, traveling back to Cymru would take too much time, besides we need to warn them. No king or reeve in these lands anymore, archbishop is the most powerful in the land at Eoforwic. Can you help me with that?" The last part was aimed at Alcuin.

The old man nodded. "I know Eanbald well, miserable stick in the mud but loyal and capable. He knows Ealdwulf is coming. He's heard dark rumors but now he needs to know more." He gave Aindrea a fierce look. "It's true? They plan to make more like the monster in the depths? To raise the slain?" At the soldier's nod, Alcuin gave a frightful shudder. "You are truly lost, Brother Aindrea, truly lost. It is going to take a power far higher than any on earth to forgive your part in this."

There was a long period of silence at that before Alcuin cheered and said, "It will be awfully nice to see Simeon again, how I've missed the little fellow!"

Brennus addressed Nelda, "After our business in Eoforwic is completed, we head for Francia. King Charlemagne would allow you to enter a nunnery despite your low birth, to be honest he considers all Saxons and Angles low born even the kings, and for devoting your life to Christian orders as well as the service shown warning Eoforwic, I think he could be persuaded to take Heregod into his service, maybe even to train as a knight if he shows promise." Nelda gave a nod and even looked happy for a fleeting second or two.

"The two children will be entrusted to you once we arrive in Francia," he told Alcuin.

"I will make arrangements for them to be educated and enter holy orders in time. I do not think I will see this island again once we depart," Alcuin replied.

Aindrea then spoke, "And what of me, druid or whatever you are?"

"I am to plead with you to accompany us to Eoforwic for both protection on the road and to tell both the archbishop and my companions from the Lost Hunt, who if god or the gods," he earned a filthy look from the three adults at this, "have listened to me are still alive, everything you have told us about these draugrs."

"After I've spilled my guts, the archbishop will clap me in irons and then spill my guts for real!" Aindrea protested.

"I will plead with Archbishop Eanbald for a quick beheading," Alcuin put in.

Brennus sighed. "I am not Saxon nor Angle, their laws are their own and you are stronger and faster than anyone here, wander into the woods and accept the bandit's life, it may doom us and doom Northumberland, maybe Mercia and Wessex can turn the tide, maybe not. I would however, Brother Aindrea, reflect on Alcuin's address to you. I cannot say if heaven or hell are real or not but death is not the end. I've come to understand that recently."

~

Nightfall came and the dead left their wagons, their shallow graves and pits the men had been ordered to dig for them during the way and the march south began.

"Where's the King?" Ordo asked.

"At the rear in a wagon, he has some sort of injury, nothing serious," Alecto answered, she was behind the draugrs who shuffled and swayed and groaned. Keres walked ahead of them and they followed in a horizontal line that stretched for hundreds of meters. Every now and then, a cluster would wander off and Keres would turn her lumbering head around, her black teeth would snap ferociously and the wandering draugrs would shuffle back into line. Behind Alecto and Ordo and a troop of bodyguards that surrounded them were the soldiers.

Just before leaving Bamburgh, they had been gathered into the courtyard. It was now empty of bodies, those who Keres had not chosen had been stripped of anything that could be eaten and the remains were a giant bonfire in the space where the fort's gates had been. On the cliff top, the flames could be seen for miles. Orthrus and Phaea stood either side of her. Keres had blessed her by choosing both of them. Orthrus had been a six-foot soldier in life, while gifting him with her kiss, he had resisted forcing her to make a few clicks and adjustments to his neck to make him pass out. *That idiot Ordo should have been more specific when he made them his thralls,* she thought to herself as Keres made her clicks, snaps and twists before brushing her lips on his face.

Orthrus now had a curved neck which gave him the appearance of always leering. Phaea, who Alecto suspected had been a wife and mother in life from her age and shape, kept staring at her new shaking pale hands. She turned her head at a sidewards angle and curved her lips, exposing her black teeth for the first time.

In the courtyard tied to the post behind them was Uurad, the Pict soldier who had fancied himself the rebellion leader. Ulf had marked the Picts as the ones most likely to desert as they knew the wild lands to the north so well and knew the army was unlikely to pursue. He bribed Picts with worthless seeds that both Ulf and the Picts believed was gold and Alecto was among the first to hear that the Picts were planning not only to desert but to set the draugrs alight as they slept before fleeing.

So that was why as the sun set on their final day in Bamburgh, every single Pict, Saxon, Norseman and Angle was packed into the courtyard and forced to watch Orthrus and Phaea eat Uurad's face while he was still alive and conscious, Alecto remembered enough from her Londinium days to come up with the right ingredients in her powders to ensure Uurad would feel every last thing.

It worked, they were broken, some wept, some vomited, most stood blinking slowly, their head bowed slightly but unable to turn away from the sight. None would ever think about disloyalty ever again.

Uurad was still alive, his lips, eyes, ears, chin and nose all missing, just crimson stumps and twists of flesh by the time Uurad took his last breath. Phaea grabbed the jaw, she wrenched it open, eager to take the tongue and backed away a little when the sparse remains of Uurad's face began to groan and twitch. More vomiting and weeping from the watching troops. Keres' children had her power! They could create!

Now on the march south she had Orthrus and Phaea walk one on each flank of the soldiers so they could always feel them, smell their stench, hear their growls and always know that they were just a few feet away even when they couldn't be seen.

Uurad was cut loose from the other draugrs and marched alongside his former comrades, stumbling and bumping into them, snarling with rage and hunger when he brushed against them. Alecto wanted them to see him, to see what would be their future if they even thought of disagreeing with her. They had one more marching night before they reached Eoforwic. She really wanted to ungag Uurad before setting him among his ex-mates next time. Just to see what would happen.

CHAPTER 43

Simeon wrapped on the door of the archbishop's quarters before entering and deftly ducked the chamber pot that was instinctively thrown in his direction whenever the archbishop was woken. Over the years he'd had to stir the archbishop in the dead of night more times than he'd have liked with news of Northumbria's frequent rebellions and regicides. After a few hits directly in the face he'd learnt which direction to lean in whenever the pot was hurled. He would still be the one charged with cleaning the door but he could worry about that later, he was still giddy with the news he was about to deliver.

"Your Grace! Your Grace! Praise him! Oh praise him! Alcuin lives!"

~

Twenty minutes later a starved Alcuin looked on wide-eyed as Archbishop Eanbald spooned porridge into his gummy mouth while they sat facing each other on stools in the center of the huge wooden church. It was a gloomy place, he couldn't blame the archbishop for keeping the treasures in the basement but some silks for the altar or the silver to hold the candles would surely be safe and something other than the sight of wood and mud would make the place look like a fitting place for worship. He was glad the others had not been allowed to enter. He was used to long periods of fasting but he feared the sight of the porridge would drive one of them to knock the bowl out of the archbishop's hands. His coin would've been on Nelda if he gambled which he never did citing Hebrews 13:5 warning against the…

"So there wasn't any rain when the isle disappeared under the water? Could this be a miracle, Alcuin? In our land?" Eanbald's questions forced him out of the chain of thought he was using to distract from his hunger.

"A miracle? Many died, Eanbald, outside there are two children, their family…"

"How many died when he flooded the earth for thirty days and thirty nights? Praise him."

"But as I said there was no rain, something was under the water. A thing, a dead thing, a moving dead thing."

The gulp of porridge as it went down the archbishop's gullet could probably be heard outside, Alcuin thought before he continued.

"I saw the creature myself close up and Aindrea claims there are more. Eardwulf knows how to create them!"

"The pagan! Yes, I heard about him. The fisherwoman was insistent on telling Simeon his crimes! I have had him clamped in chains!"

"You must talk to him before you decide his fate. Also the Briton…"

"Him? I took him for a Loiner from his rags and stench."

"Have you heard of the organization he represents?"

"Of course, wizards and warlocks and druids with their potions and tales of shades and golems. Foul things that prefer the company of sheep to women, best left alone in their valleys and mountains."

"There was talk of Wessex once being close with them."

"Wessex, bunch of onion selling snakes in the grass! Too close to the Britons and too close to the Franks if you ask me. We have some simple slave who claims to be their king, says King Charlemagne himself sent him and his gimcrack crew of… Wait? Alcuin! Where are you going?"

Alcuin's stool had been knocked over and the sound of his goat skin shoes pounding through the mud echoed around the church.

~

"My dear boy! How wonderful it is to see you again, I am truly blessed!" Ecgberht had been cooking breakfast in the Loiner camp with Nessa and Nabila when he'd heard the cries of his old teacher.

"I've been looking for you, we split up in Dorestad but Brennus said he was going to get you," a relieved Ecgberht said, wondering when the older man was ever going to let go of his embrace.

Finally free, he introduced Alcuin to the two women, "This is Alcuin, he's the wisest man in Northumbria by far. He was the one who taught me Frankish." Ecgberht wasn't sure how Nabila kept managing to achieve an expression that displayed being more unimpressed each time but she managed it.

Soon the Dorestad reunion was complete with Brennus and Nelda finding their way to the breakfasting group. Tegen, Hopcyn, Cathwulf and the trio of children who had come from the north with their guardians all sat around a campfire as Nessa tried to feed everyone a thin gruel of oats and various leaves she had collected boiled in goat's milk, Tegen cracked an egg she had acquired somewhere into the broth. "Gotta make it taste of something for the young 'uns'" she chided Nessa.

"Baga says my gruel is the best he's ever tasted!" the other Dumnonii woman complained.

"He says that about everything here! That Loidis place must be grim if that's what excites him!"

"How about we compare our experiences," Ecgberht said. "Brennus says that he, Alcuin and Nelda have direct knowledge of what is coming from the north."

So, one group learned about Norsemen from the far north, walking corpses with strength to make the waves swallow an island, a treacherous monk, and that their arrows worked against these draugr.

The others learned about the civil war to their south and an unstable Mercian king.

"Coenwulf is of no use, Eoforwic must be our last stand against the dead," Ecgberht said. "If we fail, then Mercia, Wessex and East Anglia will collapse too."

"The Briton kingdoms will hold out," Hopcyn said a little defensively.

"How?" Brennus asked. "Yes, we have knowledge of older arts that will help but aren't you forgetting the whole reason we lost this island to the Saxons in the first place was their numbers? Aindrea said they have a creature that can turn dead bodies into draugrs. The one we escaped from was once mortal. Nelda and him were… I mean young Heregod here is… nevermind! The point is if the Saxon kingdoms are taken and the Saxons rise as something else entirely, then we are fucked once more. Each village the draugrs march through will create new ones with unnatural strength and unable to be harmed by most weapons."

"The arrows," Ecgberht said, "we have some already but if the archbishop and other holymen such as Alcuin started blessing them now…"

"It should make them potent," Brennus agreed, he turned to Hopcyn, "can you get as many tree trunks into the city walls by sundown, bring them in one by one, I'll start whittling them down. Alcuin, can you arrange the rest?"

The holyman nodded and said, "And who will fire the arrows?"

"Cathwulf is serviceable with a bow, although sword and spear are his strengths, same for me really," Ecgberht said.

Cathwulf confirmed, "There's about four lads on the walls who have promise with a bow but are out of practice, been giving most of what his majesty says are magic arrows to them."

Brennus nodded. "Of course, Nabila is our best arch..." He caught sight of Ecgberht's frowning and stressed face and decided to stop. Everyone went quiet for a bit.

Except Nelda. "What in god's name is wrong with your hand? It's withered away to the size of a crab's pincer!"

Trying to hold back tears, Nabila said, "I'm working on a way to use my feet to draw the bowstring, my toes are as strong as my fingers were, it's just a matter of getting used to the new angles. I've been practicing."

Looking unconvinced, Brennnus said, "There's one more person who is skilled with bow. I fear keeping him alive by the time the draugrs get here might be tricky." He nodded to Alcuin and Ecgberht. "Come with me."

CHAPTER 44

"Water..." Aindrea gasped to his captors only to be answered with small stones and pebbles to be flung at his face. He winced and tried to push the pain away as he spat out a gob of bloody phlegm. The red blob was probably from the punches to the stomach but the dislodged tooth in the middle of the blob was from the stones. He finally got water, water sprayed in his face, water that was warm and smelled of piss. He choked and spluttered, trying to spit the foul stuff out. His eyes blinded and watery from both tears and piss cleared to reveal one of the city guards stuffing his cock into his leggings. "Brother was at Bamburgh!" he snarled in explanation.

"I had two there," said another guard stepping up to the wooden post Aindrea was tied to. "Well, one was me wife's husband and I never took to him, he beat her black and blue you see so I'll just take your fingers and toes for him but for my Aiken and his brother." He jolted his thumb at the guard who had stoned and pissed over him. "I think we'll take your eyes and your cock. Rats or monsters whoever comes first can take the rest."

"Stop right there!" rang out a shrill, high-pitched cry from a gap in the city walls from which its owner stepped out into the land between the city wall and the Ouse where Aindrea was tied.

"Bugger off, you old braying ninny goat or I'll..." The guard swung his head toward the wall and yelped in astonishment. "Oh Father Alcuin, I am so sorry, I thought you were my wife, she sounds just as squawky and no offense, please don't tell the archbishop, and don't tell my wife, also when you talk to god, can you not tell him please I..."

"Some time alone with the captive, Sibwine and your secrets will be safe with me. Also I do not believe Archbishop Eanbald has decided the Hibernian's fate yet so talk of rats is premature!"

The chastised men retreated into the small wood hut filling the gap which they probably were planning to anyway with it beginning to piss down. Ecgberht silently hacked at Aindrea's rusty chains but when Aindrea turned to thank him, he was greeted with a head-butt so spent his first moments of freedom sat arse down in a muddy puddle holding his nose. "We need an archer, we had one, better archer than you, better person than you despite that she's never spent one day of her life as a Christian. She crippled herself saving me and the others from slaving scum like you. You go where she goes, you shoot who she tells you to shoot and she's got one good hand left to gut you if it looks like you're turning craven or Judas again."

Ecgberht turned and walked back into the city. The two older men helped Aindrea back to his feet. Alcuin said coldly, "It's two days' walk from Bamburgh to here, if they started their march just after us, you may be needed tonight. A final chance to save your soul, one you do not deserve but one that the Lord in his infinite wisdom has offered you." Alcuin too turned heel and walked into the city leaving Brennus to help the delirious, starving man to follow him.

~

The day passed like any other. Ecgberht and Cathwulf now out of smocks and in tunics and mail smashed their spears and sticks against straw dummies and wooden posts with such force and strength, it attracted a crowd and Ecgberht hoped would give confidence to the townsfolk who were expecting an army of men. Alcuin and Archbishop Eanbald with staggering little Simeon following them like a shadow held a special service loudly calling for divine intervention to strike down these demons or foreigners, which to Eanbald was more or less the same thing. Their procession left the church and marched up and down the main street running through the city, chanting and burning incense while throwing alms to a growing number of townsfolk and peasant refugees who trailed after them grabbing and scraping at the floor.

The holy procession came to the Loiner camp outside the church on its return where Brennus with the help of the Loiners had whittled and carved as many arrows as they could, around fifty, Alcuin guessed, made with haste rather than quality in mind, as long as the sticks were roughly the right length, then pointed rocks were glued to the tip. Guts from freshly caught fish from the Ouse were used as the glue. The three holy men clasped their hands and chanted in the loudest Latin over the sticks as they were still being made. Alcuin knew this would work, he wasn't sure how much Simeon believed but the usually cynical and whiny Eanbald was feverishly praying and chanting his blessings. Did he have knowledge of their power, or blind faith or fear? Hopcyn arrived with two more massive tree trunks under his arms.

Nessa was preparing a tent next to Nabila's small garden to be a hospital for the wounded. Tegen was giving a final lesson to the city's women and children in hand to hand fighting, with attention on how surprise, teeth and sharpened sticks or dirty knives coated with all manner of foul substances could be a great leveler against a larger foe. Nelda, Heregod, Gymi and Hagona were among her rapt students.

Up on the city walls, a one-eyed Pagan and a one-handed Muslim got ready both knowing they were almost certainly the only ones standing between this ancient Christian city and complete destruction, a form of hell on earth.

Dusk fell and the city went as silent as the grave. An hour passed with nothing on the horizon.

Then the mist came.

CHAPTER 45

"Perfect," Alecto had smiled a few hours earlier as their army marched through the boglands north of Eoforwic. The bogs were a feature of this island she enjoyed. The bogs just south of Londinium yielded many herbs and plants that couldn't be found elsewhere, the Romans having turned the bogs into gardens and scattered the seeds of their ancestors centuries before. Once the Romans were gone, the bog reclaimed the land and Alecto honed a lot of her arts from her trips there. Even before the crux gemmata had given her the power to walk in the light, she could spend all day in the bogs chanting and inviting visions to teach her. If the sun ever got threatening, she would submerge herself into the depths and spend hours there dreaming and learning.

After Londinium's fall, she had visited the bogs where the East Angles had settled. That was for another reason however. That was where Psyche and Vitium had retired to after the loss of everything. They were no use to her in their current forms. *A cure for both of them surely exists in the Hunt's lair,* she thought. When her draugr army marched into Cymru, it would be one of the first things she looked for, but not the first.

She snapped her mind back to the present. These Northumbrian bogs were breathtaking. They stretched for miles, mist and heather as far as she could see. Where there was heather, they'd be deer so she sent out hunting parties with the promise that any who returned empty handed would be thrown into the bogs where the draugr were bathing and resting. Ordo still sulked in his cart, not wanting to take advantage of the natural protection the mist and wet of the boglands provided. "I am a creature of the night!" he had petulantly hissed at her suggestion that he rest in the bogs. She ignored the pretentious bleating sheep, she would find use for him tonight. For now she needed to concentrate.

~

Ordo rose at the first sign of dusk. He had one thrall, a survivor from Bamburgh whose job was to wake him, feed him and provide all other needs. She held out her arm, tears falling down her face, onto the red raw scratch on the side of her neck which made her powerless to resist any of his commands. Ordo's fangs sunk into her flesh and he drank. When he next took a rest from feeding, he looked around and noticed something strange, several strange things. "Where did it go?"

His thrall answered in the same annoying choking, crying voice that she always spoke with, "She sent the soldiers away, I don't know why, the monsters are still in the bog."

"I meant where is the fog?" he said.

Alecto spoke from behind him, she'd been there the whole time. He told himself to whip the thrall for not giving him a hint, she said, "The men are on the banks of the river, they will use the mist to cross it. I intend them to be bait. The rest of the mist I've arranged to move south until it floods the city."

"You've moved the mist? It was everywhere, how did you... nevermind." He sighed. "So the men are clouded by the mist on the river and people inside the city will be blinded... what is your plan?"

"To create a little chaos inside Eoforwic, the more distractions the better. I'm not sending the draugrs into the city until I know that Aindrea didn't make it down there with his arrows. If he's armed the archers already, the men will act as bait, you on the other hand can start paying your way around here. Leave the wench to me, I'll find some use for her. You don't need a skiff or to swim to cross the river so I want you make haste and be the first inside."

Ordo watched the terrified woman be pulled away into the darkness of the wooded area behind the carts and called out, "Those arrows are dangerous to me as well!" When no answer came, he turned south and began to hover in the air.

~

Ecgberht and Cathwulf along with the rest of the city guard were outside the city walls marching in a patrol of the perimeter, they were the only thing Nabila and Aindrea could see from the top of the walls. Twenty meters out from where they were patrolling the southern riverbank, the river itself, the rest of the world as far as they could see were covered in mist. "Something isn't right," Aindrea said. Nabila felt it too. "It's too cold," she said. The pair both looked back into the city. From the height above it was like looking into a black pit at night, the occasional torch illuminated houses near the center owned by merchants, an inn or ale house, the market if trade was going on late and of course the gargantuan church which took up so much space and was built even higher than the walls. These however were just little pockets of light, much of the city was a sprawling puddle of darkness.

Now every section of the city looked the same, a dull grayness draped itself over the city, it silently embraced every house, inn, shop, shack making them invisible to people standing just yards away.

"I'm not from around here," Nabila began, "is this common in this region?"

Aindrea shook his head. "Half a day's walk are the moors, vast tracts of bogs, that's where the mist settles, it never usually makes its way over the Ouse."

The mist drew in closer from the river, Ecgberht and Cathwulf with the rest of the guards becoming enwrapped in it.

Ecgberht gave her one last look before he disappeared. "This is unnatural!" she said, "Someone has caused this!"

Before Aindrea could answer, screaming started from below them on the riverside of the wall. The city guard were under attack.

~

Ulf was controlling Uurad with chains. His two strongest Norsemen were each holding a chain connected to his neck, Ulf doubted he'd be able to control the beast himself, not with his hands as the burns on the palms still caused him great pain. He tried to put the thought of what he had seen when he went up the tunnel to free Heregod out of his mind and yelled commands to the men in charge of restraining him to keep him close to the rest of the men, he was ungagged and his black teeth jutting out of his ruined face, snapping and growling at them would confirm their compliance. Truth be told, even though Uurad was one of the stupidest and weakest of the draugrs, Ulf was sure he could snap the chains with ease. Perhaps Alecto had gotten a message to him somehow. Perhaps the other draugrs had some way of communicating and giving orders to each other, perhaps some link with Keres his "grandmother" or his "parents" Orthrus and Phaea existed.

It was more likely a message from Alecto. After all she had managed to bring the mist forty miles south from the moors. He turned to see how the other draugr they had brought with them was faring. It was the giant peasant who had felled three Norsemen during the chaotic battle for Bamburgh. He was focused, whatever spell or charm Alecto had used on the monster was working… for now. He kept up his task of throwing tree trunk after tree trunk that he tore up at a rapid pace into the river to clog the river's current and allow enough footing to cover the river on foot. Both draugr were under pain of death and Ulf knew exactly whose death she implied, to be kept on the northern bank of the river while the attack was going on.

One of the Norsemen the giant peasant had killed was currently gurgling at the bottom of a bog with the others, he wondered if when the two draugr line up together on the battlefield, would they have any idea that each is responsible for the others death and therefore second life.

Ulf was snapped out of this uncharastically philosophical thought with news that the logs had secured enough of the riverbed for the men to wade through waist deep. "Good enough," he snarled.

"Odin Owns Ye All!" cried out first from Ulf but then from the other Norsemen, even some of the Picts were getting into the act. The Saxons touched the crosses around their necks but he saw them smile. After the horrors of what they had seen, what they had done, especially since leaving Segedunum, a night of slaughter was dearly needed.

The chanting grew louder as they crossed the river.

CHAPTER 46

Nabila and Aindrea noticed the chanting first, it seemed to cut through the mist upwards and the words meant nothing to her. "Ghuls," she whispered.

"No," Aindrea said, "Norsemen, they are chanting about Odin."

"Who is that?"

"War god," Aindrea said with awe in his voice.

"What are you waiting for? Cut them down! Give the others time to get behind the gates!"

"We should save the arrows for the draugr!"

"We can get the priests to make more!"

"But…"

"Do it or I will and I'll make sure that fish-faced bishop takes your head!" To Aindrea's amazement, the bow Nabila had brought with her was in position, her good hand was clutching the grip and the bowstring was being drawn back by the foot with her toes, her feet were in a seemingly impossible position and her back was twisted into an agonizing looking shape. It took a tremendous amount of effort but she managed to fire off an arrow. It was an amazing feat even if the arrow had no aim and Nabila had no control over where it flew. It drooped upwards and disappeared into the mist on the outer side of the wall.

Aindrea, a little shamed, took aim and rapidly notched and fired as many arrows as he could into the chanting part of the mist.

~

Even if the Norsemen hadn't been bold enough to chant their intentions, Cathwulf spotted them early coming across the Ouse, the Centishman had abnormally good eyesight. "Men not beasts!" he yelled, "Armed with axe and shield!" The spearmen thrust out their weapons and the men stuck close to the wall. They would use it to find their way back into the city, either through the gates or the small gaps in the crumbling parts of the walls. A shield wall formed around the spearmen as the chanting and crying got louder. They were grateful to hear a hissing sound from the wall and the chants turning into screams as men were downed by arrows and their comrades blinded by the mist too were tripping over the bodies of the fallen men.

"They will get to us before we find the gates!" screamed Ecgberht. "Get into the city if you are near a gap and reinforce it on the other side, if not then get behind the shield wall and spear and swords out at all times." He took position in the shield wall, fumbling for space, in the mist he was completely blind and waited trying to guess from the pitch of the Norse cries when they would crash into the shield wall.

~

Ulf had suspected that despite the mist the city's archers might find the chanting too tempting so had taken position at the flanks, or at least what he assumed was the flanks of the attack. He was as blind as anyone, he just moved away from the chanting. He was sure he was far from the center of the attack so should be safe from arrows when one hit him in the shoulder. He fell to his arse cursing and screaming in pain. How had an arrow ended up all the way over here?

~

Cathwulf was jolted with fear, confusion and pain when

the enemy charged into the shield wall. It was a reaction all soldiers got when it happened, some recovered a second later and went on the offense and others froze; just standing whimpering an easy target as the axes smashed their shield to pieces. Cathwulf knew one day it would be his turn to freeze, it had nothing to do with courage or valor or faith or any of the guff the priests and tavern storytellers came up with. It was down to how your body reacted on that day, many men froze their first time and never got a second time but Cathwulf had seen warriors who survived fifty shield walls freeze and be hacked to pieces on their fifty-first time. That first second of freezing lasted longer than he would ever like but he knew today wouldn't be the time it was permanent.

Straight after being winded, the rage filled his stomach and he thrust his sword out of the wall and plunged it forwards, the invaders' leather armor was well worn, some had clumps of iron plates sewn together on the arms. It was no match for mail and the flat of Cathwulf's sword clunking against the plates saw them fall apart making the arm a tempting target that he hacked at rendering his foe's axe useless. He did this more and more and saw most of his line were doing the same as they kept their backs to the city walls, they shifted leftwards toward the gates hacking and killing as they went.

They suffered losses, Cathwulf could make out Cady, a big Loiner lad with no experience but as strong as an ox who had volunteered for the patrol, this would be his first and last shield wall, he had frozen and his shield was just splinters. Cathwulf made out the silhouette of an arm, axe in hand, against the mist crash into the sixteen-year-old Loiner boy's chest. Others had been caught in the wrong part of the shield wall. Blindness on both sides had led to an uneven number of attackers surging at parts of the shield wall. Screams of fear and agony rang out from both sides.

~

Bishop Eanbald was aghast at opening the church basement but Alcuin showed uncharacteristic strictness when he ordered the church to open its doors. "This mist is an invitation for every cut-throat and rapist in the city to go door to door doing as they please!" Soon despite coming to an agreement to limit admittance to women, children, the aged and the lame, the church became packed quickly forcing Alcuin to throw open the basement doors.

The sighs of relief as torches lit up the vast basement soon turned into mutterings at the display of riches.

"I remember three winters back, the weak harvest. Archbishop halved the number of alms. My youngest wasn't strong enough for the cold, maybe a fuller belly would have got her through…" said one haggard looking woman staring at a golden chalice draped in silks, next to a carved bronze sculpture of Jesus.

"Aye, I remember," said a younger woman next to her, "my mother and father left the city walls one evening and wandered into the woods. Didn't want to be a burden, they said." Her head was then caught by the large cross propped up on a high table. It was encrusted with scores of jewels, some of which were colors the cityfolk had never seen before.

"Simeon! Simeon! Quick! Get coverings over all these things before unseemly comments are made by the unwashed! This is a house of god, not one of your shacks or stys, the more earthly rich goods be bestowed on this place, the happier he is! Do you braying hens think you know the mind of god better than me? Your Archbishop! That sounds like a certain path to damnation and the fire!" The archbishop's eyes were bulging as Simeon threw linen sacks over anything that looked precious. Both women looked petrified and bowed their heads weeping profuse pleadings for forgiveness.

Brennus was very interested in the cross, he had seen another like it in the past. Nelda observed the berating of the two women coldly. Foolish cows to question the archbishop's plan but there was something in the archbishop's voice that she disliked.

No doubting, the windbags' bravery though. "I will check the city gates in case assistance is needed and see if the fog has cleared, everyone please listen to Father Alcuin if you have concerns. Simeon! If anyone touches the precious things, kick them out, leave them for the cut-throats!"

~

Archbishop Eanbald trotted up the rickety wooden staircase and emerged into the main building of the church. He shouted instructions at two guards who had been left to hold the church doors and a stocky merchant who acted as the church treasurer that he had left in charge of those seeking refuge in the main building. Then he took a torch from the wall and stepped out into the mist.

He could hear the screams and grunts and cries from just outside the gates; the attack had started! He reached into the leather sack he had collected from the church and pulled out his bow. He had been a decent hunter in his youth before he had taken holy orders and he didn't quite trust a pagan or a Saracen controlling so much of the wall. He would go to keep an eye on them and to thin out the enemies numbers, he wanted assurance that they wouldn't be swarmed before he ordered the gates open so a first hand view of what was going on down there was also necessary.

He limited himself to the five arrows at the bottom of the sack, he was confident that he could make them all count. He hustled himself to the wall, the unholy sounds from outside getting louder with each step. At the foot of the hastily put together ladder lay a beggar or a drunk, his body covered in filthy soiled robes. Eanbald snarled, drunkenness was this city's bane, this must be one of the husbands of the frightened women in the church, he regularly arranged sweeps of the city to ensure beggars and lepers were kept outside the city walls and the coming threat had not daunted him from this. Loiners could stay if they contributed to the running of the city and with defense materials and supplies from their home but the Eoforwic useless mouths had long since been kicked out. No, this must be a drunkard, once this menace was over, Eanbald planned to confiscate every cask in the city walls and put the brewers to work digging ditches… well he wouldn't, even Eanbald knew not to go too far in his rule but he ranted and threatened enough and his hatred of drunkards was genuine.

He kicked the body. "Get back to your shack! Your brothers are out there willing to martyr themselves for this city and its holy history and…" He gave a shriek as the robed figure shot upright at a speed that defined nature and then screamed with pain as he felt his cheek being slashed in half.

Eanbald lay whimpering on the floor as the long-haired, yellow-eyed man stood over him licking the blood off his long fingernails.

"Throw that bag away from me, as far as it'll go, I do not like what's inside!" the creature said to the wounded archbishop who found himself getting to his knees and obeying the man's commands.

The man smiled revealing sharp teeth, far too many for a normal man's mouth. "My name is Ordo. Holy thralls are the most delightful, getting you to deny and curse your god just seconds before you go to meet him causes your type such exquisite misery. But that's for later, in the meantime I have a few jobs for you, priest."

CHAPTER 47

Ulf couldn't believe what he was seeing, even in the mist his men were succumbing to the arrows at a rapid rate. Why were they wasting the weapons that could defeat the draugr on his men? Did they have more? Then he realized this was Alecto's intention all along, have the arrows sticking out of Norse bodies and away from her pets. The Saxon shield wall was getting stronger the more of Ulf's army fell, if the mist didn't hold then they could break out and they were all trapped between the city and river.

His shoulder was in such pain that he could only move his neck, the rest of his body was feeling more and more numb, he remembered the skipper from the first time he set foot on this island. Thorleif, he'd taken an arrow to the leg and surely died. He'd never seen him again after that, they left him alone here. He was getting delirious. At least he couldn't feel the burn wounds on his palms anymore, he'd got them when he'd wrenched the grate trapping Heregod out of the tunnel entrance it was… his hands! He had to get his hands to his axe or sword in case he died out here. Dying with a weapon in hand was the only way to enter Valhalla! He tried to move his hand but nothing happened, everything below his neck was useless. He began to scream, that stray arrow had cursed him to Niflheim.

~

"Did you hear something?" Nabila shouted over the din from below. "I think there was an argument or fight around the ladder." She pulled her foot back and grunted as she sent another arrow into the distance.

"We should conserve the arrows! Besides you're going to cripple yourself by contorting your back like that!"

"Alright, I think Ecgberht, Cathwulf and the rest have them well in hand for now. I'll go and refill our quivers." She put her back and leg into that toe curlingly impossible position once more and loosed a final arrow. She then looked back into the city where screaming had started. "Oh, for Jannah's sake what now?"

Both of them looked at what had caused the screaming, visible through the mist and both said the same thing at the same time in their respective native languages, Aindrea in Goidelic and Nabila in Andalusi Arabic. "Shit".

~

Ulf saw the hulking silhouette cutting through the mist, from the smell and shape it was undoubtedly a draugr. He was briefly confused, she had ordered them to stay on the north side of the river until the rest of the undead army arrived. Did this mean she was near? The final attack so soon, after him and his men were used as sacrifices? He was supposed to become a king, she promised him wealth. Was it all lies? No! The draugr was a sign he told himself. The draugr could take him to Alecto, she could cure him, make the rest of him under the neck move again. "Help!" he tried to get the draugr's attention. A faceless beast soon peered over him. It was the formerly rebellious Pict Uurad. "Take me to her!" Ulf pleaded. It backed away sniffing with the stubs of flesh that were all that remained of his nose. He gave a despairing moan. The thing wanted to eat but somehow due to the link it had with the draugrs that made him and ultimately Alecto with her spells and the hold she had created with the draugrs over the years was forcing him onwards, no food until Eoforwic.

Uurad shuffled away making a low moan that almost sounded like weeping. "Please, please, at least place my axe in my hand… Axe in hand!" Ulf's voice rose to a desperate pitch, enough for the creature to turn around and start to shuffle toward him once more. Then far from the fighting yet another stray arrow flew through the air and pierced Uurad in the lower back. It stuck out of the draugr's stomach and Ulf couldn't move, he had to watch everything.

~

Aindrea and Nabila ran toward the giant fire in the Loiner camp they had seen from the top of the city walls. It certainly took care of the mist problem as it revealed the church it was next to and the church dwarfed the rest of the city's buildings so much, the flames illuminated the whole city's skyline. The problem was it was so huge it was going to engulf the Loiner camp soon and then the church and then the whole city if they didn't put it out soon. It was being defended by a wild one-eyed Archbishop Eanbald. His right cheek a ruin of red and the left side of his face with the hair singed off, his left eye was missing, blood poured from the empty socket but he didn't seem to care. He waved a wooden pole manically while circling the fire and chasing off anyone who tried to get close. Baga lay prone by the fire, blood pouring from a gash to his head which lay at a terrible unnatural angle. The other Loiners, intimidated by the older man's surprising skill and strength with the pole and his towering rank over them, cringed as they backed away. Nessa was there, with no such fear of the holy man, she had darted in and avoided the pole enough to wound the man evidenced by her clutching his eyeball in her hand but it hadn't fazed him and he had managed to strike back. She now lay dazed arse down on the ground, her chin damp red with gushing blood and her teeth sprayed on the floor around her.

"What are you doing?" Aindrea screamed at the crazed

archbishop. The fire gave a sudden explosion and Nabila screamed in fury.

"The arrows! The arrows are in there! What happened?" she cried.

Baga's wife looked up from tending to her husband and sprayed spittle across the mud.

Their sullen son interpreted, "We noticed 'im screaming n crying while 'e was making t'bonfire, da says is common with holy men coz god is their friend but then 'e throws our ale onto t'fire making it light up n da got cross at that…"

The archbishop had used ale, goat fat, flour and most of the Loiner's sparse possessions to get the fire so high. Some of the plants from Nabila's garden had proved good fuel for the fire and Nessa's makeshift hospital had been ransacked of herbs and medicine which had cost the archbishop his eye.

"He's too strong for such an old man…" Nessa's groan came from the floor. "Baga's neck is broken from one blow and he…" Talking became too painful, she just pointed at her smashed up jaw.

"The arrows! They aren't burning!" Aindrea said, "I can still get in there and rescue them…" He charged forward and with one sweep of the pole, he felt greater pain than he ever had, he'd been wounded in battle, he'd been taken into slavery, he'd received beatings and suffered through hunger and disease but nothing was as bad as the feeling when his ankle exploded when the archbishop gave an almost lazy sweep of the pole and smashed his shin bone.

Silence hit the onlookers, they had all heard bone crack and crumble. This was clearly not a feeble old man standing before them anymore. The archbishop gave a pained grin, like he was smiling against his will. "Satan stands among you, strike him down, use the arrows!" This confused everyone standing. Nabila took a breath and stepped forward. Nessa had done them a boon. By removing one eye, if she could pluck out the other, then it would be simply a case of retrieving the arrows, she couldn't afford to lose the use of one of her feet or her good arm, already being one limb down. She made careful paces around the fire, desperately searching for an opening but finding none. The one-eyed old bastard was as alert as a wolf eyeing its prey. Nothing else in the world mattered to Eanbald as protecting his fire.

~

Ecgberht quickly understood that these Norsemen relied heavily on the element of surprise and shock tactics of impacting as much bloodlust in as short a time as possible to smash the enemy's morale and make as many of the opposition soldiers freeze or flee as they could. Faced with a well organized shield wall and with the mist blinding both sides equally, the men from across the northern sea were showing fragilities the Anglo-Saxons were exposing with glee.

The invaders were trapped, if they stayed in place, their weathered shields and armor were not holding out against the much sharper steel of the men of Eoforwic, Eanbald might be stingy when it came to alms but he ensured the city smiths had pockets full of silver and were hard at work day and night. If the invaders fled, then they were trapped by the river and whatever lay beyond it that was if they could escape the onslaught of arrows that rained down.

It was weird that none were fleeing however, regardless of options when a man broke, he fled if he had wind to his back but the surviving attackers were broken that was for sure but just staggered among their comrades' bodies, some gave a fleeting look back, some succumbed to arrows and others made half-hearted swings at the Anglo-Saxon army before being hacked to pieces themselves.

The shield wall now scattered and the battle won, Ecgberht called for the city gates to open and saw the moon was beginning to shine through the mist. He pulled Cathwulf off a Norseman whose face was now nothing more than pink and purple mush and raised his sword to cover him as they staggered back inside the city. Despite their victory, none of the defenders had escaped without withstanding savage blows and both men were bleeding and bruised all over. They needed some rest.

They came across a lone surviving attacker on their way back. A youth, not much older than Cady, he had lost his axe head at some point and knelt shaking, his tunic soaking with blood, praying not to be noticed, "Oh my lord, forgive me! Give me shelter, find me a way home I promise…"

Ecgberht stopped, the boy was praying in Saxon and he knew that dialect. "You're from Wessex?" he demanded with a soft kick to the boy's throat.

The boy looked up. "Never meant to leave, but the overseer he was a bad man…" the boy whimpered on. His story would have been tragic under other circumstances. Ecgberht only had time to get the smatterings of the life of an orphan boy who grew up handsome and strong and was the target of overwork and buggerings from the village overseer and beatings and scaldings when he refused. One day he was big enough to bury the harvesting sickle into the man's stomach and fled north.

His brawn developed into genuine fighting skills which meant he was a welcome addition in fyrds and bandit crews up and down Mercia, deserting when restless. One day he and the crew he was with heard of more coin than they could ever hold for men who weren't afraid to get their hands dirty up in a place called Segedunum.

The gates were opening, the boy's eyes pleaded but Ecgberht wasn't going to let the bastard in, one potential turncoat within the city walls was bad enough.

"Run! Go back to your masters and tell them the king of Wessex spared you." Ecgberht had no idea what Eardwulf would make of that. "Tell him that Wessex will always defend Northumbria from foreign invaders."

The boy wept, "It's not the King who's in charge, he ain't even the king, I reckon. Smirking bastard, can't even speak Saxon. It's her! She's the one in control and if I run, she will do to me what she did to Uurad, turn me into one of them."

"Turn you into one of what?"

"The Rippers!"

Ecgberht was tired, he'd given the boy a chance. If he wasn't going to move, a clean death would be more fitting for one of his countrymen than bleeding out on the dirt outside a foreign city. He raised his sword and froze at the sound from inside the city.

Scratching, faint scratching but done by such a large number of things that it had become a rumble. Then the chirping, thousands of thousands of chirping noises at once, the noise became piercing. Cathwulf pulled Ecgberht out of the way just a split second before thousands of rats poured out of the city gates in a swarm. They ran straight forward heading for an unknown destination toward the river.

CHAPTER 48

Ulf stared upwards at the faceless beast who showed no initial ill effects from the arrowhead sticking out his gut, he wasn't sure if Uurad even noticed he'd been shot. It must be a regular arrow Ulf reasoned, the draugr didn't have fire rocks growing on his face like Heregod nor was he engulfed in fire like the draugr all those years ago on Lindisfarne. He tried one more time, "Axe in hand please..." The creature's head turned, he had heard him!

Then Ulf heard the scratching and chirping and squeaking getting louder and louder until it pierced his ears. He was a sailor, he knew the sounds of rats scratching but never in this number, on the mud it was more of a pitter patter that became a thunder due to the volume, the chirping made him want to cover his ears and he screamed in frustration when he remembered he couldn't.

He turned his head and saw from the direction of the city, a surreal-looking flowing gray river passing rapidly through the mist. The noise increased the closer it approached and it appeared to be heading straight for him. He screamed as the never-ending flow of rats swarmed over his belly, he was instantly winded, there were so many of them but having lost most of the feeling below the neck, he didn't realize until his throat closed and he became unable to breathe. Feeling nothing but sheer terror, his vision went blurry, one final futile attempt to move his useless arm toward his axe and he spluttered, a tear rolled down his cheek as he prepared for the coldness and loneliness of Niflheim.

His eyes flashed open at the most ghastly sound that pierced his ears. This wasn't just a screaming sound, he could still hear those from the direction of the city, besides he'd heard so many unnatural screams over the past few days, he was getting used to them. This sound was different somehow and it was coming from near him.

It was a gurgled, splattering kind of rumble coming from Uurad, his ability to make sounds had been lessened due to the bits Orthrus and Phaea had taken from him when he was being made. He was only really capable of a low groan and a snapping snarl when irritated. This sound was not coming from Uurad's lipless mouth. It was coming from his stomach. Ulf's eyes widened in horror when he saw bulges furiously appear in the draugr's stomach, the bulges were fighting other bulges and the rumble was turning into a brittle shrieking sound. Uurad raised his head and opened his mouth in pain. Although any sound he made was drowned out by the shrieking sound inside him. Rats were all around his feet, ripping and tearing away, the most noxious chewing sound coming from the flurry. One rat noticed the creature's mouth was open and shot up its legs and torso before squirming its way into the mouth. Soon another bulge appeared, fighting, squirming and feeding inside of Uurad's body.

Ulf tried to get away using just his neck and a small part of his shoulders that still worked but couldn't get more than a few inches away. He felt a slight tickling, the tiniest of sensations that he could still feel on his stomach as something climbed onto it. His eyes saw them, hundreds, thousands of rats. All desperate for dragur meat but they couldn't all find space around or on Uurad who was now completely engulfed in a gray furry swarm. More tickling from his legs, dampness, blood or piss or Odin knows what, he lacked the sensations to feel but he knew rats were now on him. Then he felt a harsh scratch as one climbed onto his neck, another on his cheek, the parts he could feel.

He prayed that he would bleed out from the wounds being inflicted on the numb parts of his body before the rats on his face started eating. The last thing he remembered was the look of horror on the face of a beautiful young woman as an arrow was forced into her mouth in a stone basement he had never seen before. Three, no four, five sets of incisors started to rip his face apart as he screamed in the sheerest agony.

~

A blow from the old man's wooden pole had smashed Nabila's cheekbone and cost her the sight of one eye, she and the archbishop were evenly matched on the eyesight score but she should be knocked over and unconscious after such a blow. Something was keeping her standing. Baga dead, Nessa maimed, Aindrea crippled, somehow the adrenaline was still surging through her body. With the townsfolk either fighting outside or hiding in the church and the Loiners too petrified to attack one of the most powerful people in the land, it was all up to her. She darted in again and backed away quickly before he could strike her again, she was unarmed so taking his other eye or his balls with her nails was her best bet. The bastard must have known this as he kept his pole upright, close to the center of his body, swishing in all directions to deliver a fatal blow if she got too close. The old bastard was too good, what had gotten into him. She needed a distraction.

The squeaks started under the fire. Sleeping rats in the firewood, she wondered, why hadn't they woken up when the fire was lit? It wasn't important, she told herself. They were only small rats, it was the big one she had to kill. The squeaks turned into a rumble, dust began to rise from the dried mud. Nabila's jaw opened slowly as she realized the rats were beneath their feet. There were underground burrows under them, the constant digging to build shacks and repair older buildings in the Loiner camp and the nearby church and houses had resulted in lots of burrows under them and the rat population had gotten huge living under so many people.

The first hole burst under Eanbald's feet causing him to stagger and drop the pole as a gray chirping flow of rodents swarmed from the hole running away from the fire. Nabila screamed, ran forward and gave the archbishop a furious uppercut punch to the jaw sending him crashing backwards into the fire. He screamed as his robes lit up and from somewhere in the crowd, the most foul shrieking moan came but the watching crowd was soon scattered due to rats, rats everywhere in massive groups hurtling at a speed no one knew rats were capable of.

There was no time to wait for water, the well was outside the city walls where the fighting was taking place. Nabila jumped into the fire, climbing over the flailing burning man, using him as a ladder and stepping on his head as she leaned over and pulled the arrows out of the flames. She was in torturous pain as her hair was singed off, her smock burnt away, her skin blistered and cracked and she choked so hard, she felt that she would cough her rib cage out. But she did it. With one mighty reach and biting on her tongue to distract from the burns, she clutched her good hand around the arrows and got as many of them in her hand as she could before flinging them to safety.

Some Loiners pulled her to safety. She saw the unconscious archbishop also dragged out of the flames. She passed in and out of consciousness. She remembered seeing Nessa's bloody face peer over her. She tried to feel her feet, several of her toes were burnt to a crisp. She would never fire an arrow again under any circumstances, her smock was just tattered rags; most of her body exposed. She saw angry pink blotches on her brown skin. The fire had destroyed her, she just wanted to rest. Nessa propped her up and carried her away. Aindrea was there, he was hopping on one leg but he was helping her to a tent somewhere on the outskirts of the camp. She saw some people throw dirt on the fire to try to control it. *Pick up the arrows,* she tried to say, *someone give them to Aindrea and find someone who can carry him up the ladder he's the best archer left. Me? I just need to lay my head, I've done so much and it isn't enough, it's never enough...*

She was nearly asleep when a group of Loiners armed with rocks and with red deep scratch marks on their faces fell on the three wounded heroes, easily knocking them to the floor and pounding their faces into the dirt with their rocks and bare feet. Standing over them was Baga's son, a lad of no more than fifteen, his scratch mark going from ear to chin, he gave a chilling grin as he held up a filthy-looking dagger.

CHAPTER 49

In the church basement, they could feel the heat and heard reports from townsfolk who had managed to sneak past the very amateur guards Eanbald had managed to find. These reports were mixed, everyone agreed there was a huge fire outside and most thought the Loiners had set it off by mistake which caused all manner of chattering and worry as the well was outside and all the men of strength were fighting. Alcuin looked quite pale and led the basement in loud prayers. Another intrusion claimed that Archbishop Eanbald himself had started the fire and was fiercely beating anyone who dared come near it.

"Shut your blasphemous hole!" cried Nelda at the woman who had given the news. "The archbishop is god's voice in this town, why would he do such a thing? You're one of those grubby little peasants from Loidis, probably half pagan and in league with Eardwulf!"

"I'm Eoforwic born, you slug brained sow!" the woman replied. "My husband runs the city kilns…"

"Helps run, it's a task which many of our flock…"

The woman cut Simeon's interjection off, "Keeps you all in bread and ale. Makes me one of the ladies of the city, look!" She grabbed her skirts which were faded green from some ancient dye unlike the plain brown hemp Nelda wore. "My husband is out there now shedding pagan blood, where is that one's father?" She wagged her thumb at young Heregod and howled in outrage when Nelda bit it.

"Enough," said Brennus, he spoke softly as ever but a mixture of his accented Saxon and his appearance which no one ever got used to somehow commanded silence even from people who clearly had no love for the man. "Are you quite sure this was the archbishop? The mist I mean and it doesn't exactly sound in character from what I've seen of the man."

"He was in his robes, got no idea who you are, you foreign bastard but known the archbishop since I was a girl and who else knows about him below, the devil," she spat on the floor, "he was saying strange stuff through, first the devil was here in Eoforwic then that he was the devil and the devil had given him his mark, nasty looking wound on his…"

"First, I'm not foreign, my ancestors were living on this island while your ancestors were getting hacked to death in the forests of Germania because they couldn't tell the difference between a Roman testudo formation and a tree and… wait, a mark? What did this mark look like? Did the archbishop only begin behaving… differently when the mark appeared?"

The woman explained as best she could. Brennus nodded. "Shit, there's a strigoi in the city."

"May I ask what a strigoi is, my dear friend?" Alcuin's tender voice sounded almost song-like compared to the gloomy Briton accent that had just spoken.

It spoke again, the rest of the room was completely silent, making each word bounce from wall to wall. "I believe I made mention on our travels from Bamburgh about the origin of the organization I represent."

"Yes," Alcuin replied. "These stories we all learn from the cradle. A haunted Roman city, giants walking the land, a man with a snake for a tongue… but these beings aren't mentioned in the holy books and writings about demons and spirits in Rome. Surely stories to scare children just like the Shellycoats." He paused for a while. "Charlemagne believed, a mighty king, god has blessed the Franks with such a king, we on this island are yet to be such blessed. Yes, he believed, letters and messengers went from Francia to the Briton lands frequently it was said. He was right, wasn't he?"

"There are writings about us in Rome, they're buried deep but that's a story for another time. Yes, before the Saxons came to this island and for a time after when the Saxons prayed to the same deities, beings and heroes the pagan raiders do so today…"

"Heresy!" Nelda said with a nodding Simeon beside her but Alcuin cut them off.

"Brennus is right, god's blessing came to us later than others but as Solomon says in Ecclesiastes 12.1…"

"Could we hear more about what has happened to the archbishop?" the Kilners wife asked, sucking her thumb and glaring at Nelda.

Brennus continued, "There were many beasts in this land at that time, as Alcuin said you've heard of many in your childhood yarns, well they are all real," he turned to Gymi and Hagona, "even the Shellycoats!" They both gave a shriekish gasp. "Or at least they were real, a long, long time ago a brave group of Britons and Saxons entered Londinium and when the survivors left, the beasts were slain."

"So, what's out there?" Nelda asked. "The draugr come from over the sea but the Norse never mentioned a seaboy, doesn't sound very scary anyway."

"A strigoi!" Brennus snapped. "They were the worst of the beasts because they looked human, if it weren't for the yellow eyes, they could walk the land without suspicion, only at night of course. Blood drinkers they were. Spurius gave them some cheap theatrics such as the ability to fly short distances and bastard strength but it was the mark that was their greatest instrument. Once they have a sample of your blood under their nails or teeth, then you are enslaved by them. A handful of creatures escaped Londinium or were away from it when the city fell but we had had no sign that a strigoi was among the escapees; we had hoped that the species was extinct like the deers with twelve foot antlers that roamed these lands once." He paused, out of breath. "I fear your archbishop is truly lost to us, I must leave here. Forgive me, Alcuin. I need to take some things that may be precious to you."

~

The Eoforwic army satisfied the foreign army had been repelled were now back inside the city walls. "I fucking hate rats!" Cathwulf complained.

"Well, you're in luck, there probably isn't one in the entire city anymore." Ecgberht shrugged. "Maybe they smelled the dead, never heard of it happening in battle before, flies yes but not rats and even the flies ain't that fast."

"Rats up here are as peculiar as the people, smell better through," Cathwulf said and the two southerners shared a laugh.

"No, they're alright really, brave bastards getting in a shield wall in the mist," Ecgberht said, "reminds me, I should go to the Loiners camp and let Cady's people know…" Cathwulf nodded and they parted.

The blaze at the camp was smoldering, enough dirt had been thrown on it to weaken the flames. Most had retreated into their tents, the archbishop had declared the church a sanctuary for Eoforwic citizens only so a few men loitered outside tents, holding clumps of wood they had found somewhere. Ecgberht thought the Loiners were enough of a close knit group they didn't need the protection of the church walls against rapers or cut-throats but he also knew Archbishop Eanbald's objections about space were really about letting outsiders see what treasures were in the basement.

He heard shouting from a short distance and recognizing the voices, broke into a run.

~

Ordo had just created his new thralls to take revenge on the bitch that saved the arrows when he was shaken at what he saw coming through the city gates. A victorious army bothered him a little, he would have liked the Norsemen to thin their ranks out a bit further but ultimately the Norsemen were bait for the arrows, the draugrs would make short work of this city. What made his blood run even colder was the man at the head of the crowd. Standing next to a large blonde-haired man, it was her! It couldn't be, it had been hundreds of years and that was a man he was seeing but the same messy mop of brown hair, the same kind brown eyes and if he got closer, he was sure he'd see the same crooked canine tooth that the peasant woman who had deceived him in Londinium all those years ago had. It must be a descendant of the long dead woman, he reasoned. Ordo worried if this was a cursed sign but then took it as a sign that if he disposed of this man with the features of the woman who had been tormenting his thoughts for the last couple of hundred years, another scar of Londinium would be erased. A good omen for the land Alecto wished to create. He postponed his plan to slip inside the church and make enough thralls to create a stampede and crush and headed in the direction of the large blonde man who had parted from his target and currently had his head submerged in an ale barrel.

~

Ecgberht thinking it odd that a few grubby Loiners were overpowering his two friends and Aindrea all known to be capable fighters and he got his answer when he grabbed one of the standing figures pelting rocks onto the bodies on the floor and one almost casual shoulder swing sent him sprawling.

Picking himself up from the mud, he gave a mystified shrug and unsheathed his sword. He smashed the flat of the sword against the back of the improbably strong middle aged man who had shook him off. The man gave a cry of pain and fell to his knees. Three others turned their eyes toward him. He saw Baga's son with a twisted grin on his face on his knees laughing as he stuck the dagger he was holding into Nabila's thigh. It was then Ecgberht noticed all three had deep, painful looking slashes on their face, made recently enough that their faces were leaking blood. Ecgberht screamed in rage and swung the sword as hard as he could. Baga's boy's head left his body and soared, disappearing into the mist.

One of the other two men was quick to pick up the dagger. Ecgberht had frozen, he had never decapitated anyone before, nor had he ever killed anyone that young. The dagger slashed at his face and would have ended up in his throat if not for a bull, a Wealas bull charging out of the mist. Hopcyn smashed the man with the dagger's rib cage into pieces with a ferocious charging headbutt to his back. The other man bent over to fumble for the dagger but then unleashed a bloodcurdling scream as he fell to the ground clutching his groin, the lower half of his body drenched red as he bled out. Tegen stepped out of the mist behind the screaming man clutching the prize she had taken from him in her long curved nails.

On the ground, the three wounded figures began to stir. Aindrea and Nessa propped each other up. One had a broken ankle and the other a broken jaw, somehow they were able to overcome the monumental amount of pain they were both in and support each other. Nabila naked, the lower half of her body red with gashes from the blade as well as angry pink boils and welts jolting out of her torso's brown skin. Unbelievably, she sat upright and asked, "What news from outside?" in the same tone she asked Nessa what was for breakfast most mornings.

Despite the grimness of the trio's condition, Ecgberht found himself smiling, they were alive, not for much longer but they had made it through more than he ever expected to be thrown at him in his lifetime. "Where the fuck were you two?" he said to Hopcyn and Tegen although both of them being half-naked already told him the answer.

"If it's going to be our last night alive, might as well get an early dose of heaven right…" Hopcyn's banter suddenly stopped and his mouth opened aghast.

Ecgberht felt nothing at first, he heard Cathwulf's voice from behind him saying, "I'm so sorry, it's a curse, I'm cursed. Find him, the yellow-eyed one… but don't let him touch you and kill me please, quickly, send me back to Cent." Then he felt the punch-like feeling but unlike being punched, the pain shot up and down, all over his body. He couldn't breathe well and started panting. He looked down and saw the small blade of a seax sticking out of his stomach before his vision went hazy and he went to one knee.

CHAPTER 50

The world went silent for Nabila, she saw Ecgberht crash face first to the floor in slow motion and Hopcyn gore Cathwulf with a tackle to the stomach. Nessa ran to Ecgberht and Nabila regained her hearing and dashed after her. The first sounds she heard were Dumnonii curse words being shrieked by Tegen as she stood over Hopcyn pounding an unresisting Cathwulf with fists. Soon the sound of bone crunching came from Cathwulf's face. She and Nessa put their hands on the hole the blood was gushing out of at a rapid pace. Among the dim, she remembered Nessa propping Ecgberht's body up and somehow with one leg Aindrea coming to do the same. Then she passed out.

~

The strigoi hunt was more crowded than Brennus would have liked. Alcuin was not letting him leave alone with what he had taken from the church and that meant Gymi and Hagona had to come along. Little Heregod had been distraught at the thought of the loss of his companions and Nelda had turned a little pale at being left in the basement with all the Eoforicians she had annoyed so the two of them had stuck with their traveling companions.

"Did the Shellycoats all get killed in that Londinium?" asked Gymi, her brother nodding in approval at the question.

"No, Spurius, he was the head monster at the time, didn't seem to request their presence for the event that precipitated his fall, the Hunt has flushed most of them out of their caves and while we still get reports that a sizeable population resides in Pictland, we are confident we've cleared them out of the civilized part of the island," Brennus explained.

"And this Spurius? He is the same one that gave you the idea for tonight's foolishness?" Alcuin was furious but his anger was more borne of concerns for the others than himself. "Can the arrows not do to the creature what they did to the golem in Bamburgh?"

"Yes but we appear to have misplaced the arrows, I wager the archbishop's fire had something to do with that and besides none of us can shoot a bow unless one of you has been hiding some talents? Nelda dearest, how are you doing with that crux gemmata?"

"Ugh," came the response from her. She had been delighted to touch it for the first time but had quickly realized it was deceptively heavy.

Alcuin prayed, no one minded, it was probably a good idea for someone's voice to be bouncing off the city walls they were groping in the darkness to keep them all together.

"Spurius was defeated when one of the heroes of Londinium rendered him unable to move with the light of the crux gemmata and the other pierced him with the blessed Roman sword that they found in Chichester with the three magical pagan pugios," Brennus told them.

"And do we have this sword or these ghastly sounding daggers to aid us?" Alcuin asked.

"The sword, the crux gemmata and one of the pugios are secured safely under lock and key and with men sworn to defend them with their lives under the mountains of Eryri. However we do have something that may work," Brennus declared, reaching into the tatty sack he was carrying and pulling out one of Saint Cuthbert's thigh bones, waving it in the air like a warrior with his sword about to recklessly run into battle.

"Oh my," murmured a worried Alcuin.

"Urgh," grunted Nelda.

~

"Turmeric, we have some left, right?" Nabila's voice was hoarse. "If we mix it with some thyme and keep the wound damp, he may heal." Ecgberht's body had convulsed violently as they carried it to Nessa's makeshift hospital tent but was now silent, only making the most shallow of breaths.

"I don't think it's enough," Nessa said with each word sounding slurred and causing her enormous pain, she was on the verge of passing out until Aindrea crawled behind her and dug both his thumbs inside her mouth and clenched his fingers around the bottom of her jaw, wriggling them into place. A struggling and furious Nessa tried to bite down but barely had the strength or the teeth left to cause much pain. His fingers wriggled some more and then Nessa's head went upwards and a little pop sound that made Nabila wince came out. Nessa fell to the floor screaming and then jumped on Aindrea bellowing Dumnonii curses and about to pluck his eyeballs out until she realized her jaw was working.

Nabila found a yellow flower that she knew was good for burns and smashed its petals to mush, the mush had a greasy interior that she smeared over the most painful parts of her body. It didn't do much but at the heights of pain, even the smallest relief is a boon to the mind.

Just barely able to concentrate on the dying man who claimed to be a king, she said, "The Chloris can help him."

"The stuff that crippled you? Left you with a crabby hand, have you lost your wits, you daft Moor!" Nessa had climbed off Aindrea and her voice and manners were back to normal.

"But before it made me powerful, I freed them with only

Cathwulf's help." Nabila shuddered at the name. What had caused such madness in their former friend? "It took something from me after it made me strong, maybe that's how it works? It'll fix him but take something?" Nessa looked very unsure at her friend's rantings.

She left the tent, each step was agony and she soon had to walk on her knees for balance. The mist had largely faded and the moon was strong. She walked past the smoldering embers of the fire. Hopcyn and Tegen were gathering the charred but surviving arrows in their arms and placing them in piles. They were both calling over members of the city watch and arguing with them, most of the men who had fought with Ecgberht and Cathwulf or manned the walls with her and Aindrea thought the danger was over with the Norsemen dead or dying outside the walls. She heard the humming squeaks of thousands of rats outside and she made a quick dua for any Norsemen still alive but dying out there even though she was quite certain that making dua for pagans was forbidden. She had passed Cathwulf's corpse, his skull reduced to pulp. She saw Archbishop Eanbald half-naked, burnt and weeping by the embers of the fire.

Everything went silent for a minute, although she could see Hopcyn's mouth moving as he tried to communicate with the guards. Her hearing must have left her again.

It came back when a fist went through the section of the wall from the outside creating a hole like a spear going through parchment. Then another fist smashed another hole, a third fist then a kick made a larger hole. Something from outside was destroying the walls with ease using only their bare hands and feet.

"*Ghuls!*" she screamed.

CHAPTER 51

Alecto levitated herself over the river, the draugr waded through it. Some kept their heads above water by walking across the logs that had piled up on the river bed, others just submerged themselves completely as they crossed. Draugrs breathed but a lack of air for prolonged periods was merely a discomfort for them.

She could sense the city walls ahead of them, she waved her hands to clear the mist. She had no need of sight of course and the draugrs moved on instinct, at least she thought, but she wanted the townsfolk to see clearly what would be the last ever thing they saw... at least as a human. It was then through unnatural hearing and smell she knew the rats were there and how many.

"Twenty four thousand, four hundred and seventy two," she said to herself. About ten rats for each person in the city but they were all outside the walls. What were they doing here?

Coming across Uurad seconds later gave her the answer. All things living or dead had their own unique smell to her so she knew it was him despite that he gave no sound, nor any of the unique vibrations that Alecto used to identify what was happening around her. All she could sense were rats. Hundreds of them covered every part of his body with more trying to squirm their way onto him.

"Get away!" she yelled. The thousands of rats tearing around the acres of mud between the river and the city walls appeared frenzied but uninterested in the newcomers. The ones near

Uurad's engulfed body had been driven insane by not being able to feed on the draugr. She doubted they would attack moving targets but the half eaten skeleton near the tormented draugr made her choose caution. She had never expected "King Eardwulf" to take his crown but she also hadn't expected him to meet this fate either. "Psyche sends her regards," she whispered, surprising herself. What on earth had made her think of her old friend at such a time?

"Girl!" she snapped and Ordo's former blood maid, now a gaunt and waifish draugr shuffled forward groaning and gurgling with a wooden circled shield she held up as she walked in front of Alecto. Two other draugr did the same from each side of her. She instantly knew what had happened to Uurad, she knew what had caused the rat infestation.

She and her three shield carriers walked alone to the city walls where they found the huge man who had killed the Norsemen with his bare hands as a human whimpering at the proximity of the arrows that were scattered all over the section of the walls where the Norse army had collapsed. Arrows were sticking out of many, others had ribs crushed by spears or skulls bashed in by axes. Rats had rendered most of the remains near skeletal and there were no survivors for Keres or her two children. They had added to their ranks by hanging seven deserters they found north of the river. Keres had woken three of them with her kiss.

Alecto turned to the cringing draugr and said, "The time is now!" She was getting better at communicating with the draugrs, Keres was always her main conduit, she spent hours whispering into the creature's ears in every language that she knew. She used the creature's black veins as a code, each bump she felt told her more and more. She made every incantation and spell that her sire had taught her and ones she had studied when she had the gifts of Londinium's books and treasures. However Keres communicated with the other draugr, she was getting across the message that Alecto was to be listened to. It took a few tries but the barrel chested draugr with an almighty snarling roar threw his fist into the wall. It went through it as if he was punching straw.

Alecto left one of her shield bearers to assist the wall wrecker in his duties and returned to the waiting draugr army to launch her commands.

~

Nabila was the first to see the monstrous figure in the space it had created in the walls. It was over six feet tall, a broad and deep chest was deathly white with black veins circling around it, below the rib cage had expanded so much that two ribs were poking out of the flesh. The creature's thick neck had a deep gash in the side making its head rest in a diagonal position. Its milk white eyes bulged with small black dots for pupils that glinted when they were in the shadows. Other than rags, it was completely naked, the black veins crossed and swirled across its stomach, arms, legs, even cock. It opened its mouth revealing ink black teeth and gums.

Hopcyn and Tegen were closer to the arrows and it was Hopcyn who grabbed one and charged toward the intruder. A faint black smile faded and froze when it realized what Hopcyn had in his hand. With one leap, it reached the top of the wall and plucked off a piece of jagged rock. He threw it down at a strength that no one witnessing had ever seen before. It missed Hopcyn by inches but created a crater in the ground with mud and earth flying everywhere. A huge chunk of mud hit Hopcyn on the back sending him sprawling face first on the ground. He flailed for the arrow that had spun out of his hand and raised his head to see a second monster was standing in the gap.

A guard ran forward and thrust his spear through the belly of the beast. Black blood gushed from the wound but the monster didn't pay any attention to it, instead clasping his hands around the mailed torso of the guard. Screams rang out from every direction as the man's torso was detached from his legs and his guts and insides poured onto the mud.

The ghul on the top of the wall leapt down landing on his knees. Happy that the arrow was no longer in his range, he ran in the opposite direction disappearing into the darkness where the other one had stepped into still holding his grisly prize. Screams soon followed from their direction.

Nabila grabbed Tegen's arm, she had picked up a bundle of arrows and was preparing to charge into the darkness following the ghul. "Please no! We need them for our archer, if you go after it, it'll kill you before you can stab it. Hopcyn got lucky he wasn't squashed like a bug."

"I've known that from the start, straight after selection Merlin called us into his lair, looked each of us in the eye and said we would never see Dumnonia again! We die so that others live! That is always the way!" Tears were streaming down Tegen's face as she screamed this into Nabila's face, surprising the other woman.

Then they heard groaning and snarling in that the same guttural sounds the two intruders made but from outside the wall and in a rising number that began to drown out the squeaking of the rats outside. Another fist plowed through the wall, more hulking figures appeared in the gap that had already been made.

"I'm going to need your help. We need to get something to help us fight back and save the others. Please come with me!" Nabila pleaded.

CHAPTER 52

Ordo breathed a sigh of relief at the sound of the draugr breaking the city walls. That strange looking bitch had fished some of the arrows out of the fire but now the humans had bigger and more pressing targets, he should avoid them if he was careful. His plan now was to jump the city walls to the south and head to some of his and Alecto's little Mercian hidey holes waiting for her and her much bigger army to set foot in Mercia.

Mercia should fall quickly, the land was easier to cover and half the Ealdorman hated this King Coenwulf from what he heard. Any Hunt reinforcements from Wealas would be easy to sense due to the spells Alecto had cursed the earth of Offa's dyke with and they would meet Mercian resistance, Coenwulf's paranoia and centuries of hatred between Briton and Saxon meant the Hunt warriors would not be seen as saviors. Ordo had one question on his mind for when they victoriously marched into the mountains of Eryri. Alecto would be eager to reclaim the crux gemmata, the mighty sword that had doomed their sire and the pugio that allowed its user powers to travel outside of this world but he only wanted to know if there was anything buried down there that could cure Psyche.

A city full of frightened bags of blood however, it would be a shame to leave right away. He took advantage of the chaos to find the big young blonde lad he'd marked to kill, the man whose resemblance to the woman from his past that had chilled him so much. Not an awful lot of the man's face was left, a lot of blood would have already left the upper half of the body. He pulled down the woolen leggings and took a bite of the thigh. He spat it out immediately, disgusting! Beyond the now smoking fire he viewed the church. He was going to eat before he fled this city now he'd had a taste.

He left the corpse and found the first one he had marked sobbing by the fire. The priest or bishop or whatever they called themselves. He was finished, a deadman despite still breathing. He smelt of piss and fear and despair, it was almost as if his flesh had started to stiffen even while blood was still pumping, the brain dulled, close to complete shut down but still functioning. Ordo reasoned this man was not unlike the draugrs; a corpse reduced to the bare essentials of consciousness, only without the super strength Keres and her gruesome offspring. He would give the old man another hour of this state of living without living before eating him and sending him off to meet his god. He wondered if this thralls extreme ennui would give him a unique flavor, but first he held the man's chin in his cold clawed hands and said, "I'm not finished with you yet, walk to the church."

~

The group from the church were still groping the wall for guidance. They planned to stay on the fringes of the parts of the city the strigoi was likely to be active in; the market square, the Loiners camp, the courtyard that the ale shacks and cesspit bordered on, the priory which took up much of the land on the southern half of the city, and a street of merchants houses behind the church which had wide alleys separating them. These were the areas the devil would hunt for prey. They would wait in the shadows for him to reveal himself, then they would charge with their weapons.

Alcuin had fretted about the church and those inside. Brennus had calmed him, "A strigoi cannot enter a premise without an invitation."

"But the archbishop!"

"The invitation cannot be from anyone the creature has enslaved. Besides, the archbishop is surely dead."

Alcuin wasn't convinced and was about to protest more when a fist thrust through the wall inches from Nelda's face. Screaming, she smashed the crux gemmata onto what was now an outstretched arm and they heard a scream of pain as the arm recoiled. Two more arms shot through the wall, one just in front of the group and the other just behind them. They panicked and bolted away from the wall. They would have all lost each other in the darkness if not for the jeweled cross Nelda was holding that was now shining a bright light from the previously dark blue jewel in the center of the cross.

Brennus looked awed but unsurprised. Alcuin crossed himself as tears welled up in his eyes. It was up to Nelda to gather the children around the cross and using it as a torch, she and the children disappeared into the city's shadows with the two adult men running after the light from her cross.

Behind them more fists, more legs smashed and crashed themselves against the ancient Roman stones and bricks until a crashing explosion was heard and in the gap stood three hulking white skinned figures with black veins entwined over their body, they stepped into the city, behind them were three more, behind them more still. They all entered the city.

~

A stunned but full of rage Hopcyn stood guard with his axe while Nabila dug deep with her one good hand with Tegen helping. She found what she was looking for in the depths of the sunken ditch that had formed in a part of the wall that had been built on lopsided ground. Clutching the sack in her hand, she tried to hold back tears from the shame as she told the pair, "I can't walk anymore, it hurts too much and I can't keep up on my knees. I need one of you to carry me."

On Hopcyn's back she found herself eye to eye for the first time with the much taller Tegen. "I've got stronger shoulders and Tegen can swing an axe as well as me," he explained as she swayed on him.

"We need the arrows for Aindrea," she said.

"I'll go, I'll meet you back at the tent where the Hibby cripple and the dead king are with Nessa," Tegen said.

"He's not dead! Yet."

~

"Archbishop Eanbald! You're alive! Praise the lord!" Simeon was so overjoyed, he practically screamed the news from the church doors. "My lord what happened to your face and your eye! I will send one of the guards to the priory to get the monastic physician, unless you would prefer an escort yourself to the priory. That might be for the best, you will need beer mixed with honey administered through your nose to stem the bleeding and the priory would have far more..."

"I... I have a physician here with me. Would you please invite him into the church, Simeon?"

Simeon froze at the shadowy figure standing just behind the archbishop. He shook at the sound of stones smashing and wood breaking from the distance and then screaming from different directions in the town.

"Simeon! Now!" The archbishop wasn't in his usual rage though. He was pleading in desperation.

Simeon beckoned the two figures into the church. The one behind the archbishop gave a vile, unnatural sounding hiss. The archbishop, now with tears spilling out of his one remaining eye said, "No, you have to invite him in verbally."

"Jerb-belly?" The younger man was confused.

Before the archbishop would have beaten Simeon black and blue, cursing the day a distant cousin from his hometown of

Carlisle arrived in Eoforwic demanding her eldest son be given an education in the church just as Eanbald had, he would have left scars and broken bones despairing of the younger man's feeble mind but not now.

Now all he could say was, "Invite him in with words, Simeon, please my dear boy, I beg you!"

Simeon didn't know what to do. He then heard another hiss and a flicker of a torch on the wall caught sight of a pale faced, gaunt youth with murky yellow eyes. It was only for a second but it was the most unsettling thing Simeon had seen in his life. He slammed the door shut so hard that the torch on the wall went out. He stood there in the darkness shaking.

He walked back into the church's main building and opened the trap door so those below could hear. In a booming voice he didn't know he had, he told the packed refugees, "We are alone, my mentor and oldest friend has been cursed by a rotting of the mind, let us pray for him…"

The animal hides that covered the windows didn't cover the sound of the screams from outside. The torches inside the church flickered out. Mumbled whispered prayer descended to silence as they heard a shuffling sound from outside. A low groan came from outside the church's wooden walls, then another and another.

~

Nelda's group were running aimlessly. "Stop!" pleaded Brennus. "We must use the bones and cross to hunt the strigoi."

Nelda disagreed, "They are coming from the north, from Bamburgh way! We go south as far as south goes!" They were behind the church on Merchants Row, a long line of wooden huts with spacious front and back mud gardens for pigs, chickens and slaves to live in. The only light was coming from the cross. She shined it onto the houses. No animals or slaves were out in the front mud gardens and no candles or torches shone from inside the huts. "They fled south days ago I suspect," Alcuin offered, "perhaps some of the fishing families took their boats down river?"

"And they took their pigs with them?" Brennus said with doubt.

"Of course they took the bloody pigs," Nelda scowled, "woods from here to Mercia will be full of bandits, deserters from armies that Coenwulf routed if that big Centish lad was talking true. Will need a pig or a slave, probably both to offer as protection before they get to Snotengaham, if they lose their coin on their travels then it'll be the caves for them when they reach Snotengaham and…" Nelda stopped as she realized the implications of what she was saying.

"So going south with only children to trade is not an option," Brennus concluded. Both Alcuin and Nelda shook their heads. "To the Loiners camp?" he suggested, "Not all the arrows can be destroyed and Alcuin could bless some more? We just have to hold out for six more hours, daylight will force their retreat!"

Then the slurred growling started. Two thuds hit the mud in front of them. Nelda used the light from the cross to see what the thuds were. Two dead women, one young, one old, probably related, Nelda thought. Two women without male protectors who either felt safe to walk at night or more likely were forbidden from the church at the archbishop's insistence. Their uncoifed hair, bloodletted cheeks and swollen lips from self inflicted pinches and slaps gave away they drank at an ale shack known for being a welcome place for whores who could attract drunk and foolish men.

Now, the young one's neck was snapped, her head slumped uselessly against her shoulder. The older one had bled out, she was missing an arm. Nelda felt bile in the back of her throat as she raised the cross to reveal the milky, black veined face even with the eyes reduced to shapeless blobs with a single black dot she knew that face. She knew it well.

"Grimwold!" came out in a tearful whine.

The growling had suddenly come to a stop. Brennus had noticed, "Nelda, take the light off his face!" The growling resumed and the eyes began to glint, Grimwold took a step forward. "Back! Back! Shine the light on him again!"

Nelda did and the growling stopped and Grimwold remained rooted to the spot.

CHAPTER 53

Alecto waited outside the biggest gap in the city walls. The draugr would stagger out carrying two or three bodies and gently leave them carefully laid out next to a raised embankment on the outer walls. The undamaged part of the wall acting as one barrier meant she only had to summon a half circle of fire to surround the bodies to prevent the rats from swarming them. Even so a few hungry and brave rats braved the pain and attacked the corpses. *So they begin their second life missing a few toes and fingers, they can live with that or not live with that as it'll be,* she reasoned. Keeping the flame going was a distraction that was giving her a headache, but she couldn't think of another way to keep the corpses fresh for Keres.

Once the draugr laid their bodies on the ground, they turned and slowly returned into the city. Alecto saw sixty bodies already, the city had a population of around two thousand, assuming Keres saved around half of the dead bodies from becoming rat food, she wanted at least several hundred bodies so her army could significantly increase in size. Eoforwic would be a rare opportunity with the city guard spent and exhausted due to seeing off the Norsemen. The Mercian cities they would approach next would have the surrounding fyrds summoned and behind the city walls well in advance. She wanted the maximum number of new draugrs so as well as Keres, Othrus and Phaea had been kept well back. She saw Keres in the distance and thought no time like the present, she waved her over before clutching her head in annoyed pain; the headache caused by the fire spell had been aggravated by the shrilling of the rats suddenly increasing sharply.

~

The draugr sniffed the hide and growled. It was deer, he remembered that and he tried to remember what a deer looked like, it was a hound but faster and taller. He could visualize a hound in his mind, at least for now. The hide was covering holes in wooden walls and beyond those walls were people. More people than there were inside the other wooden buildings, at least fifty odd inside, probably more. Just one flick of his finger and the wall would come down and he could pull a few legs and arms off them before giving the rest of them to the big one, *mother* he told himself. Keres was what the green woman called her and he had to listen to the green woman, he didn't know why but there was something about the way she spoke to Keres and the way mother Keres spoke to them, but not speaking she just gave them looks and they knew what she wanted.

This was why the draugr stopped. If there were too many people to carry, how was he to get back outside the wall without being scolded or beaten by mother? If he returned empty-handed, she would be angry but if he returned with only two or three bodies, she would know that there were others either alive or dead that he had left there for the rats even though there weren't any rats. He rubbed his head confused and took another sniff of the deer hide and gave a gurgled snarl. He felt a thud in his head, a sudden memory of hunting deer once. That had been fun but the memory faded like the smoke from the old fire that had been put out. The draugr rubbed his forehead, he was going to make a decision soon. Smoke! Again! Had they started that big fire again? No, the smoke was coming from inside the building. The curious draugr gave a flick of his finger. turning a third of the wall into splinters. Screaming humans ran straight toward him. *This is easy*, he thought as he slapped them on the chest, shattering their rib cages. They had been instructed not to hit or pop the heads. Headless bodies could be brought back but it was a lot more difficult.

~

"If the wretches won't let me inside, then we will bring them outside, won't we thrall!" Ordo screamed. A whimpering Eanbald gave the deranged yellow-eyed monster a pleading look but was simply told, "Kick down the door and run inside." Ordo abruptly left, Eanbald started kicking the wooden door but his kicks were so feeble, he doubted those inside could barely hear them. Then he doubled over and clutched his stomach in pain. Something was inside him. It had jumped on his back and seeped through the skin, it had slid up his arse, it was curdling his insides, it was *him*; the monster. Unbeknown to him, Eanbald's remaining eye flashed yellow and his kicks became stronger and stronger, the door began to splinter.

Ordo had returned with a bowl of some greasy substance he smeared over Eanbald's face and hair, "human fat," he said more to himself than anyone else, "found a few bodies leaking it and not all draugr made, I must note." He smeared more on the archbishop's robes and whispered into his ear, "As soon as you get inside, grab the first torch you find and light yourself up."

"No!" It took massive strength for the archbishop to resist that much but seconds later the door was kicked to shreds and and wailing a hellish sound, Eanbald charged into the church. It took a minute but he then heard the archbishop scream in sheer agony and flames were visible from the doorway, screaming from those inside and below started. Ordo took a sniff of the smoke and stepped back.

"This is just magnificent," he said as watched the church burn.

~

The draugr was poking his fingers into the stomachs of those fleeing the burning building, it punctured them and left shocked looking faces sinking to the ground, choking and gasping as the life poured out of them. It also meant he could lick his fingers and get some of that salty red stuff down him. A couple even winded him by running into him too fast but he was able to swat them aside, a few heads went pop and others fell off their owners but mother would just have to understand that there were too many was his last thought before he felt a sharp pain in his arse and his blood froze cold as something screamed in the back of his mind, a scream of terror, a scream that told him he was in big trouble.

~

Tegen had been at the site of the first fire collecting the arrows when she saw the church begin to smoke and then ignite. The tent where the others were recovering and making their plans was close but she decided she didn't have any time. Nabila, Hopcyn, Nessa, the crippled traitor and the dead king were all capable of looking after themselves; those in the church had no one, no one but her. She charged toward the burning building.

She saw a swarm of people trying to pile out of a hole in one of the church walls, they were blocked by a naked figure who was slapping and poking at anyone who tried to get past. Blood and body parts were spraying everywhere and some unfortunate were freezing or trying to retreat backwards causing a crush. She could hear bones snap and the desperate wailing of women and children. She ran faster.

Tegen had grown up in a family that had sent its children in rickety skiffs across the Celtic Sea to train at the Hunt's headquarters for generations. She had seen otherworldly sights before. Despite most of Spurius' creations dead or fled, sirens still haunted the coasts of her Dumnonia homeland and in Wealas similar creatures called Mogens had her combing the beaches of Cymru with net and spear. She'd waited with her spear, neck deep in swamps for days waiting for a water leaper to appear. But this was the first time she'd seen dead human flesh rise and move again.

She remembered her training and launched into a scream. It alerted the thing that she was coming but it also made her take in her breaths through her mouth suppressing the smell. The thing didn't turn around, he was distracted by the screams and moans of his victims. She clutched the arrow like it was a lover's hand and shoved it into the beast's exposed buttocks, piercing one of the hideous black veins.

Everything seemed to slow down, the monster sank to its knees, adrenaline shook Tegen out of her frozen state and she rushed to move the injured out of the way of the crush of bodies in the wall's gap before pulling and screaming as she tried to wrench people out of the swarm of bodies.

Then she heard the screech of thousands of rats pour through the ruined city walls.

~

It had gone according to plan for Ordo, he was standing on the edge of the church doorway; as far as he could go without an invitation looking directly down at the trapdoor with a wooden ladder descending downwards. Another crush of bodies was trapped on the ladder as panicked masses were desperately trying to escape the church basement. Screeching and wailing soon started, some were passing out already. A sound of bones cracking and then a thud as the first dead body fell from the mass pile and smacked the basement floor. Ordo listened for creeking; when the roof came down, the structure ceased to have protection from the likes of him and he could stride in.

"Help us!" came a strained shout from the blockage in the trapdoor, it was joined by more. "Please for the love of god, do something!" "I can't breathe!" "My children are trapped beneath me!"

"Well," said Ordo, "I wonder if that counts as an invitation?" He took a step forward and found that it did.

CHAPTER 54

"Extraordinary," said Brennus.

"A miracle, right here in Eoforwic," said an emotional Alcuin.

"My arm is hurting! I can't keep this up all night!" complained Nelda. Her arms had already slipped twice, allowing the draugr she told them was called Grimwold to howl in rage and get dangerously close to one of the group. Gymi and Hagona were propping up an arm each while young Heregod pushed up his mother's back.

Then they smelt the smoke, the church was only a street away so the flames quickly became visible.

Alcuin gave a shrill moan and sank to his knees. "Out of the ashes, we rise, for this is the way of the cross. This is our penance for the pain and suffering of the crucified Christ..." Even the normally pious Nelda looked irritated.

Brennus dragged the weeping man up. "You can build a new church but you can't bring back those trapped inside once they are gone. We must make haste and save them!"

"What about Grimwold?" Nelda said. "Even if he wanders off and doesn't bother us, he's still going to kill some other poor wretches."

"Take him with us, come on move!" Brennus started to run.

~

"Are you sure she's coming?" asked Aindrea, his ankle had a crude smattering of twigs wrapped around it in an optimistic attempt at a splint. Nessa had done her best to try to heal and reset the shattered bones but the lack of light, her own pain and the fierce damage the archbishop's staff had done all made standing possible for a few seconds before the pain was unbearable and walking impossible. Deep down Aindrea knew he was unlikely to ever walk with the ease he once did again.

"Don't you worry about Tegen, she said she was bringing arrows, they're as good as here, just cover me! How many arrows do you have left from the top of the wall?" Hopcyn was guarding the edge of the linen sheeted border Nessa had constructed as her hospital in the corner of the Loiner refugee camp.

"Three, no four," Aindrea replied.

"Once his majesty is awake we can move out and take those dead fuckers down with the arrows, maybe Tegen will meet us halfway but we need all of us on our feet and ready to move as our archer has to be carried." Hopcyn had his axe in hand and was watching the outside darkness like a hawk. Screams and cries punctuated the air, some worryingly close.

"What if he doesn't wake up? How much longer do we give him? He took a sword all the way through, any man would…"

"Shut up, you one-eyed crippled traitor! He will wake up! He must wake up! If not for him and Brennus, I'd still be tormented by nuns!" Nabila spat out the words one by one. She had the green flowers crushed to mush in a clay bowl and she and Nessa were rubbing the paste onto Ecgberht's gaping wound.

~

Tegen hated rats, live rats anyway; the way she lived, a couple on a stick skewer over an open fire was sometimes a necessity and she had grown accustomed to the taste, gamey and greasy. The live ones though, she had too many childhood memories of sleeping in a narrow cave or ditch during her training and feeling rats crawl over her, their scratchy little feet pricking through her clothes and the damp slimy tails slapping against her face, all the time knowing if she woke up or screamed, the lead trainer would beat her black and blue.

She howled in disgust as one crawled over her foot as she yanked at the arm of a girl no older than ten. The girl's face was deathly white and blood was coming out of her nose and ears. One massive yank and she freed the girl from the mass of bodies. The girl rested lifeless in a puddle for what seemed like an age before gasping for air and panting. Tegen had no time to check on her, she grabbed another limb, the more she freed, the more in the center of the mass would live.

Finally someone came to help her, a city guard in tattered mail and vacant dead eyes piled in wenching body after body out. They both clenched their eyes shut and tried to blot out the backdrop of thousands of screeching rats and the tortured howls of the draugr buried under them being eaten alive. "Where are your mates?" screamed Tegen over the din.

"Dead, dead or fled, those things are dragging bodies out of the city walls, in the same direction the pagans came from," he said. "Where are your people?"

"Dead," she said thinking of Cathwulf, "or dying," thinking of Ecgberht and Nabila. The Saxon was already dead and although she didn't know it yet, the Moor girl didn't have much chance of coming back from her injuries.

The guard and Tegen shouted at each other some more, they wanted to overcome the hellish sound of the rats and draugr rather than converse but still exchanged information.

"It was the archbishop that started the fire in the Loiners camp! He's probably responsible for this." Tegen said.

"Me and my crew were guarding the church gates when he left the basement, after that we followed the screams and interrupted those things attacking the townsfolk. Got a few jabs in and slowed them but not enough, I'm the only one left."

Tegen looked harder, the man had no other wounds than cuts and the bottom of his tunic and his leggings were stained brown; he had run away. *Happens to us all,* she told herself and at least he's here helping now. "The only thing that will work against the dead is the arrows, fuck, I only have one left. There's more near where the fire was. Wait, basement? The old goat was hiding down there before he lost his mind, who else was there?"

"Most of the women and children who couldn't fit up here," the soldier told her. Then before she could suggest splitting up to help those still trapped out of a swirl of mist, peered the lumpy milky face of another undead beast. Looking at the trapped and injured bodies freshly freed from the church, it gave a sickly black smile. The guard found his courage and plunged a dagger into the monster's eye. The monster gave him a curious and irritated look before sending the man's head flying off his shoulders with a casual swat, but the distraction was enough. With a scream that drowned out the rats, Tegen planted her one remaining arrow into the beast's forehead.

Half the rats jumped off the first draugr's body and latched onto the one with the arrow sticking out of its brow. The screeching intensified as more rats from the outside, having stripped anything they could to the bone, smelled fresh undead meat and made their way to the burning church to feast.

The crush was now loose enough for Tegen to pull further bodies out and finally wrench out some planks that had been loosened by the crush, a tumble of bodies followed. Some crashed lifelessly into the mud and didn't even stir when damp rat fur nuzzled their cheeks and incisors tore into earlobes and cheeks; the rats were now so crazed, anything that didn't move quickly was at risk. Most however managed to stagger their way to safety; despite massive wounds and trauma, sheer instinct sent them fleeing from the burning building and the two undead figures writhing in agony under a mountain of rodents.

"Head to the Loiners camp, my friends will help you, they have weapons that work against..." her voice faded to a hoarse gasp. She doubled over and vomited bile. She raised her head and gave sky a primal scream before searching the headless corpse of the guard, finding a seax sword and heading toward the church entrance to look for anyone trapped in the basement.

~

Ecgberht found himself in a stone bath house, he was submerged to his waist. He had been to the Roman baths in Aachen and other parts of Francia but this was a new place, it was a dark place, ruins really, it looked as if no one had been inside of here for years and years. Except he was not alone. She was here. She was submerged on the opposite side of the bathtub. Her hand was back to its normal size, she had none of the burns that climbing onto the fire had given her.

"I'm not really here, neither are you, you are unconscious in Eoforwic and I'm trying to fix you." Nabila was speaking in perfect Saxon or maybe she was speaking her native tongue and Ecgberht could understand it perfectly. He wasn't sure. She continued, "I think I'm part of your mind trying to bring you back but something is different, I know things I shouldn't. It's that bastard plant I'm sure of it!"

"What are you talking about?" Ecgberht's question was cut off by the hiss of a snake somewhere in the corner of the room.

"This city is full of gloom, we have been here before and we will come here again, maybe we will even recognize each other." She smiled. "I'm leaving soon, I have to, we can't both walk out of Eoforwic and you are more important."

"Leaving the bath you mean?"

Another sad smile. "It's not you that's the important one, it's your descendants. The Norsemen are merely a warning. There are pagans far more dangerous than them and it is those who come after you that save this island. Your job is to make sure they are born and that means defeating the draugrs by any means necessary. So they can be born, so anyone of this island can be born." She stood up, Ecgberht expected to be transfixed by her breasts but it was the way her birthmark shimmered on the water that took his breath away. Before he knew it, she was standing over him.

"New evil always comes so if we defeat the current evil, we may meet again someday, both older and far away." With that, she put her hands on Ecgberht's chest and her arms turned green. He gasped and opened his mouth to scream as his chest burned, his chest was glowing green too.

~

Ecgberht shot upright, he coughed so hard he thought his throat would rupture. Blood trickled down his chin and another fierce cough splattered a blob of it over the three figures standing over him. He saw Nabila who smiled, Aindrea who gave a stony faced glare and Nessa who wiped blood off her face and cursed. "He's awake?" He heard Hopcyn's deep brittle accent from a few meters away. So he was alive, five of them had survived whatever horrors the night had brought and was still delivering.

Nabila took a step back. "Can you walk?" she asked as Ecgberht looked down at the part of his lower chest where Cathwulf's sword had exited through. She and Nessa had rubbed as much of the Chloris paste on there as they could, not knowing if it would cure or kill him. It appeared to have done the former. Ecgberht was moving with vigor that should be impossible for someone so severely injured. He was staring at the exit wound where the skin had turned bright green, the same color as the flower. His back where the sword had entered his body was the same color; a flower shaped blotch of green.

Nabila felt her ruined hand clench up even though that was impossible now; a phantom feeling. If the flower had worked and returned the king of Wessex to full health then just as she had, he would pay for it with a sacrifice. Would he be rendered blind or crippled or would the old man's disease that makes the cock only good for pissing strike him?

Ecgberht showed no signs of these, well the first two at least she judged as he got to his feet and gave a lopsided smile, he certainly appeared to show no ill effects yet. He immediately asked for what had happened while he was out cold and hearing that their archer couldn't walk, Tegen was in no man's land getting the arrows and the dead were walking the streets of the city. Ecgberht decided to show some leadership. Aindrea and Nabila were limited by their injuries, Tegen was god knows where, Hopcyn was brave but charged into situations too recklessly, Nessa was an unknown quantity on the battlefield.

He began, "Me, Hopcyn, Nessa and the traitor will go out and secure the arrows ourselves. Judas, I'll carry you on my shoulders, the three of us will keep close and you can hop onto whoever gives you the best vantage point, we three will have axe and sword to slow them down, we'll take a couple of arrows too but you have our only bow, we stab them with the arrows only at close quarters so not to waste any and…"

"Could you call me something else?" Aindrea asked.

"What about me?" Nabila said.

Ecgberht looked like he wanted to be anywhere else in the world as he puffed his cheeks out and sighed. "Nabila, I… it's just… look, you can't fire a bow and your burns are still fresh, I think you could be in serious danger out there and I don't want to lose you, I don't care what you said in the bath house, we will both walk out of Eoforwic, I promise you! I swear!"

Nabila looked like she'd been punched in the gut. "What are

you talking about? I can help, I can use my feet."

Silence at that, finally Hopcyn turned to Aindrea and said, "Brother Judas, how well was her foot aim up on the walls?"

Aindrea said, "Please, my name is Aindrea. I was impressed with how she fought through what must have been an enormous amount of pain. It's just that she didn't get her arrows anywhere near the Norsemen." He looked Nabila in the eye while saying this and gave her an apologetic nod.

"That settles that," Hopcyn said. "Gather up the herbs and plants, Nabila, make a good collection in case one of us comes back wounded." He raised his axe and roared, "For Merlin and the Hunt! For the island! For our ancestors! For Aebbe and Milian! For all the heroes of Londinium!"

The last Nabila saw of them was their backs as they walked out of the Loiners camp.

CHAPTER 55

Ordo drooled at the swarm of bodies trying to escape the trap door. He hunched down in a squatting position and took a long deep sniff. A white, pale arm in the middle of the mass appealed to him, its owner was fading fast, the brain wasn't getting enough air to it, in fact it was probably too late to save it. He used his strength to yank the arm's owner out with ease. The girl he now carried in his arms was drooling too but hers was more due to brain damage than hunger. She didn't have long left which made Ordo feel ambivalent. On one hand her brain injuries meant she wouldn't feel much or even notice his presence which disappointed him greatly. On the other hand the taste he would take would be the last seconds of the blood flowing freely through a living body before it began the process of turning into clotted, jelly like, gruel-tasting shit that had made up too much of his diet over the past two hundred and fifty years.

After he'd opened the girl's neck to screams and groans from those trapped that could see what he was doing and were still capable of making such sounds, he took gulp after gulp after gulp until he was satisfied he'd had as much of the good stuff as there was left and now feeling even stronger he searched for a new victim from the crowd.

Some space had been loosened by both him removing the first girl and others fallen to the basement floor, their bodies crushed and their lungs full of black smoke. It meant some of the basement were trying to wriggle free and crawl to safety. One actually made it, a pretty young woman in a faded green dress, rather she nearly made it. She got her whole body out of the trapdoor and made a giant stride for the church entrance but Ordo grabbed her ankle and wrenched it sending her sprawling to the floor.

He crawled over to where she had landed and wrapped his hands around her throat. He didn't know what his touch felt like to those he laid it on but from the way their skin ran cold, he figured it wasn't very nice. "Just what I've been looking for, my dear," he said.

"Please, my husband, he has coin he can..." Ordo, irritated, slapped the woman across the head.

"Your husband is a corpse if he's lucky, could well be walking around with black lines across a white vacant face right now. I'll save you from that at least, love." He retracted his lips to an inhuman degree to reveal sharp spiked teeth and made for her throat.

Then he felt an incredible amount of pain in the back of his head. It felt like someone had stabbed him. Giving a low howling groan, he felt for the source of the pain groping for the back of his head and he gave a shriek of disgust when he found a blade had been rammed straight in. He whimpered as he felt pieces of his own brain begin to ooze out. They would regenerate soon but for now he felt weak, worse he felt vulnerable.

He turned and saw through the church's entrance a woman. Not without beauty but hard living had given her plenty of lines across her face and her cheeks and arms revealed several scars that showed she had survived a fair few knife fights. Her jet-black hair reminded him of Psyche briefly, although his former comrade had never had flashes of white in her hair. She was helping the stunned woman in the faded green to her feet. She blinked in surprise when she saw Ordo looking at her, she had expected the blade to kill him, she thought him just a common rapist or cut-throat she didn't know what he was.

That couldn't be good.

She had worked out by now that something wasn't right. She propped up the other woman and screamed "run!" and both of them disappeared through the doorway into the night.

Ordo was still drooling but now it was a brain injury and not hunger. He slid the blade out of his head and swayed as if drunk, his vision blurry making his way to the door. His brain should be back to normal within minutes he reasoned, he'd only lost a little bit, and then the hunt was on.

~

Tegen ran as fast as she could holding the arm of the stunned woman who had just escaped from the basement. She knew what she had just seen, the worst, the ones the Hunt were sure had all perished in Londinium, a fucking strigoi. She knew some of the monsters still existed, some trolls in Hibernia, sirens in Dumnonia, water leapers in Wealas and the Redcaps and Shellycoats up in Pictland. Some were Spurius' creations, others like the pixies and fairies predated him and any other Roman. Others like the draugr and the nain rouge came from across the sea. The woods and mountains of every corner of the island held horrors, it was why the Hunt continued to this day but they were sure the strigoi were extinct! They had been very clear on that in training!

"Who was that awful man?" the woman groaned.

"Someone who shouldn't be here, someone who shouldn't be anywhere," Tegen said. Then she felt it, a chill above her. She remembered the stories, they could fly. Not far and not well but within the city walls, it was a crucial advantage for the foul thing.

"Head for the Loiner camp!" she screamed as they both pounded their feet into the mud. Tegen noticed her companion had leather wrapped around her feet while she only had rags.

They only made it five meters further when two feet came flying out of the sky each one smashing into the women's jaws.

~

Ordo went straight for the woman who had stabbed him. He tripped over a stone and nearly missed her, his vision was so poor. He pulled her upright and screamed in her face, "You fucking *lupa!* Look what you did?" He held out the parts of his brain he'd fished out of his wound and shoved them in her face. His brain was taking a bit longer than he expected to regenerate. He felt weak and dizzy, he needed blood! In a crazed temper he shoved the bits of brain into the woman's mouth, she choked and he was sure that yanking her up made her swallow part of the brain. He didn't care, he bared his fangs and tore her throat open covering him from head to toe with blood. He cursed, in his rage and mental slowness he had forgotten to make small incisions in the shoulders and neck. Now all the good blood was drenched onto his tunic or mixed up with the mud.

In temper he threw the black-haired woman's body into the mud where it made jerking, jolting motions and walked toward the other woman, the one with the green dress.

This time he would make the necessary incisions and he nearly had his lips brushing against her trapezius when he was jolted out of his pleasure by a giant hand clutching the wounded back of his head and with immense strength lifting him up in the air.

~

They had gotten to the now extinguished fire and secured the arrows when they heard the screams and smelled the smoke from the church. They also heard the growling punctuated by solo screams from the town square where the muddy streets and alleyways criss-crossed to make an empty patch of mud behind the row of merchant's houses. It had market stalls, ale shacks and cesspits rammed into each spare corner of it, and was full of bustling shoppers, beggars and drunkards during the day and night.

"Which way?" Hopcyn shouted, Aindrea's condition meant splitting up was not an option.

Ecgberht winced at the sounds of the screams but the arrows were the most important tool they had and would be useless to those in the church. Hopefully they could be saved by any remaining guards. He said, "Forward, to the beasts!"

Ecgberht and Hopcyn led the way, still squinting from the tiny torch they used their weapons to clear away obstacles while Nessa propped up Aindrea five meters behind them.

The growls were getting closer and the two front men hacked wildly at black veined limbs that lurched out of the darkness. Angered, a draugr stepped out. This one was different from the others as it was fully clothed in tunic, leggings and some weak looking mail. Nessa gave a heave as she lifted Aindrea up and an arrow went straight through the beast's neck. The man was as quick as lightning, sending arrows through the left eye and forehead respectively of two more draugrs that appeared.

The three draugrs sank to their knees moaning and whining in an agonized guttural grunt and the four humans heard the incoming screech of rats, even the sound of their tiny feet on the mud made a thudding noise that signaled their approach. They had heard similar noises coming from the church a few minutes before they had left the camp and started their mission. They weren't quite sure what it meant but all four understood it wasn't a good sound.

That instinct had Nessa throw Aindrea into a ditch and the other three flung themselves in. Not a single rat followed them into the ditch. They heard a sickening squelching sound as the rats threw themselves to unnatural heights as they tore into every part of the bodies of the three undead monsters.

The group in the ditch watched wordlessly and began to wriggle their bodies forward past the gruesome sight. Ecgberht broke the silence. If the others thought he was just trying to drown out the squealing and the screeching from above, the words made them realize otherwise as their blood ran cold.

The Wessexman began, "The first one, the one in mail. He was alive just a few hours ago. Caddy his name is or was. A Loiner lad who fought in the shield wall with me and Cathwulf, he fell to a Norseman's axe, I think. Someone out there is making new ones from corpses."

CHAPTER 56

Alecto was unsettled by both how the supply of new corpses was slowing and how the rats were now inside the city. It was clear the Hunt had people armed with the magicked arrows that could kill them inside. The screeching of the rats was making some of the draugrs outside moan in discomfort. From the direction of the river where there was a small forest came other vermin; stoats, weasels and mice. "Faster, Keres, please make haste faster!" The draugr gave Alecto a snort and bared her black gums and teeth in frustration; for some reason this was taking too much time. Keres had only brought back three corpses since the assault on the city had started and Othrus and Phaea were even more useless, they hadn't managed one!

"We must take the city before sunrise!" she urged. They still had a few hours but she needed all the draugrs in the same place and all the attackers dead so she could cover them up while she took control of her new fortress. She should have saved a few Norsemen for assisting her in that, she thought. Ordo was useless during daylight hours. "Useless at night too," she said to herself, the strigoi hadn't managed to secure all the arrows like he said he would.

Alecto was running out of ideas and time. "Inside, the heat and the fresh bodies, would that help?" Keres gave a snort and a groan with a twist of her bent and misshapen neck. Alecto cried out in dozens of languages all at the same time orders for Keres, Othrus, Phaea, her two remaining shield bearers and a handful of draugr who were yet to enter the city to follow her.

"How on earth did you do that?" Brennus asked.

"God's hand is sweeping through Eoforwic tonight," Alcuin cried.

"What's that pink stuff being squeezed out of his head?" Hagona said.

"Will you all shut up?! It's bad enough holding this bloody thing but he only does what I ask if I concentrate. He's going to drop the devil any moment!" Nelda said in fierce breaths. Her nose and ears were bleeding but she continued to focus all she could on the light from the cross that hit Grimwold in the center of his forehead. At first it had prevented the now undead Grimwold from attacking them, rendering him immobile. Then to their amazement as they moved away, Grimwold followed but at a slow pace far from them.

Nelda moved to the right, Grimwold moved to the right.

Nelda moved to the left, Grimwold moved to the left.

As long as the light shined on him, he would follow it. At first they bickered what to do. Brennus urged them to take the light away from the beast so it would wander in the opposite direction. Alcuin was eager to use the cross in any way they could and their decision was made for them when two further draugrs shot out of an alley and lumbered toward them. All unarmed and frail from either old age, childhood or having to hold a bloody golden cross aloft all night, they were going to be easy pickings for the two crazed cannibals. Nelda in desperation screamed, "Help us please, anyone help!" Grimwold turned his head and staggered toward them.

Several minutes later all six of the party of old men, a woman and children were safe and well. Apart from Alcuin who was vomiting at the sight of Grimwold sitting cross legged elbow deep in the stomach hole of his foe and fishing the pipe shaped insides out of the groaning beaten draugr who was lying on the mud. Once he had fished them out, he sucked them down his throat. The second draugr was alive and groaning but he wouldn't be chasing after them; Grimwold had plucked the beast's legs from its body like they were flowers in the ground. Aside from Alcuin, the only other casualty was Nelda who had earned herself a nosebleed by asking or commanding Grimwold to help.

They had decided to keep Grimwold as their bodyguard as they passed the front of the church on their way to the camp, hoping to find surviving comrades and weapons.

It was not far from there they heard the thud of a body hit the mud and the torch held by Brennus revealed it to be the twitching butchered body of Tegen, one of the Hunt members who had come from the south. They saw shadows and heard a scream. The torch flickered on a faded green dress, the one the kilner's wife wore and a tall silhouette shadowing it, the silhouette's mouth seemed to be an unnatural shape, it reminded Nelda of a ghastly looking fish that had washed up on the Lindisfarena shore once, five feet long, a large fin and a mouth full of jagged, cruel looking teeth.

"Please save her," she communicated to Grimwold, her ear as well as her nose bleeding and a blood vessel on her cheek bursting.

~

The woman in the green dress had fled. He couldn't see the corpse of the one he'd just killed but Ordo wasn't concerned with that, however much he struggled, he couldn't escape the grip of whoever or whatever was holding him aloft, squeezing the back of his head.

"Let me go!" he screamed in bloody fury. He began to flail his legs wildly, kicking into the stomach of his captor but he may as well have been a mouse scratching at mountain for all the good it did. The rage turned to panic, what if he was trapped in this position until sunrise? Surely Alecto and her ever increasing army would have secured the city by then?

"I will give you gold, untold riches, eternal life," he said, only half lying with the last one as he'd never actually seen a draugr die.

"And the devil led Him up and showed Him all the kingdoms of the world in a moment of time, Luke 4:5," came a voice from behind him, a whiney voice, a human voice.

A second human voice came from what he now knew was a crowd of blood bags behind him. He could smell them, the three were very young. He was going to enjoy leaving them last. The second voice, a female one said, "Put that thing down Grimwold."

Thing? He landed on his arse raging and turned around only to be blinded by a brilliant flash of light. Everything went black. He was still conscious but had lost nearly all of his vision. He saw three large red blobs and three smaller ones. A seventh blob was a flickering white color which soon disappeared as if it just floated away. The light seemed to trap him, he couldn't move one bit while it shone straight into his eyes. He began to feel very scared.

~

Keeping the shining cross trained on the yellow-eyed monster meant Nelda had to release Grimwold from the cross' servitude. For a minute that felt like an hour. He stood next to her and the children, a simple swat with those rock-like hands would turn her and the children into red goo or worse, fine on the outside but every bone on the inside shattered beyond repair. Their bodies to somehow be reanimated like his. Grimwold gave a confused sniff and slurring growl before turning his back. He could smell them but not see them. The cross' blinding effect hadn't worn off yet. He shuffled into the darkness and she called out to the skies, "Lord God, when that beast's body is turned to dust, remember what he did and care for his soul."

"I'm not sure it's wise to be so noisy, Nelda!" Brennus said.

"It's important words that must be said, my dear friend," said a huffing Alcuin as he pushed half of the strigoi's body in an upright position. Brennus wheezed as he did the same for the other half. Both old men were exhausted as Alcuin handed the thigh bone to Brennus.

The two attempts to stab the fiend with the bone were futile. Finally Brennus said, "Fuck this!" and pulled out a dagger, he slashed at the stomach of the strigoi with surprising strength, he spat and screamed in long-dead Celtic curses as his hands became covered with the sticky black blood from inside.

Alcuin decided to relieve Brennus of the bone and screamed, *"Satanam aliosque spiritus malignos..."* Brennus was sure he saw terror in those yellow eyes as the holy man shoved the bone into the creature's wound with mighty force.

~

Ordo felt a second of relief as the massive pain he was in began to fade then he heard the Latin and the numbness crept over every part of his body and he wanted the pain back, he wanted the sun, even the arrows. Surely anything other than this. He tried to scream but it was too late. It was far too late for everything.

~

Brennus doubled over and vomited into the mud. Alcuin wept. Nelda went to embrace him. The children stood open mouthed staring at the gray stone statue that had been a monster just seconds before. The bone was embedded into the statue's stomach.

Brennus joined the other two in their embrace. "You did it,

Alcuin, the strigoi is gone, they are vanquished from this island at last," he said, weeping himself.

~

Inside the statue Ordo gave a never-ending silent scream.

CHAPTER 57

"More of them? Where do they come from?" Nessa had just been pulled out of the way of a well-hidden hole in the ditch they were crawling through. Aindrea had caught an undead beast in his sights and given it an arrow to the gut. At least a hundred rats had shot out of the hole Nessa had narrowly missed.

Ecgberht remembered something Alcuin had taught him when they were both at Charlemagne's court. "The Romans had tunnels under the city, they used pipes and smaller tunnels to wash the turds and piss away, probably thousands more rats down there."

"That's a great idea, where did all the pipes go?" Nessa asked.

"Pipes would have rotted or been stolen years back because it's a rubbish idea. You don't want to live on top of a mountain of shit! Just leave it on the streets and allow the rain to wash it away," Hopcyn said.

"Well, it does rain an awful lot in Wealas and you don't have a lot of cities," Ecgberht said, "but I suspect the whole system was never replaced because no one could agree who was to pay for it. There needs to be more central organization in a kingdom, I see that now. A king cannot live far from the cities prancing around in jewels and silks he must…"

"Got another of the bastards," Aindrea grunted. Further howls came from above them, hundreds more rats fled from the hole. A few crawled their way out of a hidden hole Hopcyn was sitting on, making him curse as he got bitten in the arse but he could cry as loud as he wanted, nothing was drowning out the anguished throes from above.

"Anyway," Ecgberht continued, "they didn't live on a mountain of shit. The waste flowed out of the tunnels into the river."

Hopcyn said, "That gives me an idea, one of us splits off and leads anyone trapped to the holes. If they are far from the creatures, then they can't be used against us."

"They also wouldn't suffer an unearthly fate," Aindrea added.

"Yes, that too," Hopcyn spat out, he was getting excited. His plans seldom attracted support. "Nessa can go through the shacks that are still standing and search for survivors and bring them back…"

"What do you mean 'Nessa can'? You think that rescuing is a woman's work, you horrible dwarf! You are smaller than me so good for the shit tunnels plus I'm 50% of our archer. He can't stand without me!" Nessa said with her usual outrage.

"So you're saying you are irreplaceable unless we find a stick."

"I should have your eyes out, you Wealas windbag!"

"Enough," Ecgberht said, "sorry, Hopcyn but she has a point about the size, you can lead survivors and cut through any obstacles that are in the tunnels. We need to find Alcuin first, he knows the city like the back of his hand, he will know where all the tunnels are."

~

Alecto was past the period of unsettling and now into full-blown rage and panic. Worst of all, she had no one to take it out on. The Norsemen dead or walking dead, Ordo fled into Mercia, she presumed. She had to keep her fears and anger to herself, she especially couldn't let the draugrs accompanying her see her anxiety.

"Where the fuck is everyone?" she moaned. There were no mass graves, no piles of bodies ready to be reawakened. Everyone the dragurs had killed was now outside the walls, there were no fresh bodies here. She saw the church – now on the verge of collapse. Getting the draugrs to walk toward fire would require too much effort. Indeed most of the buildings in the city appeared to be partly aflame. She put her hands on her temples and started thinking furiously.

The city guard had been destroyed, for some reason turning the corpses outside the city was difficult, surely enough of the citizens had died or fled into the woods for the draugrs to rest during sunrise even if she had failed in adding to their army in large enough numbers. They could always flush out the bodies and attempt to reanimate the corpses outside tomorrow night as long as the city was secure. She tried thinking of spells that would protect the city walls from any would be intruders while the draugr slept and ones that would stop these fucking rats and mice from eating up all the corpses before Keres could get to them.

Finally she calmed herself. The city was secure, the bodies would walk again even if it took a few nights for Keres and her two children to find the same sense of serendipity that they enjoyed in Bamburgh. The only problem on the horizon was the arrows that were bringing the rats into the city to feast on draugr flesh. The Hunt didn't have an army or even a battalion in the city. They didn't fight that way anymore, not since the doom of Avalon.

She decided to call all the draugrs back beyond the wall. Let whatever squad of hairy, drunken Britons the Hunt had sent to challenge them step forward and the draugrs can rip them to pieces, maybe even a Hunt member for her new army – wouldn't that be just the most delightful thing. More importantly the draugrs could be a shield for her, Keres, Othrus and Phaea. Let the Hunt exhaust their arrows on the draugr standing in front of them, they couldn't kill them all, not with just one archer.

She walked up to Keres and stroked her face a few times, breathing heavily. As usual this was enough to communicate her wishes to the mother draugr and Keres threw her head back in the air and made a sound, a continuous minute long cascade of growls and howls that could be heard by everyone in the city and beyond.

Now all she had to do was wait, stand well behind one of the draugrs she was using as a shield and wait. She stepped back to leave the city and after casting a quick sensitivity spell, she was certain nothing was behind her. She waited, the two shield-draugrs filled the draugr-made gap in the city wall in front of her.

Then she sensed something, something fast, something really fast. "Ordo?" she asked, he was capable of such speeds. Then she felt it clearer from inside the city, a swish, someone running faster than any mortal or draugr. Two light thudding noises happened and then both her draugr guards standing in front of her started screaming and howling. The arrows! Alecto started to shake and tremble, but no rats came. When the injured draugr sank to the ground, the two who in life had been Ordo's blood-maid and one of Osbald's warriors sent to raid Segedunum, both revealed a green gooey substance that covered their eyes and was causing sheer agony.

CHAPTER 58

Nabila was a dead woman walking, she knew that well. She had twice, maybe three times the amount of Chloris in her mouth than she'd had while assaulting the cave-dungeons of Snotengaham and was constantly littering the ground with green gobs of spit to stop herself from swallowing any but it was going to be futile. She was going to get poisoned. The main thing was to destroy as many ghuls as possible with the time she had left. The Chloris had healed her wounds and given her speed far beyond what she was normally capable of and she'd disabled two ghuls before they even knew she was there.

She saw on her left a tall female ghul, this one looked like it had been a ghul for a long time. Only a few strands of black hair remained, one eye was hanging out of the eye socket and the stench from her was much stronger. Behind her was a squat middle-aged woman and a lean well-built young man, at least they had been once; now they were white-skinned ghuls in rags with the power to snap her spine with a flick of their little finger so she had to be quick. She wanted to take out more than two before dying.

She lept an amazing distance and was soon within spitting distance of the first ghul; the heavily decayed female one and skillfully dodged a punch that would have popped her head like a grape. She sprayed the green mist into the eyes of... a woman with no eyes, a woman whose skin was already green.

This monstrous looking eyeless creature gave her a confused look for a microsecond before screaming a curse in a tongue

Nabila had never heard before. A second later Nabila had been flung thirty meters from the three ghuls and was laid on her back. She now knew what the side effects of the Chloris had been this time. Her bones had shattered as if they were made of chalk. Every single part of her body was broken beyond repair. The eyeless woman walked toward her as she got closer the sharp nails and unnatural razor-like teeth came into focus. This was it, she wouldn't scream. She would go to Jannah fighting the demons to the end. She tried to raise her arm an inch and the pain was intense.

~

The group gave one last look at the statue, its mouth was trapped in an eternal scream of panic and its arms were in the same flailing position they had been when Grimwold let him down. The cross' light had faded and it was now flickering.

"The crux gemmata that was used in Londinium still sits in our home at Eryri, it has not shone since the day Milian, one of the surviving heroes of that battle handed it over to the Hunt for safekeeping," said Brennus.

"Should we see the morrow, I would like to keep both the cross and statue in Northumbria. I may take the cross to Francia to present it to the King but here should be its home I think," Alcuin said.

Just as the cross flickered its last, Hopcyn's face emerged in the light. He was out of breath and the sudden appearance of his scowling face made the child squeal.

"Calm down, children. It's not a monster, it's a Briton," Nelda said, "I am told they are quite different even if it's not immediately obvious."

"Hush, woman," Hopcyn spat, "it's the priest I've come for. Father, we've had an idea to evacuate the city but I need your help and…"

Then they heard it. "It's like a herd of bulls," Brennus said. The thumping noise got louder and louder, drowning out even the shrieks of the rats.

"I think we need to get out of the mud," Nelda said, looking nervous.

Minutes later they made it to one of the empty merchant's huts seconds before a hoard of draugrs ran through the muddy paths in the same direction destroying all in its path. One draugr ran through the hut destroying much of its foundations and just missing the humans who were clinging to the inner walls of the hut.

They emerged to find the town to the south quiet, save the occasional surge of squeaking from a stranded, howling draugr covered from head to toe with rats. The beasts had all run toward the northern riverside wall from where most of them had entered.

They walked by the church where the fire was just beginning to burn itself out. A single draugr had run through it and was trying to make his way to his mates despite screaming as he was engulfed in flames. There were corpses too, choked or burned to death from the smoke and fire or their insides crushed in the rush to escape.

"This job might need all of us," Hopcyn said, "the dead need to come with us as well as the living, so if they come back, they can't create more."

Nelda and Hopcyn shoved the dead bodies down the holes that led to what Hopcyn called the "turd tunnels" guided by Alcuin while Brennus and the children called out to the smashed up and burning buildings on each street looking for survivors.

When they passed the statue, it had been knocked over but was very resilient, not a crack on it as it lay face down in a pile of chicken shit. "We'll prop it up later," Brennus told the laughing children, "we have a lot of work to do yet."

~

Ecgberht, Aindrea and Nessa were clinging onto each other on a thatched roof of what had been a large hall, probably once used for gatherings of merchants or to host VIPs. Now it was a half collapsed shack, the two families who had sheltered here had, through either blind luck or deft timing, managed to skip from hiding place to hiding place avoiding the draugrs whenever they investigated the hall. Now with the two families hiding in the turd tunnels, Aindrea had his bow notched and the draugrs were making themselves an easy target by running in a clump all in the same direction. The only problem was they were running in a collision course with the building they were standing on.

"I think I can get off two before we have to jump," Aindrea grunted resting on a weary Nessa's shoulder.

"Make them count," Ecgberht told him.

He notched his bow and dropped it instantly as the whole thing from the nook to arrowhead lit up in flames. The arrow lit up a few strands of the thatch roof as it bounced to the mud. The quiver laid by Aindrea's side exploded and in panic Ecgberht kicked it off the roof before the straw they were standing on became an inferno.

Then they felt the first of several giant thuds as the stampeding hoard plowed through the streets, colliding with anything that got in their way. "Hold on tight!" Ecgberht screamed.

~

Ecgberht woke and coughed heavily, the back of his throat was full of mud and whatever else made up these streets, but he was alive, still alive. He gazed at the moon and the black sky. There can't be many more hours to go, he thought. The monsters hadn't killed enough to be able to sleep safely in the city surely? But there was no chance of the city withstanding a second night's assault. Where would the draugrs retreat to? Could they hunt them though the forests and bogs that they would hide from the sun in? Surely Coenwulf had heard news of the danger to the north and… no it's no use, he thought. He looked at Aindrea, alive but with his arm limply hanging off his shoulder bent in a painful looking position. Their archer's archery days were over. Nessa was breathing but unconscious. He didn't know when she would wake up or if she would wake up. They were all exhausted.

It was over, the draugr had won. The handful of townsfolk who had made it to the turd tunnels would flee while the draugr slept and the dead would walk the north from now on. Mercia was the only hope, he needed to find Nabila and the others and flee to Mercia…

"Ecgberht, Ecgberht, come here, please help! I need your help please! Ahhhhh," a long and feminine scream faded away after the voice had started strong. The voice he knew well, Nabila's voice. Like in his vision when the wound had taken him away, her voice was calling to him in fluent Saxon, her accent still audible but the words clearer.

He propped Aindrea in a position far from the flames, rolled Nessa over so she wouldn't swallow her tongue and began to run in the direction of where the voice had come from, the same direction the draugrs had been running to.

CHAPTER 59

Alecto licked the blood off her fingers, she needed every bit of energy after destroying the arrows. She remembered the gargantuan effort it had taken to destroy just one in Londinium all those years ago. She wasn't sure if she could do it again, years in the wilderness had dulled much of her advanced spell-casting powers but once she had sensed the number of arrows was down to an acceptable level, she unleashed chants that she hadn't uttered in centuries and now with a bloody mouth, bleeding ears and the biggest headache she'd ever had, she had done it. They had won!

She breathed in deeply, the smell of the draugrs calmed her, they were all here now with her. She still needed more blood for the headache so reached into the stomach of the young woman at her feet to retrieve more. A pained whimper, tough girl was still alive. The woman's birthmark offended her, it reminded her of the foul man and his companions who had ruined everything for her. She decided she would rip it off next.

What on earth was that green substance that had disabled her draugrs so much? Her two bodyguards were still blind and screaming in agony, she had sent them to the riverbank to recover and was considering letting them burn up in the sun come the morning, their wounds showing no sign of the quick healing that draugrs like all creatures of the night had.

The green goo hadn't affected her one bit despite taking a shot right where her eyes once were when she was a human. She figured she was as immune to it as she was to the sun, perhaps because of the same magic. Regardless she bent down and brushed her lips against those of the tortured woman.

Then she had her voice and thoughts. "Ecgberht, Ecgberht, come here, please help! I need your help please! Ahhhhh," Alecto said in a voice that was not her own. The scream would hopefully make the arrowless Hunt scum come to their doom a little faster.

~

Gasping, Ecgberht came to the northern wall, just down from the gate he and Cathwulf had led the city guard out from to fight the Norse army. It seemed like a lifetime ago. He was greeted with a horrific sight.

Draugrs, how many he guessed, half a hundred, maybe more. A demon, a green-skinned eyeless monster in the shape of a woman, raven colored hair flowed down its back and its bloody mouth revealed jagged notches in its fangs to create more razor-like blades. Its smile was what he imagined the gates of hell looked like.

Three hours, maybe two until the creeping sun would make it too uncomfortable for these creatures to continue to stand in the open. He had to hold them off until then to ensure Hopcyn and the others could give the survivors a chance, the chance of him seeing sunrise was bleak he knew. He thought to himself, May god be with you now, Coenwulf, this is your battle now, may you be a better man than me. He unsheathed his seax; it wouldn't kill them but if he was quick, he could wound enough to cause a bit of chaos giving the others precious seconds. Then he saw the worst sight so far.

The crumpled up pile of rags by the demon's feet stirred and he knew the hand that crept out of the rags. Even if it had been the other hand, the one that the mysterious plant hadn't ruined, he still swore he would have recognized it. He walked forwards. "Nabila?" he called. "Nabila, get up and come to me. I will get you out of here."

He got close enough to see it was of no use. Nabila would never walk again, never speak again, never move again, never breathe again without pain surging through every section of her body. Cruel enough to take away her talents with a bow but it wasn't enough. Ecgberht felt a furious surge of anger toward god for this and instantly clenched his face in shame.

The green thing chuckled – she fucking chuckled, he thought as his rage boiled up and his fist clenched around his seax handle.

"So you are the best the Hunt warlocks and priests could find? If that is the case, our march west will be easier than I hoped. The jeweled cross that once spoke to me so beautifully along with the sword that doomed my sire will be mine. The dagger that allowed that bitch to spy on us and crossed the realms to other worlds, believe me I have plans for that."

Ecgberht looked up, nearly unable to see his eyes were thick with tears. She was still speaking with Nabila's voice.

"Ah, she meant something to you. Well get your revenge, young man. I'll allow you one slash at me before I turn your insides into boiling liquid. The herbs from the bogs are in this potion that will keep your friend alive for the next sixty or seventy years like this. I was hoping to keep King Eardwulf as my pet but there isn't an awful lot left of him now so a Hunt assassin living in perpetual agony will suffice as a replacement."

Ecgberht looked her straight where her eyes should be and

raised his seax.

~

Alecto gave a grunt of annoyance as the Hunt assassin pulled his sword out of the girl's neck. The potion kept her blood flowing but couldn't do anything, air escaping from the now opened throat. The girl gave a gurgle before her soul jumped to the other side.

"Very noble," she said, "but all you have done is ensure she will be my pet for a lot longer than sixty or seventy years, my friend." With that, she gave a deft flick of her fingers and a tiny flicker of lightning sprung from her fingers and hit Ecgberht on the forehead spraying him to the ground, his body shook violently and his limbs jolted at furious speeds.

"Not enough to kill you my dear," Alecto said, "but you won't be moving for a long time, enough time for my newest draugr to eat you alive." She walked to Keres and stroked her decayed face, her cheeks were the texture of vomit now but she rubbed them tenderly all the same.
Keres understood and walked toward the corpse.

~

Ecgberht's body was giving him the strangest sensations, whenever he tried to sit up, a pain unlike anything he'd ever felt before struck him. It was like something was moving inside his body. He shuddered with fear even as the pain subsided enough to allow him a view of what was happening.

He could only move his back a few inches up, his legs and arms were useless. He could shift his arse and neck ever so slightly but the twenty meters away he'd been thrown may as well have been twenty miles. He saw the most degraded of the beasts raise Nabila in its arms. He cried out as the creature lifted Nabila's face to its own and put its foul black lips onto Nabila's plump lips and pushed down deeply.

It was over. The beast put Nabila's body down almost tenderly and took a step back. It then threw its head back and emitted a howl.

It was the loudest thing Ecgberght had ever heard, louder than a charging host of Norsemen, louder than the draugrs being eaten alive by rats, louder than the biggest storm.

~

In the turd tunnels, Alcuin crossed himself and Nelda covered the ears of her son, and gave a chiding command for Hopcyn and Brennus to do the same for the other children.

~

In a ditch, far from the fire that had claimed the wooden hall, Nessa and Aindrea held each other for comfort. The scream made Aindrea think of Gjallarhorn blowing signaling Ragnarok. Nessa remembered a story from her childhood told by a Hibernian priest who came to their village about giants living under the sea. Giants who would awaken one day with a massive screech and rise up to walk the earth.

~

In the forest south of the city walls, a confused figure made their way through the tangled branches and roots in pitch black darkness while clutching their throat with both hands. They were several miles south of the city when they heard the scream. It made them stop for a moment before they continued south.

~

For Alecto, the scream elicited terror she had not felt since a deadly arrow had been inches away from her face in Londinium centuries ago. "Keres, look at me," she said in a light trembling voice. She almost sounded human.

Keres seemed to take an age to turn her head in Alecto's direction. When she did, the demon's worst fears were realized.

Black tears dripped from Keres' egg-like eyes and around her mouth was a frizzling bubbling green texture. It had already eaten away her lips and half of Keres' jaw stiffened. The flesh of her face just seconds ago a vomity porridge-like mixture was now rock hard. It was stone-like and the stone began to crack.

Half of Keres' jaw crashed to the ground and even on the mud it smashed into pieces. Whatever substance the green goo had turned her flesh into, it was as brittle as it was hard. Robbed of the power to unleash her howls, Keres sank to her knees and pounded the mud with her fists, one of her wrists cracked and the fist came off. She then sat sullenly clutching the detached fist to her chest, trembling as her ears began to crumble.

Alecto calmed herself, It's a blow yes but it needn't be a mortal one. I have Othrus and Phaea. I can still build my army with them... She was cut off from that thought by more howling this time coming from Othrus. He was screaming at Phaea, she herself had received excessively slowed senses even for a draugr when she was turned so hadn't yet realized half of her left leg had dried and stiffened into fragile brittle chalk-like rock. She gave a scream when she caught Alecto's eye and tried to move toward her only for that leg to explode in a plumb of dusty powder.
But they didn't touch the green substance... then the next logical thought hit Alecto like ice being poured down her ear and making every bone in her body run cold. Keres is their mother, they share some connection, when Keres suffers so do Othrus and Phaea. But Keres is mother to all of them...

More howling and wailing came from the other draugrs as they noticed their own bodies betraying them, fingers and toes and soon limbs and guts were falling off, and out of their bodies before turning to dust on the mud. The noise soon hushed as some lost jaws while most of the others felt their throats turn dry and crack as the metamorphosis hit them there.

Alecto got on her knees and started chanting at the top of her voice in Latin, in Greek, in Norse, in Frankish, in every Celtic and Saxon dialect there was. Even in languages that mortals were forbidden from speaking but it didn't stop the tide. More and more bodies crumbled to dust, she was choking on the remains of what had been her unstoppable army just minutes ago.

~

Ecgberht still couldn't move but he was overjoyed with what he saw. Each draugr turned to dust was one that would no longer inflict misery on the world. Nabila had done it! With her last act on this earth, she had saved this island. He was only saddened that he would never get to tell her how heroic and brave he had always thought her.
He would die soon, he imagined. As soon as the green demon noticed him again, it would tear him to pieces in rage. He thought he would sleep a while now. His eyelids were heavy, his body felt like it would sink deep into the mud. He slept well.

When he woke, the sun had risen. The city was destroyed, the night of carnage had left barely a building untouched but the draugrs were gone, so was the green demon.

~

There had been ten crumbling draugrs left when Alecto noticed they were leaving through the holes they had made in the northern wall. One had lost both its legs so was pushing its torso forward with its hands. At their head was Keres who somehow still survived, long outliving Othrus and Phaea. Keres now with one arm and half a face was somehow communicating with the survivors and directing them... somewhere.

Alecto chased after them. "Keres, listen to me, let me try to help you, where are you going?" Then she saw, the river. They were going underwater to stem the pain from the dry, cracked, brittle ruins their bodies had become.
Alecto watched nine of them disappear into the water, one had crumbled to dust just seconds before it could submerge itself

and she sensed large white shapes move on the river bed. They didn't seem to be in distress anymore and then they moved away, heading east in the direction of the sea.

Before she could wonder what she should do next, she sensed something else. Something on the river bed, it was hot, boiling in fact but it wasn't affecting the water at all. The heat and wetness co-existed. It rested on the river bed, it glowed bright orange and she could tell it was waiting for her.

"Impossible, you got struck with a cursed arrow. Your flesh and bones are magma now! It can never change. Facing the sun is the only way to end your pain!" Then she remembered keeping him down in the bowels of Bamburgh. "How did you escape? How did you find us? Did you tell Keres to come to the river?"

The river didn't answer.

She turned to flee, a smoking bright orange arm with streaks of black running down, it emerged from the water and grabbed her by the ankle pulling her into the water.

The draugrs were gone.

CHAPTER 60

Eoforwic, five days later,

"Incredible things can be done simply if one tells oneself that it is going to happen," Brennus gave his opinion on the rapid rebuilding work going around the city.

"Yes, we all heard the same speech Merlin gave when we completed our training and took our vows, when was that for you? It can't have been when we spoke like this," Nessa said in Cornish.

"No, we had one tongue then," Brennus said in Western Brittonic but to change the subject he went on, "I mean they're working so fast, by the end of the winter, the damage will be hard to spot."

"The sooner the town looks the same way it was, the sooner people will forget what happened here that night. This is what always happens when creatures terrorize a village. The people rebuild, they remarry, they have more babies to replace those they lost, they forget about siblings and parents who didn't make it. They forget."

"That is certainly true for the villages back home," Brennus said, "but this is a mighty city, home to two thousand souls. One of the holiest cities on the island…"

"We shall see." Now Nessa wanted to change the subject. "When will you return to the base in Eryri?"

"Tomorrow, we have waited too long as it is. Hopcyn is just going to have to accept that her body was lost in the chaos. They must have burned at least a hundred the next morning and it's understandable; they didn't know if the dead would stay dead. Tegen's body was taken to the pyres with the others. When we get back to Eryri, we will slay a few sheep and perform the rites as best we can for her soul. You will return south with us tomorrow?"

"No, I don't think I will." To break the silence, she asked, "What about Nabila's body? What are her people's rites?"

"Alcuin has read bits and pieces of what goes on over there. Body is to be washed and buried and something tells me that explains Ecgberht's and Alcuin's absence for the first few days after the dead left, anyway help me carry these logs to the remains of the town square… Nessa, where are you going?"

~

About a third of the church's basement had survived and that's where Ecgberht, Alcuin, Aindrea and a shaken, somehow still alive and now acting Archbishop Simeon sat on piles of dirt and charred rubble they had shoveled into piles. Every ten minutes or so, Simeon would squeal and Alcuin shudder as one of them discovered a piece of bone in the piles.

"Alcuin and I have decided that the installation of Archbishop Simeon will happen this Sunday and straight after the new Archbishop Simeon will immediately anoint Eardwulf as King."

A commotion broke out among the other three.

"Eardwulf was slain with the Norsemen!"

"Eardwulf is a pagan and our enemy!"

"Eardwulf was put to death at Ripon, the pagan is an imposter!"

Ecgberht raised his hand. "Eardwulf is dead or fled but his name drew legitimacy and followers, I propose we put an Eardwulf on the throne for stability's sake but we ensure it is someone who is competent and trustworthy. A former monk perhaps..."

"He is a traitor and a pagan and..."

"I'm aware of this, Alcuin but you and I must return to Francia soon, King Charlemagne expects reports! He probably has dozens of the hairy-arsed Britons at his door now asking questions about the silence from Eoforwic. King Charlemagne made a great many deals and promises to a great many people and he needs our help which I intend to give, especially as one of those promises was made to me!"

He stood up. "Aindrea or King Eardwulf as we shall call him from now will save Northumbria from plunging into anarchy the instant we leave."

"I will?" Aindrea said.

"With one eye, one good leg and one good arm, I think your days of leading Norsemen across the seas are over, you can use your mind to rule. Besides, you will only be making half the decisions, if you're lucky! Your queen will rule as your equal and as a fast friend to both Britons and West Saxons. I think the Queen of Northumbria will be the true power in the north but for appearance's sake, you King Eardwulf will wear the crown."

"My queen?"

A familiar frizzy-haired head stuck its way down the charred trapdoor. "Did you tell him yet?" it said.

"Ah hello, Nessa, yes, we were just talking about you. With you ruling to the north and me to the south, Coenwulf is about to find himself with some nasty neighbors."

Nessa entered the basement. "Oh look, the statue of whatever his name was. You did well getting the chicken shit off the face, missed a bit here."

Soon Alcuin and Simeon were giving thoughtful nods. Aindrea looked almost draugr-like in his shock.

~

Ecgberht awoke and spluttered the salt water out of his mouth and lips. He looked up and saw Nelda standing over him with an empty jug. "King Drunkard needs to know that our ship departed an hour ago, we're about to join the Trent and then into the sea, there are strong waves so King Drunkard needs to be awake and not be going for a swim!" She stomped off.

"You will be one hell of a nun, Nelda!" Ecgberht called after her, meaning it. His head felt like a horse was kicking it, his tunic had crusty vomit on it which he gave a coat of fresh vomit to the instant the ship lurched in heavy waves. Why was he so drunk? Ah, he remembered! He had been standing in the mud surrounded by burnt jagged planks of wood sticking in every direction in what remained of Eoforwic's church.

Simeon's installation as archbishop after which he was to be known as Eanbald II had taken two hours, so he was three jugs of wine in when it came to King Eardwulf's coronation, he'd been on the mead for that one. Nessa and Eardwulf's wedding straight after was his last memory, he'd been thinking that Nessa scrubbed up alright in the blue dye woolen dress Angle brides were fond of and then the next thing he remembered was spitting out the sea water Nelda had poured over him.

He walked up to the bow where Alcuin was standing. Alcuin was crying. "Thank you for getting me on board. I assume Nelda told you to leave me behind."

Alcuin gave a smile despite the tears. "Dear Ecgberht, how good it is to see you at this moment. Soon we will leave the Trent and depart into the sea. I feel I will see my island home for the last time then. I will die in Francia."
Ecgberht didn't know what to say to that but was quickly awed. Alcuin pressed something wrapped in cloth into his arms.

"The cross... the..."

"Crux gemmeta, I do not think we should show it to Charlemagne after all, he would find it too difficult to return it. But I did not want to leave it with King Pagan and Queen whatever she is and you still have a kingdom to claim. Return it to Northumbria someday but first please hoist it on the beaches of Wessex when you return to take your throne."

~

Brennus and Hopcyn were close to Offa's dyke when they set up camp for the night. "Mercians are less likely to loosen arrows in our direction if we cross the dyke during daylight, of course as long as it's in a western direction," Hopcyn said.

Brennus poked at the fire, he hadn't heard a word of the smaller man's chatter for hours now, every sense in his head told him they were in danger but how? He knew these woods better than any man on this island bar one, he knew where the creatures of this region slept and hunted, he knew where the villages were, he knew where the Mercian guards and fryds would patrol right down to the last blade of grass. Something new was here, something bad.

~

In the tree above them naked, save a piece of linen wrapped around her throat to disguise the horrific looking wound, the strigoi waited. Her fangs salivated with drool at the thought of the two meals beneath her.

Tegen's yellow eyes gave an almost playful glint as she dropped from the tree branch onto her prey and screams rang out around the forest.

EPILOGUE

848 AD, Wintanceaster,

Charlemagne walked the halls of the Roman palace carefully. It had been thirty-four years since his death but he still kept his cowl tightly stretched over his head. Thirty-four years since his tomb in Aachen was opened and the Hunt warlocks found his corpse sitting on a throne, wearing a crown and holding a scepter. He gasped when he was awoken. He had agreed to inherit Brennus' gift and had forsaken heaven to do so but it still shook his very soul to be awoken in such a way.

On the boat over the sea, he had asked the hooded men,

"Where is Brennus?"

"Long dead," was the reply.

"How long am I to assume his position?"

"As long as you are needed."

In the thirty-four years since then, he had been Merlin's eyes and ears across the island and the massive continent beyond.

He had counseled kings, he had seen Ecgberht outlive Coenwulf and he had led Hunt warriors from the west to ensure Ecgberht smashed Coenwulf's successor at Ellandun. He had seen Mercian supremacy fall and Wessex become the dominant kingdom of the Saxons. Finally hundreds of years after King Cynric and his successors, another Wessex king took his seat at the Hunt's table.

That had been the peak. King Ecgberht's madness had started about three years after Ellandun. Merlin had muttered darkly when he had reported that the green discoloration on the King's chest; once a source of pride that he had shown off in battle was now causing him unspeakable pain and that the King claimed it spoke to him, whispering dark thoughts and desires into his mind.

The final ten years of his reign saw a decline in fortunes as tribes from both Wealas and a furious tribe from over the sea calling themselves Danes attacked. With the King bedridden and half-crazed, Mercia clawed back power and the growing strength of the East Angles meant the island was more divided than ever at Ecgberht's death.

The Hunt was determined to keep Wessex in its folds despite the King's madness and fall. So Charlemagne was to report on King Aethelwulf's sixth child, a sickly babe who even if he lived could expect a bishopric at best.

He was stopped by a grubby-looking guard. "Oi mate, no beggars inside the palace walls, hop it!" Charlemagne flashed his palm, the spear piercing a snake's head symbol was tattooed on both palms and the guard froze and bowed offering apologies to the ragged robed old man who did look like a beggar.

To think I was once an emperor, he chuckled to himself. He

didn't regret his decision to inherit Brennus' position. He had already done more good than he ever could as an emperor and there was more to be done from what he had learned, a lot more.

Finally another few flashes of the tattooed palm and he was in the King's private chambers. The lean King gave a slight bow; he had known Charlemagne all his life and knew who he once was. That didn't mean he liked the secrecy of Hunt business at all. "Danes to my south and Mercians to my north and here comes the big man to bless son number five. I really do not have the time for this."

"The Danes and Mercians will soon fight each other over Londinium and neither will find joy in such a haunted city. It will be explained the next time you travel west to treat with your other Hunt representatives. Merlin said it was important I inspect the boy."

The mention of Merlin's name chipped at something in the King's mind and he nodded to the bed. His wife Osburh was laying on furs by the fireplace. She had only given birth two days ago and looked as if an ox had run her over. "This is the last one I swear, he tries to make me have another, I'll geld the bastard with my teeth," she said in Frankish which her husband pretended not to understand.

Charlemagne held the baby aloft. It cried weakly, this was not a healthy baby but it would live. The purple birthmark on the left side of its face told him that. Over half a century after her self-sacrifice, she had returned.

"Call him Alfred," he said as he handed the baby back, "and bring him west with you as soon as he's old enough to travel. He has a lot of work to do."

AFTERWORD

Author's notes

Fear the Draugr is set in the same universe as my first book Dark Age Demons. Alecto, Ordo and Brennus are characters that were introduced in Dark Age Demons who due to their various powers are still alive at the start of Fear the Draugr. Other Dark Age Demons characters do appear in this book but in new bodies as they were mortal so died and were reincarnated. I've dropped hints about who was who. If you didn't read Dark Age Demons (feel free to give it a go, it's not bad for a first effort IMVHO) then I hope Fear the Draugr works as a standalone story. There's the odd reference or even chapter that relates to events in book 1 but the intention was to create a story that anyone could understand and hopefully enjoy.

Again if you are reading this you probably bought/rent/found a copy and read to the end so my sincere thanks. If you enjoyed it then leaving a review on the page you bought it would be wonderful.
Here is a link: https://www.amazon.com/gp/product/B0BBQFC4R2/ref=dbs_a_def_rwt_bibl_vppi_i1

This book was very fun to research because a lot of it happened! Granted there's no evidence of draugrs terrorizing York for one night but Ecgberht was a real person who came of age in exile, he returned to claim the Wessex throne in 802 and his descendents unified England and ruled it until 1013. Northumbrian politics was like Game of Thrones on steroids. The Mercian king Offa did create an earthwork barrier between Mercia and Wales called "Offa's dyke" bits of which still exist today. The Viking raids on Portland and more famously Lindisfarne happened. Alcuin, Osbald, Odberht and a few others are all real people with real lives just as outlandish as their book counterparts.

Dorestad, the city in which Brennus, Nabila, Ecgberht, and a newly arrived Nelda and young Heregod live in for a while also existed. This is a cool video I found about it: https://vimeo.com/505137652

Al-Andalus and the Saxon kingdoms had no recorded interaction I could find but given the proximity between Spain and England, it's possible some occurred. Nabila was created to bring a new culture into the story as I felt the Briton vs Saxon cultural differences had been exhausted in book 1. The differences between Islamic life then and now give me a bit of license but any errors are on me. Nabila soon became one of the characters I enjoyed writing the most so her importance and her role got a lot bigger quickly.

Now I have to start thinking about book 3! What era will our lads and lasses find themselves reincarnated into and what foes familiar or not will they bump into? Late Viking age? Norman conquest? 1st Crusade? I think I might go down the pub and mull it over while drinking several beers. If you want then please feel free to get in touch with me on social media or email for an update on how it's going.

Neil Kay, Yokohama, Japan, August 15th 2022.

ABOUT THE AUTHOR

Neil Kay

Neil Kay is a British teacher currently living in Yokohama, Japan. He has been interested in both history and creative writing for as long as he can remember. His favorite historical fiction novels are Shogun by James Clavell, Hawaii by James Michener, Hilary Mantel's Cromwell trilogy and The Baroque Cycle by Neal Stephenson. Dark Age Demons was his first attempt at trying it for himself, he found horror is a natural companion for historical fiction and he enjoyed it so much that he wrote Fear the Draugr as the follow up. Away from writing his interests include Indian food, Kirin beer and Crystal Palace FC.

He can be found at the following links:

Twitter: @neilkay1979

Facebook: https://www.facebook.com/neilkaywrites

Website: www.neilkay.com

Email: neilsbooks@neilkay.com OR neilkay1979@gmail.com

BOOKS IN THIS SERIES

The Lost Hunt

Dark Age Demons

Dark Age Demons - A Historical Horror Thriller.
Britain, 540 AD. Britons, Saxons, Jutes and Angles war with each other for land. They have no idea they are all just meat to the monsters that dwell in the abandoned Roman city of Londinium.

The monster's leader, a former Roman soldier turned demon, sends his creatures across the land to forage for food and increase their numbers.

When one of these creatures destroys their village, two brave Saxon sisters and their stubborn but determined brother form an unlikely team-up with a Briton bandit who has knowledge of the island's darkness. Saxon newcomers from the old country and a Briton-born slave, raised and abused by Saxons complete the fearless squad.

Vampires, shapeshifters, and unnatural beasts chase and confront the heroes forcing them to turn their attention to the smoldering ruins of Londinium.

Horrors Of The Harrying

A man must eat.

The year is 1070. Frithger, a former housecarl for the defeated King Harold, is charged with solving a series of grisly murders in the ancient city of York.

The North has been devastated by King William's Harrying. Every plant and grain burned, every well and river poisoned. The northerners stripped of sustenance. Tens of thousands starved to death. The city now fears a mad butcher is within its walls.

Frithger is in a race against time to find the killer before the King's return to the city. He is aided and hindered by a collection of the city's characters; a deranged Norman torturer, a degraded knight, a limbless former soldier forced to beg, two streetwise prostitutes, and a Welsh wise woman who uses the practice of sin-eating to see through the eyes of others.

Fearing that the Harrying has forced a nest of vampires into the city, two members of the secret demon-hunting society, The Lost Hunt, arrive in the city to complicate matters.

Frithger and his crew of misfits track the vampires as well as a bloodthirsty English rebel frenzied with murderous rage at the Normans, but there is a third candidate for the killer.

Someone who survived the Harrying for all those hungry months by doing whatever he had to, someone who enters York with unnatural tastes and a never-ending hunger.

After all, a man must eat.

Printed in Great Britain
by Amazon